The ... **ng.**

HER EYES FLICKED FROM ONE QUICKLY APPROACHING threat to the other. In one direction, the blizzard swept angrily toward them, and in the other, the plane grew larger, carrying men who would do absolutely anything to find them. "What are you thinking?" she asked, afraid she knew the answer.

"I'm thinking we're screwed."

"Right." They already knew that anyway.

Closer now, the wind whipped ice crystals into the air, like sugar spinning into cotton candy. Even through the whistling, she thought she heard the sound of an engine. "What do we do now?"

"We run." Expression grim, he turned and led her straight into the coming storm.

Everyone is talking about
Adriana Anders

"Scorching hot and beautifully emotional. A pulse-pounding, edge-of-your-seat read."

—Lori Foster, *New York Times* best-selling author, for *Whiteout*

"Strong heroines, sizzling tension. Heart and heat abound! Do yourself a favor and start this book early—you won't be able to sleep until you finish."

—Molly O'Keefe, *USA Today* bestselling author, for *Whiteout*

"Emotionally riveting page-turner... Readers will be hungry for more from Anders's pen."

—*Publishers Weekly*, STARRED review for *Under Her Skin*

"A dark and emotional tale that will make your spine tingle as well as your heart."

—Sarina Bowen, *USA Today* bestselling author, for *Under Her Skin*

"The perfect romance...a hint of danger, a whole lot of spice, and an HEA you believe in."

—Anne Calhoun, award-winning author, for *Under Her Skin*

"Passionate and heart-wrenching."
—HelenKay Dimon, award-winning
author, for *Under Her Skin*

"The romance I've been craving—smart, edgy, brimming
with heat and heart."
—Cara McKenna, award-winning
author, for *Under Her Skin*

"Incredibly sexy, heartbreaking, and intense."
—*Kirkus Reviews* for *Under Her Skin*

"It is just something about how Adriana Anders writes that
makes you enjoy the story and want more."
—*Fresh Fiction* for *By Her Touch*

"For those who enjoy living in the emotions the characters
are going through, I would highly recommend this author."
—*Harlequin Junkie* for *By Her Touch*

"Anders excels at creating sympathetic characters who will
win the reader's heart."
—*Publishers Weekly*, STARRED review for *In His Hands*

"There is truly an art to writing darker, touching romance
and Anders is definitely onto something."
—*Smexy Books* for *In His Hands*

Also by Adriana Anders

Blank Canvas
Under Her Skin
By Her Touch
In His Hands

Survival Instincts
"Deep Blue" in the *Turn the Tide* anthology

"Through endurance we conquer."
—Ernest H. Shackleton

"It is the power of the mind to be unconquerable."
—Seneca, *The Stoic Philosophy of Seneca: Essays and Letters*

WHITEOUT

ADRIANA ANDERS

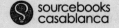

sourcebooks
casablanca

Published by Sourcebooks Casablanca, an imprint of Sourcebooks
P.O. Box 4410, Naperville, Illinois 60567-4410
(630) 961-3900
sourcebooks.com

Printed and bound in the United States of America.
OPM 10 9 8 7 6 5 4 3 2 1

To the scientists and those who support them in the world's most inhospitable places. You are real-life heroines and heroes.

CHAPTER 1

Ice Tunnels, Burke-Ruhe Research Station, South Pole

AIR WHOOSHED FROM THE DYING MAN'S LUNGS AS HE landed on hard-packed ice. He couldn't move, couldn't see, couldn't breathe. Was he conscious?

He shifted and groaned, the sound swallowed up by darkness.

Hurts.

Yes. Yes, conscious, once the wave of pain passed. Barely.

Only one eye opened. The other was swollen shut. It made no difference anyway. The world was pitch-black, the absence of light so complete that he could be in only one place—the tunnels beneath the ice.

Entombed.

Something frantic and animalistic twisted inside his chest at the thought, shoving at the pain, giving him the strength to roll to one side, press a bare hand to the ice, and scoot up to a seated position, his back to the frozen wall.

He wheezed through three inhale-exhales, making an effort not to think of the blood bubbling from his mouth or the way the hole in his chest whistled with every breath. By God, they'd torn him apart.

He'd never met anyone like the men who'd questioned him. They'd beaten every inch of him until his body was nothing but a bag of pulp and splintered bones. They'd broken him so methodically that this decision—to let him die alone and afraid in this underground tunnel—most certainly had to have been purposeful.

Just when he'd accepted that it was over for him, they'd grasped him under the arms and heaved him into this terrifying place, as carelessly as a child chucking a chocolate wrapper in the bin.

He pictured the man who'd led the interrogation and flinched. Pure evil.

"Think I'll kill you?" the leader had asked, his smile almost tender. He'd leaned close and whispered against his face, "I'd rather count the minutes as you take your last breath. Know you're suffering while everybody else is up there, partying it up." The bastard had winked, rubbed gloved knuckles down the side of his face with something like affection, and thrown him in here.

A violent shudder overtook the dying man, rattling his bones and clacking his teeth. He shut his eye and stopped fighting for a few seconds. Fighting hurt so damned much.

He dragged in a lungful of frigid air. It snapped through him as quick as a current, deadening his nerves and easing his pain. A number popped into his brain, as they were wont to do: *forty-three below zero*. The average yearly temperature in these tunnels.

Thirty seconds. That's how long it would take for his bare skin to freeze. And frostbite was just the first phase. He'd be gone soon.

If he just stayed here, it wouldn't hurt anymore. If he didn't fight the ice's pull, then that horrible man couldn't change his mind and return for him, find new ways to torment his shattered body.

He couldn't feel his feet, which was…*good*.

A sigh left his mouth—so much simpler than the struggle for deeper breaths, so much less work. Oh, this was nice. No worrying about frostbite, no bothering to swipe the rime from his beard or wiggle his fingers to get the blood flowing. *I'll stay here. For just a bit.*

Can't! He pried apart flash-frozen lashes, the lassitude briefly fading. *Have to warn the others.*

He found his gloves in his pockets.

So cold in this place. Where was he again?

Concentrate.

Antarctica. The tunnels. *Right.*

He'd only been here a few times, but he could envision it, carved from the ice deep under the station. If he could stand and walk, he could find a way out. *The* way out, since he couldn't very well climb the emergency ladders in his current state. If they'd even left them for him to find. Perhaps he could open the door, locate someone, warn them, stop those people from doing the terrible things they planned.

His attempt to rise was pitiful, pointless, his muscles no longer functional.

The pain had changed, he realized in a detached sort of way. It didn't crackle sharply through nerve endings like it had when they'd shot him or beaten him or hacked at his fingers. Now it filled every cell, swamping him, melding with him so that they were almost interchangeable. On some level, he wondered if the deep throbbing was keeping him alive.

Something clanged outside, and fear hit him like a religious experience, set him—an atheist—to praying as only near-death could do.

A laugh tightened his abdominals and shook his chest. Mum would be pleased to know that he had finally found God. There was an odd comfort in that thought. That he wasn't alone down here.

No, focus. Walking out of here wasn't an option, but he

could leave a message, in the vague hope that someone would open the tunnel door and discover him in the morning, before it was too late.

Slowly, as if wading through thick, near-frozen water, he patted his pockets in search of something, anything... It was all gone. No pens—not that a ballpoint would work in this cold. No phone. Nothing to communicate with at all.

A hard, razor-sharp cough wracked his body, scraping the bottom of his lungs, sending a rush of warm, thick fluid spewing from his mouth.

Blood.

That was it. If he'd been in better shape, he might have laughed at the old sense-memory urge to turn to one of his students and offer up his palm for a high five. Oh, he'd seen the way they looked at him when he did that, knew they thought he was an absolute *wanker*. A "science geek," as the Americans called them. But he'd never been one to waste time caring about what people thought.

Look how little it mattered, after all.

Slowly, his limbs robot stiff, he removed one of the gloves he'd just struggled to put on, reached for his wound, dipped an unwieldy finger into his own oozing blood, and felt for a surface. When he tried to slide his finger, it wouldn't budge. Stuck to the ice. *Shit.*

He pulled it away, the digit too numb to register the pain of tearing skin.

There had to be something else he could use. He pictured the tunnel, cold and blue-white, its walls shimmering like glittering diamonds.

Slowly, hoping that he'd got his directions right, he worked his way toward the left, the movement scraping, insect-like. A thrill ran through him when his palm *thunked* lightly against a slab of wood. A storage crate of some sort. Perfect.

Another touch of finger to blood before he pressed it awkwardly to the surface, just stopping himself from wasting time on explanations or articles. He'd add them at the end. Wouldn't want to leave them with improper punctuation. Perhaps, while he was being fanciful, he'd add a footnote. A bibliography.

The blood kept solidifying on his fingertip, so he wasn't sure if the **C** worked or not. And then, because he needed his final thoughts to be good ones, he decided that yes, it had most certainly worked, and so would the next.

He'd just completed the **H**, with a bit of a flourish, when he heard footsteps. It was them, coming back to kill him after all.

Frantic, he hurried to finish, fingers clumsy with death and that endless frozen dark.

Field Drilling Site—22 miles from the South Pole

Ford Cooper couldn't wait for the summer crew to leave.

Given Coop's general disposition, that would surprise exactly no one at the Burke-Ruhe Research Station. But still, this particular year seemed worse than most.

It might be the recent influx of newbies, sent by the National Science Foundation to replace crew members who'd been struck down by a particularly virulent flu. The new operations manager, in particular, rubbed him the wrong way.

A second—very distinct—possibility was that he was getting grumpier with age.

Or it could be the station's cook, Angel Smith, whose presence put him on edge like nothing had in years.

Just thinking of her—too loud, too enthusiastic, too fluid with regulations—annoyed him.

Instead of sitting through another meal surrounded by all of that bright, colorful messiness, Coop took his usual approach to anything involving humanity and gave the entire research station a wide berth.

Which meant spending even more time alone on the ice, away from the oppressive heat and noise and constant, unpredictable movements of so-called "civilization."

Though it felt like just moments, he'd been out here for hours, working at one of his field sites. A storm had come through this week and done some damage to his drill, giving him the perfect excuse to stay out all day. He huffed out a laugh. As if he needed an excuse.

Not that anyone was checking up on him. He worked solo because he liked it.

And possibly because no one wanted to work with him.

He squinted out at the wide, welcoming landscape, trying—and failing—to estimate the time based on the sun's position. After all these years, the eternal daylight of austral summer still confused his internal clock. He checked the time—after eight.

Though he ached to take advantage of the continued light and stay out here, working, safety dictated that he pack it in for the night.

As he climbed onto the snowmobile, the stiffness of his limbs confirmed that this was the correct choice. On cue, his stomach gurgled. He hadn't eaten since this morning's breakfast, which wasn't all that smart in the land of vanishing calories.

He revved off across the hard-packed ice, directly into a headwind, as usual. Some days were like that: headwind coming out, headwind going back in, as if they followed him purposely. The winds here defied common sense.

He frowned, thinking of a conversation he'd overheard at base between Angel Smith and Pam, the station's doc. They'd been discussing love languages or some crap. Apparently, there were people who needed gifts in order to feel wanted, while others sought quality time with their loved one or acts of service. Whatever those were.

Coop craved headwinds and bracing chills the way others did human contact. His love song was the crackling of ice underfoot, staccato and sharp as a snare drum, his language the low, melodious roar of a Condition 1 storm blasting over endless white expanses. He'd take the translucence of blue glacial ice over diamonds any day.

Angel Smith, of course, wanted *touch*.

Which he wouldn't think about. Instead, he focused on the landscape spread before him. He'd heard it described as lunar, empty, or flat, but it was none of those things. This place was as vital and complex as the ocean, its depths as fascinating as the Mariana Trench. He'd never tire of this view.

Thirty minutes into his ride, something flashed to his right.

Blinking through his dark goggles, Coop eased to a stop and stared across the wind-scoured stretch to the east, where Cortez had set up his research site.

Hadn't Cortez moved his equipment yesterday? With the coming winter, he'd planned to settle a new site closer to the station.

Coop waited for another movement, his sun- and snow-blinded eyes working hard to focus this late in the day. And then, because Cortez was one of the only people whose company Coop actually enjoyed, he veered off in that direction with an internal *Why not?* Maybe he had last-minute cleanup to do on the site. In which case, Coop could lend a hand.

Ha! a tiny voice whispered as he cut due east. *Anything to avoid her.*

He shoved that as far down as it would go. No point in dwelling on the person who turned him—an awkward man at the best of times—into a monosyllabic robot. Angel Smith would be gone by this time tomorrow. Thank God.

Cortez's site had been right around here. He slowed and swiveled his head a hundred and eighty degrees—noting nothing out of the ordinary.

Wait. There. What was that?

A pennant flag, used by researchers to mark a specific spot or, in some cases, a camp itself, lest a snowstorm cover it up entirely. This one, a reflective silver, was what he'd no doubt spotted. No Cortez, no more research site. Nothing but a lone flag in the middle of the colorless landscape. A glance at the sky confirmed that it was a rare flat white evening—the kind that pilots preferred not to fly in, since there was no way to tell the difference between the ground and the clouds above it. Earth and sky mingled until there was nothing but pale, milky white everywhere.

For one strange, discomposed moment, Coop saw himself, in his red NSF-issued coat, as a solitary drop of blood in the middle of all this vastness. If he wasn't careful, he'd get soaked up by the ice, by the ground itself. Not eaten so much as absorbed, covered, layered over, forgotten until some enterprising researcher with a drill chose this particular spot to study.

Jesus. Better nip this kind of thinking in the bud. Coop swallowed and shook his head, tried to blink dark spots from his vision. He considered pulling the flag up, and then went very still.

Rather than disappear, one of the dark spots coalesced into a stain on the ice. It didn't belong there.

Some old instinct kicked in, making him check his surroundings with jittery eyes before getting off the snowmobile and crunching over to look.

About six feet away from the bright red mark, he stopped and stared, unblinking.

It *was* blood. Had to be, or maybe Cortez's team had used a dye to test something out here and left some of it behind. But that was unlikely, given how obsessive most scientists were about keeping this continent clean. Coop knew for a fact that Cortez wouldn't contaminate future research by leaving something, even a thimbleful of blood, behind.

Funny how half his mind flew immediately to the new slew of crew members, while the other half fixated on that stain with absolute certainty as to what it was.

Yeah, it was blood all right. And since no flora or fauna lived this far inland, it had to be human.

It was as bright red as his parka, which shouldn't have surprised him, given the low temperature. Still, he always thought of blood as brown when outside the body for any amount of time. If it weren't so grisly a sight, it would be pretty, actually. It wasn't massive—maybe the size of his hand, bright and colorful as a bouquet in this pale place. A sprig of tiny red flowers haloed on one side with the lush, deeper red of velvety roses beyond. Not a huge stain, but enough to make him curious.

In an absurd feat of human self-deception, Coop's

useless sense of smell gave him the sweet, rusty stench of blood, viscous and battlefield fresh. He stumbled back from the shock of hot, dusty, diesel-scented memories he'd never expected to follow him here and did nothing but breathe for close to a minute.

There'd be an explanation for this. All he had to do was return to base and find Cortez. Probably one of his research assistants had cut herself or something and they'd had to rush back without cleaning up the site first.

Right.

And because he'd never been one to accept bullshit—especially his own—he climbed back onto his snowmobile and took off for the station, full of the knowledge that something was very, very wrong.

CHAPTER 2

Burke-Ruhe Research Station, South Pole

ANGEL LEANED OVER THE BAR AND GRABBED A GLASS OF
water. Around her, the Skua's Nest was raucous, teeming
with that last-day-at-camp energy. It was fun.

It *should* have been fun.

Sucking in a deep breath, she turned and leaned back
against the worn wood, taking it all in.

By this time tomorrow, she'd have left behind this odd,
imperfect, wonderful bunch that had been thrown together
from every walk of life—folks who worked their butts off,
people she'd been honored to cook for; every last one, jan-
itors, researchers, fuelies, her own kitchen crew. God, she'd
miss them.

With a brittle crack of a smile, she waved off a heavy-
machine operator's invitation to dance.

Oh no. Don't do it. Don't cry.

It was easiest to focus on Jameson, in all his big, bearded,
bearish glory, who thrashed on the rickety stage, pouring
his ever-loving guts into his guitar and vocals. He was at the
point in the evening where he'd started taking requests and
this one was a hard-core version of a Violent Femmes song.
Predictably, the crowd was eating it up, half of them crying
while they sang along, arm in arm, lighters in the air.

She wouldn't be alone if she let it out. That was good
at least. Except, these weren't bittersweet goodbye tears
pressing at the surface—they were the deep, ugly tears of a
woman who'd lost sight of herself somewhere along the way.

She turned down a couple more friendly invitations to dance, lifting her cup as an excuse. With a smile that felt jagged at the edges, she started to spin back to the bar and froze.

The door opened and before she'd even looked, hope lifted its sad little head, immediately followed by crushing disappointment and, on its heels, embarrassment. What an idiot.

Would she ever stop being a glutton for punishment? After what had happened back in the U.S., she should know better than to pursue a man—especially one who disliked her as much as the Ice Man did.

Too many feelings sprouted up when she thought of what *should* be waiting for her stateside. But there was nobody. Nothing to look forward to. Which was good. Perfect. A clean slate. How many people got a fresh start like this? The opportunity to build on her strengths instead of focusing on the past. And the fact was, unless it involved slicing, dicing, sautéing, baking, or anything cooking-related, Angel Smith was pretty much crap at it.

Jameson hooted from the stage, joyous as always. Maybe instead of dwelling on things she couldn't change, she'd take a page from his book and enjoy herself. Turning, she yelled over the bar, "Hey, Pam, would you grab me one of those?"

"Bourbon and Coke?" Pam raised her gray eyebrows, adding an unspoken *Are you sure?* to the question.

"I'll be fine. It's the last night." Angel made a face and put out her hand to receive the cocktail in its plastic cup. "Thanks!"

Pam, the Burke-Ruhe station's physician, gave her a long look. "What took you so long getting here tonight?"

"Once I'd printed out all my recipes, I realized they needed to be...you know, stuck together."

"Collated?"

"Mm-hm. So I did that and then—"

"We'll be able to boil pasta, you know."

"I know, but Jameson loves my puttanesca, and what'll Alex and Rowe do without my mom's empanadas?" So she was going overboard. She knew that, but it didn't stop her from making sure these guys had everything they'd need once she was gone.

"You include the brownie recipe?"

Angel nodded. She'd cry on the plane, dammit. "And I'll bring what's needed up from the supply arch."

"There's nobody like you, Angel." Her friend's eyes narrowed. "You gonna be okay, hon? You thinking about the acci—"

"Great!" She pulled from her selection of well-worn responses. *Good, fine, awesome!*

Pam circled the bar and tapped her cup against Angel's. "All right, then. To new beginnings!"

She grinned, for real this time, and nodded, her entire being swollen with affection. The crowd swallowed up her too-quiet "Cheers," and instead of riding this self-pity train any further, she took a swig and yelled, "Hell, yeah!"

When she'd come here, there'd been nothing to look forward to. No future beyond this crazy stint as a cook at the South Pole research station. And, yeah, coming here had felt a whole lot like running away, but it couldn't be if there was nothing left to run *from*, right?

These last few months were supposed to show her the way. And they had. *They had!* She'd landed here in pieces, like a broken doll or one of Jameson's machines. Which was okay, because sometimes, it turned out, you had to take something apart before putting it back together again.

Never mind the cracks it left behind.

"Wipe that look off your face, Angel, honey. You *deserve* a fresh start." Pam put a thin but strong arm around her and pulled her into her fleecy, disinfectant-scented embrace. "Stop kicking yourself and accept that. Okay?"

Nodding, Angel squeezed back, refusing to let this morose mood mess tonight up.

"The world"—she lifted her cup toward Pam with a forced smile—"is my lobster roll."

Pam toasted, laughing, and the two women drank.

Angel watched the dance floor as she nursed her cocktail. This place had changed her outlook if nothing else. It wasn't every day you met the best people in the world. Poleys—the folks who lived and worked at Pole—were special, a population apart. She'd never find anyone quite like them back home.

Swallowing back more sentimental tears, she looked on with affection as one of the smaller scientists lifted a big guy onto his shoulders, the two of them collapsing to the floor in a fit of laughter.

"Jesus. I'd better stop drinking right now." Pam handed Angel her cup. "Half these idiots'll be in my clinic before the night's over."

Angel watched Pam stomp over to the guys and give them a talking-to. The station's doctor might be half their size, but she wasn't intimidated. Then again, why would she be? This was the best group of people Angel had ever known.

The only bad thing about this place was what lay outside. Hunkering down in the middle of all this vastness, this absolute endless *nothing*, drew people together. She looked around at her team. No, more than that. Her family.

Where else would a thirty-one-year-old chef and a fiftysomething emergency room doc like Pam be thrown together? Or Jameson—a rough-looking ex-army oil rig mechanic who'd never managed to fit into civilian society? The man looked like he could chop a redwood in half with his teeth, but he was the biggest marshmallow in the world. She'd never have met him back in Pittsburgh. Or any of these people—scientists or maintenance folks.

Aside from a few outliers—like the new group that had arrived a few weeks ago—she'd miss pretty much everyone from Burke-Ruhe.

The only thing she wouldn't miss was the ice.

Her *stupid* mind chose that moment of weakness to swerve right back to the Ice Man. He spent every waking hour in the elements, aside from the torturous moments he took to eat in her galley. Dr. Ford Cooper actually *enjoyed* the cold. He liked it so much he'd become a part of it, let it seep into his veins, transform him from a warm-blooded person into some soulless...cyborg.

A *creep* who, since her first day at Burke-Ruhe, had looked at her as if she were nothing but a speck of...whatever it was he looked at out there all day.

"How can I get just one screw?" Jameson's voice growled from the too-loud speakers, stirring her annoyance up into something hot and reckless. She slugged back the rest of her drink. No, wait. She coughed. That was Pam's. Straight rum burned to the ends of her limbs and pushed her away from the bar.

"Come on." She went up to Pam, grabbed her hand, and

tugged her into the heart of the ripe, overheated crowd. "Let's dance."

Maybe if she closed her eyes and let the music take her away from thoughts of cold ice and colder eyes, she'd forget for a few minutes that she had absolutely nothing to go home to.

Back at the research station, Coop parked the snowmobile in the vehicle hangar and stepped onto the ice, head cocked to the side.

What the hell was that pounding?

It wasn't until he'd made his way closer to the main cluster of buildings that he realized it was coming from the Nest. Jesus, with decibels like that, the little hut should have been visibly shaking. He pictured it reaching such a fever pitch that it exploded out all over the sunlit night.

"Shit." He rubbed a hand over his stiff neck, annoyed that he'd told Jameson he might put in an appearance tonight.

Later, he decided with a sigh. First, he needed to figure out what the hell was up with Cortez. Halfway to the central building, he heard a sound from the supply arch entrance. Was someone in there? At this hour? He'd bet that every single person, from cleaning crew to mechanics to researchers, was in the bar right now. Except, possibly, for whoever'd left that bloodstain on the ice.

He changed course and stalked over to the open arch door where he hesitated, staring into the deep black interior.

"Somebody in here?" he called, his voice immediately swallowed up by echoing space.

Nothing.

After a few seconds, he slid quietly inside and groped along the wall for the light switch.

A scan of the enormous, arched interior showed two rows of high shelving along the walls, filled with cardboard boxes. Food. Enough for a siege. Beyond, past the wooden door to the ice tunnel, he glimpsed the dimly lit area where he stored his ice core samples.

Nothing looked out of the ordinary.

He'd just flipped off the overheads when he heard a sound, so light and scuttling that he couldn't be sure it was real. Muscles spring-loaded with tension, he headed farther into the dark, cavernous interior, oddly hesitant to turn the light back on. Had the noise come from the tunnel? *Ridiculous.*

He'd advanced a half-dozen steps when a prickle of wariness made him go absolutely still. Slowly, he turned as someone stepped into the doorway, blocking out the exterior light. Had this guy made the sound? The arches were a strangely echoing place.

Coop squinted, unaccountably spooked by the unmoving silhouette. He forced his hands to loosen at his sides.

"Who is that?" His old throat injury kept him from yelling, but the guy, who was only a few yards away, had to hear him.

"Bradley Sampson," the man finally responded, sliding in and moving to push the door closed.

"Don't shut it. Headed out."

The pause was shorter this time. And maybe, just maybe, that could be explained by the awkwardness of getting caught together in the dark or even by the lingering hostility between them, since he'd never made a secret of the way he felt about this new operations manager.

"Everything good?" There was something careful about the way Sampson spoke. It was as off-key as Coop's singing voice.

"Yep." Coop didn't bother faking a smile. The man would see right through that, if he could see at all in here. "Just trying to find a friend."

"Oh yeah?"

"Yep."

Did he imagine the shift in Sampson's shoulders? "Maybe I can help. Who're you—"

"Coop!" another voice sounded from farther off, cutting through the tension like hot metal through ice.

Relief shot through him.

"Hey, Sampson. You see Coop in there?" Alex, part of the meteorite search team, came into view and Sampson subtly shifted away from the entrance, letting in more light.

"I'm here." Muscles tense, Coop immediately moved the last few feet to the door, and then outside. "What's up?"

"Coop, bro. Been lookin' all over for you."

"Just got in."

"Your presence is being requested."

"Hm?"

"Everybody's waiting for you at the Nest, man."

"Why?" Coop stopped, flummoxed. He never went to the base's bar. Or at least he'd stopped going since Angel Smith had started showing up there. The last thing he needed was one more opportunity to stutter like a fool in front of her.

"Jameson's got his eight-thousand-year-old bottle of scotch out. To celebrate the summer people leaving, he says."

Oh, right. Jesus. He didn't have time for this. "I'll pass." He shifted subtly toward Sampson.

"Yeah, well, he's not opening it unless you show up. Says you promised." Alex shook his head. "Things were getting so tense I came to find you."

Coop couldn't help giving a dry huff of humor. Jameson playing games, as usual. He knew damn well that Coop would feel obliged to go. Or maybe he figured that he wouldn't go, in which case Jameson could hold on to his precious bottle for one more season.

He glanced at Sampson, who looked smaller than he had moments before, his stance casual. Had Coop imagined the threat he'd seen in the man's silhouette? "Cortez at the Nest?" he asked, keeping Sampson in his peripheral vision.

"Yeah. I think so, man."

"All right then."

They set off, side by side, just three buddies headed to the bar for a drink. Alex showed no sign of sensing the strain beneath the surface, but Coop felt it, as present as the thump of music in the air.

The last of the quiet blew away the moment Sampson swung open the door to the Nest.

Within seconds, Coop was swallowed up by the crowd. Sweaty arms landed on his shoulders, pulling him deeper in, yanking off his coat, and helping with his gloves.

While every instinct screamed at him to get away, he used his height to scan the bodies for Cortez.

The closeness, the noise, the smell, all of it made him want to head back into the cold, where he could breathe unimpeded. And *think*.

He shook his head to clear it, blinked away the tunnel vision threatening to take over, and did his best to respond to the greetings thrown his way, all while trying desperately to find Cortez. He couldn't get that bloodstain out of his head.

"Hey, Coop!" Someone slapped him on the arm and another thrust a drink into his hand. Coop blinked at it for a few seconds before setting it on a table.

On the tiny stage, Jameson looked like a youngish, demented Santa Claus with his flaming-red beard and hefty frame. He stopped singing abruptly and pointed Coop out with a whoop. "Coop's in the house! Let's open her up!" Jameson yelled before throwing his guitar and mic to someone else and stomping toward the bar, where he grabbed his bottle from the place of honor it had occupied these past couple years.

With a sigh, Coop gave in and concentrated on fighting his way to Jameson instead.

Just before he reached the bar, his eye latched on to something, sending his breath into overdrive before his brain registered what it was.

Angel Smith. *Dancing*.

By some sort of witchcraft, his gaze separated her out of the faceless bodies writhing on one side of the room. He focused on her sinewy movements alone, while everything else blurred away into background noise.

He half acknowledged Jameson thrusting a drink into his hand and clinking their glasses together, caught just a whiff of the shot's smoky fumes, and barely registered the peaty burn of barrel-aged booze as it slid its way down his throat. All his senses were pointed at the place where Angel turned and twisted to the rhythm of the music—bare, glistening arms stretched high, head swinging back, river of dark hair cascading behind her. Her face...

"Good to see you here, my friend. Been a while."

"Mm-hm." Coop blinked back the haze and squinted at Jameson. What was it he wanted to ask again?

"So, listen to this, Coop. I've got a plan for the 300 Club that you're gonna love. We're gonna do freaking margaritas or some shit and get someone to take pictures like we're in goddamn Club Med. I'll wear my hula skirt, Pam's got that…"

No way was he running around the South Pole buck naked after sitting in a two-hundred-degree sauna. Coop shifted his head, doing his best to listen to all the ways the winter-overs would freeze their nuts off in the spirit of macho stupidity.

It was a lost cause, since he was only able to focus on one thing: her. Part of it was normal—the single-focus part. It went along with the other traits that separated him from the crowd, literally: his issues with outside stimuli, discomfort with closeness, inability to handle certain sensations or touches or smells. Not to mention the noise.

It was a sensorial processing thing. He knew that, had spent ages researching it, since research was his solution to most things—how he grasped ideas, solved problems, answered questions.

It was too loud and too crowded here, which was why he never came to the Nest with the summer crew in residence. He didn't mix with the horde, didn't even attempt to blend in.

Out on the ice was where he belonged, his only company snow and sky. Not standing in a crowded bar, staring at a woman who might as well be a different species.

He'd just decided to take off when she turned and caught his eye.

CHAPTER 3

IN A SPLIT SECOND, ANGEL WENT FROM BREATHLESS AND happy on the dance floor, to…she didn't know what to call the thing that Ford Cooper's intense scrutiny did to her. Torn open? Seen?

Her feet faltered, making her stumble and grab on to Pam, who giggled and helped her upright, saying something about mixing booze and tunes. But Angel's reaction had nothing to do with either of those things and everything to do with the hungry look on the Ice Man's face.

She shut her eyes tight and felt the room spin around her.

Oh, she thought with something like relief. *Pam's right. I'm drunk. That's all this is.* When she looked again, expecting him to have disappeared into the crowd, he was still there, head and shoulders above the others, eyes fixed on her, drawing her in with their tractor-beam pull.

Instead of ignoring him as she'd done since her first week here, she let that *now or never* thrill take hold. She'd never seen anything aside from irritation on his face, but at this moment, he looked like he could *consume* her. For some reason, that hint of interest pushed her to forget every one of the unfriendly one-sided conversations they'd ever had. Every curt "no salt," "too spicy," or just plain "no" he'd thrown her way, without a single hint of a "please" or "thank you."

What if Pam and Jameson were right about Ford Cooper? What if he was misunderstood? A good man who deserved another chance?

What if that thick veneer of cool disdain hid an actual person, with thoughts and feelings?

Someone slid a drink into her hand—a clear liquid in a shot glass—and rather than worry about her 4:30 a.m. wake-up or the packing she still had to do, she let the unexpected thrill of the man's interest goad her into toasting with the rest of the crew and slinging it back.

She barely heard the round of cheers, barely felt anything but the sultry rhythm of the bass thrumming through her veins.

This was it. One chance to scratch the Ice Man's flash-frozen surface before she left this place forever.

And because she never learned from past mistakes, Angel let the booze and the curiosity and the million foolish impulses drag her through the crowd toward where he stood, as tall and remote as an iceberg in a sea full of people.

"Missed you at dinner." Jameson moved close again. "What convinced you to come out tonight? Was it the scotch or…" His eyes cut to Angel, then returned to Coop.

"You, of course." Coop finally pulled his attention away from *her*, blinking hard as he worked to remember just what it was that had made him stop in here. "Actually, it was Cortez."

"Yeah?" Jameson let out a sly laugh. "Somehow doubt that, man."

"You seen him?"

"Uh. Hm." Jameson ran a thick, blunt hand over his grizzly beard and cast an eye around the room. "Yeah. Feel like he was in earlier? Those are his students over there."

"Right. You see if he was injured?"

Jameson gave him a funny look. "Pam didn't mention anything."

"Hm." Coop scanned the little huddle of students. No sign of Cortez there. Hopefully his colleague had gone back to his room, because he couldn't take another minute of this suffocating heat. "Gotta go."

Jameson nodded and gave him space, knowing him too well to try to get in his way.

With grim determination, Coop shoved his way toward the group.

"Where's Cortez?" he asked, ignoring the looks the students exchanged at his abrupt interruption.

"I think he was in his room," said one of the women. "Sick."

"I heard he hurt himself, out on the ice." The voices layered up, two and three of them coming at him simultaneously.

"Didn't someone say he was—"

"Phil talked to him. Nosebleed or something, he said."

"I heard him hacking up a lung in—"

Okay. Okay. Throwing his hands up, Coop backed away. He'd heard enough. A quick check on the way to his quarters would put his mind at ease. But for now, it was time to get out of this swamp. What an idiot he was to have come to the Nest on the most crowded night of the year.

He made it about halfway to the door when a hand landed on his arm, stopping him in his tracks.

"Hi there." Angel Smith smiled at him.

Was she drunk? She must be, judging from the slight sway of her body, even standing still, and the stubborn thrust of her chin. It was tilted high, squared off like he was a challenge to her. A nut she wanted to crack. He imagined she wore that expression when faced with a particularly large fish to gut or...a wild boar to butcher or something.

He lifted his own chin in a wordless greeting, but kept his eye on the coat pegs beside the door, wishing she'd go away.

"Hold on." Her voice, warm and rich, almost melodic, should have been too low to carry over the din, yet somehow he heard it perfectly. "Don't go yet."

He blinked at the row of near-identical outerwear, then started pawing through the coats. His should be easy to find, since it was older than most, more worn. Bigger, too.

Where was it? Behind him, Jameson screamed into the mic and everybody went wild.

"Doctor Cooper?" Angel shifted closer. Too close.

"It's not 'Doctor Cooper,'" he said over his shoulder, his voice cracking in a dozen different places. "It's Coop."

He caught her wrinkling her nose. What was it about his name that made her do that every time? Or was it him? Probably him, though he'd barely said two sentences to her in the months she'd been here. If it was him, then why the hell was she bothering him now?

He bent to retrieve a coat. Not his. Shoved it onto a peg and grabbed another. *Shit.* Another and another, all too small. *Breathe, dammit.* He was about 3.5 seconds from squeezing into somebody else's Big Red when his hand found the familiar rough nap of his patches. Thank God.

"Okay then. Coop. Wanna dance?"

Arms halfway into his sleeves, he stuttered to a stop, turned fully, and squinted down at Angel Smith, his features tightening in disbelief. After their few stilted interactions, this woman wanted to dance with *him* of all people?

He ignored the pull of that smooth stretch of lush-looking

skin, the overly large dark eyes, and lips that had no right to be as plush as ripe fruit when everyone else's were dry and flaky and shriveled up like old prunes.

"Dance?" *Why?* he almost asked, but that would open the conversation up to more—questions, discussion, even intimacies—and that was the last thing he needed.

She looked hesitant, like maybe she regretted whatever impulse had pushed her to ask in the first place. Good. Things were better that way.

"Of course not," he finally said, doing his best not to notice the hurt in her eyes. He nodded once.

That done, he turned and pushed out into the cold night, where he blinked blindly at the sunlit sky and counted out his breaths, waiting for a sense of relief that never came.

It was Cortez, he thought. That was why he couldn't seem to get rid of this tension.

He tromped back to the dorms and straight up to Cortez's door. If he'd been thinking clearly, he'd have knocked lightly, but his brain felt scrambled, his cheeks overheated. The spot she'd touched on his arm itched like a rash, so he made a fist and pounded. "Cortez! You in there?"

"Who's there?" The voice was scratchy and hoarse, the accent definitely English.

Relief washed through him like sun after months of austral winter. "It's Coop. You, uh..." He sniffed, suddenly conscious of how paranoid he'd been. "You okay?"

A pause. "Why?"

"The blood, on the ice."

"Nosebleed." Another few seconds passed before Cortez coughed, hard, and went on. "Wouldn't...stop."

"Lot of blood for a nosebleed, man." He saw the stain again, blossoming on the ice. It hadn't been all that big, he supposed.

"Bloody Crud's got me. I'm sick." It was true, the Crud had hit Pole hard since the last group brought it from McMurdo. Out here, a simple cold could put a man down for a week.

"Right." More hacking had Coop cringing and backing up a step. "Sorry to bug you."

"No worries."

Coop walked back to his room, annoyed at himself for blowing this thing out of proportion. Still, it took him a little longer than usual to fall asleep—and not just because he couldn't get Angel Smith out of his head.

It wasn't until hours later, just before his normal wake-up time, that his eyes popped open, the echo of two words running through his thoughts.

I'm sick, Cortez had said. Not ill, *sick*. Which didn't seem British at all. And, damn it, but even down with a cold, something had sounded *off* about his friend.

He threw off the blankets, jumped from his bed, and dropped quickly to the floor to do his usual round of get-warm-or-freeze-his-ass-off morning push-ups before heading out to figure out what the hell was going on.

CHAPTER 4

Angel hated the silence.

That was one thing she wouldn't miss. Well, that and the cold and the ice and being surrounded by miles and miles of nothing.

She hid her face in her pillow, the throbbing behind her eyes reminding her of everything she'd done last night. Drinking, dancing…embarrassing the living bejeezus out of herself.

If only she could stay right here.

Ugh, no. The whole crew expected breakfast and she'd stupidly told her staff to take it easy this morning, so she'd better get a move on. She groaned.

A long slow stretch beneath the blankets popped her joints and pushed through her knee pain before she reached for the clothes she'd shoved under the blankets last night. The dry skin of her fingers caught on the fleece of her leggings as she slipped her feet into them, then yanked them up over her long underwear. She struggled into one layer after another—merino wool, fleece, Gore-Tex—all of it blessedly warm.

Three…two…one. Now up. One cool lungful of air, then, as fast as she could, she added a second layer of socks, put her foot out, stuck it into a boot, then did the same with the other. She planted her feet firmly, tensed her thighs, and pushed to standing, gritting her teeth through the burn. Darned knee hated the cold.

When, exactly, did I turn into an old lady?

She huffed out a laugh, pulled her hair up, slid her chef's coat on, followed by a puffy, lightweight inner jacket, then the massive Big Red coat she'd been issued at the start of this trip. Last, she slid her fleece gaiter over her head to protect her neck and the bottom half of her face, pulled on gloves, and grabbed her knives. She lifted the blackout blind—a nighttime necessity at the South Pole in summer, the land of the midnight sun—and sucked in a bolstering breath before opening her door.

The long, brightly lit dorm hall stretched out in both directions and she shivered, not from cold this time but from the absolute dead quiet and the feeling that someone—or something—watched her, ever ready to spring out. From day one, trudging around Burke-Ruhe had spooked her in a way that was vague but bone-deep, as if she were always on the alert for…what? An alien attack? Jack Nicholson to pop out wielding a bloody knife? The abominable freaking snowman?

As if anything could survive this continent.

Even dry, her boots squeaked on the rubber hallway floor, then down a long set of metal steps. At the bottom, she pushed through a door into the chilly vestibule, then took a quick breath, counted down, and shoved the heavy outer door open, stepping into—*holy crap*—cold. Cold, cold, cold.

Wind ripped the air from her lungs and shut her brain down, stunning her into momentary stillness. Everything was a shock to the system—the subzero temperature, the achingly bright daylight. Not to mention the place itself.

Nothing lived here. No birds, no insects, not a solitary penguin on this most remote part of the East Antarctic Ice Sheet. Just three hundred and sixty degrees of sky and ice—blue and white—fighting for dominance.

Not to mention a sun that played its strange game of hopscotch, bouncing along the rim of the sky but never quite setting. Almost sunset, sunrise, almost sunset, sunrise.

Thank God she wouldn't be at Pole for that final sunset of the season, because she didn't think she could handle twilight blending into months of eternal night.

The wind whistled between the buildings in a ghostly catcall, and because she wasn't about to accept that kind of disrespect, she whistled right back. The sound didn't carry past the fine weave of her neck gaiter.

Each exhale puffed loudly in her ears as she tromped across the snow, unwilling to glance again at the vastness beyond. It was too big, too scary. If she wandered outside the limits of the station, she'd become an insignificant blip swallowed up by the continent's angry jaws. No, not angry. Aloof. Antarctica didn't give a crap about her.

Geez, she laughed at herself, *this freaking place.*

Finally, she hauled open the door to the central building, which housed the gym and entertainment center, along with the lounge and communications office and—most importantly for her—the galley.

Relief flooded her, along with blessed warmth.

She'd never understand people who chose to come here and trek around, living in a tent out in that frozen wasteland, *for fun.* Explorers or adventurers, they called themselves, but she knew they were just masochists with too much time and money on their hands. Sunburn? Chapped lips? Frozen digits? You didn't have to fly thousands of miles to find those.

And the landscape? Well, it wasn't even a landscape, exactly, since that insinuated actual *land* beneath a person's feet, whereas Antarctica was an ever-evolving ice sculpture. A *presence.*

Okay, Debbie Downer. Time to lighten this party up.

After stomping the snow from her boots in the vestibule, she shed her coat, hung it on the hook, and beelined down the hall.

Finally, in the sanctuary of the galley, she let the door close and flipped on the overheads, watching as they illuminated rows of white rectangular tables, each with their own napkin holder and salt and pepper shakers. The one at the front—Jameson's table—held his requisite bottle of hot sauce.

The view through the galley windows was different from the one outside. Beyond a few smaller metal structures—the ancillary building, Pam's clinic, and a huddle of tents belonging to visiting scientists—there was nothing but white. But maybe the view wasn't different. Maybe she was. With the glass separating her from the outside, she could appreciate the beauty.

Would she miss more than just the Poleys—the people—once she was gone? Would bittersweet memory turn all that powdery, dangerous snow from a splintering wall of pain into a cozy wintry landscape, covered in a delicate dusting of confectioners' sugar? Would she remember the marrow-deep ache of the wind as just a sweet, mellow breeze?

The sky was blue today and went on forever. No reason to cancel the flight with weather like this. Which was good, she mentally repeated for the bazillionth time—it was time to go back and face the music. But first, Angel reminded herself, she had to face breakfast.

She went around the food service line into the bare-bones kitchen. Nothing, she decided as she got the coffee going, would ruin her last day at Pole. Not this cold seeping into every pore, not the lights flickering above, not even the hangover chipping away at the inside of her skull.

Of course, there was the stupid thing she'd done last night. *That* might ruin today.

Oh, shut your piehole, brain. She slid a mug under the first drizzle of coffee, which would be too hot and too strong, but she needed something to knock the stupid right out of her.

Once her tongue had been scalded to her satisfaction, she shoved the frozen bacon into the microwave, pulled out the dough she'd thrown together last night, and punched it down with more vigor than usual. Then she went to work laminating the croissants—layering and rolling and layering and rolling. One advantage to cooking at Pole was that she didn't need to refrigerate between stages. Until she turned the ovens on, the air in here was bracingly cold.

After an hour spent julienning, dicing, sautéing, and baking the ingredients of her last meal in Antarctica, she savored the aroma of thyme-laced veggies, glanced at the clock, and pulled out the fresh buns before sliding the croissants into the hot oven.

Soon she'd be snug in the cavernous belly of an LC-130 Hercules airplane, heading to McMurdo, then Christchurch, better known around here as Cheech. From there, she'd hop another flight to the United States, and finally, home to Pittsburgh.

First, though, it was time to run the gauntlet of one last breakfast in this place, which would be an absolute pleasure if not for the presence of a certain man.

Ugh.

Dealing with the guy most days was a trial, but after last night, it was the stuff nightmares were made of. Well, high school nightmares anyway, when crushes made or broke you.

She slid the covered pan of bacon onto the service line, added dishes of stewed tomatoes and crab cakes—a crew favorite—and fought the fresh, hot wave of embarrassment that washed over her.

What an idiot to have hoped that a dance might heat up that man's subglacial eyes. Why did she have to go and ruin a clearly defined…what was the opposite of friendship? *Enemyship*? Didn't sound right.

She sent a final glance at the clock and—

The door swung open, more violently than usual, and there he was, right on time, too-wide shoulders filling the doorway, perma-scowl on his annoyingly handsome face: Dr. Ford Cooper, the Ice Man himself.

Coop shoved open the galley door.

"Doctor Cooper," Angel Smith said in greeting. She did not seem happy to see him. Unsurprising but not a problem. If the weather held, it would be her last day. The last time they'd be forced to converse.

In response, he grunted through scarred vocal cords, already raw from the morning's arid cold. And then tried again. "You see Cortez?"

She didn't answer right away. Just blinked at him, followed by a slow, deep inhale. "No. You're the first person here." She scowled. "As usual."

Shit.

He'd just woken up all of Cortez's students and half the people on his floor by pounding on the man's door again.

That had not gone over well with any of them. "He's out on the ice," they'd told him, with big intimidated eyes.

"Why?" Coop had asked the frightened-looking kids. "He was sick, right?" *Ill*, not sick. He was ill. "Why'd he go out again if he has the Crud? Was he feverish? Delirious?" he pressed. "What's going on?"

The students had all glanced at each other, their expressions saying that both Coop and Cortez were batshit crazy anyway, so who knew what the hell he'd gone out for.

"Did you actually *see* him?" A few head shakes, so Coop had set off—he'd go out on the ice himself to find the man if he had to. This wasn't normal. None of it was.

He'd made it about twenty feet before his stomach had produced a long, low grumble, however, telling him that he'd better feed himself now or he'd regret it. Sustenance was essential everywhere, but in Antarctica, where bodies consumed calories as fast as the generators burned fuel, eating was key to survival.

With a bitter sigh, he'd changed directions and stalked toward the central building.

On normal days, getting food from Angel Smith was a pain. Today, it was an annoyance he didn't have time for. A necessary evil.

"You see or hear anyone else walking around this morning?"

She shook her head with a sniff and turned her back to him, leaving Coop to suck in a calming breath.

Just a few more hours of this and the place would empty out, only the die-hard winter-overs left to carry on the work meant to keep the station alive through the dark, cold months. For some of those months, even Coop would have to stay indoors. Which was fine, because after today, it would be just him and a skeleton crew of trustworthy souls. That knowledge brought relief flowing through him so fast and hard he could have sunk to the floor with it.

Angel Smith would leave and take her excessive *everything* with her. She was too curvy, too boisterous, too gregarious, too loud. Had she not noticed that people here liked quiet? Okay, not entirely true, judging from the unholy din the Poleys had made at the Nest last night.

The plates rattled as he grabbed one, still peeved that he'd gone there at all. But the Cortez thing had burrowed under his skin—a mystery he needed to get to the bottom of.

Hurriedly, he opened the first serving dish. His belly went wild as the warm fog of bacon hit him.

He'd just grabbed a croissant when Angel started sharpening a knife with a slow, even cadence that seemed oddly grim to his ears.

Slice. Slice.

His eyes were drawn to the enormous blade she dragged back and forth along the steel rod in her left hand. Each long, sharply ringing pull made his teeth clench so hard he could feel it in his balls.

Was he imagining the implied threat here? *Christ*, he thought, letting his eyes, for one brief moment, slide down her back, *I need to hurry up or she'll—*

Why was she standing like that, her shoulders curved forward, her head tilted at a strange angle? The posture was different from anything he'd seen from her—a woman who didn't seem to have a grumpy bone in her body. At that moment, she looked…defeated? Tired?

Swallowing back an unwelcome wave of discomfort, he picked up a sticky-looking bun, threw it on his plate, then paused as he scanned the food. She'd put out a feast. A riot of smells and shapes and colors vibrant enough to rival the bright red of his coat.

It was so over the top, even he could see that there was something behind it. A celebration?

Maybe, but she didn't seem all that festive right now.

Yeah, well, I don't usually bring that out in people.

He could only surmise that she was sad to be leaving. And here he was, being his usual curt self in the face of all of this…generosity. She worked her ass off to feed the Poleys and he'd barely done her the courtesy of thanking her. With violent suddenness, his face heated. *And* he'd refused her a silly little dance.

He needed to say something.

In preparation, he inhaled the buttery scent of fresh pastries, and his mouth watered. Something smelled like Christmas. Cinnamon? Was that what that odor was? A neighbor used to bake them cookies when he was a kid, and they'd smelled exactly like this—only not nearly as fragrant.

Stop procrastinating.

He forced himself to speak. "Ms. Smith."

She half turned to face him, expression blank, brows and chin lifted, ready for a fight. As if to illustrate how little he mattered, her hands continued their smooth slide, scraping steel to steel. His breathing picked up.

"I'm…sorry." There. He'd said it. Or mumbled it at least.

He turned to go, plate only half-full, then sighed, swiveling back. Shit. The woman had fed him for the past few months, and though her presence perturbed him, hers was admittedly the best food he'd eaten on this continent. Or possibly anywhere. He shut his eyes, breathed in, and opened them again. "And thank you. For everything."

He punctuated his words with a single nod.

Okay. Done.

Ignoring her open-mouthed expression, he took his plate and left the galley, intent on fueling up as quickly as possible and heading out to find Cortez.

CHAPTER 5

WHAT WAS THAT?

Angel stared at the door, so tense waiting for a punch line that she jumped and nearly dropped her knife when it swung open again a couple seconds later.

The sight of Jameson barreling in deflated her—with relief. Probably.

"Saw Coop rushin' off with a plate full of food." He raised one red brow at her. "What'd you do to him?"

"Me?" The word came out a little too shrill. "Are you kidding with—"

"Yes, gorgeous." He winked as he walked up and grabbed a plate. "Just teasin'. Coop's the best man here, but Lord knows he's not good with…"

What—words? Women? Mere human beings?

"…emotion."

Squinting, she opened her mouth to grill him on what emotion *she* could possibly be responsible for but then stopped abruptly. There was that totally weird apology to consider, after all. Not to mention the most out-of-the-blue, awkward thanks she'd ever received.

She glanced at the door, thinking of the way Ford had stalked out, wolfing down his food.

Actually, "wolf" was a good description for the man. A lone one—fierce, unapproachable, with that rough, rarely used, gravelly voice. There was something kind of wolf-like, too, about his face with its broad, flat, angular features, lips that somehow looked both hard and curved, and square jaw. He was remote, stiff and smooth as sharply carved ice. Except when he looked her way.

She let out a humorless sound. Right. She alone was responsible for chiseling that extra line of annoyance between his eyes. The one that made him look angry.

What the hell had he thanked her for anyway? For slinging institutional food his way? For asking him to dance? And the apology? That was—

She caught Jameson's eyes on her and quickly looked away, flushing hot.

Thankfully, Pam chose that moment to sail into the galley, followed by a couple researchers and a little cluster of interns. Pam's "Hey, y'all!" led to a long, sappy breakfast, full of teary-eyed farewells and hugs in a quieter, more sober version of the night before.

"Didn't realize leaving would be so hard," Angel told her friend during a lull.

"Could just stay." Pam grinned, knowing full well that wasn't an option. She could return next summer, but cooks didn't over-winter. From here on out, the crew fended for themselves.

I wish. The thought surprised her.

Behind Pam, some of the recent summer arrivals crowded in and Angel rushed to make more coffee.

Someone shifted and sidled up close to the food. Bradley Sampson, the new operations manager. Okay, so maybe she didn't like *everybody* she'd met here.

"You gonna miss me, Angel?" His jaw tightened as he crunched down on one of the Life Savers he always seemed to be sucking on. The sound was like bones breaking.

"Sure." She gritted her own teeth and moved back, wondering how he'd managed to enter her personal space with the food still between them.

"You really mean that?" She was always unsure how to respond to the guy. He shifted close enough to press his hips to the counter and leaned all the way over the glass divider, his voice friendly, expression innocent. "Sure wish we could take you with us."

Angel went very still. Her skin prickled from the top of her head to her toes.

"*What?*"

"You know. 'Cause you're leaving today?" He gave her a quizzical, innocent smile, but somehow even that got her heart racing.

"But you're not."

"Hm." He winked.

"Okay," she muttered weakly before heading back in search of something to do with her hands. What the hell? Had she misheard him? Because if she hadn't, that was the weirdest—

The door opened and someone stuck their head in to yell, "Sky's clear! Plane's taking off from McMurdo!"

A cheer went up and everybody ran to get ready. No time to worry about what she had or hadn't heard now.

With the help of a couple crew members, she quickly cleaned the kitchen and then stepped back to give her domain one last look. The shelves were a little sparse. And though she hated the supply arch with a passion, she wouldn't leave the winter crew without supplies. One last task before she said goodbye to this place forever.

Heaving a sigh, she left her warm kitchen, suited up, and descended the long, dizzying spiral staircase that led from the central building to the supply arch, which housed dry storage, mechanical equipment, items needed for the field sites, and everything else that could be kept at a constant deep freeze. Sewage was packaged in one of the arches and prepared for removal. Jameson's shop, where he and the other mechanics worked on equipment, was in yet another, while many of the researchers counted on the arches' deep freeze to keep their field samples from melting.

Every clanging step took Angel farther underground, the air around her growing noticeably cooler. By the time she reached the bottom and pushed through the door into the yawning space, her eyelashes had frozen stiff.

It always took a few moments to psych herself into leaving the relative safety of the tin-can-like stairwell for the enormous supply arch.

She was going to call out to see if anyone was there, but that was totally the kind of thing the first victim did in horror movies. Besides, it wasn't really a creepy, dark snow tomb about to crumble under the weight of a bazillion tons of ice. That was just her imagination. She peered up at the corrugated warehouse ceiling. Well, the dark part was true. Only a few of the lights seemed to be working. Were the others out? She felt along the wall and flipped the switch. Nothing. Okay, great. Fine. A quick check confirmed her Maglite was still in her coat pocket.

From the outside, the arches were snow-covered, nothing visible but brightly shining metal doors, but inside, the place was more shadows than light. In the next arch over, the power plant's bright-yellow machinery busily chugged out electricity and heat for the entire station. And in the farthest one, Jameson coddled hardworking vehicles into lasting another season, another year. But this arch was silent, dark, lifeless, the type of place where you'd expect to see bats hanging from the ceiling. Except, of course, nothing could survive down here.

Swallowing hard, she avoided the tall rolling ladders lined up on the concrete floor like stairs to nowhere and peered into the shadows behind the massive metal storage shelves lining the long building. The coast was clear. Nothing but a bright red POSITIVELY NO SMOKING sign.

Oh for Pete's sake. Relax.

She walked farther inside and grabbed a sled, onto which she'd pile supplies before dragging the whole thing out through the big arch entrance, up the ice ramp, across the snow, and to her kitchen. It was a long haul, but she couldn't carry the stuff back up the steps.

As fast as she could, she yanked big bags of pasta from wooden pallets, a few canned items, then on to paraffin-coated eggs and frozen veggies and fruit. Those were a necessity here, since aside from the freshies coming in on today's flight, there'd be limited produce. And her people needed their vitamins.

It was at moments like this that she hated being short. The darned canned tomatoes were at the back of the second shelf, which meant the ladder wouldn't help. And though she stretched as high as she could, she couldn't quite get her hands on them.

Grumbling under her breath, she pulled the sled into the shadows between two big units and the wall, then slid behind one of the metal structures. Her boobs made it a tight squeeze, but she managed to shuffle down, strained up, and slid a can off. She just caught it before it brained her, and—

What was that?

Every nerve ending in her body vibrated as she went still and listened hard for that strange scuffling sound.

Buzzing, nerves on high alert, she held her breath and stared hard into the shadows, willing a familiar figure to walk by. But nobody appeared. And when it came again—a slow, stealthy dragging sound straight out of every one of her childhood nightmares—she screwed her eyes shut and crouched low, trying to make herself as small as she possibly could.

It was absurd to be afraid of the dark. She knew that. She *did*. But there was something out there. Or someone. And she couldn't for the life of her fathom why they were working so hard to be quiet.

CHAPTER 6

A DOOR SLAMMED AND ANGEL STARTLED, JUST BARELY tightening her hold on the can of tomatoes before it clattered to the ground.

Okay. This was ridiculous. When would she stop being so spooked? Forcing herself to relax, she started to call out when someone spoke.

"Down." Though it was spoken quietly, some strange acoustic trick made the word so loud she obediently ducked before realizing the order wasn't meant for her. She should make a joke right now. Bark or yell *Up!* or something. But she couldn't even catch her breath.

"S-swear I told you everything I know."

Wait. Who was that? A second guy? Whoever it was sounded scared, his voice high and shaky.

"Look, Stickley." Stickley. Alex Stickley. A climatologist maybe? Or maybe he was one of those guys who searched for meteorites. He liked hash browns. That she knew for sure. "If you can't show me which tube it's in, I'll have to—"

A dull thud made Angel jerk so hard she rattled the metal shelf, then put out a hand to still it.

Was someone hurting Alex?

No way. This had to stop. *Now.*

She'd half stood, ready to march down there, when the next sound hit her. A pop like a nail gun, quick and loud.

Then screaming.

For a few long moments, her mind went completely blank. Those sounds knocked all understanding from her, the way a word lost its meaning after repeating it too many times. Nothing made sense—not the noise or the voices or even the sight of her own gloved hands grasping metal.

Dumbly, she focused on the industrial tomato can with its '50s block lettering, then slid her eyes to the shelves and stared until the holes in the metal brackets lined up again.

This nightmare was actually happening.

She had to get out of here and find help. She started sliding toward the end of the storage area, an inch at time, her body so tightly wound it was a shock she could move at all.

The man's next words made her stop and listen. Though she truly didn't want to hear them.

"No, no, no, no, *Alex*." That was Bradley Sampson speaking, in his soft, singsongy drawl. "See, bro, you're not dead. You know? Just a kneecap," he scolded affectionately. "It'll heal."

Alex's response was too garbled to understand.

"Look, this isn't about me. We answer to a higher power." Apparently there was something funny about that, because someone laughed. Was there a third person there? "This is bigger than you or me, man." Sampson lowered his voice, so she had to strain to hear. "I'll put it to you straight: you help me figure out which of these core samples to pull, right here, right now, and this little cutie?"

"*No, no. Noooooooooooooo.*" The word was long and low and full of so much pain that it stood the hairs up all over her body.

"This li'l lady and her mama back in Ann Arbor? Well, they might just survive this. But we need the ice samples. Today. Right now."

A scream welled up inside her—a bubble that needed to burst, only instead of being hollow, it was filled with the horror of this new reality. They'd threatened to kill his wife. His baby, for God's sake. *Oh God, Alex.*

Half ready to spring into action, half paralyzed by fear, she willed the scream down and listened.

It took a while for Alex to respond and she couldn't make out the word. Maybe "okay," though it might just have been an expelled breath.

"Cool." Sampson's voice turned those fine standing hairs to ice picks. "Here." Footsteps crunched. "Let's get you…"

The rest of the sentence was lost, but she didn't need to hear it to know what was happening.

"These five?" A pause. "You're sure about that?"

"If there are more, I don't—" Alex coughed long and hard before speaking again. "Don't know. But we all got a chance to see them. They were so…extraordinary." Another cough. "See? There."

"Right." A pause. "And these numbers right here? That's the date?"

"Y-yes."

"Great, that works!" Sampson said this like they'd just made lunch plans for next Tuesday. "Now, kneel."

"I c-c—"

"Do it," Sampson said, all friendliness gone. She pictured him putting a hand to Alex's shoulder and pushing. "If that *fucker* hadn't gone out on the ice again today, we'd have the damned thing already. Ford motherfucking Cooper. Dude is—"

He abruptly stopped speaking. The clomp of footsteps told her he, or someone, had moved a short distance away. "Go ahead," Sampson said in a completely different voice. Deep, all business. After a long pause, he asked, "How many missing? This is confirmed?" Another pause. "Shit.

Can't contain the whole group here and the aircraft's just for today. We've got to get to the Facility." He might have listened again before uttering a curt, "Good. Ignore those assholes and tell the pilot they're all accounted for. Tell them…I'm the operations manager, dammit. And if I want to hire her on for another damn season, I can. Tell them to take off without her." He paused, then in a louder voice clearly meant for his companions as opposed to whoever was on the other end of the headset, said, "Summer plane's taking off right now. Missing the cook, apparently."

The plane was leaving already? How was that possible? She hadn't even heard it land.

No. Oh, please, don't leave me here. Angel opened her mouth and shut it tight, not trusting herself to keep quiet as the unmistakable drone of the plane's engine cut through the corrugated metal and layers of snow overhead to reach her sensitive ears.

"All right. Let's do this *now*."

A few seconds ticked by, as hopelessness and fear warred with Angel's need to intervene. To help Alex. To stop these monsters.

She had to do something. There was no choice, was there? She either did something to stop them or… Without waiting for that thought to gel, she set the can down, quietly, so quietly, and scooted along the wall. Slowly, carefully, breath held. If she could get a look at them, maybe she could find a way to intervene.

"I said kneel." How could Sampson sound so casual?

"Please don't."

Her heartbeat picked up, frantic. What was happening? Faster, she sidestepped until she couldn't move farther without going out into the open, and bent forward. Alex said something, his words coming at her as an incomprehensibly jumbled flurry.

The prickle she'd felt earlier buzzed to life again, heating her face, slicking clammy sweat wherever fabric rubbed skin.

There, three top-lit silhouettes. One doubled over on the ground, his arms thrown up to protect himself.

She watched in slow-motion horror as Sampson reached out. For a few seconds, it looked like he planned to give the cowering man his blessing. But then the gun materialized—long and thin and deadly. Was that a silencer? She'd never seen one in real life, but it sent something visceral through her. *Please, no. Please.*

He pressed it to Alex's head and, without ceremony, pulled the trigger. The resulting pop seemed too small to kill a man, to cut him off midplea. How could something so quick, so casual, end a life?

Disbelief. White noise. Nothing for a handful of seconds but void, filling her brain like television fuzz.

Suspended on that spinning sphere of shock, she couldn't move, couldn't get air, couldn't believe what had just happened.

And then, with warp speed, reality hit her, as painful and real as a cast-iron pan to the face. Her entire frame heaved. She had to keep the scream inside, so she shoved her gloved fist into her mouth and stared at the ice-coated wall opposite, deaf but for the buzzing in her ears. It was a trick of her eyesight, she knew, or her brain probably, but the ice, like cloud shapes, offered up an elephant, its trunk raised. Beneath it was a cherry. No, a double. Double cherry. The kind she'd hung over her ears as a kid to make round, shiny, ripe earrings.

"All right. You acquire the samples." Sampson didn't sound like a man who'd just committed murder.

"Yes, sir," said the other one. She couldn't even be sure who it was at this point. Didn't want to turn and look at what they'd done.

"Bring them to the surface. We're moving out now." He switched to that other voice. "Alpha Team, you are a go in five."

Go? Go where?

Oh God, she couldn't think, couldn't figure any of this out.

The plane was gone, and she had no idea what she'd find up there. Was she alone with these murderers?

She squeezed her eyes shut, only to be assailed by Alex's death again—that smooth, snakelike movement that had changed the scene from benediction to condemnation. The point of no return. The moment her life went from complicated to nightmarish. Worse, because she'd always woken up from nightmares.

But this wasn't a dream.

Now poor Alex would never speak again. Never breathe, never eat or see his sweet little girl, and all she could do was find cloud shapes in the ice.

No. No, that wasn't all she could do. She was alive, wasn't she? She had no idea what or how or if she'd die in the process, but she was going to find some way to stop these men. Now.

Something wasn't right.

Coop already knew that, but he hadn't seen Cortez out here—or any sign of him on the ice at all—and as he drove on, the feeling of unease grew and ripened inside him like a rotten fruit about to explode.

A lot of vehicles seemed out of commission lately, so he'd been forced to bring the big PistenBully out to fix the drill he'd been unable to repair on-site. He'd have to haul it back and pull it apart. Besides, he'd figured he'd be able to bring Cortez back if his friend had run into an issue. Now he pushed the machine as fast as it would go, wishing he'd taken a snowmobile instead.

He approached his field research site, watching the horizon…and pulled to a stop.

He confirmed his current coordinates on the GPS unit and looked up again.

Usually, he'd see his site from here. Today, there was nothing.

Twenty minutes later, he pulled up beside his site.

Or what had been his site.

He threw open the door and jumped to the ice. Nothing remained but a hole in the ground, along with a few discarded items—including the bright-red tent that had protected his drill through all kinds of weather.

His drill, dammit. His life's work. *He'd* designed and built the damned thing. He'd dug the hole and put it in the ground.

Jesus, who the hell would steal another scientist's work, not to mention the tools they needed to do their work?

He picked up the tent and threw it to the side. They hadn't just taken his drill; they'd slashed the fabric, smashed the rest of his on-site gear to smithereens, and ground it all into the ice in what felt like a deliberate insult.

Whoever had done this didn't just want to steal from him, they wanted to screw him. Hard.

Head thrumming with foreboding, he climbed back into the tractor and set off for the next site on his route.

CHAPTER 7

THIS WAS FEAR. NOT HER USUAL FEAR OF BEING ALONE in the arches or the uneasiness of staring across the ice and knowing she meant nothing at all.

This was terror that had changed her for good. It sparked things she'd never be able to control on her own, ignited entirely new systems in her body, rearranged them into popping, cracking networks of reactivity. Synapses? Was that the word? Or just nerves that she was no longer in command of. Like when a driving instructor took over the car, she felt a weird sort of relief. *I don't have to do anything. I'm not in charge anymore.*

The other man—who looked like Ben Wong, another of the new crew members—went to one side of the arch and returned dragging something big, which he flopped down onto the floor. A shipping case, maybe?

Then, once he'd lined it up, he pulled a long metal tube from its slot along the wall and dropped it into the box with a loud thud.

"Watch out with those," Sampson said, sounding peeved. "No payload, no pay, remember."

"Yes, sir."

"All right. We've gotta move." He spoke into whatever communication device they were using. "Bravo Team, to the generators."

Sampson headed away from her, leaving behind the

inanimate lump that was once Alex Stickley without so much as a backward glance.

Angel looked on as terror stoked something inside her. Energy? Courage? She wasn't sure, but it ran through her body like a jolt of electricity.

Whatever it was spurred her to step over her half-empty sled, careful to walk on her tiptoes.

Angel's eyes slid to the side, where bags of rice filled most of the metal shelves. Farther up, where Ben worked, was nothing but row after row of those metal tubes. Could Ben see her crouched down here? Maybe not. Maybe her silhouette blended in with the bulk supplies.

Once all five cylinders were loaded into the case, Ben grabbed the handle and started pulling—right toward Angel. She popped back behind the shelf and waited, wishing she could roll herself into a tiny ball, but she was stuck in this too-tight, too-visible place.

Please don't see me. He walked closer. She couldn't move, could only listen to the fingernail-on-the-chalkboard sound of plastic scraping over concrete. It was a horrible sound. But not the worst. She couldn't think of that other sound—the sound of gunfire, of death—or she'd do something stupid.

And suddenly, holy crap, he was right there. Close enough to touch, if she slid her hand from the back of the shelf, over the rice, and out to where he stood, in the center of the arch. And here she was, trying to meld with the wall, shaking like a jackhammer. She ignored a lancing pain in her knee and did her best not to breathe, to stop the shaking. To stop existing, if she could.

How can he not hear me?

He stilled. *This is it. I'm dead.*

Every muscle tightened in anticipation of whatever

he'd do or say. She couldn't kick him from here, but if she shoved some of the food aside, she could maybe hit his crotch and—

"Still in the arch. Headed out." He paused, clearly listening, while Angel used everything she had not to breathe a sigh of relief. "Shit. Yeah. Okay. I'll intercept them." Dropping the handle, he took off at a jog, back toward where he'd come from, then around the corner.

Before she even realized what she'd planned, Angel's lizard brain took over, some prehistoric, instinctive part of her she'd never had to tap into.

Run.

Mustering every ounce of her courage, she stepped out from her hiding place, turned, and almost tripped over the silver shipping case. She stared at it, then, like a zombie, reached out and flipped open the top to see the dull gleam of metal.

Run! The fear voice was right. She should go…

Almost calmly, she turned and eyed the row of cylinders lining the wall farther up the arch.

And then she was walking—only not to safety, the place where the arch opened up onto the bright outdoors, but toward those other tubes, following in Ben Wong's footsteps.

What the hell am I doing?

She slid a tube out. *Whoa. Heavy.* Still, she could do it. She *would* do it, because if these men were willing to kill for these, then she sure as hell didn't want them in their hands. Bending her knees, she grabbed another and humped them back to the shipping container. Crap. She hadn't thought this through.

Doesn't matter. Do it.

Somewhere in the distance, she heard Ben talking. Was

he talking to friend or foe? Should she yell? No. No, she'd seen the carnage these people were capable of. She'd make it worse if she wasn't careful.

First do this, then find a way to warn the others.

As fast as she could, she pulled the cylinders from the case and slid them under the shelves. The fifty-pound bags of rice that drooped over the edge like fat, juicy steaks hanging over the rim of a too-small plate hid them perfectly.

Once it was empty, she loaded the case up with the first two cylinders she'd grabbed. Crap. There was a label, right? She dropped to her knees and felt around until she found a tube and pulled it out, then took a deep breath before yanking off her gloves and working at the sticker with her ragged fingernail.

Relief flooded her when it came off easily. She slapped it over the sticker on one of the new tubes, and did the same with the second.

In the distance, Ben laughed, the sound resonating in that weird way the arches had, echoey but also swallowed by the ice. Was he coming back?

Don't come back. Don't come back, she mouthed silently as she raced to pull more dummy samples, hauled them back and placed them in the case painfully slowly, so as not to make a sound. Finally, she went through the whole cycle for the last cylinder. Now for stickers. One…two… She worked to peel off the last sticker, breathing so hard now that she almost didn't hear the exterior handle's telltale squeak.

For a split second, she couldn't move.

But when that door opened, whoever was there would see her, clear as day. Maybe it was someone she could trust, but if it wasn't…

Forget the last sticker. With one hand, she slammed the cover shut, gave herself up to that lizard brain, and ran like hell.

Something cracked in the distance, everything shook, and the arch went dark.

Gone. Every one of his drills. Into thin air.

And nobody at base was answering. Not the station manager, not Jameson, not the communications office... nobody. Which made zero sense. Somebody should pick up. Coop had tried putting a call through to McMurdo, but the sky had chosen that moment to cloud over and he couldn't get a *goddamn* signal. He needed to tell somebody what was going on, so they could stop whoever was responsible before they left the continent.

But who the hell was behind this?

None of the researchers, because it wouldn't make sense when they shared scientific data freely between them. Just recently, in fact, he'd pulled probably the most interesting core samples of his career and shared them with pretty much every researcher here.

Operations staff was even less likely to be interested in what he was doing out here. The mechanics would have the know-how to pull the drills apart, but with their sixteen-hour, six-day-a-week schedules, they lacked opportunity to do so. The same went for kitchen staff, fuelies, and sanitation folks.

Was it pure, angry sabotage?

He squinted hard out the windshield, willing the machine to go over twelve miles per hour.

The new guys had done it. Had to be. He should've

listened to his gut about them. Not that it would've changed a thing.

An image of that blood came to him again. Jesus, he hoped Cortez was all right. If only he'd busted through his door last night.

If only he'd been paying more attention, he would've noticed trouble before it fell all around him. Somebody'd asked him about his drills recently. Who was that? Alex? No. No, it had been one of the new guys. Ben something. He'd claimed to have an interest in engineering, said someone had mentioned Coop's drills. Damn it. Was he the guy behind this? Or that whole group?

Those assholes had never fit in here from the moment they'd arrived. Cleaners and mechanics, ostensibly, along with the new operations manager. But he'd seen the way their eyes took in a room. Cautious. Hypervigilant. And more than a little arrogant.

In hindsight, that arrogance was particularly telling. Not to mention worrisome.

He was grinding his teeth now, fighting the urge to get out and run. No matter how slow this machine felt, he couldn't outrun—

Something cracked beyond the engine's low rumble, and seconds later a gray smudge appeared on the horizon.

What the hell?

He yanked off his sunglasses, rubbed his eyes, and squinted in the direction of the Burke-Ruhe Research Station, where a plume of black smoke reached up into the white antarctic sky.

CHAPTER 8

ANGEL HAD NEVER STARED INTO SUCH COMPLETE DARK-
ness, never strained to hear a sound in such absolute silence.
Was that an explosion? Was it the power plant?

Please, God, what's happening?

"Got company!" Sampson's yell broke through the
silence, stern and matter-of-fact. Through the pounding in
her ears, Angel couldn't tell which direction his voice had
come from.

She slid around until she found a spot behind another
shelving unit filled with big cardboard boxes. Toilet paper,
she remembered. Great weapon to have at a time like this.
For a split second, the idea of mummifying Sampson almost
made her laugh.

Light sliced open the dark, solid as a knife through
butter, blinding her, while footsteps converged from both
ends of the arch.

They were coming for her.

Go!

It was some sixth sense that led her to the wall, instead of
straight down the arch, and pure instinct that sent her to the
low wooden door leading to the ice tunnels. Jameson had
shown her around once. He loved it down here, had even hand-
carved a few of the passages himself, but to her, they'd felt
like a frigid tomb. Didn't matter. She needed a place to hide.

The steps pounded closer, someone breaking off to
search the tool room, someone else another storage area.
There was no time.

With shaking hands, she slid back the lock and pulled. It wouldn't budge. Another pull, with both hands this time, and still no give. The door, her only escape, was frozen shut.

No, no, no.

A wild look over her shoulder showed them approaching, one flashlight carving through the darkness within a few feet of her. She'd seen the emotionless way they'd killed Alex. Ten more steps and she was as good as dead.

No time to be quiet.

She tightened her hands on the door and heaved.

It flew open, smashing her nose in the process. It took every bit of control she had not to cry out. Quickly, blindly, she stepped in, pulled the door closed behind her, and waited. *No, no waiting.* She had to lock it, somehow, to keep them from following her in.

Oh God, was there even a lock on the inside?

Breath coming in hot and hard, she scrabbled at her pockets until she came up with her Maglite. *Wait.* If they hadn't already heard her, then it was best not to alert them to her presence. But they'd figure out eventually that she was here. They'd think to search the tunnel, right? And the place was so unfamiliar, she needed a quick look. It was worth the risk.

She turned it on, blinked twice, then immediately slammed her eyes shut. They burned from the light and the cold, but mostly—*oh, please no*—they burned from what she'd just seen. In the split second after closing her eyes, she turned off the light again.

The image was seared into her corneas like a brand into skin. A body. A person, stretched out, frozen on the ice. Even now, on the backs of her lids, she couldn't unsee the bright red Jackson Pollock-esque splashes and stains.

Jamie Cortez. Dead.

That man. That sweet, funny—

Stop. Think about it later. The important thing now was that there was no lock, no way to keep them out.

Something thumped just outside the door and her body went absolutely still. Only her eyes moved, along with her madly beating pulse—racing, racing, racing— until she pressed one gloved hand to the ice wall and forced herself forward. Each crunching step led her farther into the massive ice maze, like walking into a tomb. She counted out her own steps, heavy as death knells. One, two, three...

The door swung open behind her.

She lurched forward and around the first bend just as the light grazed her shoulder.

"Who is that? That you, *Angel*?" It was Sampson, his voice smooth and Southern, the charm as real as his bright-white smile. His light laugh made her curl in on herself. Or maybe that was the unbearable weight of his attention, after everything she'd witnessed.

Never had she felt so much like an animal. Prey, making itself as tiny as possible—playing dead and begging the hunter not to notice.

"That you, darlin'? Ford Cooper wouldn't be down here hiding from me, would he? You guys are the only two we're missing. Nah. Ain't his style. It's you, Angel. I can feel it. Heard you missed the plane." He let out a low, sad sound. "Actually, word up there is that you decided to winter-over with the others."

Slowly, she put a foot down on the hard-packed snow. *Crunch.* The sound was light, barely audible, yet too loud. Another step, another, each one painting a bigger, brighter target on her back. She had to get away or he'd kill her.

What was down this way? Impossible to remember after just one visit.

Didn't matter. She had to move, *now*.

With Sampson's slowly oscillating flashlight to show her the way, she forged ahead, doing her best to remember the layout. There were holes, lots of them, cut from the ice like false starts; tunnels that were never meant to be. Some were altars that Poleys from previous years had set up as odes to their experiences working at Pole. But most were small and high and impossible to get into.

Sampson's light drew closer and she picked up the pace, almost running down the seemingly endless white tunnel, until the darkness ahead revealed three passages. Shit, which way? Which way?

Right.

Another crossroads. She went right again. Not thinking. Not waiting to consider. Not slowing to listen, just running, slipping over the ice, catching herself on the frozen walls.

Calm down. Breathe.

Wait, there! A shadow to the left.

Suddenly, everything got brighter, which meant Sampson's light was closer. Too close. How? How were his steps so measured and still so fast?

She pushed herself. Her breaths came out in audible puffs, as if this fear were too strong to stay inside her. It had to be out in the open, vocalized, real. Never mind that he'd hear her if she couldn't find a way to shut up and *hide*.

She turned another corner. Another hall. Darker. No way to tell how deep it was, but the steps behind her seemed to fade. Maybe she'd lost him.

With no choice now, she threw her hands out in front of

her and sprinted, the sound of her feet on the ice like a dog chomping on bones.

She connected with something, hard, and almost went down, only managing to grab on at the last minute. A horizontal pillar or a pipe. A pipe. Okay. The piping that brought something to the living quarters… Heating? Hot water?

Who cares?

She put a hand on it and used it as a guide.

And then, headfirst, she crashed into a wall. Dead end.

Literally.

Why did she feel like giggling? She pushed the irrational impulse down and spun, hands out.

He wasn't far; she could feel him. The prey instinct ratcheted unbearably high.

Desperate, she scrabbled at the walls. Stuck. Caught like a rat. In a maze, no less. She ran her hands up and down, to the ground. A sob had just crested her chest, about to break through her tight throat, when right above the floor, her gloved hand met nothing but air.

A hole. So low she almost hadn't found it. Afraid to feel even a glimmer of relief, she dropped, just as the light hit the wall opposite, and backed into the pitch-black of an unknown void.

CHAPTER 9

Trapped in a slot no bigger than the space under a kid's bed, Angel counted his footsteps, trying to remember how long this section of tunnel was. Ten steps? Thirty? She'd come too far, taken too many random turns to tell. She'd been running when she'd veered down this way, but Bradley Sampson walked at the pace of a Sunday stroll.

At some point, his footsteps interwove with her heartbeats, until suddenly, she couldn't count anymore. Couldn't tell what was him or her or the creaking of the ice around them.

Crunch…BOOM. Crunch*boom*. Crunch, crunch. Closer. Closer. Careful steps, carrying out a methodical search.

"I know you're around here somewhere, Angel, darlin.'" Crunch *boom*. "Wanna know how?" A long, low chuckle that would have sent shivers down her spine if she wasn't already a shuddering, spinning mass of goose bumps, suspended here waiting. "You're bleeding."

Was she? She almost shifted to check the place where the door had slammed into her nose, then stopped herself. There wasn't room to move in this hole she'd stuffed herself into. It would scrape her coat against the ice and give her away.

Something clanged. "Ow. Fuck!"

Angel went very still. *He's right here.*

Was her hood sticking out? Her hands? Would he trip over her? Breathing much too fast, she resisted the desire to ease back, to curl tighter. If she shifted now, he'd hear her.

Something tickled her nose. Blood, dripping out. It

stopped almost immediately, froze on her upper lip. Just as she'd managed to ignore the itch, his voice cut through their shared silence.

"Followed her into the tunnels."

She startled, her whole body jerking so hard that the scrape of knee and boot and glove to ice might as well have been an explosion. She was so sure, in that moment, that the jig was up that she almost breathed a sigh of relief.

Almost.

But then she heard another sound, so ordinary, so completely out of place in this horror-movie moment that it almost didn't register—the crinkle of a wrapper, followed by the crunch of a Life Savers in Sampson's mouth. It was so clear, so loud, that she could have sworn she caught a puff of that telltale cinnamon flavor.

He was breathing hard, which struck her as almost funny. Here she was, quiet as a mouse, while he huffed and chewed and cussed his way around.

"You clean 'em up?" This time, when he spoke in that curt boss voice, she didn't react. Didn't move a muscle. "Yeah. Fine. I'll be right there."

There was a beat of silence, of stillness, and when Sampson spoke again, it sent a shiver down her spine. "Know you're in here, Angel, darlin'. No place for you to go. No way out." He released a long, annoyed hiss. "Why'n't you come on out, huh? Promise I won't hurt you."

Yeah right. She knew better than to believe this psychopath.

"We're about to take off and we could really use your skills where we're going, so..." Sounding impatient, he went on. "Look. There's no time to wait around for you to make up your mind." His feet crunched slowly past, so close she could reach out and grab his ankle. The beam of his flashlight hurt her eyes.

"You either come with us now, or I lock you in and you're de—" He muttered a curse under his breath, then louder, said, "Tell him to hold his horses." Another pause, while he waited for the person on the other end to respond. "Fine, I'm coming up." He exhaled loudly. Took a step. "Last chance, Angel." There was a long silence this time—so complete that she held her breath with it, strained into it, hoping. Then, on a laugh, "*Got you.*"

Light and sound and pain ripped through her all at once.

One second, she'd almost made it; the next, he had her by the arm, dragging her out, his painful hold nothing compared to the angry backhand to her temple. She flew back, landed on her rump with a heavy *oof* sound, head ringing, vision strobing. Instinct pushed her into a few frantic crab-crawled steps, but he was on her, spewing curses, his hands grasping her like claws, tearing into her.

This was it. She shut her eyes, used every muscle in her body to pull away, to shrink back from his blows, only they didn't come down. Instead, he shoved one hand into her hood, seized her ponytail, and pulled.

She screamed and grabbed on to his forearm, flailing to stay on her own feet as he dragged her back through one long hall after another.

The cursing had faded into grim silence by the time they made it back to the door. "Shit. Idiot said he'd cleaned up." He tightened his grip, drawing her face close to his. "Don't try anything or I'll leave you down here to freeze to death."

Abruptly, he dropped her like a sack of potatoes and turned to shove Jamie Cortez's stiff body out into the arch. The fall knocked the air out of her but not her common sense. Fast. Faster than she'd moved in her life, she flipped to her stomach, pushed up onto hands and knees, then up to her feet, and ran.

She made it maybe ten feet before he realized she'd run. But it was enough. She'd seen something on the way back and had just enough time to take hold of it and dive around the corner before he came after her.

An axe. Or a hatchet, actually. Whatever it was called. The name didn't matter. The only thing that mattered was that she had it and she wasn't afraid to use it. While Sampson had quickly yanked Jamie Cortez's body out into the arch, she'd make sure hers wasn't so easy to clean up.

"You fucking *bitch*." He was breathing hard. Good. He wanted a fight? She'd give him a fight. "I'll—"

The second he appeared, she swung, wide and hard. He stumbled back, snarled, came at her again, and she retaliated with another attack, sending him around the corner into darkness.

There came deep breathing—powerful as a bellows— then his clipped voice as he growled into the other end of the line she couldn't hear. "No, dammit, I don't have her. Tell him to—Shit!" He sounded insane now. "Hold the goddamn door open! Be right there."

When he spoke again, it was quieter, more venomous. Just for her. "You wanna die in here? Fine. Freeze to death." Was he moving away? His steps seemed to fade, but it was so hard to tell. Hard to hear with the way her ears rang, hard to concentrate with her own fury running through her veins. Oh God, please let him leave. She'd rather face the cold than his anger. His final words drifted back to her from the doorway into the arch. "You missed your ride, Angel. Plane's going wheels up in two minutes, so I'm gonna scoot.

You stay here and become a Popsicle. They'll find you here in the spring, you stupid, stupid c—"

The door slammed, muffling his last words, then the lock slid into place.

She half collapsed and gasped for air, the hatchet tightly gripped in one hand. For a few seconds, she could do nothing but blink into the darkness, suspended at the unfamiliar crossroads of adrenaline, relief, and absolute soul-deep terror.

She wallowed there for maybe ten seconds. And then, because there was still breath in her body, she stood up again, tightened her hold on the hatchet, and went back to the door.

Coop watched helplessly as the second LC-130 Hercules sliced through the air, its departure as loud and final as the telltale whistle of an IED. What was that second plane all about?

The first flight was normal, right on schedule, picking up the summer folks. But the second?

And what the hell awaited him at the station right now?

When he finally got close enough to see what had happened, the place looked remarkably innocuous—*if* he ignored the black smudge hanging overhead like a cartoon storm cloud.

He pulled up, shut off the engine—beyond wary—and did a quick scan of the place. Nothing. No sign of life and no movement, aside from the dark, noxious-looking smoke billowing from what used to be the power plant arch.

Not once in his decade coming here had he wished for a weapon. Until now.

Shit, he didn't want to get out of the plow. Getting out meant going on the offensive and he was in no way prepared for that. But he didn't exactly have a choice. Coop reached under his seat and pulled out a toolbox, which he yanked open. A wrench. Not much, but better than nothing.

He threw open the door and listened. Sounds reached him in phases—the ticking of the plow's engine a baseline. Layered atop its steady rhythm came the ominous crackling of fire. An occasional bang added an off-key treble to the mix. What was that—was someone hammering?

Heartbeat keeping time with the uncanny symphony, he jumped down, crouched, and waited, taking in every possible detail. There, to the side, the door to a metal storage shed blew open and slammed shut in the wind.

The thriving research station he'd left this morning had become a ghost town and he couldn't figure out why. What had turned the power plant into a burnt-out crater? And where the hell was everyone?

Staying low, he made his way to the first building—the living quarters. To the door, then on an inhale that was more Hail Mary than oxygen intake, through it. It was still warm here, but dark. He reached out and flipped the switch. Nothing. Backup generator wasn't working. With eyes wide-open, limbs heavy and flush with adrenaline, he grabbed a Maglite from the vestibule, threw open the inner door, and slid inside, poised against the wall. Watching.

Nothing.

He shone the light methodically from right to left, down and up. Aside from the deep shadows and absolute silence, everything looked as it should. Well, mostly.

A few rooms stood open, letting a dull, grayish light into the long hall.

Cautiously, he made his way to the first door and kicked it all the way open. A glance inside showed an unholy mess, which was 100 percent Jameson. The guy lived like a freaking hoarder from one of those shows. Must have a system, though, because when he needed something from his quarters, like magic he'd pop out with the item in his hand. A quick visual search didn't reveal a radio or satellite phone or laptop.

He sucked in a breath and crossed the hall, opened the door, and looked into another room. This one was totally stripped, as if its occupant had moved out. That made sense, too, since he was pretty sure this one belonged to a couple summer folks who'd left today.

They'd have been on that plane.

Had everyone evacuated and left him behind? The wind picking up said bad weather could be on the way, which might very well have precipitated the flight's early departure. Maybe with no power, the operations manager had called it, leaving the lone straggler to fend for himself.

That would be unlikely under normal circumstances, but given that the new manager, Bradley Sampson, had no experience at Pole, anything was possible. Jesus, it sure felt like he was alone here.

A search of the entire building showed more of the same—messy piles of belongings in some quarters, nothing in others. If they'd evacuated, then they'd done it fast, without grabbing anything personal.

And that felt wrong. He sniffed. No toxic leaks, as far as he could tell. But what the hell else could it be?

He returned to his door, which he'd saved for last, and pushed it open to find the same mess—someone had gone through his belongings.

Shit. His sat-phone charger was nowhere to be found. No computer, no wires or backup batteries. Not a scrap of electronics remained in any of the dorm rooms.

Definitely not an evacuation.

He checked the other buildings, where he found more of the same. All comms mysteriously...gone.

He opened every door, checked every bed and space he could think of. The place was as big and echoing as that hotel in *The Shining*, though not half as cozy. Frankly, he'd welcome just about any sign of life right now—"Here's Johnny" with a butcher knife, creepy twins chanting "redrum," Jack the freaking Ripper, hallways full of blood.

Anything would be better than this emptiness.

It took an hour to go through the galley and the other communal living areas. The gym was empty, as were the screening room, game room, labs, and offices. Pam's medical clinic sat cold, her data uplink smashed to pieces, generator silent and broken.

It all reminded him of something that he couldn't put his finger on, though his body showed recognition. He couldn't get rid of the goosebumps climbing up and down his arms.

Tightening his jaw, he made his way through the remaining common areas to the communications room door, which was wide-open. The utter destruction inside tested his forced calm. They'd taken a sledgehammer to the place.

Pure sabotage, deliberate and devastating. Violent.

Unease growing in his gut, Coop headed over the ice to the power plant arch, which had hummed with life for as long as he'd been here. Nothing was left of it now but a misshapen pile of melted plastic and blown-out metal, crackling with invisible flames. He couldn't get within a hundred feet of it without choking on the fumes.

Innards roiling with tension, he turned in a circle. What now?

He exhaled a puff of vapor and blinked, sorting through the pieces in his head. Stolen drills, destroyed power plant, no communications.

What was he missing?

What did they want with his drills? Why destroy years of work? Not just his work, but this entire place. And where the *hell* had everyone gone?

That last question sent something dark and queasy through him, sour as bile and heavy as sludge.

Unless he'd grossly misread the situation, no help would be coming, and unless the airplane truly had evacuated the winter crew to safety, no one would even know there was a problem until they reached out to the station and couldn't get through. That could be days or weeks away, given how spotty communications were here in the winter.

Desperation sharpened Coop in ways that might dull someone else. He'd been deployed in enough war zones to know how to use fear to get shit done instead of letting it drag him down. Heat and food. Those were the only things he'd need to survive. There was plenty of the latter, and the former would be impossible to find, unless…

Wait. There was one backup generator they might have missed.

Instead of checking out the supply arch as he'd planned, he hurried to the ancillary building, the base's emergency locale, equipped with its own generator, in case of an outage. Camp beds, cooking supplies, MREs: it had everything needed to survive for a day or two. Maybe longer, if he could locate more fuel. Maybe, just maybe, the people who'd carried out this destruction hadn't known about it.

Hopeful for the first time since he'd gotten back, he threw open the shed door to find the ancillary generator in one piece. Relief flooded him. *Hallelujah.*

If they'd forgotten this, he thought as he got it up and running, maybe they'd left other things behind. A charger for his sat phone, for example. That would be helpful. Thus far, though, he hadn't found a single charger—solar or otherwise—which spoke of a highly organized, premeditated operation. A full-blown assault.

Burke-Ruhe felt like a war zone.

He looked up at the sky, picturing the plane he'd watched flying away earlier. Had it been full of refugees from some terrible accident, or hostages?

In a flash, his brain fed him an image of Angel Smith, dancing like a hot-blooded goddess in the coldest place on earth. Had that been just last night? Felt like ancient history.

Where was she headed right now? The safety of McMurdo Station? Christchurch? The fucking Bermuda Triangle?

Dammit!

He squeezed his temples, willing his brain to think. What were they up to? And who were they? What had they done with everyone? There was no blood. No signs of violence, and he'd checked everyth—

The supply arch. He'd been headed there when he'd remembered the ancillary building.

Suddenly, the image of that airplane full of Burke-Ruhe's population changed into something entirely different. What if the supply arch was filled with corpses instead of food, rows and rows of—

No. He had to stop thinking like that if he wanted to be in any state to search for possible survivors.

Angel Smith filled his thoughts again, and he gently

pushed her aside. He needed his wits right now, had to treat every move with as much seriousness as a military recon.

Filled with a sick dread and armed with a baseball bat, he headed into the supply arch.

CHAPTER 10

As Coop stalked silently down the long ice ramp toward the arch's entrance, a deep, disturbing sense of déjà vu washed over him.

He'd been here just last night, looking for the missing Cortez. He couldn't help but wonder: What if he'd found him then? What if he'd insisted on seeing his friend's face, rather than accepting that scratchy whisper through the door?

He stood to the side of the open entrance and paused.

The long, metal-arched structure, which had been built on top of the ice years ago, was now so deep underground that the entrance had to be plowed out on a pretty continuous basis. Especially in winter.

A perfect place to hide something. Like bodies.

Or it could be empty.

He needed to get a grip. He'd be useless if he let *what-ifs* rule him. After a silent, calming count of three, Coop slid inside, stepped to the right, and waited for his eyes to adjust to the complete dark. Nothing. Not a sound, not a ticking clock or a scuffle. Not a sign of life.

Dead. They could all be dead. Jameson, Doc, Angel Smith.

He couldn't push the thought from his head, couldn't stop the way images long buried mingled with scenes of gore freshly painted by his mind. A mind that was all too aware of how barbaric death could be.

He couldn't stand the idea of Angel Smith—so alive this morning—snuffed out like a too-bright, too-hot flame.

Taking a crushed-ice breath, he set off, sticking to the

wall, where the shadows immediately engulfed him. The crisp fall of each cautious step was the only sound, aside from the loud pounding in his ears.

Once the last glimmer of light was swallowed by the pure black of the arch, he had no choice but to switch on the flashlight, though it would make him a target. He hefted the baseball bat and hungered for the weight of one of those ultraheavy law-enforcement flashlights or, even better, his rifle.

Memories assailed him, as brutal as a Condition 1 storm: dust and diesel oil, sweat and fear. The polar opposite of this place, until today. He shut off the light, paused, breath suspended, and waited out the feeling of being watched.

Stress. This is stress. He knew it, recognized it, did his best to push it back, and finally moved ahead, his feet as stealthy as they'd been on dozens of raids, his body primed for attack.

He didn't question this need to be quiet—instinct drove it, not well-thought-out strategy.

Given that instinct had saved his ass more than once, he listened.

One step, foot down, leg bent, no scuffing, barely a sound. Which was hard in boots that turned feet into blocky hunks of ice.

He sniffed the air. What was that? A spice, maybe. He knew it but couldn't put his finger on it.

His foot kicked something that skittered across the concrete floor to land with a high, brassy bell sound, and it hit him—that odor was gunpowder. It was here in the still air. Not heavy, but... He inhaled through his nose. He'd never forget the smell.

It had no place here.

He switched the light back on and shone it on the ground, picked up the gleam of a shell casing, and stepped toward it when—

Something moved to the right. He snapped off the light, canted his head, quiet as the grave while alarm bells tore up his insides.

There. Again. A metallic rattle. Like a machine trying to work and failing. The vibrations lasted for a few seconds and stopped, started…stopped. Spurred on by the possibility of company, he headed toward the entrance to the ice tunnel.

As he watched, the wooden door shook, rattled like it'd fall off its hinges, and then stopped. Behind the sound was a low humming that raised every hair on his already chilled body.

He leaned in, startled to see a heavy-duty slide lock where he didn't remember there being one before. The fresh-looking drill holes confirmed it.

His jaw went diamond-hard, crackling the thin layer of ice coating the new growth on his chin. "Who's in there?"

The moaning went on, and the rattling picked up.

He reached for the handle and hesitated, horror movie images flashing through his head, *The Thing* high on the list. Bat fisted in his gloved hand, he stepped to the side, grabbed ahold of the slide…and pulled.

Inside, the sound stopped.

He pulled again, but the damned lock appeared to be jammed. He bent closer, ran his light up and down then door, and… *Sonofabitch.* There was a second latch, at the very bottom, in a place where most people would never think to look. And this one was padlocked shut.

He'd have to cut it off.

"You okay in there? This is Serg—" He stopped. "This is Dr. Ford Cooper." Christ, he'd almost given his rank. That was how fucked up this was. He shut his eyes and went on. "It's Coop. Who's in there?"

Moaning. Just moaning, with another bout of shaking and a thump, but the voice was one hundred percent human. And female. And she wanted out.

"I'm gonna get you out, okay?" He tried to soften the hard army edge from his voice. "Hold tight."

He spun, ready to tear the place apart in search of something to pry open that lock.

Tools. Jameson's shop was in the utility arch, but there'd be something here. There—a fire extinguisher.

Without hesitation, he pulled it from its red metal case and returned, squatted in front of the door, and beat the shit out of the lock.

It popped off after three good hits. In a rush, he threw the extinguisher to the side, pulled open the door, and just avoided getting brained with a hatchet.

"Whoa! Whoa. Hold it." He threw his hand out and snatched the tool from her, which wasn't much of a challenge, given how hard she was shaking. "It's Coop. Ford Cooper. Not here to hurt you."

He didn't need to see her face under the layers of cloth to know this was Angel Smith. Holy shit. As if he'd conjured her.

"I've got you. Got you, Angel. Got you." Shaking from adrenaline and anger and relief, he put an arm around her and shifted into the tunnel. He went still at the sense of déjà vu when he spotted drops of red against the ice, mostly hidden by a messy pile of crates, like the last bit of evidence left from a hasty cover-up.

"What is that? Is that blood?"

"Jamie C—Cor—" Her shuddering took over. "Cortez."

The name fell on him like an avalanche, covering every bit of hope he'd harbored until now. Shit.

No time for thinking about his abysmal failure at saving his friend. Angel sucked in a wheezy breath and shuddered so hard he almost lost his hold on her.

Sticking the flashlight into his mouth, he bent to slide one arm through her legs and hauled her up and over his shoulder in a fireman's carry. No time to check on her. No time to ask questions. No time for stealth or mourning or regret.

He'd get her warm, keep her alive, and worry about what the hell was going on here later.

As he turned, her foot caught on the pile of crates, over-turning the top two and spinning the bottom one out.

Letters had been scrawled across the previously hidden side of the bottom crate. They spelled out **CHRONOS COR**, which was interesting. But what made him stop and stare in absolute shock wasn't the words themselves so much as the sloppy, thick, fingerprint-smudged blood in which they'd been written.

CHAPTER 11

SOMETHING POKED AT ANGEL. "*MMMMMM*." SHE TURNED away.

Water in her mouth, steaming hot, trying to drown her. Coughing, flailing, hands trapped. *Stop. Stop it. Stop!*

"Drink."

She froze. The syllable was so scratchy and deep, it was more grunt than word. She should open her eyes, but she didn't want to. She wanted to stay asleep. To play dead.

"Drink," the rough voice ordered again. "So you don't die."

Let me. Let me die.

"No. No way, Ms. Sm—*Angel*."

Everything was fever-wrong. Clammy-hot, shaky-cold, and heavy. So heavy. Was someone *sitting* on her?

"'swrongwithmyhans?" Her tongue wouldn't work.

"*Drink*."

Something pressed against her mouth. Fighting the need to gag, she gave in, opened up, let it flow into her. Warm and sweet, sunshine coated her insides. No, not sunshine, but...

Good.

"More."

"Okay." Prying open her eyes was like pulling apart thick, cooling caramel. Finally, she got one, then the other. She immediately shut them again, hard. "'stoobright."

Something landed on her face. Sunglasses. "Try again."

This time, things were slightly darker, no blazing shaft of agony.

"More." That rough voice cut in and out, as if it couldn't

quite find a note to cling to. As if part of its register had been ripped out, leaving swiss cheese holes.

Something about it irritated her. She shook her head—or tried to. It ended up as more of a side nudge. And her head was big and cotton-filled.

"You want to die?"

No. No she didn't want that. Her lids weighed a ton. They shut again.

More sweetness trickled down her throat, followed by a bigger mouthful, then a gulp.

"Wha's going on?"

"You tell me." The bed shifted beneath her. *Bed. What bed?* "Sit up."

Turning to face the seesawing mattress, she pushed hard on hands that felt like lead, shifted up and back, away from this incredible, firm warmth, and managed to crack her eyes open one more time, focusing on—

Holy mother of God in Heaven above.

She'd have done the sign of the cross if her hand had worked, because the sight of the Ice Man half-naked and *right there* was too much for her poor, overwhelmed senses to handle.

She could only slam her eyes shut, but that did nothing to obliterate the image, burned into the inside of her eyelids.

He had one of those thick, wide, flat-planed male bodies that she'd only ever seen in movies, his pecs slabs of squared-off stone, with a light fan of dark blond, almost reddish hair, leading down to...

She swallowed and squeezed her eyes tighter to clear away the hallucination.

I must be dead. And this is what Dead Me wants: the dude who rejected me with his shirt off.

But common sense followed right on that thought's heels. *No. No way would Dead Me settle for that. She'd want the bottom half, too.*

She leaned back and cracked an eye open to see thighs covered in tight merino wool.

Oh well.

Besides that, the mean expression he wore, too intense and hard to be anything but the real Ice Man, confirmed that she wasn't dead. He'd be much nicer in the afterlife. Besides, the sun-, wind-, and ice-burned red of his face wasn't something she'd ever conjure up on her own, nor were those hard brackets around his mouth.

Almost angrily, he put one of those muscle-packed arms around her and pulled her back into his heat. She was about to protest when he asked, "What the hell happened here today?"

She blinked. It all came back in a three-second flash that sent her careening into hell again.

"Gonna throw up." She lurched to side and just made it into the trash can Ford Cooper held up for her.

The memories hurt, scraped her insides and tightened her stomach, reminding her of how indelible those deaths were. Of how she'd done nothing to stop them.

Alex. Oh God. Poor Alex. And Jamie Cortez.

The tunnels. Even now, they were closing in, darkness crowding the edges of her vision. Those footsteps, slowly approaching.

"Angel."

"I ran." He bent close to hear her whisper. "They killed him and I just…ran."

"Cortez?"

"Alex." She blinked at him. "Cortez…" She couldn't think of that bloody mess and the sweet, silly Jamie Cortez she'd known. Her body tried heaving again and she held it back, breathed through it until she could talk. "He was already in the tunnel when I got there." Deep-frozen. Blood everywhere. She put a hand to her face. Her nose was swollen and hot where she'd hit it on the door.

Ford swiped something warm and wet over her mouth, her cheeks, then tightened his hold on her, pulled her into his body.

"You're safe now. Safe."

Slowly, she loosened a bit, let him take a little more weight.

At least Ford was alive. At least she wasn't alone. Or frozen through, like Sampson had threatened.

"I've got you."

Nodding seemed like a good idea, particularly since it rubbed her damp cheek—*when did I cry?*—against that wide, solid expanse.

"Where is everyone else? Did you find any more…" She wouldn't say *bodies*. Just the idea that there could be more made her ache.

"No one else." With something like relief, her gaze shifted to the five o'clock shadow over his Adam's apple as he swallowed. He opened his mouth, but nothing came out. With a curse, he tried again. "Gone."

The shaking started again, although this time it wasn't from hypothermia—it was an overdose of pure, raw emotion.

I know you're around here somewhere, Angel, darlin'. Wanna know how? Her heart thumped in her chest, too fast, too heavy, and so loud he had to hear it. That trapped feeling rushed out of the recent past to smack her in the face. *My God, that was just this morning.*

"He planned this," she finally said.

"Who?"

"Bradley Sampson was the leader, I think, though he mentioned higher-ups or the powers that be or something. Kept talking about some payload they were after." And then, because she couldn't be the only one to know this, she said, "I watched him shoot..." *Air. Breathe.* "Alex. In the head."

Beneath her ear, Ford's heartbeat picked up speed, but he didn't respond.

And, honestly, what was there to say?

Her nose, pressed into him, couldn't help but take him in. And it was good. Everything about him was more human than she'd have guessed from a man who'd seemed stone cold: the smell, the heat, the give of his flesh.

"Bastard didn't get me."

"Good," he whispered, arms tightening, head low, voice terrible in its intensity. "*Good.*"

"Why do you keep hugging me?"

"It's not a hug. I'm sharing body heat. To keep you warm." His voice rumbled against her ear. She could feel it in her bones, as comforting as a purring cat.

"Oh, that's nice."

"What?"

"Talk again."

"Excuse me?" He cleared his throat, tried to shift away, probably to look down at her, but she wouldn't let him. He felt too good. "You want me to—"

"Like that." It was the rumble of his voice that calmed her, echoing through muscle and bone. It was comfort, home. His deep, slow words flashed her back to a time when she was just Papa's little girl. No responsibilities, no pressure. No evil murderers chasing her through frozen tunnels. "More. Say more."

"You…" He cleared his throat again, more awkward this time. But she didn't care. That awkwardness made him real when, before today, he'd been the stiffest, chilliest, hardest-ass prick she'd ever met. She knew secrets about him now: he was warm. And he smelled good. "Want me to talk?"

She nodded, getting in another clandestine rub.

"I'll, uh, tell you about ice, I guess?" He paused and she made a sound of assent. "Ahem. Um. So, the thing is, ice is like amber, or fossils. Except better. So cold, pristine, and untouched that it's the perfect receptacle for trapped data."

"What kind of data?"

"History. The history of the world. Everything from soot to bacteria, with layers that perfectly delineate eras, changes, shifts in temperature, climate…major events, disasters. The ice and every air bubble inside it is a time capsule."

"I didn't realize that." He'd never used this many words in her presence before. And his voice, though almost painfully rough, felt good against her ear. She needed him to keep talking. "So. You study ice."

"Mostly. Glaciers. Movement, cycles, patterns…"

She closed her eyes and pictured layer upon layer of ice. "Are they different colors?"

"What?"

"The ice layers."

"Sometimes. It's actually quite beautiful. Volcanic ash, for example, is black or gray, which makes dating and identification easy when we know of an event."

"Sounds like an opera."

"What?"

"Pastry. Layered buttercream, coffee cream, almond cake, chocolate… All paper thin." She swallowed back a mouthful of saliva. "It's complex and, when done right, amazing."

He didn't respond, which wasn't a surprise, since before today, the man had never strung more than a couple words together. Not for her.

It was disappointing, though, that he'd shut up.

She arched back enough to look up and had to curl right down again when the sight of him hit her.

This suddenly felt an awful lot like a morning after—or even worse, the *moments* after. She lay, limbs heavy and used up, in the arms of a man who was uncomfortably sexy.

And the worst part was that even that hesitant, building excitement in his voice when he talked about ice was appealing. He made it interesting. To a woman who'd never gotten better than a C- in science, that was saying something.

She swallowed back discomfort at this unexpected closeness and asked the first question that came to mind. "What do you go out there for every day?"

"You really wanna hear this?"

She nodded.

"Well. I have"—his jaw tightened—"*had* multiple sites, each equipped with a drill that bores down into the ice. Heat helps them slice right into it. The technology's great because it avoids contamination and—" Another throat-clearing rumble, followed by a gruff scoffing sound. "You don't need to know the details."

"Go on."

"Um. I get ice core samples. From the drills. I collect these long cylindrical tubes of ice, which I examine initially and then send back to the States to be—"

Something prickled through her. "*Whoa.* Hang on.

Hang on." She rolled away from him, groaning as her feet hit the frigid floor.

"Sit, Angel." He reached for her, but she stood and staggered just out of reach, noticing vaguely that she was wearing just her base layer. "There's nothing we can—"

"No, wait. Listen. They talked about *you*. Sampson said… Crap. What did he say?" She put a hand to her suddenly aching head. "Boy, he was *pissed* that you weren't around."

"Why?" He stood.

"They were *yours*." She tilted her head back to meet his intelligent blue eyes. "They must have been. Those metal tubes, the uh, core thingies? You kept some in the supply arch?" Heart racing, she swayed and put out a hand to steady herself. It landed on his hot, heavy forearm. It took her a good three seconds to refocus.

"Ice cores. Yes."

"That's what they were after." A slow smile curled her lips as she felt something other than a sick dread. "But there's a chance they didn't get them."

"You *what*?"

"I took them back." She looked excited. Not quite smiling, but satisfied, like a runner who'd just beaten out the competition in a close race.

"The cores?" He pulled on a shirt, racing to catch up with her.

"Yes." She stepped into her boots.

"Where are you going?"

She blinked. "To get them." Might as well tack an eyeroll and a *duh* onto the end of that.

"Stay here. I'll go."

He did get the eye-roll then, which sped his pulse up. Dammit, the woman was a loose cannon.

She was already sliding into her coat, so he went to the door and opened it.

"Where are they?" He grabbed his flashlight and baseball bat—because whatever was going on here was dangerous as hell even if he was fairly certain the people responsible were long gone—and led the way toward the arch. Even the way he walked had changed, he noted with detached interest. No more stomping across the ice, head in the clouds. As if the years had been stripped away, his situational awareness was back online, his muscles loose and ready, buzzing with that almost electric tension he associated with being outside the wire.

"Under one of the food supply shelves. The rice." He couldn't see her face behind her glasses and gaiter, but something like worry had threaded its way into her voice. Which was good. Caution was good.

Wait, was she limping?

He opened his mouth to ask, but she spoke first. "Must be something pretty special in those tubes, huh?"

Well, *he* thought they were special, but the normal ash or trapped air bubbles that got him riled up wouldn't send anyone else into—

He paused, an idea spinning brightly in his brain. Those samples he'd pulled a few weeks ago. They'd contained a different sort of finding.

Suddenly, he had an idea of what Sampson and his team were after.

They arrived at the still-open door to the arch, which sent him into hypervigilance. "Stay here."

"I'll come." Breathing hard, she went on. "No way am I staying here alone."

He stared at her gloved hand clenching his arm, wondering if she felt the same thing—a memory from last night—the Skua's Nest was worlds away now. Something a lot like shame washed over him before he shoved it far, far down.

This wasn't the time for such pointless emotion.

After a few steps, she broke the silence. "I don't *think* they saw me."

"What?" He turned to look at her. She was nothing but a darker shade of black.

"I mean, if they saw me replacing them, then your ice tubes are gone, right?"

"Right." He walked on as he considered the ramifications. It would be very bad if those men had gotten ahold of certain ice cores. Because what they contained…well, their actions pretty much confirmed that it was dangerous.

But if after all of this effort, they'd taken off with the wrong cores… His flashlight shone on a pile of heavy-looking white bags, hanging over the shelf like big, fat lolling tongues trying to lick the floor.

Angel crouched. He bent beside her, focused the light, and let out a long, slow breath.

"Still there," she breathed. "I switched the date stickers but never got to one."

He pulled them out, eyeing them one at a time until he got to the one that still had its sticker on it. "I know what their payload was."

"What is it? What's worth all these lives?"

"I found something in a core a few weeks back. It looked like…" He shook his head, sure now. "Cortez has…had a colleague back in the UK. He sent her images and she confirmed that it's—"

Something heavy and dark rose up from his chest, stopped his air and cut off his voice.

"What?" The word was less than a whisper.

"Shit. It has to be linked. She died. House fire. Cortez was devastated when he found out."

Angel let out a sound—low and pained. Her eyes were massive in the dark. He couldn't look away from them. Didn't even try.

"It's a virus, Angel. A very old virus, buried deep in the ice."

"A virus? What do they want with that?"

"I don't know." Even as he said the words, an idea occurred to him—the kind of worst-case scenario that couldn't possibly be real and yet clicked right into place. All the deaths. The military precision. The warning scrawled in blood. "Maybe…maybe a bioweapon?" Shit. This was bad. Worse than bad. If his gut instinct was right, it was potentially catastrophic.

"What can we do?"

The tubes sat beside them, gleaming innocently in the dim light.

He had an idea of what they could do—what they had to do—but he wasn't quite ready to share it yet.

"We'll uh…figure it out." He stood, heavy from the sudden weight of what lay ahead. He swallowed and shined the light up the long length of the arch. "Where did they—" There was too much crap in his throat. He tried again. "Alex. Where'd they kill him?"

"Up there." Her usually musical voice was no better off than his. "By the rest of the tubes."

He squinted. There was nothing there now.

"You sure?"

"Yes." Ah, there was the voice he knew. "Of course I'm—" She turned to look at the spot where he shone his flashlight. "Where is he?" She spun. "I swear he was—"

He reached into his pocket, then grabbed her hand and slapped the 9mm bullet case he'd found into her gloved palm. "I believe you." He leaned down, caught her eye, and held it. "Even without this, I'd believe you, Angel."

She stared at the object in her hand before looking up at him. "Okay. Okay, then."

He opened his mouth and closed it again, then headed toward the door.

"What? What are you not saying?" She ran to keep up.

"The ice cores." He didn't pause until they were back outside, on the bright, clean ice. "When they open up the dummies, it won't take long for them to figure out that they've got the wrong ones."

Her hand flew to her mouth. "You think they'll come back?"

"Yeah." He nodded without hesitation. "They'll be back."

"What do we do?"

"We leave." He threw his head back to look at clear blue sky. "Now."

CHAPTER 12

COOP WENT TO WORK HURRIEDLY GATHERING EVERY-thing they'd need to survive a trek across the continent, while Angel prepared their food. He'd located skis, snow-shoes, camp stoves and fuel, a tent, sleeping bags, and pads to protect their prone bodies from the ice. Most of this he amassed in the eerily empty living quarters, which added a layer of discomfort to his growing anxiety. Rooting through his friends' private belongings while they were likely in trouble somewhere felt as dirty and wrong as looting the recently deserted homes of nuclear disaster victims.

But it couldn't be helped.

The rest he found in the "skua" pile, named after the rapacious sea birds that plagued Antarctica's coastal research stations. Thank God people dumped things they no longer needed when they left or Coop and Angel would have been out of luck. While Coop had skis and boots already, they'd been incredibly fortunate to find a pair that *almost* fit Angel. A little big, which they could compensate for with padding.

The second he stepped out of the dorm, relief flooded him. There, on the horizon, were clouds. And while bad weather was usually a pain in the ass, today it would keep aircraft at a safe distance.

Good.

The stress inside him had coalesced into hatred now. It burned so hot he could have taken off his coat out here.

Murdering bastards.

What they'd done to the rest of the crew was anyone's guess, but two people, at least, were dead. He'd taken a precious half hour to search the rest of the tunnels and arches and found no sign of either body, which meant those assholes had taken them, since you couldn't hide that kind of evidence under the ice without time and a big-ass digger.

Two lives snuffed out. Two preeminent researchers—gone. Friends, dammit. Men with futures, families. That wouldn't go unnoticed, surely.

He pictured those two planes taking off, maybe an hour apart. From what Angel'd told him, Sampson had said something about the summer people leaving on the first aircraft. He'd apparently wanted to bring her along on the second flight. Had they taken the winter-overs with them? Or evacuated them on the first plane?

Why, damn it? He paused, shut his eyes, and pressed his thumb and forefinger to his eyeballs, hard. Why do this? Why bring violence to the most peaceful continent on earth?

No matter how he turned it over in his head, he couldn't seem to come up with an answer.

Though it was light out, it was the middle of the night when he shoved open the ancillary building door and got a faceful of heat—nothing like in the main building when the power worked, but better than the current exterior temps of -25 Fahrenheit. They were lucky it was sunny out.

No point thinking about how low that temperature would drop out there on the ice when cloud cover could instantly lower it by twenty-five degrees.

No point thinking about how alone they were. No point wondering what kind of spin this whole thing was getting in the outside world. Shit. Did the world even know?

Angel sat at the table filling small baggies with

easy-to-consume food rations. The fattiest, highest-calorie, lowest-weight items they could put together.

He didn't spare her a glance as he grabbed a protein bar and headed back out to unload the sled's contents by the door. He was so caught up in his thoughts, with so much tension in his body, that when Angel appeared beside him, gloved and coated and prepared to help, he almost jumped out of his skin.

"Thought you were kidding about this stuff." She picked up a massive pack of butter that would need to be cut into bite-sized portions. "We seriously need this much fat?"

He glanced at her and forced out a grunt, barely audible through the wind, then squatted to shift gear onto one of the expedition sleds he'd found.

"How many calories?"

He squinted up at her. "What?"

"How many calories will we burn through in a day?" While she piled the butter by the door, he considered the sled, staring at it like it was a game of Tetris.

"Six, seven thousand, more or less. The fat'll help us pack in the calories more efficiently."

"Wow. Well, I'm pretty sure I don't need it, Ford."

His scalp tingled at the use of his first name. Nobody but his brother called him that. "Need what?"

"All this butter." She stood up, rubbed her hands on her thighs, and yawned.

"You will."

"Huh. Silver lining, I guess, 'cause I'm a fool for butter."

He threw her a confused look. "What?"

"With all the trekking, maybe I'll finally tone some of this." He averted his eyes as she patted her hip, then turned

again and squatted, unconsciously giving him the opportunity to check out her rear end. Which was perfect, as far
as he was concerned, but then, her curves were none of
his business.

He searched the sky. No approaching aircraft. Good.

"Almost done."

"Wow. Okay. Better get my knives."

"Knives?" He blinked. "What do you need those for?"

"First, I'll need something to cut all this butter into
chunks. But also, you know that burning-building question?
Like, what would I run back inside for?"

He nodded.

"My knives. That's what I would grab."

"Why?"

She cocked her head at him, squinting like he was of a
different species. "They're the tools of my trade." Something
in her face changed, as if she'd suddenly figured him out.
"Like you and your drills."

Understanding hit him like a fist to the solar plexus. He
stood up. "I'll get them for you."

She opened her mouth as if to argue and then closed it
with a nod. "Thanks."

"Wind's picking up."

"This is good for us, right?" She eyed him.

"Sure." He turned to go.

"Wait." She put a hand on his arm. "Why don't you take
a break?"

Instead of looking her way, he stared at the bright yellow
of her glove against his red coat and shook his head. "Too
much to do."

"Okay. Be honest with me. Are we screwed?" When he
didn't answer, didn't move at all, she went on. "If it's that

bad, how about you take a few minutes, huh? Rest. Tell me how screwed we are."

He shot her a surprised look. Of everyone in this place, Angel Smith would have been the last one he'd have looked to in a crisis. He'd have asked for a partner with a more scientific mind or maybe someone athletic and strong. Not her, with her effusiveness, her musical laugh, and spice cloud aura.

Wordlessly, he met her molten-magma warm eyes.

She looked tired and anxious and, for the first time since he'd glimpsed her in the galley all those months ago, pale.

"Aren't we better off staying here and fighting?"

"No power. No fuel. No weapons. Winter's on its way. We stay here, we die eventually. Whether or not they show up." It wasn't a question of if but when. Today, tomorrow, or in a few weeks, when the sun set for the season and temperatures plummeted. Nothing could survive without power out here in the dark of austral winter.

Breath held, he steeled himself for histrionics or maybe, on the opposite end of the spectrum, flippancy.

What he got was something he'd neither expected nor wanted: a hug.

Ford Cooper didn't do hugs—not as a kid or as a sniper in the U.S. Army, nor as a research scientist in the most unwelcoming field on earth.

But after a few breathless seconds in the soft circle of this woman's arms, even he had to admit that there was something to be said for comfort in the face of impending doom.

Certain death, he recalled after years without its specter hanging over him, had a way of blowing old hang-ups right out of the water.

She pulled away. "So, where are we headed?"

"Volkov Station."

"Volkov? Don't they close down for the winter?"

"Normally. But I understand they brought a construction crew in to renovate this year." He didn't let himself imagine what it would be like to winter-over with a handful of Russian workers…and Angel.

"What about the South African station? Aren't they closer?"

"Eighty miles closer, as the crow flies."

Her jaw dropped.

"To get there, we'd have to either climb some of the continent's highest mountains or go around them. Don't like our chances." He shook his head, sure of his decision. "I thought about it, and Volkov's the best choice." Their sole chance at survival. "Those are the only two options within five hundred miles of here."

"Five hun—" She looked like she'd be sick. "How far is it?"

"It's a straight shot. Fairly steady downhill slope, given the elevation here, and without—"

"*How far?*"

"A little more than…" He cleared his throat. "Three hundred miles."

"*What?*" She didn't sound happy. "How long's it gonna take us?"

"We'll drive the big plow for the first fifty or so. The rest could take as little as twenty days." Unlikely, but possible. They'd have to ski thirteen miles a day at that rate and he had no notion of her skill level or endurance.

Her eyes were massive. "*As little?* Are you nu—No. No, let's think about this." She backed up, put more space between them. "Okay. So, what other options do we have?"

"None." He shrugged. No point arguing against facts.

"Anyway. Backup generator'll run out of fuel. We need to get our gear together, pack up these sleds, and go. Sooner the better."

"Right. No fuel, no heat." Looking shell-shocked, she eyed the sky. "Once we take off, what's to stop them from coming after us?"

"Nothing." No point in lying, was there? "It's why we need to head out, ski all night, if we can. Put some miles between us and this place."

"We're heading out into the most dangerous place on earth with killers after us?"

"Yeah." He couldn't help a grim smirk. "Better hit the road."

CHAPTER 13

Harper Research and Testing Facility, East Antarctic Ice Sheet

"WE DON'T HAVE THE VIRUS."

"What do you mean you don't have it?" The director's voice crackled over the sat phone.

"I've been given the wrong ice cores."

"How on earth could they make an error like that?"

"I'm not certain." *Because you hired monkeys, obviously.* "It's a pretty major issue."

Without sparing a glance at the man responsible for this colossal error, Dr. Clive Tenny, MD, PhD, waited for the director to respond.

Her breathing was audible through the line, as if she'd been running. Or was in the throes of some kind of fit. Having seen her in person, it was likely the latter, since Katherine Henley Harper, head of Chronos Corporation, was getting on in years and it was perfectly obvious that she did not run.

"Go back and locate the samples. Drill some more if you must." Of course she'd say that. Of course. It was what he'd said, too. "We need the virus. *Now.*"

"Well…" Clive hated being the bearer of bad tidings. And, honestly, he shouldn't be the messenger here, since he wasn't the one who'd fucked up. He threw Bradley Sampson a poisoned glare. The man was incompetence itself. He'd been given weeks at that research station. In fact, in the time it had taken that paramilitary bozo to do basically nothing at Burke-Ruhe, Tenny had been in charge of outfitting an entire vaccine research and testing facility. In fucking Antarctica, for God's sake.

"*Well* what? Tell me."

He pulled in a long breath. "The drills don't work."

"I provided you with engineers as requested. Have they not—"

"They were unable to acquire a sample at the original site. Apparently, they melted straight through the ice. The engine overheated and the entire mechanism died." He paused, enjoying this just a little. "Seems the design wasn't as simple as they'd assumed. The engineers didn't have time to—"

"And it's too late, I suppose? Were they left at—"

"I had the men retrieve them and load them into the plane, so we've got the drills here at the Facility."

He cringed, ready for another dressing-down, but she surprised him. "Smart."

"Anyone would have done the same, ma'am." Which wasn't strictly true. If Sampson had been in charge, the drills would have stayed at Burke-Ruhe, smashed to smithereens, no doubt. Instead, Tenny had made sure the team worked all night to retrieve them.

"Have that man fix them. The glaciologist. They're his drills after all."

"Ah." His hand tightened on the phone. And he sucked in another breath, wishing he had an actual drink in his other hand instead of cold coffee.

"*Please* just spit out whatever it is."

"Cooper. The researcher. The one who retrieved the virus and designed the dril—"

"You've *explained* who Cooper is, for God's sake, Clive. Now get to the point."

"He's still there."

"There?" The word dropped into the phone like a stone into water. The ripples reached him, even here at the bottom of the earth.

"At Burke-Ruhe." Clive swallowed audibly. He wasn't made for this nonsense. He was a virologist, an immunologist, and a physician, not some covert operative. "Apparently Sampson was unable to locate him. And…"

Sampson shifted at the other side of the room.

"There's more." Not a question.

"There has been some unexpected collateral damage." All thanks to Bradley Sampson. The man was a wild dog, a barely domesticated mutt who, in Clive's opinion, ought to be put down. He was uncomfortable in the same room with him.

"We've lost four, counting Cooper." He dreaded this part. "One of them was summer crew." When she didn't speak, he went on. "The, uh, station's cook was left behind. The two scientists questioned by Sampson are—were—winter researchers, but they did not…" He dragged in a shaky breath. Not at any point during his long, difficult climb had he foreseen his career winding up this way. An accessory to murder? No. No, he was—

"Yes?"

"They didn't make it."

"I'm extremely disappointed." An understatement, obviously.

"I understand that, Madame Director. We're not sure how—"

"You were *sloppy*. That's how. Inexcusable."

Clive tightened his lips. A hot flush spread up his neck and face as he fought the urge to hang up on her. There was no point reminding her that he hadn't been present at Burke-Ruhe. His job had been to oversee the Harper Facility, ensuring that everything was in place for the trials. And it had been perfect. He'd taken her millions and turned what was once a poor excuse for a research station into a state-of-the-art vaccine research facility. That, of course, wasn't something she'd remark upon.

And it didn't matter anyway, because he couldn't run trials on a vaccine if he didn't have the damned virus.

The director sniffed and he waited, needing this to work—the virus, the vaccine, the bonus.

He wiped a hand down his face and forced a tight, bitter smile.

Whatever happened, he'd continue to do as he was told. Though he hated to admit it, his career would have been long over if Katherine Harper hadn't allowed him to keep this position. The money certainly sweetened things. It would be a hell of a lot sweeter if those damned mercenaries hadn't ruined everything.

Tenny hated the feeling of owing this woman something when, really, she was the one who owed him! He'd been the one to identify the virus from Cortez's email, hadn't he? He'd followed the trail to Antarctica.

Without him, her mission was dead in the water. Unlike her famous father, she was just a suit after all.

So he'd do what he always did—dig his nails into his hand and wait for the next wave of insults to wash over him.

What came instead chilled him to the core.

"All right then." He heard a creaking that he could have sworn was the sound of her spine straightening. "Since you're in charge down there, and you've got the most to gain"—*Lose!* he wanted to say. *I've got the most to lose, you selfish bitch!*—"I want you to go with your security specialist colleagues. To Burke-Ruhe. Get the virus. And the missing scientist, while you're at it."

"Director, that is simply impossible. We are on the brink of austral winter. Imprisoned by the ice and the weather until the first fli—"

She must have shifted, bringing the phone closer to her mouth, because when she spoke, her voice cut straight through his—low and quiet but also perfectly clear, as crisp and sour as a New England apple. "You will outfit yourselves. I believe the Facility has every cold-weather supply known to man, and I intend for you to use them. You will take the team, you will find those samples and that troublesome scientist, and you will return to the Harper Research Facility, where you will run your trials as planned. Do you understand?"

"Yes, Director." He'd made the mistake of calling her Katherine once. That wasn't something he'd do again.

"Now, with a missing summer crew member, you've left me with a lot of smoothing over to do." As if he was somehow responsible for this clusterfuck! No, this whole insane venture was *her* brainchild. He was just the poor schmuck freezing his nuts off on the ground. For nine fucking months of austral winter. "An expedition gone wrong, I suppose. I'll have to get the story out." She shifted on the other end. "See that their bodies are collected."

"Yes" was all he could manage through too-tight lips.

She let out a long, annoyed exhale. "You of all people understand how important it is that the virus not be lost. This entire project—Chronos Corporation's entire mission, our *future*—necessitates that it be in your possession." She paused. "Quickly."

"I understand, Director. Of course I underst—"

"And, Clive." He'd never invited her to use his first name, but she'd been doing it for years. Man, did it piss him off. "You will stay on that continent—you and your colleagues—until the virus has been retrieved, the vaccine tested, and the *proper results* obtained."

She hung up, leaving him with the phone in his hand and one smug special-forces-type operative—or whatever the hell people like Sampson were called—sitting on Clive's desk, watching his every move.

"Boss lady's not happy, huh?"

"No." Clive rolled his eyes up to glare at Sampson's wide, movie-star grin. "But I'm not the one who fucked up."

"You sure about that, Clive?" Sampson chomped on his mint and jumped off the desk. "When do we suit up?"

Clive almost spat out the last of his coffee, "How'd you—"

"Come on, Clive, buddy." Sampson patted his shoulder, then tightened his hold for a second too long. "What do you say we go get ourselves a virus?"

CHAPTER 14

Burke-Ruhe Research Station, South Pole

COOP EYED THE SLEDS, WHICH WERE LOADED UP WITH everything they'd need for twenty-one days on the ice. Beside them sat the five metal canisters containing the ice core samples.

They'd have a better chance at survival if they left those behind. Not only would their load be lighter, but Sampson would have no reason to pursue them.

If only he knew what those assholes wanted the virus for.

Did it matter?

Absolutely. But their immediate survival mattered more.

Which made it a no-brainer. Hard to stomach, but a no-brainer.

Decision made, he stomped inside.

"You ski?" Coop asked as he pushed open the ancillary door for what might be the last time.

Without looking up from stuffing baggies with coconut oil and chocolate and trail mix, Angel shook her head. "Downhill. Once, in New Hampshire. Must've been about eight years old and the slope was like one hundred feet long."

So that was a no.

"Practice."

She gave him a strange look. "Didn't your mother teach you any manners?"

"No." He forced the word through tight lips, annoyed and...embarrassed? Was that what this was?

She put down the twenty-pound bag of granola and stood. "I'll get ready."

He blinked in surprise. No argument. Huh.

Twenty minutes later, exhausted and cold, they returned to the ancillary building to eat a quick meal before leaving.

She set to preparing it in silence while he hung their outerwear up to dry by the heater. Once they'd settled onto the only two chairs in the place, with the table between them, Coop took a scalding bite of couscous. The taste—spicy and fragrant—shocked him into speech. "'S good."

"Yeah?" She met his eyes with a small smile. "Did what I could."

He shoveled back a few more bites. "Good…job."

"What?" She yawned the word.

"You did well out there."

Was she choking? No, that was a laugh, apparently. "You kidding me? I was a mess." Her smile faded when he didn't reciprocate.

"Even after the day you had, your…" He waved at her nose. "Injuries and so on. You didn't stop till you got it right." Grudgingly, he went on. "Admirable."

It was what he'd want in a teammate. Grit, not strength, was the decisive factor when it came to making it out alive. That and some elusive survival instinct that couldn't be taught. After everything she'd gone through, and everything she'd done in the arch, he figured she just might have what it took.

He'd seen it over and over again. It wasn't the big guys who made it out of tough situations. And it wasn't the ones who'd planned and prepped and made it their life's work to be in shape or perfectly trained. It was the ones who *wanted* it. The ones who acted without thinking, who paid attention to instinct and took cover before they even registered that they'd heard a detonation.

Brows up as if he'd shocked her with his compliment, she compressed her lips and nodded in acknowledgment. She gave him none of that effusiveness she always exhibited to the rest of the crew. Why was that? Why'd everyone else get her laughs, but never him? Why'd she keep her smiles tight and short when he walked into a room, but wrap her arms around Jameson like he was the second coming?

Didn't matter. None of it mattered at this point. Not the way her hips undulated when she danced. Not the way her face hardened when she caught sight of him or the way her breasts looked in that one soft-looking, bright-red sweater she'd worn at Pam's birthday celebration.

Coop looked up and, steeling himself, met her eyes. "One more thing before we go."

"Yeah?" The word was swallowed by another yawn.

"Waste disposal."

"Okay." She glanced to the side, then back at him, as if to say, *Yeah, what about it?*

"You are aware, of course, that according to the Protocol on Environmental Protection to the Antarctic Treaty, we are required to evacuate all waste. Um…" Damn it, his face was scorching hot. "Including human waste."

"Ooohhh." She blinked a couple times. "You want to discuss *our* waste."

"I don't *want* to." He swallowed hard. "We will bring a bucket for initial disposal, as well as sealable bags for transport."

"So we…do it in the bucket and then dump it in the bag."

"Correct. Here." He handed her a wide-mouthed water

bottle. "This is for nighttime disposal. And there is the additional, uh, issue of…"

Her brows were almost up to her hairline now as she watched him, like a rubbernecker at an accident, waiting to see how bad it would get.

"Of your…menstruation."

"Holy crap, this is painful." She hid her smile behind her hand.

"You would have to—"

"Not that this is any of your business, but…" She raised a hand and closed her eyes for three long seconds. "Between my IUD and the cold, I haven't *menstruated* in months."

"Good." He nodded once. "Then that's done."

After that, they ate in silence, eyes on their bowls. Focused on nothing but filling their bellies.

Except it wasn't just that and he knew it. The food was good in a way that fed his starved soul, too. Which was possibly the crux of his whole issue with this woman. Coop, who'd never had a mom and never been too sad about it, wasn't a man to wish for anything. Ever. He had what he had and worked hard to get what he wanted. Which was mostly peace and quiet.

But here, across from a woman who was the antithesis of everything he'd ever known, who'd fed him food that burst with flavor and worked as hard as any soldier he'd ever fought beside, he let himself wish—for just a second or two—that he could be the man who made her laugh.

CHAPTER 15

Day 1—302 Miles to Volkov Station—21 Days of Food Remaining

THE DOOR FLEW OPEN AND FORD STOMPED INSIDE. "Time to go."

"Yes. Right. Okay." Groggy from lack of sleep, Angel pulled on another pair of socks, planted her feet on the floor, and tested them. Would she even be able to ski with her crap knee?

Yeah. If there was one thing being in that ice tunnel had shown her, it was that she'd walk, ski, crawl, or whatever the hell else she needed to do in order to get through this.

Ford was different somehow. She couldn't say exactly what it was, but there was something younger-looking about him. Even tense as he was, he seemed more approachable. Had exhaustion rounded off his edges? Or maybe the five o'clock shadow on his perpetually clean-shaven face made him look more human. The dark blond hairs glinted along his square-cut jaw, looking rough as sandpaper.

Drowsy from exhaustion, she stood and hobbled a few steps closer to him before she realized that she couldn't just stroke his face out of the blue, despite their physical closeness earlier.

Jesus, woman. Snap out of it. And whatever you do, don't touch the wildlife.

Except he wasn't an animal, was he? He was a bit of a weirdo, for sure, but weren't they all, in their own individual ways? Especially at Pole. The place attracted some pretty odd characters.

As she'd finished getting their food together, she'd spent way too much time thinking of the way this man had looked when she'd asked about his mama teaching him manners.

No, he'd said. Which meant what? Had his mother not been there for him? Had she not taught him to say *please* and *thank you*? Or the possibility she kept coming back to—had there been no mother at all in Dr. Ford Cooper's life?

And why, oh why, did that make her want to hug him when nothing the man did said *take me in your arms*. He was pretty much the definition of standoffish. And yet…

"Here." He held out a couple protein bars and her face heated when their gazes met, as if he could read her thoughts. "Eat."

She opened her mouth to tell him she'd just eaten and she wasn't hungry and maybe he could cool the bossy thing. Thinking better of it, she grabbed them and put them in her pocket. No point protesting when he was right.

He *was* the boss now after all.

"You okay?"

Surprised that he'd ask this—or even wonder it—she thought about her reply. "Scared, I guess."

He nodded. "Your nose better?"

She touched it lightly. Not broken, she didn't think, though it was still a little sore. With her coat on, she slipped mittens over her inner gloves, stepped into her pants, and drew a ski mask over her head. "Are you? Scared, I mean."

He stopped chewing his protein bar, looked to the side for a second, as expressionless as a robot searching its motherboard for some elusive data, then shocked the hell out of her by saying, "Yes." It came out in a voice she'd never heard him use before. It was a toss-up as to whether the admission sent more fear running through her or relief that she wasn't the only one. "But we'll be fine," he added, back to himself again.

She sucked in a deep breath, comforted. If he said they'd be fine, then they would be—

And then he ruined it. "I mean, there's a chance we'll make it."

"A chance." She glared at him, then compressed her lips into a semblance of a smile. "Great. Good. That's... Thanks." She pulled her ski mask over her face to keep from adding something snarky. He was just being honest.

With a breath in, she followed him outside and looked up at the massive, bright-red snow plow, waiting for them on the ice. "So this is our ride, huh?"

"Till the fuel runs out. First fifty miles or so."

"Then we'll only have two hundred fifty miles to ski." She glanced at him, blank behind all his outdoor gear, and forced a laugh. "Piece of cake." Her eyes landed on the sleds. "Where are the tubes?"

"Tubes?"

"Your ice thingies. Why aren't they on the sleds?"

"We're leaving them."

"What do you mean we're leaving them?"

"Too heavy."

"Then take them out of the casings."

He shook his head. "Can't risk contamination."

His nonchalant act was good. Really good, since it was pretty much his schtick to begin with, but something about it was off. The careful way he watched her, maybe? The slight tick in his jaw? Whatever it was, she didn't believe it for a second.

"You're suggesting we just hand them over? After everything those evil jerks did?" She yanked the ski mask back up and pulled her neck gaiter down. "Look, Mr. Ice Man, I didn't go through hell to give the bad guys their damned *payload* back, okay?" When he didn't respond, she went on. "I'll dump the damned butter if I have to."

He opened his mouth to say something, then narrowed his eyes and kept quiet.

Good response.

Without a word, he set to work rearranging the sled contents to make way for the tubes.

With everything once again packed up and secure, she took one last look at the station, her throat working convulsively. This had been home for the past few months. The only safe place for miles around.

But then it wasn't all that safe in the end, was it?

Tears blurred her vision. Which they pretty much always did out on the ice. The only difference was that these tears hurt from the inside out, not the other way around.

"I'll miss it."

"Hm?"

She shook her head and accepted his hand up onto the massive hunk of machinery. "Nothing." She had to yell to be heard above the engine until the door slammed.

"Heat'll kick in soon," he said as he pointed the plow away from the base, shifted into gear, and rolled forward, into white so big, so powerful and pure in its nothingness that it felt almost like...God.

She cleared her throat, a little embarrassed at the crap her mind was feeding her. "How do you know where we're headed?"

"GPS."

"It works?" She brightened.

"For now. Gotta keep it warm so the batteries don't die." He patted a pocket. "Brought extras."

"Could someone track us on that? The GPS?"

"No." He glanced at her, unreadable behind his goggles, though the grim set of his mouth was visible since he'd pushed his neck gaiter down.

"Okay." She closed her eyes, halfway relieved that she'd wound up with a guy who knew apparently everything there was to know about this place. Her other half was stuck in a spiral of hopelessness, spurred on by the enormity of what they were doing. "What if it breaks?"

"Got a backup," he said as if it was only natural. As if you'd be crazy not to have a backup.

"Of course you do."

"And a backup for the backup."

Her eyes cut over to him again. Was this an actual Ice Man joke? Nope. Same stern Batman mouth, hard and somehow kissable all at once.

What the hell? *Not kissable.* She craned her neck to look behind them as they pulled away.

What is wrong with me? His mouth was about the most rigid thing she'd ever seen. Kissing it would be like putting your lips to a Greek statue.

Except she didn't actually believe that anymore. And suddenly, the hot-blooded, reckless part of her that had tried to get him to dance demanded that she find out.

"*No.*" The whispered word popped out hard, low, and guttural.

"What?"

"Nothing." The station was invisible now, behind a hazy screen of wind-blown snow.

When she finally turned back toward the front, she caught him eyeing her for a few long beats.

"Also brought a compass," he offered.

"I thought those didn't work at the poles."

"We're far enough from the magnetic pole for it to work. Besides, the farther we get from ninety south, the better off we'll be."

"Good. Good." She nodded and let the passing landscape blur into one big white nightmare, feeling... *alive?*

How was that even possible?

Well, I'm not dead.

She turned to take in the man beside her. And because this man had saved her life, because he was the only hope she had, because her world right now wasn't this landscape they chugged slowly across, but *him*, she leaned forward to place her gloved hand over his, and spoke. "Thank you, Ford."

"Don't thank me, Angel." His voice was uglier than its usual croak, as if *thank you*s rubbed him the wrong way. "'Cause things are gonna get a lot worse before they get better."

CHAPTER 16

Day 1—254 Miles to Volkov Station—21 Days of Food Remaining

THE PISTENBULLY CUT OFF SUDDENLY, ITS SILENCE filling Coop's head as fully as the engine noise had. They came to a slow, eerily quiet stop.

Above them, the sky was a perfect blue, the sun's focused rays heating the vehicle's interior so that they'd needed only a couple layers for the ride. Aside from minor variations in the surface of the ice, there was nothing outside to break up the view.

Coop knew exactly how much this vast place contained: limitless untold secrets inside each layer of ice, each molecule. It was beautiful, this pure, endlessly repetitive landscape.

But then he looked at the woman passed out in the seat beside him and the ice had never looked so unpredictable.

He forced his eyes away from her. "Angel."

She stirred with a sleepy sound that went straight to his groin.

"We're, uh…" He cleared his throat and stared outside rather than watching her slow, sleepy awakening. "We're out of fuel. Time to start skiing."

"Oh." She sat up, appearing alert and ready. "Right. Right. I'm awake."

"Let's have a snack in here and get going."

Without a word, she dug into the pack at her feet, handed

him a bar, and opened up one of her own. No argument, no questions, no delays. He wasn't sure what he'd expected from her, but it hadn't been this.

After polishing off his protein bar, he put his hand on the door, caught sight of her, and paused. Instead of eating, she sat rigid, staring out the windshield.

He opened his mouth to tell her they didn't have time to waste and immediately closed it again. The woman had gone through a hell of a lot in the past—what? Fourteen, fifteen hours? She'd witnessed a murder, fought off the killer with a hatchet, and then prepared for an unexpected expedition that most people wouldn't survive.

Even Coop—the man who'd never met a conversation he couldn't turn awkward—could tell that he needed to tread lightly right now.

"You okay?"

She sent him a startled look, with a high, humorless half laugh, and bit off a piece of protein bar. After a few slow chews, she nodded. "Yeah."

A glance at the GPS unit told him that it was about 4:30 a.m. Over twelve hours since he'd returned to find Burke-Ruhe deserted. A lot had changed since then.

As soon as Angel finished, he put out a hand, palm up. The move must've shocked her because she stared at it for a few seconds before putting hers on top.

"You've got this, okay?" he whispered, surprised by the emotion he couldn't seem to swallow down.

"Thank you. For everything." She put her fingers through his and squeezed, her hold surprisingly strong, even through the multiple layers of gloves. "And *we've* got this."

Right. They were a team now.

After a final squeeze, he opened the door and dropped

to the ground, straight into a cutting, ferocious wind. By the time he'd fought his way to the other door, it was too late to give her a hand down.

He hesitated, taking in her unrecognizable form. Between her coat and neck gaiter, ski mask, goggles, hat, and gloves, with her fur-lined hood covering her head, she could be anyone. It made it easier, thinking of her as an anonymous trekking partner.

"Stay behind me!" he yelled to be heard through the low howl. "Follow my tracks." Even standing still like this, the wind snatched his voice and blew it away. He leaned closer, spoke louder, straight into her ear. "If I go too fast, let me know. You need a break for water or…" He cleared his throat. "Yell."

At her nod, they quickly harnessed up, stepped into their skis, grabbed their poles, and took off, lugging probably three hundred pounds between them.

It was slow going, towing this much weight against the wind. But he'd humped enough gear to know his body could handle it. He glanced behind at regular intervals to see that Angel was struggling. He slowed, she caught up, then lagged again. He slowed more. At some point, the sky cleared, but the wind picked up, its assault a barrage of sharp, cold little splinters.

After a couple hours on the ice, it was obvious that they'd have to cover more ground than this. By his estimation, they had enough food for three weeks. At their current rate, the trip would take a month, barring unforeseen meteorological events. Of course, consuming food would lighten the load, but their bodies would weaken as they went. There'd be blisters and frostbite and other issues, not to mention the real possibility of injury.

"Ford… Ford… *Coop!*" Angel's voice barely carried

through the screaming gale. He stopped and turned to see her bent over a pole, body heaving with every breath. "Need a break."

He took off his skis and tromped over to help her do the same. They'd been at it for two hours and gone less than a mile. Not even a dent in the two hundred fifty or so miles left between them and the Russian station.

He kept an eye on the sky while they shared a silent snack. Well, *they* were silent. The wind howled as if protesting their alien presence. As if even their ski tracks sullied its pristine domain.

"The wind's so…" Angel didn't finish. Possibly because just being heard out here was a chore. Or maybe she didn't have the words to describe how hard it was blowing.

"Need a rest?" They had to put more miles between them and Burke-Ruhe. Just in case. But an injury this early in the game would mean failure.

"No. Thank you." She stood up from where she'd been sitting on the sled, grabbed the lead, and hooked it to her harness, then snapped herself into her skis. "Let's go!"

He blinked, stunned again by her strength—of body or will or both, he wasn't sure. And then, because he didn't have time to sit around thinking about how wrong he'd been all this time, he got into his own skis and set off.

At some point, the wind calmed, leaving almost total silence, aside from the slip-slide of skis and the closed-in waft of breath through fleece.

He quickly settled back into the zone, glancing at the sky and then over his shoulder every hundred paces or so. Angel forged on, as stoically stubborn as anyone he'd ever met. For three more hours they continued, their painfully slow pace only picking up slightly.

Breakfast was a snack, lunch a quick pit stop. Food, hydration, a few minutes' rest. They barely exchanged five words.

"You okay?" he asked.

She nodded.

After a couple more hours, he slowed, turned to see her leaning heavily on her poles, and came to a complete stop.

When he handed her the ice axe and cookpot with a curt, "Fill this," he expected ribbing or a complaint at his lack of nicety. He got nothing. Not a look, a significant pause, or an annoyed huff. She just nodded and tromped over to a brittle-looking section of ice, where she went to work.

As fast as he could make his heavy muscles go, he pitched the tent and put up the snowfly—the tarp-like outer layer that would provide them with extra protection against wind and ice.

After setting up their pads and sleeping bags, Coop sat back on his haunches, eyeing the space they'd be sharing. It was tight in here, as he'd known it would be.

Which was fine. They'd sleep like the dead tonight.

While she unpacked the cooking supplies, he went out to pile snow up along the base of the tent, for added protection against the elements, then dug a latrine area, which would afford at least a bit of privacy.

After that last flurry of activity, they wound up inside together, brushing off the layers of frost coating their outerwear. He pulled his boots off with a sigh.

When Angel did the same, she let out a long, low groan that shouldn't have turned him on. Not even a little, considering how beyond tired he was.

"Okay?" he croaked and rubbed his throat unconsciously. Hurt like hell from the dry wind and constant exertion.

She nodded, but he was pretty sure that was bullshit. He'd never seen the woman's face so devoid of expression, like she couldn't even lift her brows. As if her facial muscles wouldn't activate after the day's journey.

"I'll make dinner."

"I can—"

"You're not the chef here, Angel. You're just…one of the team." He set out the camp stove and got to work heating up chunks of ice.

"Yeah?" Her face changed, something flickering in her eyes. "Team of two, huh?"

He watched out of the corner of his eye as she reached up and under her clothes behind her back, fiddled with something, and then sank forward with a sigh. "Darned thing."

He opened his mouth to ask what darned thing she meant and then realized just in time: her bra. She'd undone her bra with as much relief as she'd pulled off those boots. The hell women went through just to be women.

After a few seconds of watching him pour pale, desiccated poultry and sauce flakes into the cook pot, she collapsed onto her back, wide eyes fixed on the tent ceiling. "Not much of a team member, am I?"

"What do you mean?"

"How far do you figure we went today?"

He didn't have to pull out the GPS to know they'd made it forty-eight miles in the plow and just about eight on their skis.

"'bout fifty-six miles." He worked hard to sound unconcerned.

"Crap. We only skied eight miles?"

He nodded.

"You can ski twice that much. You'd still be at it if I weren't here, wouldn't you?" Looking grim, she refused to catch his eye. "Right?"

With a half shrug, he stirred and thought about what he could say to make her feel better. Nothing. It was true. She was holding him back. At the same time… "Glad you're here, though."

"Come *on*." She looked at him finally, the sudden directness of her gaze almost aggressive. "Hauling me around's not doing you any favors. Wouldn't you rather survive this than die because of my dead weight?"

He blinked at the rehydrated chicken dish sending its mouthwatering fog into the air. Crazy how good this stuff smelled. Finally, he set the spoon down and turned to her. "No."

"Bullshit."

"Rather not do this alone." That wasn't strictly true, but it seemed like the right thing to say. *Yeah, I'd rather be alone, but I couldn't leave you back there to die* didn't have a good ring to it.

"You go out on the ice alone every single day."

"That's research."

"Ah. Research. A fine mistress." She did some weird approximation of a foreign accent.

He snorted and opened his mouth to say something, but she beat him to it.

"Holy crap."

"What?"

"*Did you just laugh?*" She sat up, humor brightening her eyes.

"Huh?"

"That huffy noise you made. That was a laugh, wasn't it?"

"Huffy?"

"Yeah. Like a grunt."

"Wasn't—"

"It *was*. You laughed. Halle-frickin-lujah. The man laughs."

That made him frown. "Course I do."

"Not with me you don't."

"What are you—"

"Oh, come on, *Professor Ice Man*, you know as well as I do that I'm the last person you'd want to be stuck with out here on the ice. Am I right?" The look she gave him was knowing and brash and close to the way she acted back on base. Except for one little difference—an almost unnoticeable moment of hesitation. Like she assumed she was right, but she really didn't want to be.

He couldn't answer right away. Partly because he didn't want to have this conversation at all, but also because he wasn't entirely sure of his own answer. Would he rather be here with someone other than her?

Whatever. No point wasting time worrying about things like that. If what-ifs had been his thing, he'd have started young with questions like, *What if Mom were alive? What would life be like then?* Or *What if I'd stayed in school instead of joining the army to piss off Dad?*

Those weren't questions he'd ever bother asking himself.

"No point."

"What?"

"No point worrying about crap like that." He grabbed a bowl and spoon and handed it over to her. "Eat."

CHAPTER 17

SHE SHOULDN'T HAVE SAID THAT *DEAD WEIGHT* THING. Because now that it was out, it hung between them like… Well, like a dead weight. A years-old salami, left too long to cure. Heavy, dry, hard as rock, obvious, and utterly pointless.

Right. Pointless, he'd said. Or, actually, "No point worrying about crap like that." Such a practical way of looking at life.

She ate without tasting, which, frankly, was a good thing, given the slop they were shoveling in. Slop that felt pretty amazing going down, though. The heat and moisture revived her a bit, made her feel more human after the repetitive hiss of skiing had taken even that away.

She hurt in ways she'd never imagined after one day on the ice. What would it be like after three weeks of this?

"Thank you," she finally managed, once she'd put away almost the entire bowl, barely taking the time to breathe.

He did another of those grunts—apparently his catch-all sound—and lifted his head. Those blue eyes, close and *here* after so many hours hidden behind protective eyewear, nearly blinded her. "What for?"

"For dinner."

"Don't."

"Don't thank you?" She blinked. "Why not?"

He shrugged and his already sunburned face got redder. "It's normal."

She thought of that final, awkward thank-you he'd

offered up back at the station. Those were meant to be his last words to her ever.

"Nothing like the food you used to make," he added.

That warmed her a little. Lit a hungry little flame inside her. "You liked my food?"

"Course."

"I didn't realize that."

He grunted again and went back to his bowl, while Angel hid a smile and did the same.

They chewed slowly, not speaking for so long that she'd thought the conversation was over.

His voice was quiet when he spoke again, as if he didn't really *want* to speak, but felt compelled. "Your meals were worlds beyond the last cook's."

"I'm not fishing for—"

"Even last night. Dried-out couscous, a sprinkle of this, dab of that, hot water. Brought me back to the Middle East."

Something about the way he said that tweaked her. "You travel a lot?"

His eyes twitched toward her and away. After a few seconds of silence, she thought he'd shut down again, but he surprised her.

"Couple tours in Iraq. Also traveled to Lebanon and North Africa, where couscous is queen." His face was softer when he met her eyes. "You ever been there?"

"No."

"You'd like it. Morocco, I think."

She nodded. "Bet I would."

"Full of…" He lifted his hands and gesticulated, as if hunting for words that wouldn't come. After a second, he tried again. "Smells. Bright, saturated colors."

"So, the opposite of this place."

Her comment lifted his lips and she froze, blindsided.

The man's smile was as mesmerizing as the sparkle of sun on ice—a million blinding diamonds there and gone so fast she wasn't convinced it was real.

Do that again, she wanted to beg, willing his face to lose that hard, wolfish focus. To relax and brighten.

"Pretty much. It's big and bright and raucous. Color, sound, smells."

What was he talking about?

Oh, Morocco. Right. That was why he thought she'd like it. Unsubtle, obvious, in-your-face Angel Smith.

She must have cringed, because he stopped talking and gave her a quizzical look. "No?"

Was this the way he looked into a microscope? Did he even look into microscopes? It occurred to her that despite seeing him trudge off every morning, she had no idea how he spent his days.

She blinked, shook herself internally, and tried to recover. "Oh. Yeah. I mean, I'd love to go one day. I've never traveled. Aside from coming here." She set her bowl down and took a long drink of water, doing her best not to think about Jerkhead Hugh and the research trips he'd taken without her. Someone had to take care of the restaurant and he was the culinary genius, after all. She was just the workhorse. The idiot who'd eaten up every one of his lies, who'd given up her dreams for his.

And here she was, thinking about him…again. No. No way. On a hard exhale, she looked at Ford, trying to picture him in a uniform. "What brought you from there to here, then?"

Stiffly, he lifted his shoulders and dropped them.

"Science." The single word was dull and uninformative, as if designed to deflect all interest pointed his way.

"Science," she repeated quietly, watching him with a slow nod.

Suddenly, with absolute clarity, she knew that he was lying.

Ford Cooper was one hundred percent full of crap. He hadn't come to Antarctica for science any more than she'd come here for the food. He'd come to get away. For some reason she couldn't explain, it softened her to him, made her want to understand him, or at least know him better. Because nobody knew this man. Not really. People at the station liked him. Some, like Jameson, even spent time with him, but he didn't let anybody beneath that thick, opaque surface. And like the surface they sat on, the man was more complicated than he appeared. Powerful and driven, but also good and kind.

Good enough to take her with him on a journey that she might not be equipped to survive. Kind enough to slow his pace to match hers when she suspected that he could go much, much faster.

"Would you still be out there if it weren't for me?"

He frowned. "What are you—"

As if to remind her of the danger of this place, a wall of wind attacked the tent, rattling it and sending a hailstorm of snow to pelt the thin fabric, startling her and cutting him off abruptly.

She set down her bowl and scooted closer to him.

"Promise me something."

He narrowed his eyes, but didn't say a word, and rather than look at that sharp blue gaze, she stared at the orange tent material above. "When the moment comes—and it will—when you have to decide between hauling my ass to safety and saving your own life, make the smart choice." She plowed on. "Promise me, Ford, that you'll leave me if it saves your life. I don't want us both to die. I don't want to be responsible for killing you." With the last of her energy, she turned onto her side and reached for one of his callused hands. She grabbed it before he could pull away and held on tight. "*Promise.*"

It took a long time for his wolf eyes to make their slow circuit of her face, to their joined hands, and back. By the time their gazes locked, something deeply frightening had happened inside her, something she wasn't ready to think about.

When he opened his mouth, she had no doubt what he'd say.

Confusion morphed to tight-jawed anger. "No."

Tingling from the top of her buzzing head to the tips of her half-frozen toes, she opened her mouth to protest. He halted her with another annoyed look.

"And don't suggest it again or I'll…"

She blinked, eyes ensnared by his, and breathlessly awaited his next words.

"Don't know what I'll do," he said. "But you won't like it."

Maybe I will, a little voice said before she snuffed it out.

It seemed wrong, as they discussed their fates, to picture his hand wrapped in her hair and his strong-looking mouth against hers. Especially when he clearly meant what he said. He'd sacrifice himself if it gave her a chance at life.

In that moment she knew, with utter certainty and complete devastation, that whatever happened in the next few days, however they got through this—or didn't—she'd met the best man she'd ever known.

Too bad they'd probably die together.

One of the things Coop loved about Antarctica was how it boiled everything down to the basics. Wind, ice, work, silence. Not exactly quiet, of course, since there were times when the wind howled as constantly and inevitably as waves breaking on land, but here there was space for thinking or not thinking as much as you wanted. What kept him coming back year after year, season after season, was the quiet in his head. The vacuum. No nightmares, no voices, no dreams at all. Just…space to exist.

He'd slept quickly and easily, as he always did on the ice. So, when screams tore through the night, sending him up and out of his protective cocoon into the freezing air, he could do nothing but gasp and blink into the early winter sunlight trying to remember where he was.

He stared at the orange canvas walls. No explosions, no pained groans, no adrenaline-laced dreams. Just the rattling wind, ball-tightening cold, and a terrorized woman. With his body shaking in an effort to heat itself, he slid partway out of his bag and bent over her.

He set a careful hand on her shoulder, not to shake her but to steady her rocking, not to quiet the moans but to soak them up.

"I'm here," he whispered. "You're okay, Angel. I got you."

Over and over, he gave her the words. He felt useless, but it was the best he had to offer.

She eventually calmed, her eyes still closed, as if she'd never fully awakened. He lifted his hands, worked his way back into his bag, and had just closed his eyes again when another sound leaked through the tent. Only this time instead of a heart-stopping scream, she paralyzed him by whispering his name.

"Yeah?" he managed to push out after a few shallow breaths.

"Can you… Would you put your… Never mind."

"What?" It seemed urgent, somehow, that she tell him what she needed.

"You probably can't."

"Can't what?"

She sniffled from deep within her bag and turned onto her side, away from him.

"Can't leave your bag. Without freezing." Another sniff and then a low, very hesitant, "Right?"

He could, if he put more clothes on. With the sun beating on their tent all night, it wasn't terribly cold in here. He sat up and reached for his coat.

"It's just that I'm…" She shuddered, her shape curling in on itself. Cold, he was sure she'd say. "Afraid."

He didn't ask what she was afraid of.

"Come here," he said, unzipping his bag as fast as he could and reaching immediately for hers. He'd noted that these two could be mated. The sound was harsh, like tearing tent canvas. Worse than the noise was the cold, instantly, completely wrapping itself around him.

Quickly, with surprising efficiency considering how hard it was to move, he scooted his pad, bag, and body toward hers, found the place where their zippers intersected, and shoved one into the other, pulled, got stuck, and shook for a good five seconds before he managed to yank it up again. All the while she waited, trembling. Another zip and they were in a single larger bag. He reached for one of the extras he'd grabbed and spread it out over them. Finally, a yank brought the tops up and over their heads and an awkward drawstring pull gave them a dark, welcome shelter.

Together, face-to-face.

Bad idea. How could he not regret it when it brought everything into pure sensorial focus?

Her shaking continued, punctuated by little gasps.

I should touch her.

Uh. No.

Except they were touching already, pressed together by proximity, from where her sock-clad toes dug into his calves to where her face nestled in the hollow under his chin.

He drew a deep, cinnamon-laced inhale and lifted his arm, which skated audibly against the nylon.

Outside their dark, tight, intimate shelter, the tent shook, battered by winds. But in here, everything was slippery, slow movements, hesitation.

She sighed, the sound as full of pleasure as a slide into hot water, and rather than fight it, he let himself wrap around her. Just his arm, but it felt like so much more. Particularly when she stopped shaking, stopped making those noises, and melted into him.

Each of her exhales puffed hot and intimate against his neck.

It felt good to hold her. As good as it had yesterday in the ancillary building, when he'd taken off his shirt to give her his body heat. Two bright spots in an otherwise hellish twenty-four hours.

Angel let out another deep, satisfied-sounding breath and twisted so that instead of being face-to-face, he spooned her, the position so natural, so warm, that he couldn't help but tighten his hold.

For the first time in as long as he could remember, he gave himself a break.

Why shouldn't he share a bit of warmth? Why shouldn't he get some comfort in the process? There was no harm, was there, in closing his eyes and soaking in this connection for just a few seconds?

Who would it hurt if he let himself like it?

No one was the answer.

Within the snug circle of his arm, her chest rose and fell with comforting regularity, until it stuttered for a second and he could have sworn she whispered something—probably not his name—before settling in deeper and finally falling asleep.

He breathed in, filled his lungs and brain with her, soaked in her warmth and steeped in her spicy scent, and it was so good after the harsh kiss of the wind, so perfectly right that, suddenly, he knew it for exactly what it was: a lie.

There was a reason he'd avoided Angel Smith. Already, she'd started seeping under his skin, making him feel things he preferred not to think about.

And it felt so good it scared him.

CHAPTER 18

Day 2—246 Miles to Volkov Station—20 Days of Food Remaining

FORD HAD BEEN UP FOR AN HOUR MELTING WATER AND repacking what he could when he heard a faint buzz.

He'd spent so much of the past twenty-four hours actively listening for a sound just like this, scouring the sky for signs of aerial approach, that he was half convinced it was a false alarm. An auditory hallucination.

He squinted up, saw nothing, aside from the sun glaring down from pristine blue.

He'd just decided to wake Angel up when he heard it again, clearer this time, as if the wind had snatched the sound from the air and delivered it right here by some ventriloquist trick. Fighting a deep sense of disorientation, he spun, his eyes flicking around until he found it.

There.

When he squinted, a bright red smudge solidified in the sky, heading in the direction of Burke-Ruhe. One of the small Twin Otter airplanes that were commonly used for transport throughout the continent, he'd bet. It shouldn't be here.

Just the sight of that colorful speck tore him in half. First, the burst of excitement—*They're here! Evacuation!*—followed immediately by the deep, frightening certainty that no one was coming to save them. Those assholes had returned for the core samples.

Anyone's guess what they'd do when they didn't find them.

Time to get a move on.

Day 2—Burke-Ruhe Research Station, South Pole

Sampson stomped the ice from his boots and slammed the door with such gusto it shook the ancillary building. "Nothing."

Clive blinked, working hard to keep the irritation from his face. "What do you mean, nothing?"

"If you'd come with us, Doc, you'd know exactly what I mean."

Was this a joke? The gorilla couldn't possibly think that Clive planned to get involved in this man's bloodbath. He had no intention of searching for the ice core samples that Sampson and his team had misplaced. No intention of partnering with this man on anything aside from what was strictly necessary in order to carry out his trials.

"I trust you to do your job, Mr. Sampson. Which is why I did not accompany you to the supply arch." That and the fact that he couldn't stand being underground. Or under ice, as the case may be.

"Well, Doc, to sum it up for you, your ice cores are gone."

"Impossible."

"Actually, I'd say it's *entirely* possible." Sampson flashed one absurdly incongruous dimple. "Looks like our friend Cooper took off with them."

Clive almost laughed. "Where on earth would he go?" There was nothing for miles around. Like the Facility they'd prepared for their experiments, Burke-Ruhe was as isolated as an island in the middle of the Pacific. "You removed or destroyed all fuel sources, correct? Machinery? Communications? You can't possibly be telling me he took off into this wilderness on his own? With just those core samples for company?"

"I think that's exactly what he did." The door opened again to reveal two more men, whose overlarge presences filled the room to bursting. They pulled off their ski masks and exchanged looks with Sampson, who turned back to Clive with a smirk. "And I don't think he's alone."

"Who could possibly have accompanied—" Clive blinked and swallowed the burn hitting the back of his throat. Unconsciously, he reached for his roll of antacids. He had cases of them back at the Facility, but suddenly he feared those wouldn't be nearly enough. "Oh." The woman.

If they made it out somehow, with his virus…things would not go well. For him, or for anyone here, in fact.

Sampson's blond brows rose and fell while he adjusted his crotch. Clive looked away. *This* was who the director had chosen to head up logistics? The person meant to be Clive's right-hand man? Insulting.

And a little worrisome. Because far from the precise, surgical operation Clive had hoped for, everything about this man and his cronies screamed *blunt force*.

"You *have* done a thorough search." He didn't quite phrase it as a question, but the doubt was there.

"Yeah, Doc. No new bodies. No blood. Cores are gone, tunnel's empty, bitch is MIA. Looks like they took a snow plow." He popped a mint and grinned. "Guess it's time to go hunting."

Clive hadn't thought he could get colder than he'd been a moment before, but of course he was proven wrong. "Hunting?" The word was barely audible.

"Gotta get the cores back. Boss said." Sampson reached for his sat phone and checked the satellite schedule taped to the wall. "I'll check in with her. Let her know we'll need to launch a full-scale—"

"Oh no." Clive hurried to interrupt. "I'll update her on—"

"*Director.*" The shithead had already dialed. "Sampson here." He turned his back to the room, giving Clive the sudden urge to slide that enormous knife from the man's sheath and plant it in the back of his neck. "Looks like the big guy took off with the cook. Yeah. Cooper. Took the ice cores, too." The ring of excitement in Sampson's voice was absolutely nauseating.

While the man listened to whatever the director had to say, Clive worked hard to slow his breathing, willing himself to calm. It didn't matter, after all, who headed up this search, as long as the virus made it back to the Facility. Where *he* was king, not these thugs.

He pictured the Harper Facility's pristine, high-tech labs, equipped with everything needed for viral replication. It was all ready and waiting. The only thing missing were the infectious materials themselves.

He'd have the entire winter to conduct his trials in peace, and though he wasn't exactly pleased with the methods, he had what most people only dreamed of—a group of subjects entirely at his disposal.

"Yeah. Got to head back to the Facility to gear up first. But don't worry. We'll get 'em, boss." He watched the idiot talk to Katherine Henley Harper as if she were some college girl he'd met in a bar instead of one of the most powerful women in the world. Perhaps he didn't realize. Clive tilted his head. Maybe the trick was that Sampson didn't care.

Okay. He'd do the same. Not care. So, rather than focus

on these militarized idiots and the frigid hellhole around them, he let images of the future soothe him—the villa in France, the East Village loft. With the bonus he'd been promised, he'd be flying first class for the rest of his life. Not too shabby for a kid from Detroit.

"The doc?" Serene now, Clive focused back in on Sampson's conversation. "I'm afraid he's stepped out for the moment, ma'am." The man's hard eyes flicked to Clive's outstretched hand and then away. "I'll tell him you wanted a word."

Clive worked hard to maintain a placid exterior, while inside he was boiling. Was the asshole making a play for power? Was that it?

Why? What good could it possibly do him to make enemies when they were ostensibly on the same side? It wasn't like he could carry out the trials. Was this just some stupid, macho posturing, or was there something deeper happening here?

A shiver went through him as he thought of the months he'd be spending locked up with these men in that facility.

He'd have to keep his distance, he decided. It wasn't the loudest who held the power, or the strongest. It was the man who delivered.

While these mercenaries strutted around bullying everyone in their path, the service Clive provided would change everything.

So they'd have to coexist peacefully for the next several months. He could do that. He could do anything given enough motivation.

As Sampson hung up, Clive did his best to channel one of the man's easy, Sunday-morning smiles and stood. "So, it's a-hunting we shall go, then?"

"That's right." Sampson smiled. "You ready?"

CHAPTER 19

Day 2—246 Miles to Volkov Station—20 Days of Food Remaining

"Get up, Angel. Gotta go."

Something about Ford's tone cleared the sleep from her mind with uncommon swiftness.

"Okay," she mumbled, struggling out of the bag. "Up. Up. I'm up." Half-out, she paused to squint around the now-familiar interior of the tent, one eye still closed, in search of whatever had him so agitated. "What's going on?"

"There's a plane."

Adrenaline shot through her so fast she swayed. "Here?"

"Not far."

"They see us?"

"Don't think so." He was throwing things into bags, packing sloppily when yesterday he'd warned her against just that. "Better leave."

She nodded, grabbed the socks she'd hung above her head to dry the night before, and shoved her feet into them, then threw on her many layers.

"I've got the bedding." He urged her toward the door, where she yanked on her boots. "You go out and eat. And here—drink this."

She accepted a steaming cup of something, stumbled outside, and took a too-hot swig as she eyed the horizon, the freezing wind turning the cold bite of fear into something solid that slid in at the nape of her neck and worked its way down her spine. Her next sip was cold. Breathing hard, she searched the skyline. Where were they?

In what must have been record time, she helped Ford stow their stuff on the sleds and knocked back a couple of the fat bombs she'd put together at base—bite-size packs of butter and granola—glad to have something to eat in a hurry.

Strapping into the harness, she found those first few trudging steps held echoes of a weekend triple shift. Chafing in unexpected places, general aches and sharp, lancing pains. She'd deal with them later. Distance was what they needed now.

The initial push was like poking at a bruise over and over again or opening up a blister. Which was probably happening. All over her body.

Ignore it. Work through it. All it took was one hard press, the wind at her back—then another. Then another. The repeated *swish-scrape* of her skis felt as useless as treading water. Were they even moving?

Despite the blazing sun, she shivered. She had caught Ford's jitters, convinced that her movements and protective wear muffled the thrum of an engine. Maybe they were being watched even now.

She turned to the side. Blank white nothing. Emptiness. Everywhere.

Swish-scrape. Swish-scrape. Swish-scrape.

Ford had his compass rigged out in front of him on a chest harness, ensuring that he never lost sight of their direction. And in this wide-open white-and-blue landscape, where dips and crags didn't appear until she was right on them, where she could spin in circles for hours without spotting a single abnormality, *he* was *her* compass.

Swish-scrape. Swish-scrape. Swish-scrape.

With a jarring crunch, her ski jammed into a depression in the snow and she just barely kept herself from falling.

Better simmer down. She took a couple calming breaths, focused on the man in front of her, and took off again.

Unaware, Ford just plowed on, tall and unperturbed, making it look so easy. Straight as an arrow, his pace steady, his direction unerring. How the hell was he so unbothered by everything when she could barely see straight, barely push her leaden limbs on? Fueled by hot resentment, she mumbled a dark "jerk" and felt immediately guilty.

He was a good person. A good man, leading her to safety. A man who'd held her in the night and made her feel...

"Oh hell," she said this time, because being dependent on anyone rankled. But liking him rankled even more. And then, because it felt stupidly good to just say it aloud, she whispered it on repeat over and over again until the words lost their meaning.

Her eyes stayed focused so hard on his tall, red-and-black form that she didn't notice the change in the light until they stopped for lunch.

"Whoa." She blinked at what looked like a low fog bank up ahead, where sky and ground blended into one big soup.

Something pressed into her hand—a bottle of warm water. "Take this." Fingers as useless as sausages, she lowered her neck gaiter and shot him a quick smile of thanks before cupping the bottle in both palms and drinking. Wow, that felt good going down. After a few long swigs, she handed it back and pulled out a couple bags of food, handed him one, and ate.

Numbly, she stared at the sweeping mass before them,

light tendrils curling toward them in inviting wisps that were lovely from a distance. Closer to the ground, it was opaque and ominous as a swirling vortex into hell. "That just appeared out of nowhere."

Her eyes moved to Ford, who stood, head cocked. "Yep. Coming in fast." He wasn't looking at the storm.

Feeling heavy and slow, her movements off, somehow she followed the direction of his gaze and stiffened. "You hear the plane again?"

"Not exactly."

"What do you mean?"

He shook his head, and though she couldn't see his eyes through his dark goggles, the tension was obvious in every line of his body. "Can't explain it."

The prickle at her neck turned to goose bumps so painful she had to rub her arms to get them down. "Okay. Well. At least the cloud cover's good, right? For us, I mean?"

"Yeah. It would definitely ground 'em."

Right. It would ground the flight. But what would it do to them, down here in the thick of it? Back at the station, it was against regulations to even *go outside* in some storms. Was this a Condition 1 or a Condition 2 storm approaching? She turned, wondering if Ford could tell, and stopped.

Though every inch of his face was covered, something about the way he stood told her that his next words would be bad—very bad.

"What is it?"

He pointed at the sky, where it took her a while to spot a tiny red dot, no bigger than a sunspot on an old photo. "They're coming."

"That's bananas." Whoever was in that plane was out of their mind. Couldn't they see what they were flying into?

"Yeah." He swung around to look at the quickly moving storm, then back at the plane again. Was it closer than before? "They want our virus. *Badly*."

For the first time since they'd started this terrible trip, Angel almost wished they'd left the samples back at base. Almost, until that nightmarish image flashed back—that moment when Sampson had put his gun to Alex's head, and the handful of seconds afterward, when disbelief morphed into gut-squeezing shock. It would never leave her. The whole thing—the *feeling* of it—had been imprinted into her brain, into every cell, every part of her being.

Her eyes flicked from one quickly approaching threat to the other. In one direction, the blizzard swept angrily toward them, in the other, the red dot grew larger, carrying men who would do absolutely anything to get their payload. "What are you thinking?" she asked, afraid she knew the answer.

"I'm thinking we're screwed."

"Right." She nodded. They already knew that anyway.

Closer now, the wind whipped ice crystals into the air, like sugar spinning into cotton candy. Even through the whistling, she thought she heard the sound of an engine.

"What do we do now?"

He shoved his empty bag away and grabbed his ski poles, so she did the same.

"We run." He turned and led her straight into the coming storm.

CHAPTER 20

THIS WAS THE STUPIDEST THING COOP HAD EVER DONE.

Or maybe not. Maybe leaving the base took the cake. Or, if he was being brutally honest with himself—which he was, as usual—it was refusing that dance the other night.

If he'd known what they'd be up against, if he'd realized how close death hovered, well, yeah. Fuck it. Maybe he wouldn't have worried about maintaining a safe distance. Maybe he'd have calculated the danger, accepted her offer, and risked the burn.

Right now, as he fought, head down, shoulders up, through what had to be a Condition 2 storm, he wanted only one thing—and that was to be back in that warm, snug sleeping bag with Angel Smith in his arms.

He'd urged her to walk beside him, where he could see her, but even that was getting tough with the ice crystals pummeling them like tiny glass daggers. For five hours, they forged through the storm, making close to no headway and exhausting themselves in the process.

Even during their quick breaks, they'd exchanged no words—the hurricane-force gales carried all sound away— and not a look had passed between them, since they were goggled and suited and covered up to within an inch of their lives.

And even then, the ice got in. Through zippers and holes, anywhere clothing hadn't been tucked quite right, the storm delved inside, as sharp and surgical as a blade.

As he skied, his attention was divided almost equally

between the GPS unit, his compass, and the vague red shape of her. He'd developed a rhythm: five paces, a glance down, another five, a look back. He turned to look over his shoulder and found that her figure was smaller than before, so he slowed. When she didn't immediately catch up, he stopped.

"You okay?" he yelled. A wasted effort. Instead, he tried for a thumbs-up. No response.

Shit.

He stepped out of his skis and tromped over just as she slumped over her poles. When he put a hand on her arm, she shook her head slowly, every line of her body sagging in defeat. Her black mask was coated in ice crystals, as his own must surely be.

She spoke and the tail end of whatever she said reached him—a long, low *O*, which could've been a *No* or a wordless moan. He tightened his hold and leaned in. This time, the wind circled them, leaving the space between them as eerily calm as the eye of a hurricane, and he heard it. *Go,* she said. *Gooooo.*

It lit a fuse under him, as combustible as whatever those assholes had used to blow up the power plant. And just like that, he wasn't mad at the storm anymore, or at the men who'd put them in this position. He was mad at her. Enraged that she'd give up this easily after fighting so hard to survive the attack. How could she let him down like this when all they had was each other?

"No!" The one word punched a hole in the wind. She jumped as if startled. "Sit." He pointed at her sled, not waiting to see if she obeyed before turning to unpack the necessities from his.

At some point, a few minutes in, she joined him in his fight to keep the tent from being snatched by the wind's greedy hands. When, finally, he'd staked it out as best he could, he sent her inside with the pads and sleeping bags and whatever else she could carry. If the gale picked up at all, her weight could be the only thing standing between them and homelessness.

Nearly blind, he hacked at the ice beside the tent, building as much of a wall as he could.

He was bent double by the time his muscles gave out. Everything hurt, but it would hurt a lot worse if he didn't get inside. Warmth. Hydration. Angel.

He dropped a dozen pieces of ice by the entrance to the tent and forced his way in. By the time he'd zipped both layers up behind him, the storm had poured another pile of the stuff onto the tent's floor.

His heart tried to shove its way through his throat when he finally focused on Angel. She was in the sleeping bag, hunched over the stove, staring at him, her big, bottomless eyes hopeless.

"Can't," she said through clattering teeth. "Can't light it."

Wordlessly, he grabbed the fuel canister and eyed the stove, primed it, and lit it carefully.

She looked like a zombie. He imagined he did, too. Running a palm over his jaw produced a fistful of tiny icicles. They sat in his still-gloved hand like a pile of white marbles. For one furious instant, he wanted to fling them outside, to fight back, somehow, against the absolute hopelessness.

"You okay?"

She nodded from her nest where she sat huddled smaller than he'd ever seen her.

He slid into the bag and held her tight until the shivering subsided. His or hers, he couldn't tell.

"That storm wanted a piece of us."

He nodded. "Yeah, we should have stopped before." He didn't have to say what he was thinking—that they couldn't afford this delay.

Maybe food would help. Not just for sustenance, but because it meant something to her. It fed her soul. He might not know her well, but he'd gathered that much about this woman.

As he set to work doing all the things that would ensure their survival, he thought of how the GPS unit had flickered earlier. At the time, it had told him they'd gone seven miles. He couldn't imagine they'd made much more progress once it had gone full whiteout.

Seven goddamn miles when they had over two hundred to cover. Somewhere around two hundred forty now, probably. At this rate, it would take over a month to get there. Longer if the storm didn't let up. Their food wouldn't last that long.

And then there was the distinct possibility that their pursuers would come after them once the weather cleared. Maybe not by plane, now that the chill had arrived in earnest. Nobody flew here once it hit fifty below.

And they were definitely getting there.

Which made him want to laugh in a *screwed if you do, screwed if you don't* kind of way.

"Here." She jolted him from his thoughts. "I'll do it."

He opened his mouth to protest, then shut it. Working helped the time pass. It kept a person from going crazy out here.

She looked better as she took over. Tired and drawn, but more herself. After a few seconds, he turned to his own issues—the socks he needed to get out of, the blisters and chafing to patch up, the fingers and toes to check for telltale numb spots and loose skin.

Everything around them shook—the canvas, the zippers, the clothes they'd hung to dry. It all rattled as if the earth itself were shuddering beneath them. But in his sleeping bag, with an extra bag wrapped around him and the stove on, he felt human again, if not toasty. As he watched Angel cook, the color seeping back into her face, something strangely content, almost domestic, overtook him.

His eyes shot to hers. She couldn't possibly know what he was thinking.

But so what if she did? She was cooking; he'd set up the shelter. If it resembled—in even a passing way—a cozy living situation, then he'd take it.

He sat forward and sniffed, wishing he could get a whiff of what she was making, but the day's travels had burned that sense right out of him.

Apparently his taste buds didn't care if it smelled good or not, because just the sight of brown, rehydrated chicken à la king, or whatever stewy mess sent steam rising from the bowl, had saliva shooting into his mouth. It felt good, this hunger. His body had earned this meal.

She handed him his food and he dug in like a starving man. They ate, cleaned up, and prepared for bed in silence, exhaustion making extraneous effort impossible.

With the raging storm, they couldn't hear each other speak. Their language was barely suppressed groans—of pain, exhaustion, pleasure.

It wasn't until she went outside to take care of her needs that he looked at the sleeping bags, separate now, and had a moment of awkward indecision.

They'd be warmer together. But last night had been... confusing. He wanted to curl himself around her again, craved the feel of her body, soft and appealing, even through layers of clothing. And that desire freaked him out.

She came back in and fussed around without meeting his eyes. Embarrassed, maybe, at having to perform bodily functions in such close quarters. He headed out for the same purpose—into the hard, stinging, soul-snatching vortex.

Coop hadn't experienced darkness like this since last winter, before the sun had risen for short-lived austral summer. Before *she'd* arrived.

Now, he barely felt the ice and wind and snow as he stared at the half-buried orange structure glowing like an oasis in the desert.

And suddenly, he understood why he couldn't have her back then or now. Or ever.

He was a starving man and she was an oasis, a hallucination, a single sparkling drop of water in his desiccated world. And the problem with giving in, drinking that water, getting just one little taste, was that he'd know exactly what he'd been missing. And he'd never ever be able to go back.

CHAPTER 21

Day 2—Harper Research and Testing Facility, East Antarctic Ice Sheet

"GODDAMMIT!" SAMPSON'S FIST LEFT A DENT IN THE WALL.

Clive forced himself to stay rooted to the spot and watched with a wary eye. There seemed to be an awful lot of rage simmering beneath Sampson's smiling surface.

In this case, his frustration arose from their inability to track Cooper and the woman. A storm raged outside—Condition 2, according to the reports coming out of McMurdo—which meant they were stuck.

He couldn't say that he was glad, exactly, since his objective was to get his hands on that virus, but he didn't mind seeing this asshole foiled. Again. He pressed his lips together to hide a smirk.

"Bastard can't possibly survive in this shit," Sampson spat out and moved to the map on the wall. "But without wings, we're just as screwed. We need eyes in the sky or this hunt's gonna be a crapshoot. Over before it starts."

Sampson traced a circle around the South Pole and stared at the dots and ridges and wide-open spaces that made up the highest, driest, coldest wilderness on earth.

"We've got a man and a woman on their own out there. Wind chill as low as seventy-five below. Can't see. Can't move." He tilted his head, staring at that single dot marring the middle of the continent. "Why'd they leave Pole?"

"Surely, they guessed we'd return for the samples."

"And the bastard took 'em with him." Sampson shook his head, looking…excited almost. "Fucker's smarter than he looks."

"Or paranoid."

It took an effort not to step back when Sampson focused his sharp blue eyes on Clive. "Ain't paranoid if a threat's real."

Clive narrowed his eyes and considered the map. The most commonly used route for long expeditions headed through the Transantarctic Mountains to McMurdo, the large U.S. base on the coast. But that had to be close to a thousand-mile trek. People did it in the summer, but in this season? Impossible. What else could they do?

Was there some place they could hunker down through the winter? Had they left the station and hidden nearby, only to return once the coast was clear? The South African station was the obvious choice.

Or… His eyes widened as they landed on a small dot that lay a good distance across the ice from Burke-Ruhe. Wouldn't that be funny?

There was always door number three. Clive glanced at Sampson to see if he'd come to the same conclusion.

When their eyes met, he felt, for the first time, a sense of camaraderie with this monster. Which maybe wasn't such a bad thing, since they'd be stuck at this facility for months, wintering together along with the staff and researchers, not to mention the trial subjects.

"We should probably just wait for now, given the weather," Clive suggested lightly, to which Sampson replied with a smirk and a wink. He was in a much better mood apparently.

Good. It was best to keep the caged animals from getting too agitated.

Clive smiled back.

In fact, things were absolutely looking up again, weren't they? While Sampson stomped off to do whatever it was meathead brutes did in their downtime, Clive made his way to the lounge, hoping he'd find a book or two in English to read.

Day 2—239 Miles to Volkov Station—19 Days of Food Remaining

Coop reentered the tent to find that Angel had made the decision for him: the bags were zipped together.

"Is this okay?" Angel had to yell above the wind's boisterous din. His chest did an odd clenching thing.

"Good. Good idea." He nodded as he pulled his boots off, wincing when they rubbed against the raw places on his feet. He needed to take a look at them. "We'll share, uh, body heat."

"Share *what?*" she yelled through the unbelievable din of wind-shaken nylon.

"Heat!" he replied.

When she shrugged, he gave up. He couldn't yell and she couldn't hear. He wiped the frost from his face and body, removed his outer layer, and then slowly dropped to the ground, where he slid into the sleeping bag.

She turned her back to him and wiggled close, as they'd done last night. As if this were a thing they did.

He hesitated for three long breaths before succumbing to the siren's song of warmth and comfort and that other thing. The thing he'd never had growing up. The thing he'd never needed or, frankly, wanted until he and this woman had been forced to team up against the world.

Connection.

Despite himself, he sighed at the close, warm smell of her neck and the perfect, easy fit of their bodies.

Her answering sigh didn't surprise him. It seemed natural, as did the press of her rear to his groin, the tightening of his arms and the loosening of something vital in his chest.

As he lay there, a concept seeped into his head. An idea that he'd never had occasion to examine, much less yearn for. Something he'd have sworn he didn't care about or have time for or, in fact, believe in at all. How could he believe in something he'd never been able to fathom until this very moment?

Home. It floated through his mind and lodged itself somewhere deep inside, awkward but not uncomfortable. *Home,* he thought, as he let sleep take over.

CHAPTER 22

Day 3—239 Miles to Volkov Station—19 Days of Food Remaining

"ANGEL. UP."

A freight train ground overhead, smashing the world to smithereens.

The darkness split open, revealing orange-tinted shapes. Socks on the ceiling, swaying above her. Beside her, a man, bent, yelling something that she couldn't hear. She shut her eyes and pressed her fists hard to her ears so her eardrums wouldn't explode from the pressure.

And the cold.

Angel!

Her eyes snapped open again to see Ford's mouth move, but any sounds he made were just notes in the cacophony, whipped away like tiny bits of paper.

"Up. Come on."

Angel turned over with a groan, keeping her ear covered to block out Ford and the wind and the incessant rattle of straps against tent poles. "This is the worst alarm tone in the world."

He drew close and put a hand to her shoulder. "Here. Take this," he said, his voice like a chainsaw scraped slowly over metal. What had happened, she wondered—not for the first time—to damage his vocal cords like that?

"Don't..." *want it*, she meant to finish, but she couldn't quite get her mouth to function. She tried to roll again and knocked her knee to the ground, which sparked off a series of lancing, interconnected pains. "*Ooooohhh.*"

"Sit up." Only the consonants were audible through the screech of the wind.

"It's so dark." How long would they be battered by the surreal presence outside? She pictured it like a storm at sea, waves crashing over their tiny vessel. Alone. So alone. "Is it even day?"

"Yes."

She didn't know why that made her feel better. "Did we sleep?"

"Some." He tightened his hold on her shoulder, all gruff business. "Sit."

No break, of course. Days off were for regular expeditions across the far reaches of hell. Not for this running-for-your-life malarkey.

Okay. She could do this. With a grimace, she put her weight on her fists, feeling every bone as if it were bruised, and pushed up.

Once she'd worked her way to sitting, he shoved the tea in her hands and plunked her coat over her shoulders. "Where's it hurt?"

"Where doesn't it?" Every bit of her hurt. Although mostly her knee. She opened one eye and looked him over. "'S it cold out?" The question was ridiculous, obviously, but out here, the difference between -15 and -40 was substantial.

His answer—"Not too bad"—made her smile.

"Why're you so chipper?"

"Chipper?" Brows up, the edges of his mouth pointing down, he gave her a disbelieving look. Insulted, almost. Okay, so maybe chipper wasn't the right word, but she couldn't exactly ask him why he didn't look his usual level of angry. God forbid the man show a glimmer of joy.

"I feel like refried turds and you look..." *Less pissed off.* She took a sip of lukewarm tea, swallowed, and almost moaned at how good it felt going down. "Well rested."

His cheekbones went a little red before he shut it down, back to the Ice Man: cold and remote and not at all amused. He hadn't been any of those things when he'd held her in the night. He'd been her warm sanctuary, her corner of heaven. Funny how safe she'd felt with the world falling apart around them.

Don't get used to it, dummy. In three weeks, we get to safety and then...

A blank. Nothing. No concept of what awaited them there. A dangerous emergency evacuation? A winter on the ice, in some foreign enclave? Would she have a room, a bed? Would they be forced to share? Would he refuse?

She looked away, annoyed with the path her thoughts had taken. As if what was happening here were anything but practical companionship. "What time is it?"

"About five." He threw a look up, as if he could see the sky through fabric. "Storm's died down."

A strong wind buffeted the tent, showing them exactly who was boss.

"Well, some. Nobody's flying in this, but we gotta move." His head gave a fatalistic little tilt. "Temps seem to have risen, so I doubt we'll freeze to death."

"That's heartening." She'd put a hand down, ready to match her actions to his words, when he stopped her.

"Drink. Eat." He handed her a morning ration. "And tell me where it hurts."

It was an order and, since he was the man in charge of

her survival, she sipped, bit, and chewed, enjoying the give of frozen butter as solid as cheddar against her teeth, and twice as satisfying. Next, she crunched into the precooked bacon they'd brought along.

She closed her eyes and took stock.

Food: good. Drink: satisfying. Body:....

"Knee hurts. But that's pretty much par for the course. Back, too. Can't say that's a surprise." She managed a smile. "Man, this is the world's worst workout program. The Drag Your Own Butter." She tensed and rolled her head to one side, then the other, letting out a long, relieved sigh.

"What else?"

"Dude. Give me a sec." She slitted her eyes and grimaced his way. "Besides, I can handle it." She flexed her right leg. It didn't feel great, but it wasn't anything she couldn't push through. It was how she'd gotten through a million late shifts—ignoring burns and sprains and aches—and she'd do it again. "I'll be fine." She slurped down the rest of the tea and shifted, ready to emerge from the bag when he stopped her with a heavy hand on her thigh.

"You wanna survive this?" It was immediately obvious that the question wasn't rhetorical.

She blinked, gaze meeting his, working hard to ignore the magnetism of those strange, crushed-crystal eyes, of freckles and sunspots, of a strong nose, burned red from the wind, and that square, no-nonsense, scruff-covered jaw. He was so handsome it hurt. Especially with that raw annoyance focused right at her.

"You know I do."

"Then tell me what hurts." His face, his voice, even the way his body bent toward her were deadly serious.

"Aside from my pride?" Her smile went unanswered, sending her right back to the galley her first week at Burke-Ruhe, when he'd walked in and scowled. And he hadn't stopped since. What was it about this guy that made her feel like a bad twelve-year-old? He didn't respond now, of course, so she closed her eyes again and concentrated. "My knee, but like I said…" She hated talking about it. Hated it almost as much as she hated thinking about the events leading to and from it. "That's normal."

Boom! The walls rippled with the force of another angry gale.

"Why?"

"Old injury." She forced a smile, hoping he'd let it go. "My feet, however, feel like they've been steamrollered."

"Can't be that old," he yelled close to her ear.

"What?" She watched him, frowning.

"Your injury."

"What do you mean?"

"You're only what, in your twenties, so—"

"I'm thirty-one. How old are you?" The entire conversation had an odd edge confined in such close quarters yet yelling to be heard through the hard-pellet sound of ice to nylon.

"Thirty-eight." He tapped her foot through the bag. "Muscular or skin?"

"Huh?" It took her a second to realize he'd gone back to her injury. "Oh. Little of both."

He nodded and turned to rifle through the first aid kit. "Your nose okay? Fingers? Toes?"

"Um…" *My butt's bruised—not to mention my ego—from all the times I bit it out there.* "Legs are sore, but I can handle that. Just muscular." She leaned forward and indicated the place at her waist where her harness had rubbed her raw. "Chafed here."

"Okay. Let's see 'em."

She stilled. "See what?"

"Your feet, for starters."

Her head had barely begun to shake from side to side when he stopped her with a flat look. "Fine. Here." She shouldn't have been disappointed when he handed her a pack of ointment and bandages. Especially not after protesting his attentions. But she couldn't help it.

"Check 'em, rub 'em, and wrap 'em. You don't want an infection in this cold." His eyes slanted to hers, a translucent, unimpressed blue. "Did mine already. Can't afford a delay."

"Right." Feeling chastised, she grabbed the package and ducked her head into the big sleeping bag. It wasn't easy to peel off her socks and fix up her raw feet in the tight space, but she managed. And thank God, because the damage was worse than she'd realized. Not quite blistered, but close. Just applying moleskin and bandages hurt. She couldn't imagine how walking would be.

With her feet bandaged, she grabbed her belongings and followed Ford out onto the ice.

Outside, the clouds had lifted, but the wind tore at them, worse than yesterday. It tried to yank the tent from her hands, worked her hair out from under her hat, made packing up the sleds into a contact sport. As unpredictable as a sea of currents, it whirled one way, then another, in an ever-changing waltz that made her head spin.

They awkwardly strapped up and buckled into their skis, and Ford took off, as impervious to the gale's harassment as he was to everything. He'd run until his battery ran out. No hesitation or intimidation for the Ice Man. No worrying if he'd make it.

She wished—

To hell with that. She hadn't come this far to stand around *wishing* for things.

"You wanna play?" she whispered into the next taunting blast, too annoyed to feel silly or embarrassed.

This was about survival. About putting one foot in front of the other, sucking air into heaving lungs, stealing what little oxygen the atmosphere gave up, and spitting it back out again. The sound of her own breathing in the relative quiet of the ski mask reminded her of her own inexorability. Her own strength, dammit.

Nose running, eyes streaming, lungs working harder than they ever had, she leaned into the wind, forging her own path, the way Ford did, with every step. "Let's play."

Bent almost double, half-blind, single-minded, and hardly blinking for fear of losing him, she followed her companion's tall red form straight into the coldest depths of hell.

CHAPTER 23

COOP SPENT ANOTHER DAY LEADING THEM THROUGH hell, trudging on while the wind stripped them of humidity and humanity, serenading them with its harsh, atonal requiem. *Their* requiem, if they weren't careful.

He was a realist. This continent had killed and it would kill again. It was the idea of who would be killed here that did him in. He could handle the idea of his own mortality. It was Angel Smith's that perturbed him. She was too vital and full of life to die.

Or at least she had been before this fiasco started.

Now he surreptitiously eyed her as she ate. Her movements were heavy, exhausted, despondent. How could they not be when skiing ten miles out there required the energy of twice the distance? Three times? They weren't skiing so much as pushing against a constantly compressing wall. Stuck in a trash compacter, like in one of the *Star Wars* movies.

One of the old ones, from a time when he actually watched films.

His eyes slid to the side again. What kind of movies did she like? Thrillers? No. He couldn't see that. But he could picture her getting into those family food movies where you came out craving hugs and homemade Italian pasta.

"What do you watch?"

She blinked, owlish and blank. "Hm?"

"You like movies?"

"Oh." She stared at him, features blurred by the delicate

swirl of steam rising from rehydrated food. "Don't watch much."

His lips went down at the corner. "Huh." Wrong again.

After a few more seconds and another bite or two, she set her bowl in her lap. "What do you mean, *huh*?"

"Don't watch much either." He half shrugged. "Lost interest at some point."

Her nod was slow and thoughtful. "People tend to watch stuff at night, you know? I've always worked at night. And here…" She pointed her spoon vaguely to the side. "I was in that kitchen sixty, seventy-five hours a week. Not much downtime."

"Yeah." He had a sudden flash of what it would be like to take Angel to the movies. They would crowd each other, since even as a teenager, he'd been too big for those seats, knocking knees into the seat in front, rubbing elbows with the person beside him. For three out-of-body seconds, he smelled the popcorn, felt his salty, buttery fingers grazing hers in the oversized bucket, heard her low, happy laugh at whatever was happening on the screen.

He, Ford Cooper, the man who ran from crowds and closeness, who couldn't stand loud noises or excessive stimulation, could see himself there—with her.

Was he experiencing Winter-Over Syndrome? It could turn a person erratic, forgetful, slow. And he'd seen it first-hand. Shit, they'd even had psychiatrists spend winters at Pole to study its effects. Was this what Winter-Over Syndrome looked like for Coop? Wishing for things so outside his wheelhouse that they couldn't possibly be real?

"What's your favorite movie?"

He'd been so lost in his fantasies he jolted at her words.

"Will you think I'm crazy if I say *The Thing*?"

Her hiccupped laugh rang out like wind chimes in a hurricane, and shit, he wanted to bottle that sound. "Yes." She sparkled, her smile wider than he'd seen it in days, her face relaxed. It flipped a switch in him, made him crave smiles and sighs the way an addict craves opiates.

"What about you?"

"Me?" She snorted, leaning forward as if sharing a secret. "My problem is that I've never been able to pick just one of anything. I love it all. Food, movies, music. I mean, my favorite black-and-white movie? That's *The Maltese Falcon*, hands down. Actually, no, because I've always been a sucker for Cary Grant. But then you add Christmas movies to the mix and..." She shrugged, as if giving in to her own excess. "See? Depends on the day, my mood. Where I am..."

Her words faded away as she stared off at nothing. Exhausted, like him. Battered by this place.

But not beaten.

They finished dinner, cleaned up, and went about getting ready for bed.

"Better take care of those feet," he said.

A low sound of protest emerged from inside the sleeping bag, where Angel had already taken up residence. "Can it wait till the morning?"

"Frostbite's not something to mess with. Let's see them." He didn't intend to sound quite so bossy.

"I'll do it." Her words were slurred.

"You can barely move." He held on to the kit, obstinate—and something else. Responsible, maybe. "I saw you limping out there. Your knee's bugging you. Don't deny it."

She threw him a glare, but surprised him by complying.

He took hold of one slender foot and stripped it gently but quickly, since even in shelter, the risk of frostbite was real. It was light in his palm and mostly warm enough to alleviate his worry, though her toes were chilly. He touched each one. "Any numbness?"

She shook her head.

With great care, he peeled the bandages off, cleaned her skin, and reapplied fresh ones where needed, slipping the sock back on before starting the whole process with the other foot.

He couldn't say exactly when it occurred to him that he held her naked foot in his hand, but once the realization popped into his head, it wouldn't go away. Hung around like an itch he couldn't get to.

A foot, for God's sake. Ridiculous.

But the foot didn't feel ridiculous right now. He gently squeezed it and expelled a harsh breath.

It felt…improper. Especially in comparison with the rest of her fully clothed body. And secret, somehow. He knew things about her now. He knew her second toe was longer than the big one, that her arches were high and elegant, her skin already roughened from two days of marching in the freezing desert air. He knew she'd put on a bright red nail polish at some point. It'd worn mostly off, but it made her toes look like candy. And he'd never craved sugar so badly.

The best course of action, now that she was all bandaged up, was to give her back her foot.

But he couldn't.

Instead, he ran his thumb along the central curve, pressed forward beneath her toes, then down to her heel. The sounds she made were—he swallowed—*obscene*. A shocked gasp that urged him to look her way. He didn't, though, because if their eyes met, he might have to stop.

And that was the last thing he wanted to do.

Another rub, deeper this time, bearing down on aching muscles. But it didn't sound like pain when she moaned, low and guttural, and though he knew better, he let his eyes slide up her body to her face.

He froze. He'd never seen anything hotter—not on-screen or in the throes of sex or in his darkest fantasy.

Mouth open, eyes closed, cheeks flushed, everything about her screamed pleasure. Just to be sure, he stroked back and pressed again, wanting—no, *needing*—to know which notes *this* spot would play on her ever-changing face.

And she didn't disappoint. Every feature cringed, slowly, sensually, in a magnified expression of pleasure-pain. Sweeping up to caress her toes now was sheer torture, because he was hard—shocking in this cold—and her reactions, though subtle, were more intimately real than any peepshow.

He could've gone on forever, rubbing, rapt, eyes glued to her face as she showed him just how good he made her feel, picturing how amazing she'd look if he were kissing her, or—

Her eyes popped open, ensnaring his in their velvet trap.

Everything went quiet, stilling as if the storm had taken a breath. Or maybe it was him going a little deaf, like when his ears needed popping in a plane. Except he could hear the things happening in this tent. Could feel and smell with overwhelming precision every fine detail blown up under a microscope.

They shared a couple hard inhale-exhales, the tension between them as palpable as the frigid temperature.

The press of his fingers lessened, his caresses slowed, until he did nothing but grasp her foot while she just as steadily held his gaze.

"That feels amazing," she said in a bedroom whisper that he could feel deep in his bones, though it couldn't possibly be loud enough to hear.

Her mouth closed and his attention flicked down, watching her swallow with something awfully close to hunger before sliding back up to find her eyes boring into him.

And, just like that, the bubble popped.

Everything came rushing in—the unbearable noise, the killing chill, the too-intense, sizzling stimulus of this connection.

As if stung, he released her foot and backed up until he couldn't move any farther. There was no escape, nowhere to go.

He had to get out. Blindly, he put on whatever clothes he found, then his boots and coat. He tore open the zipper and went out, not once glancing her way.

Outside, he went to work with the shovel, as if he'd dig clean through to the Arctic. It wasn't until he almost broke a sweat that he slowed down long enough to admit what had happened.

He'd touched her, felt her skin, seen her pleasure, and it scared the living hell out of him. She'd burn him if she got too close. And he wasn't sure he'd survive it.

CHAPTER 24

She watched, completely flabbergasted, as he booted and suited up before heading out again.

After a few seconds, a sound came to her, through the two layers of tent fabric and a million coats of whiteout. She cocked her head and listened to the shovel. She looked around: water, food… They had what they needed.

What the hell?

When he didn't return after a good chunk of time, she wrapped up and went out.

"What on earth are you doing?"

He stopped, back bent, breathing so hard she could see the cloud from five feet away.

"Back inside, Angel." He didn't even straighten up when he spoke to her, just stayed there, stiffly bent, frozen as if he needed her to leave before he'd move again. "Please."

"Why are you doing that? We have water."

"Need more." *Lie.*

"I'll help, then. Then we'll both go to bed."

She cringed at the domesticity of her words, while he made a weird, hoarse strangled noise.

"I can't be in there right now."

Claustrophobia, she thought.

Or he hates me. That was the likelier of the two, considering the way things had started between them. But hadn't the last few days changed that for him the way they had for her? Weren't they a team? Did he not like her even a little?

"It's me, isn't it?" Her voice was higher than she'd have

liked. She hated how weak it sounded in front of this man with his big muscles and bigger brain.

He shook his head slowly, then surprised her by saying, "Yes."

It sent a punch to her gut. If she'd been back home or at the station or any other place, she'd have spun on her heel and taken off. But here, there was nowhere to go.

"What'd I do?" *Don't cry. Don't do it. Don't show him you care.*

"What'd you…" He finally straightened and stormed a few steps closer—close enough for her to see that every hair on his face was frost-rimed. It made him look older, and also, in a weird way, terribly mortal. Even he couldn't win against this weather. "What'd you *do*?"

"Yeah." She nodded, swallowing back the tears. "So I don't do it again."

"So you don't…" He shook his head and turned away, muttering, before looking back at her again. "You're so… *much*."

She stepped back as if he'd hit her. "What?"

"You've got to be *hard* to survive this place, Angel. And you're *not*. You're all softness." He waved a hand at her, then turned away. "It's already sucking the life out of you. What'll I do if you…" He shuddered. "If you don't survive this?"

Slowly, fueled by shock, her mouth dropped open.

With a frustrated huff, he threw down the shovel and moved closer. "You know what happens if the ice takes me, Angel? Nothing. Not a thing. I've been out here almost every day for years. I *like* it here. I belong here. I fully expect to end my days on the ice. But *you*, with your…" He waved at her. "Curves and lips. That laugh. The way you dive into people and experiences and eat up the world like you'll never get enough. When you look at me like you did in there." He pointed now, emphatically, at the tent. "Like I've just saved the damned planet. Like you want me to—" He cleared his throat, seemingly speechless.

What was he angry at exactly? Was it that he couldn't protect her? Couldn't keep her alive? But, wait, did he *like* those things he'd mentioned? Her body, her laugh? *Her?*

He was as confused about this attraction as she was. The realization hit her like a frying pan to the head. Which meant he definitely felt it.

All the times he'd ignored her at the station, put his head down and pretended not to hear, or walked in the opposite direction when he saw her coming: attraction. Unwanted, apparently, but attraction nonetheless.

"You *like* me," she finally said with a grin.

And, though she had no idea why, she could tell that he was not happy about it. At all.

This wasn't supposed to happen right now. Or ever.

He should've known with the foot thing. Should have stopped it right away. In this deadly environment, the last thing he needed was to lose it.

What went entirely against his grain was that he didn't *want* to resist her. *And*, a whiny little voice inside him asked, *if we're not going to survive this anyway, then why the hell should I fight it?*

Unbidden, a wave of tension stronger than anything he'd felt in a decade swept up, grabbed his body, his emotions, and every last bit of control and sent him the last three steps to where she stood, probably freezing in the polar night.

"You..." Dammit, his voice wouldn't survive this trip. But he'd say what he had to say. He'd say this at least, and then he could stop talking. He grabbed her head, except with his thick gloves and her hat and hood, he didn't get a drop of her heat. Which was good, probably, though he craved it the way he craved food at the end of each day on the ice. "*Listen.*"

She went very still, but even that stillness was almost sensuous against his hands, which was crazy. Absolute lunacy. It reminded him of the way she pressed to him in their bag. He shook his head to clear it. "You're gonna ski faster tomorrow. You'll go"—he coughed, cleared his throat, and went on, almost at a whisper—"*farther*. Because if we don't do more miles every day, we run out of food."

No way would he be responsible for snuffing out a light like hers. So bright he hadn't been able to look at it head-on until now.

She lifted her hand to his chest and took a slow, hesitant step, bringing their bodies too close, acting for all the world like he was a wild animal she needed to tame. Christ, his lungs hurt as she stood on tiptoe and pulled down her neck gaiter to reveal perfect pink lips, almost obscenely plump in a world that stole every last drop of moisture.

Denial, he understood as his eyes ate her up, had turned his hunger into starvation, desire into a need so strong he'd die of want before the ice could ever take him. He put a hand up to run it over her cheek, to soak up her heat and humanity, and paused an inch away. No point touching her with gloves. It wouldn't satisfy his inner beast any more than it would warm her skin. There was no choice now but to dip his head, share her shaky exhale, and press his cold lips to her hot ones.

He went mindless the second his mouth met hers. No cognitive abilities, all nerves and need, this unbearable tightness in his chest, this raging fire in his limbs. He couldn't slow down to save himself. His mouth wasn't just on her; he was devouring, prying open, taking everything he could. As wild and out of control as this storm that was trying to end them.

So much softness, but he needed more. He wrapped his arms around her, drew her flush to him, pressed and pulled and lifted, while his mouth ate her up.

Tilted heads, delving tongue, the rough scrape of his teeth, which she met with a long, low moan. But, hell, they had to stop or they'd freeze their faces off in this cold.

He couldn't, though. Not when she slid her mittened hands inside his hood, running them down his jaw and back up, like she hungered for just one tiny feel.

Finally, he managed to pull away, though he couldn't quite disengage his hands—one tight on her ass, the other cradling her head.

"Inside."

She nodded and turned gratifyingly quickly.

He paused just before ducking in. What the hell was he doing?

Didn't matter. He wanted this.

But did she? Had he pressured her somehow? Or even worse, did she think she had to, in order to receive his help? God no. No, he didn't want her that way.

Not that he could have her, he knew, in a tent in the freezing cold. More than fingers and toes could succumb to frostbite, and that wasn't something either of them should risk.

He had to check, though, before this—whatever the hell

it was—went any further. Quickly, he ducked inside, almost blinded by the warmth in her eyes. She was shivering, halfway undressed—clothes still on by necessity, but boots and coats shucked. After that kiss, seeing her in just her base layers was as intimate as looking at her naked.

"Why'd you kiss me?" He forced the words out, remembering the way she'd approached him, like she'd been taming the beast.

She stopped on all fours, just about to slide into the bag. She must be freezing without the subzero protection, but her eyes focused hard on his.

"*You* kissed *me*."

"Did you want to?" He swallowed. "Kiss?"

The look she threw him should've shriveled his dick right up, but contrarian that he was, it only made him hard.

"Yes, Ford. For some inexplicable reason, I wanted to kiss you."

"You didn't do it so—" He cleared his throat and went on. "So I'd take care of you? Out here?"

She blinked, her eyes losing a little of their haze and zeroing in sharply on him. This was where women usually backed off—when he opened his mouth. Over the years, he'd learned not to say much during sex.

He waited, hunched, hands in his pockets, for her inevitable rebuff. When her look turned more into a squint and her lips tightened, he knew she was about to put a stop to it all. Probably even separate their sleeping bags again, which he surely deserved.

"Would you shut up?" He'd started nodding already, resigned to the separation, as she slid under the covers and said, "And get your ass to bed."

It took him three seconds to comply.

Making out with Ford had *bad idea* written all over it.

Not like that had ever stopped her before. Hugh, who'd seemed so talented and fun, had been the worst idea of all. Of course, in reality, he'd been neither artsy nor exciting. He'd been a total fraud. A con man. She just hadn't realized it until he'd stolen her concept, her restaurant, her savings… her heart. Pretty much her life.

She sucked in a bracing breath. *Not* her life, actually. In fact, *life* was exactly what was at stake right now. And here she was worrying about stupid kisses.

Ford slid in beside her and all that ancient history disappeared.

She shivered. Whether from the cold or his proximity, she couldn't tell. But the space he took up—the sheer size of him—moved the dial heavily on the side of arousal. Her breathing picked up.

It was more than his size, if she was honest. His smell was freaking ambrosia. Crazy, considering how ripe they both should be. Although maybe not, in temperatures like these. And at least they'd bathed using wipes.

"Okay. I'm in bed." God, that voice did things to her insides. Scraped her raw, leaving goose bumps in its wake. "Now what?"

She huffed out a laugh. "I don't know."

"Don't have to do anything." He let out his own soundless laugh that reverberated against her chest. "It'd be challenging in here anyway. Impossible."

"What if I want to?" Her mouth barely moved, but the whisper was perfectly audible in their cocoon.

Crap, where was the smart woman? The one who

learned from past mistakes? The one with too much pride to run after a guy who kept pushing her away?

The problem was that, just as she'd given up all hope, the Ice Man had gone and surprised her. If he'd been different—bossy or entitled or at all an asshole—she'd have brushed him off, no problem. His generosity, this vulnerability, was like a spark to her tinder. The opposite of Hugh, who'd felt entitled enough to plow through her defenses.

That was something she'd unpack later.

Right now, the hand he settled on her hip was burning a hole through two base layers. With gloves on.

"How about another kiss then?" he whispered, the words nothing but puffs of air against her ear, so easy to ignore if she chose.

Yeah right.

The problem with being a hothead, as Mama had always reminded her, was that she didn't just make quick decisions—she dove into them headfirst. Those rash choices had left a trail of blood, tears, and regret a mile wide behind her.

Then again, they might not survive this, in which case…

"Okay," she said, before reason could stomp all over this need coursing through her.

Their lips had been cold outside, the kiss fast and hot.

This was different. Sliding into a warm bath after a bracing dunk in the ocean.

She pressed her mouth to his for one heated second before pulling away, already breathless. Already drunk.

Their foreheads met with a light *thunk*. A few breaths passed between them, like acclimation, though not to the cold or the elevation, but to this new level of intimacy.

When he finally moved, it was a gentle dip, his nose

to hers in an achingly slow exploration that shouldn't have been provocative. She strained for his mouth, but he denied her.

Like a big cat toying with its prey, he stroked his cheek along hers, scruff to soft skin. Just that move made her choke back a moan. How would it be if they could take their clothes off? If skin touched all over?

Deliberately, gently, he ran his nose beneath her ear and a sound escaped him. A tiny, tight-lipped hiss that she'd never have caught if he weren't so near.

"Ford." With her arm wrapped around him, she did her best to urge him toward her. But he denied her. The man was so freaking stubborn.

"Shhhhhh."

In frustration, she tilted her head for a kiss, getting nothing but his tight, rough jaw. He must have liked it, though, because it pushed him to lean lower and bite her, through her shirt, at the junction of neck and shoulder.

And then, oh God, then he kept her pinned with his mouth, stilling her, while he finally stroked his hand, lazy as a lion basking in the sun, from her head to her neck, then down her side, bypassing the obvious draw of her breasts, to clamp her hip, holding it still when she hadn't even realized she was fidgeting.

Owning her.

Slowly, as if he had all the time in the world, he shifted above her until she could feel every hard bit of him, put his mouth to hers, and took the kiss from her. She couldn't find another word for the way his lips explored hers, the way he slanted them and softly—but so freaking perfectly—showed her what he liked. Slow, firm, knowing.

A moan escaped her and he responded with a grunt of

his own as he pressed deeper, kept her there with his melted
Ice Man magic.

When finally he used his tongue, it was like they'd never
done it before, like outside hadn't happened. A first taste of
a rare ingredient that would change her palate forever.

A tear escaped her eye.

Had a kiss ever been so...everything?

The soft touch of his tongue was as intimate as a hand
between her legs. Good God, if he continued with this long,
slow possession, she'd be done for. No touch needed.

On the ice, in the antarctic cold, in the middle of freaking nowhere, his tongue showed her how dirty sex could be,
his body made her take it, and that dark, raspy husk of a
voice broke in to turn the whole thing up a million degrees.
"I didn't want to do this, Angel. Didn't want to open this
up."

Why not? she wanted to ask. And why'd he still sound so
unhappy about it?

A wash of cold swept through her, immediately doused
by his next words.

"Avoided you for months so I wouldn't make a fool of
myself." Another kiss, this one just lips, punctuating the
secrets he unveiled to her. "Guess I'm making a fool of
myself."

"You're not alone."

"No." He smiled against her lips. Every breath he took
pressed into her body, uncomfortable in theory, but in
reality perfect. Close, warm, comforting. "But we are." He
sighed, pulling slightly away. "*Alone.*" Another kiss, sweet
and almost chaste. "And we need sleep."

She nodded, which prompted another of those long,
slow inhales against her cheek.

"But, damn, if I didn't have enough reason to get us to a warm bed before, this..." He kissed her again, but the damage was done.

"Right." She gave another nod. Survival before making out. It made complete sense.

His body shifted to the side and she tightened her arms convulsively. *Don't go!*

He must have read her thoughts, because he scooted and rolled until she lay on top, a blanket for him, while his big, hard slab of a body soaked up the cold from the ground. Her heating pad: warm, firm, perfect. She curled her head into his chest, closed her eyes, and did her best to pretend like this wasn't some last-ditch battle to feel something before dying.

CHAPTER 25

Day 4—Harper Research and Testing Facility, East Antarctic Ice Sheet

"As I said, Director, the storm's kept us from—"

Clive took another sip of disgusting, cold Russian coffee and watched as Sampson reported their progress—or lack thereof—to the director.

Hunting scientists and cooks wasn't turning out to be quite as easy as the idiot had first assumed. Which, Clive had to admit, was pretty fun to watch, even if it did make it impossible for him to do his job.

Would vodka make the coffee better or worse?

"No, ma'am. Flying's no longer a possibility with the—" Clive pressed his lips together to hide his smile while Sampson listened, no doubt receiving the type of talking-to he deserved. "The Herc left the continent and the Twin Otter's grounded. Too windy and cold to fl— Yes, we… Yes, ma'am, either Volkov or the South African station. But there are five different ways they could've gone, at least. And given the—" Clive tilted his head, and though he couldn't hear the director—she was much too cultured to actually yell—he could imagine her directives: *No more excuses, Sampson. Get me the virus. Get the results I need. It's a big continent. You can't sit around and expect them to just stumble upon you. Go find them now, before they ruin everything.*

Fucking ridiculous. He supposed that was what

happened when you grew up spoiled and rich. You sat back and watched your minions scurry.

She didn't give a shit how cold or inhospitable this place was. Frankly, she had zero understanding of the roadblocks Antarctica threw at its inhabitants.

Sampson's team coming here to collect the virus was one thing, but having Clive perform his vaccine research on this remote continent was absurd.

The director was punishing him, he was certain, though she'd couched it in other terms—a private facility, unlimited access to test subjects, absolute control over the environment, and so on. And, yes, this facility provided all of that and more.

But it was stuck in fucking Antarctica. Not Mexico or Bolivia or some private island where he'd have had all the time and space he needed to work on the Frond virus vaccine. No, the old bitch had sent him to the coldest, most inhospitable place on earth to conduct his trials.

And now, due to this jackass's absolute ineptitude, Clive didn't have an actual virus to work with. Over a dozen subjects languished in their perfectly air-tight cells, waiting. For nothing.

Not for the first time, he wondered what that man had done with the original virus. The one with which the director's father had created the live virus vaccine. How in the hell did one of the biggest pharmaceutical companies on earth let someone just walk away with such an important asset?

"I understand, ma'am. Yes, they're on foot, but we've got no idea which route they've taken or… We head out there, we're going blind… It's a deadly—"

Half-annoyed, half-entertained, Clive sloshed a shot of vodka into his cup. Until he could get started on his work, he was officially off the clock. And, frankly, everything tasted like shit here, so who cared? As long as it did the trick and made him stop dwelling on how he'd been screwed over and over again, he'd drink it.

He sighed just as Sampson ended the call, looking pissed.

"She didn't need to speak to me, I gather?" Clive asked, nonchalant now that things were out of his hands.

Sampson ignored him and turned instead to his men. "Head out at zero six hundred hours, storm or not. Tonight, we prep."

Without another word, the men stalked out of the communication center, leaving Clive to slug back the rest of his coffee with a fatalistic sigh.

Day 4—230 Miles to Volkov Station—18 Days of Food Remaining

A couple hours into the next day, Angel began to hate the ice. Not the way she had before, like an object or an idea, but like a person.

She cursed it with every slide forward, every painful drag on the sled.

And the bitch spoke to her in return.

It crackled beneath her skis, the pops and hisses as vicious and alive as a creature from the underworld. So big its back curved off in the distance. So vast she'd never meet it head-on.

Swoosh, slide, crack. The wind, still working against them, whistled hard and loud. Even covered as she was, it ate at her skin, tore at her flesh, chapped her lips, and sucked the blood from her veins.

Behind her fogged-up goggles, she could barely see Ford, which left her alone with her thoughts.

And, honestly, her thoughts were a mess. Along with pain and hunger was the thrill of last night.

The more time passed, the more she doubted her own sanity. Had she hallucinated the whole thing? It had sure felt like it this morning, when she'd unstuck her eyes to find him stoic and cold again. As if nothing had happened between them.

How could he be so normal when everything was in such turmoil, inside and out? It had been business as usual for His Royal Stiffness.

She was mad about it, actually. So riled that her pace picked up, every sliding step drawing her closer to that wide, straight back. In fact, when she caught up with him, she'd let him know it wasn't okay. Between the stupid ice and the stupid wind and the stupid man who wouldn't even throw her a morning-after smile, she wanted to—

Her ski caught on something, wrenching her leg to the side and slamming her body painfully to the ice, so hard it forced the air out of her lungs.

Wheezing, she rolled onto her back, stared dumbly at the sky, and waited for her eyes to focus. Her arm throbbed from breaking her fall and her head smarted. How about her knee? Slowly, she shifted to the side, taking stock as she attempted to put weight on it. Oh hell.

Maybe she could stay here for a second or two. Just a few minutes to catch her breath and rest.

The wind, bastard that it was, said her name, trying to get her to come up and play, toying with her like some evil force from the deep.

"Leave us alone!" she managed to get out.

When something grasped her arm, she pulled away, then froze for a few confused seconds.

Ford, not the wind.

Oh. Okay. So, this is it. I've officially crossed into delirium.

Maybe it was time for a snack or something.

"Here," he said as he reached for her again. "Let me ge—"

She put out a hand to stop him.

No. She was done with the weakness and the falling and accepting help from this man. Done craving things she had to pull out of him by force.

She hadn't fought her way to the top of the restaurant food chain to let this place turn her to mush.

It was do this or die trying. Which was almost funny, because if there was one place she could actually die trying, it was here.

"I need some space, Ford."

After a moment's hesitation, he stepped back.

She undid her skis and rose, stacking sore bones over swollen joints with the help of petrified muscles.

"Okay?" he asked.

Good question. It all hurt, but pain was the new normal. She did a quick check, opened and closed her hands, rolled her head, tensed her shoulders, stretched her leg, and ran through a few exercises to see how the bum knee was doing. Aside from stiffness in the knee, she was fine. All systems functioning. "Amazing."

Under his ski mask, his eyes crinkled. "Here." He shoved an open bottle into her hands and it was almost warm. He must have kept it against his skin, under his coat. Or close to it.

"Are you laughing at me, Ford Cooper?"

"Hell no." He leaned so close the wind had to work hard to keep them apart. "But I am smiling."

The miracle was that, despite everything, when they took off again, she was smiling, too.

CHAPTER 26

DESPITE A FEW HICCUPS, THEY MANAGED A WHOPPING eleven miles, with occasional stops to shove calories into their mouths.

Every time Coop looked back at Angel, slowly but steadily plowing across the ice, his respect for her rose. He'd seen the woman's feet, for God's sake, rubbed raw. They were more blister than skin at this point. He had enough blisters of his own to know what she was up against. And, though she hid it well, her limp had gotten worse in the past day or so.

By the time they stopped and pitched the tent, they were both bent double from the effort of battling the constant headwind.

He glanced at the shelter, where Angel'd already heated water, made dinner, and had started on physical therapy exercises for her knee.

Or she could be in the sleeping bag, waiting for him. He dug faster.

A long shiver that had little to do with the cold worked its way down his body, trying its best to get him hard.

Not gonna happen out here.

In there, however, the rules had changed. The life-or-death situation had flipped a switch in him, moved the paddle in a pinball game, opening a new path. In the tight confines of their bed, his debilitating need to control himself had been blown apart.

Damn, it was liberating.

He was drunk on it.

Now, in the bright light of day, he could see that he'd let his excitement get the better of him. Dangerous. Losing sight of his rationality in forty or fifty below could kill them both. But if the kissing motivated her, somehow, to ski eleven miles instead of seven, then…

And here he was, making excuses for wanting her, like a horny teenager.

With the protective ice wall as high as it would get, he trudged the few steps to their home—a tiny, low bright-orange cone in the middle of this vast white expanse—crawled into the vestibule, then hesitated for a few seconds before unzipping the tent itself. He was dying to rush inside and show her where his mind had been all day. And that scared the crap out of him. He could almost stand not to eat if it meant they'd curl up in that bag together and see how good they could make each other feel.

All of this screamed *bad idea!* Or at least half screamed. The other half said *why the hell not?* What could possibly be wrong with finding physical comfort with a consenting adult out here on the ice? They weren't hurting anyone by being together, were they? Unless… Crap. He hadn't considered the possibility of her having someone back home. Had she ever mentioned a husband or boyfriend? Seemed unlikely, considering her long stay here, but people did crazier things.

In front of him, the tent opened and he blinked, wondering just how much time he'd spent between the flaps. His eyes scanned her sunburned face—*bad idea*—the taut line of her shoulders—*bad idea*—the plump little Cupid's bow mouth, turned slightly up at the corners despite the long day's slog—*bad idea*. She was smiling like she was happy to see him.

That gripped him in a place no woman had ever touched.

"You get stuck?" She gave him a full-on grin, loosening the tension in his chest and tightening other parts farther down. *Bad idea? Nah!* "Here. Hand me that ice and get in here before we freeze our tits off."

And just like that, the teenage boy was back in charge, picturing what she'd look like naked. She grabbed the container and set it down, and without waiting to take off his frost-stiffened layers, he had her in his arms, his mouth on hers, wishing he could press her up against a wall and strip her right here. Wishing what they were doing was real and not just a dream wrought of ice and danger.

When he finally managed to wrench himself away, she backed up and pressed her fingers to her lips. "Whoa."

Yeah. Whoa.

His lungs fought to catch a breath, his head spun, his vision darkened at the edges.

Overstimulation, loss of control. These were the things he fought so hard against.

He pulled off his outerwear, playing nonchalant, while inside he was anything but.

It helped to concentrate on sloughing off the layers of clothing, brushing them carefully, then hanging them around the tent to dry.

Seeking calm and focus, he looked wildly around before settling his attention on the tiny camp stove flame.

"Guess you missed me."

His only response was a tightening of the lips, awkward and a little embarrassed.

Despite the ever-present exhaustion, preparations went faster than they ever had. Practice, he guessed. Or maybe it was that energy buzzing between them, that wide-open *what's gonna happen in the bag tonight?*

Once they'd settled with their bowls and he'd shoved a couple steaming spoonfuls of food into his mouth, he made himself look her in the eye—a little surprised to see something like hurt there. Had he done that?

"I'm a mess." His mouth took over, pressing words through damaged vocal cords before he'd had a chance to consider. "This thing. You and me. It's screwing with my head."

She blinked, spoon halfway to her mouth, then lowered it and waited.

When he didn't go on, she took a quick bite, then another. For a few seconds, he watched her tear through her food with a vengeance. Her face got redder as she went, her eyes cast down instead of at him.

Finally, bowl empty, she set it aside and made as if to get up.

"Wait, Angel." He stopped her with a hand on her arm.

"What, *Ford*?"

"I didn't mean to say that it was bad."

She skewered him with a look. "What did you mean to say?"

"That I…" He puffed out a frustrated sigh. He was bad, really bad, at talking to women. To anyone, actually. "You've short-circuited my brain."

"Me? I short-circuited it?" Her brows went so high they disappeared into her hat and the red on her cheeks solidified into two dark spots. "You've gotta be kidding me. *I* didn't do anything to your brain. You did it yourself."

"I didn't intend to blame you. I'm just saying that—"

"You're just saying that I'm responsible for whatever happened last night." She nodded, once, hard. "Fine.

That's fine. I can take the blame. For last night. For every one of my past relationships being utter, pathetic failures. For being the ball and chain that's kept you from skiing yourself to safety, right? I'll take on all of that. Oh, and how about I take the blame for us being here to begin with, shall I? Those guys that almost killed me? My fault. Yeah. And I forced you to kiss me out there last night. The sleeping bag, obviously, was me because I was freezing cold and—"

Coop opened his mouth a few times, but she talked right through whatever he'd been about to say. He deserved this tirade.

She was right, blaming her was ridiculous.

"I'm sorry," he said. "I'm not used to all these…" He waved helplessly between them.

"What?" Her eyes watched him, hot and bright with what looked like desire. "These what?"

"*Feelings*," he said on a groan. "Angel, I don't know how…" He leaned in, reached for her, then pulled away again. "Can we…"

"Yeah. Come here."

They met in the middle. The kiss was hard, nothing like the soft, voluptuous thing they'd shared before. This was bossy, demanding…although he'd be a liar if he said it was only that. Words couldn't explain what he felt, but his lips, teeth, and tongue could.

He nipped her bottom lip, slowly released it, and pulled back, just enough to say, against her lips, "None of this…" When she opened her mouth, he went on. "Is your…" Another nip, a swipe of his tongue. "Fault."

Breathing hard, she pulled away. "Whose *fault* is it, then?"

"Mine," he said with absolute certainty. He was out of breath now, from the taste and the feel of her against him. "I should have done this months ago."

"Why didn't you?"

He let out a pained chuckle. "You scared me. I was afraid of what would happen." His body eased forward, every muscle and cell commandeered by this overpowering attraction, until there was no distance between them, no way to step back and examine this.

"And now?" She sounded like she'd been running.

"Now?" He nudged her head to the side and nuzzled her neck through the fabric again, wishing he could get to her skin and taste her. "I'm terrified."

Day 5—219 Miles to Volkov Station—17 Days of Food Remaining

Angel woke up on a shudder, breathing hard, as if she'd run, every hair on her body standing up. She worked hard, in the dark of the sleeping bag, to catch her breath, but something was off.

There. A sound, in the distance, like—

"Ford." She whispered his name, for some reason, and shook him.

"Yeah." Though still a scratchy, sandpaper scrape, his voice was immediately awake.

"I heard something."

He fumbled above their heads and let in the light, along with a good dose of bracing, subzero air. It sent a penetrating shock straight to her lungs.

Their breath was visible now, even in their nest, a conjoined vapor cloud rising out of their mummy tomb. No, not a tomb—a *bed*.

He shifted, cocked his head to the side, and listened, eyes alert.

Nothing.

"Still hear it?"

She shook her head.

"Describe it."

"A buzzing. Like insects or…"

"An engine?"

"Yeah." She eyed him, hoping he'd show no signs of worry. Just as she opened her mouth to suggest that it might have been her imagination, he unzipped the bag.

"Let's get moving."

Quickly and quietly, they readied themselves, skipping the hot breakfast part of the day, but by necessity warming water for drinking. Angel stretched out her knee, which felt frozen at a ninety-degree angle.

"How is it?"

"Stiff."

When she'd finished, Ford shoved a stick of butter at her. "Eat it all. We need to hurry."

"You don't think they're—"

"Can't risk it." Which meant he *did* think that plane was out there searching for them. "We're a needle in a haystack out here. They've got no idea where we're headed or which path we've taken, so these are random flybys. But they could get lucky."

And if that happens, we're as good as dead.

"Hold on." He stopped her from going out, head cocked. "You know what I hear?"

She shook her head, though what she wanted to do was cover her ears and hide.

"Nothing," he said. "No wind, no ice. Storm's gone."

She hurried out into a flat white landscape, pleased to find it as still and quiet as death. Days like this had bothered her back at the station, too much ice, too many clouds, too much endless nothing, but perspective was everything. With a laugh, she turned to Ford. "It's beautiful."

"Yeah?" He eyed her quizzically before sliding his dark goggles into place.

She packed up her sled, feeling lighter than she had since this trip began, stepped into her skis, and lined herself up behind Ford's sled. Just before he zipped up the contents, her eyes caught on the sample tubes, stowed like five enormous, sharp-ended sausages, gleaming in the dim light. All that buoyancy sank in a fraction of a second.

What the hell was it about those things that made everyone so crazy? What about that virus was worth so much time and money and effort? What was worth so many lives?

CHAPTER 27

Day 6—209 Miles to Volkov Station—16 Days of Food Remaining

Coop heard them again the next day.

With the storm out of the way and the cloud cover almost gone, those assholes were up there for the second day in a row, searching for them. Had they somehow spotted them and figured out that they were headed to Volkov, instead of the more obvious South African station? Part of Coop's reasoning in choosing Volkov had been to avoid pursuit, but if they'd been spotted before the storm, then that advantage was gone.

Given their slow pace, they needed all the advantages they could get.

Just thinking about Angel behind him sent a rush of anxiety through him. He couldn't hide or cover or protect her. All he could do was push himself more, go faster, get to shelter sooner, and make sure she kept up. And she was keeping up remarkably well.

He couldn't have wished for a better partner.

He did, however, wish they weren't such easy targets.

His muscles strained as he pushed, his knees tense and weak, his face burning from the wind, his eyes barely open, even behind the dark goggles' protection. The snow blindness would get worse if the sun came all the way out.

What they needed right now was another flat white day like yesterday, not a clear sky. It would force the plane to land. Although any pilot crazy enough to fly a small plane in winter here might not worry about things like an overcast sky... No. Flying in flat white was suicide, as a pilot couldn't differentiate between ground and sky.

They had to hurry, dammit. These ten-mile days would kill them.

He turned to check on Angel and stumbled. The ice behind him was absolutely empty as far as the eye could see. Disbelief made his brain stop working as he stared at the place where she should be. How many times had he glanced back in the last six days? Hundreds? Thousands? Millions? Under the harsh sun, against the beating wind, through ice and clouds and every other type of weather they'd traveled with, she'd been the only constant.

Her absence was wrong, like a missing puzzle piece.

He swung left—nothing but choppy, water-like surface. He swayed, as lost at sea as a sailor looking in vain for a familiar lighthouse. Was he hallucinating? Where was she?

Shit. *Shit.*

He swung back, frantic, her name already out of his mouth, once, twice. "Angel! Ang—"

"Yeah?"

She stood beside him, as if she'd grown tired of following him and decided to keep pace. He shook his head and blinked at the puffy red-and-black shape of her, intimately familiar now.

The sun turned the smooth horizon rough, gave it details and shadows and depth. Through a cold, wheezing breathing cycle, he focused on those variations—followed snakelike shapes to their abrupt ends, moved from one short series of lines to a larger pointed protrusion. Once he'd steadied himself, he focused back on her. Behind her, the sky was clearing to a bright, crystalline blue, the sun breaking through to limn her the way it did the dips and divots in the ice. "You okay?"

"I'm fine."

"Good." He put his hands to his face and exhaled hard.

"How about you, Ford? You seem—"

Annoyance bubbled over, replacing the anxiety from moments before. "Why do you call me that?"

"Call you what?" She sounded confused.

"Ford."

"It's your name." Her head tilted at an angle. "Isn't it?"

"People call me Coop."

"Oh, right. Coop." She popped the final *p*, clearly displeased with the sound.

"You don't like it?"

"It's not that I don't li—"

"Why don't you like it?"

"Because you're a man, not a *henhouse*." She sighed. "Not to mention, it rhymes with poo—"

A gruff laugh erupted from his lungs, surprising them both. It relaxed his muscles and broke him from the spell of almost losing her.

Jesus, this woman.

"And I like Ford. The name suits you. You're…" There was something awkward, almost embarrassed about the way she turned away now, but because she was courageous, honest Angel Smith and not cowardly Ford Cooper, she finished. "I don't know. Fording streams, forging a path for us. Coop is too…small a name for you."

"All right then," he managed to say before his bout of embarrassment clogged up his throat. "You want a break?"

"No. Keep going."

"You've got to watch that knee, Angel. I see how you're favor—"

"You heard it too, didn't you?" She didn't have to pull off her goggles for him to know she had that narrow-eyed look on her face. "The engine noise. They're still after us, aren't they?"

"Yeah."

"Then we keep moving."

"You need to rest, or we'll—"

Ignoring him, she skied ahead, leading the way. Stubborn woman.

He grinned, the feel of it unfamiliar on his features, and took off. They'd been going maybe five minutes, skiing beside one another instead of in a line, when he slowed and half turned. "Speaking of names," he said, enjoying the novelty of being heard after days of howling against the wind. "Angel's pretty presumptuous, isn't it?"

"Huh?" She slowed to match his pace.

"You live up to your parents' expectations with that name?" He figured she had. Maybe she wasn't saintly in the biblical sense, but she was kind, good, generous. And beautiful, though he worked to ignore the pulse of want that went through him, turning to stare at the increasingly textured ice. There was a pattern to it that reminded him of something. Striations breaking up the windblown desert. To avoid falls, they'd have to watch their pace with variations like these. He turned, thinking he'd mention it, but she was still laughing at his comment.

"Ha! Right." She pushed off hard, more confident on her skis than she'd been that first day. Graceful, in fact, and faster.

They hadn't heard the plane again, though the weather

was holding, with the sun bright enough to warm the air and his body and even his insides.

Who knew? Maybe they'd get those thirteen miles in today and make it to Volkov after all.

He'd just set off when she screamed, loud, primal, and frantic, then disappeared—swallowed up by the ice.

For a few valuable seconds, Coop stared at the spot she'd just vacated, mind blank.

It was fear that knocked him out of it, reaching in to twist his innards like a bony fist. Before his brain had begun to process things, he unclipped his skis and ran. Stupid, considering she'd just been eaten by the earth, but he couldn't slow his pace.

A crevasse, dammit. Those stripes. Though the ice appeared flat, there were deep cracks in it, hidden by newly deposited ice and snow. Where there was one, there'd be more, so he needed to watch his own footing—but faced with the prospect of losing her, stupid and fast was the best he could do.

"*Angel!*" he yelled as he ran, burning with fear and adrenaline.

Jesus. Please. Please. Please don't. Please don't.

He leapt over a small, wavelike sastrugi and landed, grunting when his foot smashed through a layer of ice to dangle somewhere beneath. He grabbed ahold of the hard ridge in front of him and pulled himself out, losing valuable seconds. He shouldn't be plowing into a crevasse field like a goddamn PistenBully. He should slowly, cautiously test every single inch between him and Angel.

Fuck that. Momentum pushed him forward, jarring his brain and shoving every ounce of air from his lungs.

He was up and running again before he could breathe or see straight or think long enough to let caution take over. Then, with shocking suddenness, his sprint ended, leaving him teetering on the edge of the hole that had taken her. In the split second it took to analyze what he saw—Angel alive, hanging from one bowed ski pole—he experienced countless thoughts and emotions. Lives, deaths, everything in between.

Intestine-loosening relief.

But there was no visible bottom to the crevasse. If she fell…

She's slipping. Her gloves weren't meant to grip anything—they were for warmth. To hang like that as long as she had was a miracle.

It couldn't last.

He dropped to his knees, too numb or buzzed on adrenaline to feel the impact. His body was nothing but a tool, like one of his drills, with one purpose: to save her. Beyond that, it didn't matter. He could pop joints, rip tendons, tear himself open for all he cared, as long as he pulled her up in the process.

Her ski pole, though it looked flimsy as a toothpick, was the lone item standing between her and death. It had somehow been wedged into the side of the gaping fissure, while the handle sat on top. Angel's right wrist was still caught in the strap and all of it—pole, strap, swinging body, the ice around it—created a precarious sculpture that could crumble in the blink of an eye.

One wrong move and she would be gone.

He stilled, dared to breathe, and reached.

He couldn't think about how far the hole went. He'd seen crevasses as shallow as a few feet, while others were bottomless pits. Bottomless being relative, of course, when you studied glaciers. There'd be a bottom, it'd just be—

He ripped off his bulky mitten and extended his arm.

Too damn far. A shift to the side brought him closer to her hands, but also to the ice that held one side of that pole. Stretching hard gave him an inch. Still not enough.

"Ford." His name was a whimper. It tied his chest in knots and would have paralyzed him if his body had been human. But it wasn't. It was machinery, doing its job. Stretch, reach, tighten, flex. Focused, strong. Single-minded.

"I'm here, Angel. I'm with you."

"I can't…"

Don't look at her. Don't look. Don't feel or think, just move. Do.

"I can't…can't move my hands. Can't…"

"I know. Hold on. Just hold on. I'm coming to you."

And how the hell was he supposed to do that?

Eyes moving lightning-fast, he took in details—some pointless, like the clear, glowing blue of the ice beneath the surface, others essential, like the harness still strapped to Angel's middle. The sled was attached to her. Pulling her down.

He didn't have to see her eyes to know they were pleading through her dark goggles.

"I'm sorry, Ford," she sobbed. "So so so sorry."

His chest. Christ. *Breathe.*

Another scan of the fissure showed a ledge on this side, maybe two inches wide. Without another second's hesitation, he threw a leg over, found it, and shoved his foot onto the too-small surface. If he could jam his other leg on the opposite side... There it was, a crack in the wall. Worth the risk.

A religious man would have prayed before extending his left leg and straddling the abyss. There wasn't time for God. Coop just did it, letting out a harsh little breath when it stuck.

He didn't look down, didn't worry about his own precarious position, but the precious moments he'd taken had been too damn long. As he watched, Angel's hands slipped, her fingers twisted back. Only millimeters, but more than enough, since a fall would pull this whole thing down.

"Breathe," he said to himself, though when Angel obeyed, he realized she'd been holding it in, too. And then, because it seemed to help, he spoke again. "Need to cut through the harness. You hold on. Okay? That's your only job."

She nodded so slightly he'd never have caught it if they weren't hovering together in this still, silent limbo between heaven and earth.

He reached into his pocket, removing his pocketknife and struggling to open it with his mouth, then leaned farther forward.

"Just hold on." He didn't dare speak above a whisper.

The air around them was as taut as the harness, suffocating and supporting as he grappled with the knife, nearly lost his hold, and seesawed forward before evening his weight out again.

Instead of fighting through a second futile round of fumbling, he ripped his glove off with his teeth, threw it up and over the edge, and went to work bare-handed. The metal was shockingly cold against his fingertips, but at least sensation wouldn't last once frostbite took over. He had to move fast. Wedging his feet farther into their cracks, he bent and sawed in earnest, staring hard at the strap that anchored her to this place.

"Almost there."

A few hard swipes and suddenly the nylon slithered from his grasp, a creature sprung from a trap.

Seconds later, the sled smashed into the depths, the sound deafening enough to burst their bubble. He'd just taken in half a lungful of air when the pole came loose.

The next fat millisecond stretched into eternity, and it was still too short. He reached for her hand and missed. His left foot skidded to the side. Angel's body started its freefall.

Inevitable and terrible, until she slammed against him.

On sheer instinct, he wrapped an arm around her and swung them both to one side, flattened against the ledge.

One second.

Nothing moved.

Another…

Frantic, she yanked her wrist from the ski pole's strap and chucked it up and over the side.

The ledge shifted.

"Up!" he yelled, though Angel couldn't move from where he'd crushed her between his body and the wall. Working fast, he pulled himself from the crevasse, not for one second letting himself enjoy the solidity up top, and reached down.

Angel gripped his left hand, glove to glove, flesh to flesh, bone to bone, so tight they'd grind to dust if one of them didn't let go. She climbed, he heaved, and within seconds, she was up and over, rolling from the edge as it crumbled beneath them. The pieces fell, tinkling like fairy bells, though they should have tolled like a death knell.

"You whole?" he asked quietly into the shocking silence.

Their clenched limbs were links in a steel chain. Titanium, tensile and shatterproof. Impervious to the elements, incomplete without their other half.

Her whispered *"yes"* ripped something loose deep inside his body.

Chests heaving hard in synchrony, they lay together for a few seconds before he could work up the will to move.

They needed to get away from the edge, though not too far. This whole place could be riddled with crevasses, a honeycomb of cracked ice.

For once, he saw the ice the way most people did—a dangerous, lonely place to die.

Something sounded from below, like the last hungry call of a predator, foiled by their escape. Her sled, shifting with a loud grinding noise before scraping its way down, down, down into the bowels of the ice sheet, the sound too small for such a cataclysmic event, slowly disappearing into nothing.

He glanced at Angel. Both skis and one pole were gone, along with at least half their food, swallowed up by the ice gods in exchange for her life.

For maybe the first time since his maiden trip to this continent, he cared more about what lay over the ice than under it.

The vulnerability of that was terrifying.

"Come on." Her fingers loosened when she stood, leaving him to stare at his bare, red hand.

"Ford."

He blinked. "Lost my glove."

"You took it off."

"Oh." He shook his head, startled into action again when she handed him the missing item. "Thanks."

Using the ski pole to test the ice before him, he stepped away from the hole, finally seeing it in its entirety. Where Angel had fallen was the narrowest part of the crevasse. The rest of it split the world open in either direction, as far as he could see. Angel had no doubt disturbed the camouflaging crust of ice and snow when she'd fallen into it, causing something of an avalanche inside. If she hadn't fallen in at that exact spot, if she'd walked five feet in either direction...

A final, ominous groan echoed from deep in the giant crack, before leaving them in silence, broken only by the whistle of what, if Murphy's law had its say, was sure to be another megastorm blowing up around them.

CHAPTER 28

ALMOST DYING TASTED HOT AND MINERAL, LIKE ROCKS and dirt and rusted metal. Even after gulping what felt like a gallon of water, she couldn't get it out of her mouth. Couldn't wipe it from her lips or stop herself from gagging.

Everything was so hot, she had no choice but to yank off her gloves and hat.

A laugh escaped her, as abrupt and alien as a bark. Her head shook slowly from side to side as if in denial, but she was here. She'd seen it. *Been* it. She'd died. And come back to life. No, almost died. Although for a while, everything had hung in the balance.

She'd hung in the balance.

Flexing her bare hands, she stared as if she couldn't quite place what they were and sank to the ground, surprised when her butt encountered Ford's sled instead.

"You okay?" Ford sat beside her and put an arm around her. Tightly.

She leaned into the man who'd proved himself more solid than the ground they walked on.

"I…" A slow turn brought them face-to-face, which didn't tell her much. Instead of pulling his ski mask off to see his expression, she reached for her own. His hand was there to help her, then somehow his was yanked up and his mouth was there, hot and hungry on hers.

The kiss was life-giving. It showed her just how real this was. How real they were. It proved there was blood rushing in their veins, life in their bodies. She wanted him. Badly.

She pulled away, muttered something about the heat and moved to unzip her coat. Shook him off when he tried to stop her.

"No. No, I need this. I need you." Her hands scrabbled at his zipper, fighting him. "Need to feel..." She leaned in, with all the intensity in the world, as if she'd sucked it from the air. "Alive."

"We're alive." His big hands covered hers and pulled them to his chest. "But we won't be if we get naked out here."

"If we..." She blinked and looked around. Her chest kept rising and falling like she'd run or, hell, fallen into a big hole in the ice. "Oh crap. What am I doing?"

She hurriedly rezipped her coat, reached for Ford's, and stopped when he did it up himself. "I'm sorry. I feel crazy. I could laugh or cry or... Doesn't matter. Right. Right. Let's go. Keep moving." She stood up on wobbly legs, then sank back down again. "*Whoa.*"

"You okay?"

"I'm like rubber." She braced herself to stand again and got a faceful of confetti-like snow.

"We need to get inside." He looked around. "I'll put up the tent. You get in and—"

"No. No, I'll help. I can—"

He squatted, framed her face with his hands, put their foreheads together, and spoke. "Let me do this." If he were any other man, she'd brace herself for more. Arguments, reasoning, worries, pleas. But from Ford Cooper, those four words were enough.

"Okay." She nodded, sinking all the way down with relief.

Eventually, the weather stopped cooperating entirely,

sending her to her feet to help after all, which was far better than sitting and watching. They fought for control of the tent. Angel held it while Ford hammered his horizontal deadman stakes deep into the ice so they wouldn't budge in the night.

By the time they'd gotten it up and thrown their belongings inside, they had to bend double in order to move.

She turned to dig up ice to pile against the fly, but he stopped her, stern, expressionless, and as unrecognizable as a yeti. They were covered in the stuff.

"Go!" Too bone-tired to argue, she flopped inside as fast as she could. A pile of snow had already gathered on the floor of the tent. After shoveling it out with her hands, she set to work melting water for dinner. It wasn't until he'd crawled in and zipped up behind himself, motioning for her to take off anything wet and get into their sleeping bag, that she let herself relax.

"Hey."

Her eyes snapped open. Was she sleeping? She didn't remember sleeping.

"Here." He slid in beside her, helped prop her up, and handed her a bowl of hot food. She shoveled it back as unconsciously as breathing.

Once it was gone, she put the bowl down and looked at him.

"How bad off are we?"

"We've lost most of our supplies. Won't make it with what we've got." Her insides shrank up as he looked away. "I'm ditching the cores."

"No!" Her response shocked them both. "You can't."

"Why not?" He looked at her like she'd lost her mind. Had she?

Hanging there in the void, with that solid-butter anchor dragging her into the depths, she'd felt nothing but a base animal fear—sharp and still and piercing. There'd been nothing human until he'd lowered himself in there with her. Even now, she felt changed.

It wasn't like the fears she'd cycled through when the accident had blown out her knee—that she'd never walk again, never cook again, lose her restaurant, her reason for being. Oh, and the man she'd thought she loved.

This had been a dark, scrabbly, ferocious sensation, from somewhere deep inside. *Survive*, it demanded. *Survive*.

Over and over again, this place had done that to her: broken her down into her most basic, vital components. Cells. Nothing but an Angel-shaped combination of cells. And they didn't want to die.

This time, something else had crawled out of that hole with her, a phoenix from the ashes. It felt dark, though it wasn't really. It was simple, clean, real, and as pure as this pristine place. *Rage*. So strong it cauterized her soul, scabbed it up, and gave it purpose.

Those evil bastards wanted the virus? Well, she had it. And she wasn't giving it up.

"I want to keep the cores" was all she said.

Ford held her eyes for an uncomfortably long while. "All right," he replied, no questions asked. "We keep the cores."

She nodded once and looked away, afraid of what he'd see in her face. Gratitude and affection, certainly—after all, she'd grown to like this man—but something else, too. Something she wasn't ready to examine too closely, though if she was honest, she'd admit that it put an ache in her chest, scraped at her insides, and left her feeling raw.

What made her hide, though, tender as a day-old

bruise, was the realization that, of everything they'd gone through on this hellish journey, it wasn't a near miss or a miracle that pushed her heart over the edge, but that simple acquiescence.

CHAPTER 29

Coop put his mouth to Angel's ear. "You warm?"

"Relatively speaking." Here, inside the sleeping bag, everything was magnified, whisper-close. He'd never sought intimacy before or even been comfortable with it. But this felt good. Inside and out. She felt good. Being alive felt good.

He nudged her with his head, pressed his forehead to hers, and kissed her.

It wasn't a sexy kiss but something else. Dry, tender, affectionate. Proof of life.

Part of him hated how much emotion crowded his brain right now, pushed out the logic and any semblance of control. Again and again, that moment came back. Angel on the ice and suddenly, *poof*! Gone.

Recklessness edged under his skin. He pressed harder, more desperately, slid his fingers through her hair, tightened his hold.

The deep, consuming kiss, tongues tangling, pushed noises out of his mouth. Painful against his ruined trachea. There was so much to do. He needed to take stock and figure out how they'd live for over two weeks on less than one week of food, but hell, maybe he could live off of this. Off of her.

He barely noticed his erection at first. Then, like his body'd taken over his brain, he moved against her—a slow, rhythmic press of his pelvis to hers. Not easy in this tiny, confined space, but so satisfying when she opened her legs and gave him access to that warm place, meeting every move with one of her own.

Adrenaline still buzzed in his brain, flushed his blood, made the heaviness in his limbs a pleasure rather than a pain. He rocked against her, let himself feel the pure, unexpected pleasure of sexual excitement. When had he last felt such a thrill from being with a woman? Years? Decades? He couldn't help the way his breathing stuttered and his body shook. He couldn't help grinding himself just a little harder against her.

She made a sound and he stopped. "This okay?"

"Yeah," her whisper assured him. "It's good."

"I'd do anything to be inside you right now, Angel." She'd scoured his insides, leaving nothing but the truth, clean and raw as the surface of the ice. "*Anything.*"

She let out a surprised little *puh* sound and went very still.

Maybe that hadn't been the best thing to say to a woman who'd almost died today.

Shit. The words had just puffed out, exposing him for what he was: part teenager, part soldier, part awkward science nerd.

When she didn't say anything, he nodded, trying to make space between them, as impossible as that was in this bag.

He swallowed, opened his mouth to apologize, and—

She laughed. More a semichoked cough than the big raucous sounds she used to let out at the station, but a laugh all the same.

"Me too," she finally managed through the giggles. "But the last thing we need is your penis freezing off."

"Polar penis." He shuddered with a laugh.

This woman. Jesus Christ, this woman. Just when he thought he'd pushed things too far, she went and surprised him again. Her eyes, bright and full of humor, didn't show a trace of today's narrow escape. He kissed her cheek, then let himself luxuriate in the soft feel of her against his lips and nose. Back and forth, he ran a tender trail from cheek to jaw to mouth, occasionally tickling her with his too-long scruff. Eventually, her giggles faded into happy sighs. He stopped moving and just held her into sleep.

When he slid out of the bag, he was punched in the face by the barrage of sound and icy air. He checked his fingers for frostbite. They were red, but warm, which made him hopeful. Actually, everything made him hopeful right now. He pulled his skullcap over his head before crawling over to the stove to melt more water.

It made absolutely no sense how ridiculously happy he felt. Young and free and indomitably *alive*.

Carefully, he went through the food he'd had on his sled, thankful that they'd divided it between them. Even after cutting their portions, they'd have to cover twice their average daily distance to survive.

With the fresh storm to contend with, the crevasse field to avoid, Angel on foot, and lord knew what kind of army after them, they were absolutely fucked. And yet, idiot that he was, Coop couldn't stop smiling.

CHAPTER 30

Day 7—201 Miles to Volkov Station—6 Days of Food Remaining

"NINE LEFT." ANGEL SHOVED THE BAG OF PROTEIN BARS into her pack and held up her set of kitchen knives. "But, hey, at least we've got these."

"And I've got this handy virus."

"Mmmm. Tasty." She forced a smile even though it hurt. Everything hurt. Her mouth, her feet, the knee that had wanted to buckle before she'd even gotten up today. Her heart hurt worst of all. It felt bruised and battered and swollen up to twice its size.

She desperately wanted to put the tent up again, slide back into the bag with Ford, and just hold him. Just hold him.

He tied their belongings onto the sled, glanced at her, and stopped. "All right?"

Well, we're running out of food, my body's broken, and I'm hormonal, though I'd thought that wasn't even possible for me.

"I'm okay." She nodded.

"Let's go."

Walking was much slower than skiing, but without the sled to haul, it was doable. And the freaking snowshoes were a pain in the ass.

An hour passed. Probably. Who could tell anymore? One step, another, crunching slowly forward, with nothing to think about except death. Or her past.

Funny, though, because as soon as that thought flashed

through her mind, her eyes landed on the other thing she could think about—Ford.

I'd do anything to be inside you right now.

A shiver went through her. Not the cold kind, but the realization kind. The shiver that tells you that your mind has landed on something important and your body's aware of it before you are.

I like him.

Oh yeah. *That* thought.

No, not *like*. Need. Want... Love?

Maybe.

She walked on, one high, knee-numbing step after another, and closed her eyes, remembering. Not just remembering but *feeling*. His fingers on her face, her cheek. The rough rasp of his beard, the press of lips, softer than any kiss she'd ever had from Hugh.

Hugh, with his silky words. Smooth-talking Hugh, who'd stolen everything from her.

What if I'd never come here?

That was easy to picture. She'd be back in Pittsburgh, possibly with one of the few friends who'd stuck around after the accident—laughing, drinking, pretending everything was okay. Only she couldn't pretend anymore.

That was why she'd left.

And that wasn't her anymore, anyway. *This is me.*

A body, surviving.

Did she regret it? Coming here?

Not if he's here with me.

Her eyes snapped open to a blurred world. She reached up, smeared the fog from her goggles...and there he was. Red back, straight and tall, forging through the infinite white.

When she'd woken up that morning, he'd already been busy, getting ready for the next leg of their journey. She'd watched him through slitted eyes. His movements had been fascinating—calm and slow-seeming, but oddly efficient and fast. She'd seen chefs who worked that way and it was magic.

She thought of the moment his eyes had landed on her. She swallowed, swiped a hand over her goggles again, and stumbled on. His expression had cauterized the wounds in her heart, even as it made new ones. Soft. That was the word for it. Soft—maybe yearning?

She didn't regret leaving Pittsburgh and coming to Antarctica. She didn't regret cooking for people who appreciated it. Who needed the calories and loved her food. How could she? She didn't regret setting out onto the ice with Ford, because she'd never have known how strong she was.

Nor would she have known Ford, seen the tenderness under the hard shell.

She'd never have felt this way. About anyone. Not even the man she'd thought she'd loved.

The night of the accident came back to her in a bright, loud rush of color so strong it could have been a hallucination.

The quiet restaurant, dark, still, but with that strange, hovering sense of expectation that had put every hair on her body on high alert. Why had she gone back that late? Something about the cash drawer, maybe. Right, she couldn't sleep because she'd forgotten to put the drawer into the safe at the end of the shift, but Hugh wouldn't answer his phone or the restaurant phone, and she was pissed about that: Why wasn't he answering? And why wasn't he home yet?

Through the dining room, through the dark kitchen,

up the back steps, and there—she'd forgotten about that sound. A thumping, scraping kind of sound. *Heart attack!* she'd thought, picturing Hugh on the floor, unable to reach the phone. *He needs me!*

She'd run down the hall, thrown open the door, and...

Everything after that was a jumble. First, worry—that heart attack thing she'd been warning him about for years. He was older than her, after all, and lived a rough, late-night, hard-drinking, high-fat life. Confusion quickly followed. Why was Hugh on top of their business partner—Angel's best friend—Lorraine like that? Oh God, maybe *she* was hurt.

In the next blink, she'd thought he was pointing something out to Lorraine over her shoulder. Some fine point in their business contract, maybe? But that theory had ended when they'd groaned together, looked up, and...

Kept going. They'd continued, eyes on Angel while she'd stood there, wishing she could unsee what they were doing, but also unable to move. Stuck in a continuous loop of horror and betrayal until Hugh opened his mouth and, in a voice tight with the effort of screwing her best friend, told her to get out. So he could finish.

After that, she'd half slid down the long, narrow staircase, stumbled through the dining room, knocking into chairs as she went, out into the heavy night air. Without thinking, she'd gotten into the car and sat there with the engine on for who knew how long.

When the driver's door swung open, she wasn't surprised to see him there. Hugh had the gall to look completely unruffled. Neither satisfied nor abashed, not freshly fucked nor devastated by the inevitable end of their marriage.

And she'd watched him, utterly blank, empty inside.

"Switch," he'd ordered, and out of habit, she'd obeyed and walked over to the other side of the car, gotten back in, and buckled up. She'd opened her mouth to tell him to do the same and then decided not to.

Fuck him.

He'd leaned forward to put on some late-night NPR show and turned out of the lot toward home, as if everything were normal. As if he hadn't just upended her entire existence.

Did he think they'd go home and get ready for bed together? Was he planning to somehow explain what he'd done? Would try to *make love* to her? "You need to move out."

"Come on, Ange, you know this isn't—"

"And you either buy me out or I find an outside buyer." She hadn't known she wanted out until that very moment. A thread of relief had wound its way into her, turning hurt into anger.

He'd watched her for a few seconds, then turned back to the road, his jaw twitching in the dim light. "It was a mistake. Didn't mean anything."

"I don't care. It's dead. We're dead. This…it's been dead for a while." She couldn't remember exactly when she'd lost faith in him. In them. They'd been together forever, it seemed like. She'd been twenty and he more than twice her age.

"You're tired. We'll talk in the—"

"*No!*" Her voice, punctuated by a hard slap of her hand to the dashboard, had filled the space—and because that kind of yell deserved an echo, she'd screamed it again. And again. And again.

His grip on her wrist had been a vise, a testament to

the strength in those famous hands. Hands that had held Lorraine's hips to the table while he'd pistoned into her, mechanically. Did he fuck *her* like that? The way he might take a leak? Without any expression at all?

"I'm done being your—" Jesus, what had she been? His tool? His muse, he used to say, but that seemed about as fake as his front-of-the-house smile. His stooge? Puppet? "I'm done."

"Done?" The look he'd thrown her was different from the others, more highly charged. As if he'd had a right to be pissed. "You're done with me?" He downshifted to take the next turn, cutting it close the way he always did. The tires squealed on the wet road. "After everything I've done for you, you ungrateful little..." Another turn, onto the highway this time, full acceleration. "Bitch. You think I brought you up from nothing to have you turn your back when things get bad? At least Lorraine's willing to spread her legs. You won't even let me into that—"

"What things are bad?"

"What?" He'd used that "big man, I'm the chef and you're my minion" voice.

The speedometer read over a hundred miles per hour, with the rain hitting the windshield in staggered bursts. "Slow down."

"No. What did you say? Before?"

"I asked what's bad in your life? What things?"

His laugh had been a strange hollow sound, woven into the low-pitched radio voice droning on about rising sea levels. "We're broke, sugar!" he'd said gleefully. "We're broke and you're all happy in your little kitchen, totally ignorant of how bad it is for me. All these guys after—"

With a sound like hell breaking open, the world had

gone completely still for one breathless moment in which she'd taken in so many things: his hand, too tight on her thigh; his eyes nowhere near the road but on her instead, focused and hard and more than a little desperate; and in front of them, one of those thick concrete guardrails.

And then the blurry, too-quick crunch of metal to asphalt, bone to plastic, the taste and smell of blood, inhaling it, choking on it. Another crash shoved them forward, and a roll turned her into a rag doll, heavy, limp, the world upside down.

Slowly, in the vacuum left by all that noise, she'd opened her eyes, swiped the wetness away, and looked to the side.

The last thing she remembered with any clarity was Hugh watching her, fixed and still, the oddest, shocked expression on his face.

Then darkness, yelling, sirens, flashes of light. More yelling and voices asking her to stay with them while they worked hard to get her out. *Angel*, they said over and over. *Hold on, Angel. Angel.*

That was a bad day. But not the worst. The worst was the day she'd found out he'd been right. There was nothing left. No restaurant, no home. The bastard had mortgaged it all and spent every last penny in his constant race to keep up, to be the biggest, best, most impressive chef. No health insurance, no life insurance. Nothing.

And she couldn't even yell at him because he was dead.

Her snowshoe caught on a bump in the ice and she stumbled, landing hard on her butt. It took her a few seconds to blink back to reality. To here. Now.

Ford turned and started to unclip from his skis.

"No!" she yelled. "It's fine."

Which wasn't a lie.

A half-hysterical laugh zipped through her veins and burst from her mouth.

Here she was, plowing across Antarctica, body a mess, food supply nonexistent, in a losing fight against death. But she was better than she'd been back then. She was *fine*.

Ford's hand appeared in her field of vision and she grasped it, let him pull her up into his arms.

She was *fine*. Because she'd changed through her months spent in this place—the loneliest place on earth. And unlike the woman she'd been back then, here she knew without a shadow of a doubt who she was...and that she wasn't alone.

CHAPTER 31

Day 7—Harper Research and Testing Facility, East Antarctic Ice Sheet

THE QUICK, HEAVY THUD OF BOOTS HAD CLIVE THROWING his cards down and dashing into the hall, where he nearly collided with Sampson and three of his men, monstrous and ice-crusted, emitting angry clouds of cold air like toxic exhaust.

"Get her on the phone," Sampson said roughly.

"The director?" Clive half laughed. "The satellite's not—"

The man faced Clive and, without showing his face or lifting a hand, somehow showed him just how much violence simmered under his surface. Holy shit was he scary.

"I need a line out." Sampson pulled up his goggles, baring bloodshot eyes, the pupils such narrow pinpricks that neither light nor life could possibly flow through them.

"No luck?" Clive forced a stiff smile to his lips. After a week of pointless searching, patience as a whole was wearing thin, and tempers were frayed. Fights had broken out, drunken brawls ending in missing teeth and broken bones. Most worrisome of all was Sampson's physical transformation, from bright Hollywood son to something as feral and wrong as a junkyard dog.

"Fuel's freezing up. We're grounded." Sampson huffed out a breath, snorting. "Eyes, dammit. Told her we need eyes in the sky."

It took Clive a few seconds to understand what he meant.

Satellite images. Right, well, that was patently absurd. He
shook his head. "Even without the cloud cover, the communications satellites are only available sporadically, so I can't
imagine you'll get..." He trailed off, watching Sampson
warily. There was something entirely too wired and
unhinged about him now, no doubt underscored by fatigue
and excessive alcohol consumption—or consumption of
something else. Not that Clive could blame him for that,
but it was quite an about-face from the man who'd arrived
here talking about his body being a temple.

Apparently uninterested in a reminder of the Facility's
communications capabilities, Sampson stepped around
Clive and continued down the hall toward the labs. Beyond
them lay nothing but housing for the trial participants.

"Hey." Clive's voice clearly didn't reach Sampson's ears.
Anxious now, he followed in Sampson's slippery path.
"Where are you going? There's nothing for you down there.
You can't—"

"Can't what?" Sampson was breathing hard. "Can't see
more than five inches in front of my nose? Can't get any
kind of backup from the people who sent us here? Can't
hunt down two fucking amateurs? The woman's a cook, for
fuck's sake. Can't I catch a *break* on this godforsaken mission?" With a low wordless sound that raised the small hairs
on Clive's neck, Sampson turned and put his fist through
the wall. At this rate, the place would be pockmarked.

For a few stretched-out seconds, Clive's eyes weren't
sure where to land—on the man melting down in front of
him or the mercenaries hanging back, casting glances at
each other.

Finally, Sampson stepped into Clive's personal space
on a waft of cinnamon and sunscreen and something

else—bitter and crude as the fuel they used to heat this place. "Now, I'm gonna need to ask the prisoners some questions."

Trial subjects, Clive wanted to say, but he knew better than to interject. This wasn't a normal conversation. Besides, there was nothing to ask. They knew exactly who had the virus and, if they weren't mistaken, they knew exactly where it was going. "As I've said before, Mr. Sampson, my subjects are not yours to play with. What could you possibly—"

Sampson's eyes were Clive's only warning before he moved, flat blue irises alive in a way they'd never been before. Clive stumbled back, shock and fear warring with his knowledge that he was *better* than this man. Too good to succumb to bullying.

Pride did him absolutely no good when Sampson put his forearm to Clive's throat and leaned in, as calm and non-chalant as if he were on a Sunday stroll. Pride didn't help him breathe or keep his eyes open, didn't prevent his larynx from bruising like a ripe peach.

In the few seconds spent chasing the stars that popped at the edge of his vision, head pressed into the newly formed wall dent as if it were made for him, Clive understood: They would die here. Not just the trial subjects, but all of them. Him possibly right this moment, his body just one more tossed onto the growing heap outside on the ice.

When Sampson released him, it was sheer willpower that kept Clive's knees from buckling. A compulsion to survive that compelled him to speak through his already swelling throat, eyes not leaving the other man's as something hard and wild of his own reared its head. "Think you're...strong..." He coughed, the sensation rough as nails. "With your fists and guns... There's a virus on its way." He swallowed and stood up higher, keeping himself still as he forced a smile, as false and pointless as those wax lips he used to chew through on Halloween. "Your *payload*, remember? The reason we're all here? It would serve you well not to forget that I'm the guy with the vaccine."

With his hand pressed to his throat, Clive stepped unsteadily around Sampson and his mini-army, heading deliberately away from the lab and the vaccine in question. Though his vision closed in with every step, he kept himself erect until he turned the corner and collapsed against the wall.

The bastard had gone too far.

Slowly, he made his way toward the lounge, where he gathered water and an ice pack for his throat, along with a fresh bottle of that vodka. Make that two. From there, he went to the kitchen and filled a basket with supplies. Enough for a siege.

Things were not going according to plan. Did they ever? He coughed out a dry, bitter laugh, which he instantly regretted. Shit, his throat hurt.

After a good half hour had passed, he crept down the hall leading to the lab. There, he typed in the pass code, pressed his hand to the print pad, and went in, dragging his supplies behind him. The door locked with a satisfying *snick*, leaving him blessedly alone.

Well, relatively alone.

He glanced at the shatterproof glass separating him from the four cells containing his trial subjects. At least the two-way mirrors afforded him privacy.

Time to get to work on a permanent solution to a difficult problem. Thankfully, he knew just what to do.

CHAPTER 32

Day 12—156 Miles to Volkov Station—1 Day of Food Remaining

COOP WATCHED ANGEL LICK THE WRAPPER OF A PROTEIN bar and hated himself.

They'd pushed through. Made an effort, a really strong effort to add miles, but the human body wasn't made for this shit. They'd spent twelve days on the ice, and if they hadn't lost their food, they could have done twelve more.

But after this final dinner, there wasn't a chance in hell they'd make it.

Ford couldn't wrap his mind around that, here in the tent's warm orange interior on what was possibly the last night of their lives. Or maybe that could be tomorrow. Or the day after.

He'd never make love to her. Never hear her laugh again.

His brother, Eric, would never know what had happened to him. He wished he'd reached out more often. Especially since Eric had been there for him—always.

He and Angel had saved their final dried meal for tonight, as sort of a celebration, he guessed. One last taste of something. A last shared pleasure.

He was hungry for something else, though. The only thing keeping him moving through the coldest, roughest days of his life—her. Every day, every mile, every step was made with the promise that he'd hold her in his arms that night.

In silence, they dipped into the lukewarm bag of

rehydrated food—a chicken curry, which he supposed was okay as far as last meals went. They were huddled together, for warmth, yeah, but also because this was how they lived now: as a unit.

Which didn't mean they were alone in this tent. Oh no, exhaustion hung above and between them, sat on their chests and shoulders, oozed into their pores, its presence as solid as theirs. The wind, too, made a good show of it, robbing them of their peace and privacy. And then there was the ice itself, hell-bent on stealing what was left of their humanity.

"Hate the wind," Angel said, echoing his thoughts without any animosity.

"The wind doesn't care," he said, immediately regretting how morose he sounded.

"*Wind don't care*," Angel imitated in a high, bratty voice. It was the most excited sound she'd made in days.

He blinked slowly. "What?"

"Remember those honey badger videos?" At his blank look, she went on. "The crazy, nasty-ass honey badger? You know, 'This is honey badger. Honey badger don't care.' No? Nothing?"

He shook his head, eyes bright on her.

She sighed. "Some guy redid the audio narration for a nature documentary about honey badgers. Years ago." Her words were more spaced out than they used to be, as if she couldn't get breath or kept losing her way in the middle of what she was saying. "It was hilarious." She screwed up her face, pursed her lips. Even chapped and burned, they could never be anything but beautiful. "Anyway." She motioned toward the howling wind, the joke over now, fatigue back after a brief respite. "Reminded me of that, you know? Wind don't care. Doesn't matter that we're here. Nothing matters."

Her features flattened out again, narrower than when they'd left the station, her cheeks too hollow, her eyes swallowing up her face. Those bones were beautiful, fine and sharp, with a tilt to the nose that he'd never noticed before, as if taking away the flesh put it all into clearer perspective. On a strange level, though he preferred her healthy and flushed to sharp and sallow, there was something intimate about seeing her like this.

Jesus. He pushed his palms into his eyes, hard.

"It'll blow if it wants to, won't it? Feels like it's started to wear away at me, like erosion's already begun and it's skimmed off parts I'll never get back."

He swallowed back a pointless wave of rage. There wasn't room for that shit in here. Not between them. Not now, when shoring up the good was more important than reflecting all the bad.

Later, bodies entwined in their shared bag, with the noisily crackling ice beneath them and the midnight sun washing everything in its glow, Ford felt the rare urge to talk.

"Eric'll be upset."

She shifted against him. "Eric?"

Right. That was a bit of a non sequitur, wasn't it?

"My brother. He'll miss me, though I never call him, rarely see him. Don't ever check in."

"That's so sad."

Huh. He'd never thought of his life as sad before.

"Used to fish with him. And Dad. Only time Dad paid much attention to us, really. There's this island off the coast of California. San Elias. It's right next to this deep-sea platform. Dad's spot. Hot summers, he'd drop us on the island and fish off the boat."

"Sounds nice."

He lifted a shoulder. "Dad didn't like dealing with us. Couple times he brought camping gear and put us on the island to fend for ourselves while he fished. Probably got wasted, too, but I wasn't aware of that in those days." He sucked in a dry breath, filled with nothing but Angel. "Drank himself to death. But that's not the point. The point is that Eric was a kid, too, but he was more of a man than Dad. Dad taught us to fish, to clean what we caught, but he'd pass out before we cooked them. So Eric, at probably ten or eleven, would light a fire and make sure I ate. After the second or third trip like that, he started bringing other food, too. So we wouldn't have to eat fish for the three days it took for our dad to finish whatever booze he'd brought."

"Oh, Ford. I'm sorry, that's—"

"Don't feel sorry for me. Shit happens to everyone. It was nice. Peaceful. I had Eric. I was lucky." He sighed, letting the backs of his gloved knuckles rub her rib cage and wishing there was room—time—for more. "I remember these…sensations. My feet in the warm mud. Sitting with my brother by the fire, leaning against him shoulder to shoulder. We didn't have to talk, which was nice." Behind his closed lids, winking lights appeared. "The stars. I remember watching them with him and wondering if—"

Shit. He couldn't finish, couldn't voice the childish hopes or wishes or whatever those had been. Wanting his mom back, begging the night sky for another chance. Shooting stars and their false, empty hope.

She nodded and that movement, the tight rub of her cheek to his chest, made something twist hard inside of him.

"Eric's my hero," he said into the top of her head with a weak smile. "Wanted to kill me when I joined up."

"The army?"

He hummed his assent against her.

"Yeah. Why'd you do that?"

"Piss my dad off, maybe. Though it was more than that."

"What do you mean?"

"Dad was a scientist—petroleum geologist."

"Hm. What's that?" Angel sounded tired, but present. Exactly the way he felt. Like if they went to sleep, they might never wake up again. Like this might be it for them.

"Worked for the oil companies—it was how he knew about that island, from the time he'd spent out there, planning on where to place rigs. They have geologists on staff who locate oil and gas deposits."

"Huh."

"Yeah. So, I was kinda following in his footsteps. Majored in geology when I first went to college, but about halfway through my third semester, something happened. An oil spill, right off the coast. It was a mess for months. Animals dying, people sick. Filthy water. I got so pissed that my dad had a part in that. See, while he fished, pulling animals from the water, Eric and I spent our summers on that island, getting to know the wildlife, becoming a part of it. Like, we created our own little oasis. Guess that island made me care. About nature. The world. The oil spill made me realize we were destroying it."

He smiled, remembering how enraged Dad and Eric had been when he'd gone to basic training. Dad because Coop had quit school and wouldn't become his mini-me, Eric because he knew how bad life was on the front lines. Eric had joined the navy right out of school and eventually gone on to BUD/S training and become a SEAL, also to piss Dad off.

What a way to live a life, between the three of them—as a series of aggressive maneuvers. Would they have been that way if Mom had been around?

He blinked in the dark sleeping bag, shook himself free of his memories, and focused on Angel's breathing. "My brother had all this easy confidence and swagger. I was the quiet one. Just wanted to be alone."

Although not now, strangely. Now he was happy to have her here. Well, not *happy*, because he didn't want this for her. Didn't want to see her suffer, witness all that magnificent life draining away.

He swallowed back a fresh wash of pain, skating on the perma-layer of hunger.

Why was he even talking about this stuff? Man, his brain was scrambled. But the images wouldn't stop, and the words kept coming.

"Eric knew I was different from him. Couldn't take crowds or noise. People, heat...all the shit I had to deal with in the army."

"I just thought you were a jerk."

He shook with an unexpected burst of laughter. "I know." He squeezed her tight, trying to figure out how to keep her alive. "I know."

CHAPTER 33

Day 13—151 Miles to Volkov Station—No Food Remaining

THEY'D EATEN VITAMINS FOR BREAKFAST, WHICH WASN'T all that unpleasant. It made her feel full. In a way. If she pretended really, really hard. It didn't, however, get rid of the cramps in her belly and thighs. And the cramps made walking difficult. She snickered. Well, *more* difficult.

At least it's not storming, she thought for maybe the twelfth or eighteenth or millionth time today. Or yesterday. Whatever. No storm was good.

But wait. Angel stopped, swaying like a sheet of paper in the wind. If it wasn't storming, why was she bent forward like this? The extra effort she'd had to put in for the last hour or so was really chafing her.

Her eyelashes crunched as she blinked up.

Were those mountains ahead, biting the sky like a big set of teeth? Had Ford mentioned mountains?

She staggered back, managing not to land on her poor bruised ass, though maybe she should just let go and do it. Just sit.

It would be so nice. On a soft, springy sofa. Or maybe one of those memory foam beds, molding to every aching bone. Oooohhh, a hammock.

She set off again, picturing a cloud-light bed, right beyond this rise.

Even as she daydreamed, experience had taught her to keep her eyes glued to the ground. Damn thing may look as smooth as a skating rink, but every little ripple was an obstacle, just waiting for her to happen.

Or something. That wasn't the expression, was it?

The ground rose and rose, the angle like torture, but also entertaining in a way. Variety. Variation. One of those words. Spice of life.

Spices. Her mouth watered painfully. Crap. She'd cut food words out of her thoughts a couple days ago. Damn this one for sliding in sideways. Now she'd have to cut out sayings, too, which limited her options of things to think about. Ford thought it was hilarious when she—

She raised her head, wiped her goggles, and stared at the empty space ahead.

Oh great. Now where the hell was Ford?

"I have a real good friend…lives in the hospital…I'll buy him anything…to keep him alive." Coop whispered the marching cadence under his breath as he skied. It was grim and grisly and perfectly appropriate. *"Don't…have no…legs…"*

He stopped, shook his head, pulled his ski mask up, ran his glove over his face to clear away the clinging crystals, and turned to find that he was alone.

"Angel!"

Nothing. Silence.

Frustrated, he pulled his hat and ski mask off and called again, listening hard for her response.

"Yeah!"

Relief washed through him so intensely he had to work hard to stay standing. He scanned the horizon until he saw her, way down below.

Which was odd.

There hadn't been mountains on their route, had there? His brain was on the fritz, foggy from lack of food. Maybe oxygen, too, judging from the climb he'd just done. He peered down at Angel's slowly approaching figure. Christ, how had he not noticed the change in elevation?

He turned and stared at where a series of heavily striated hills chewed darkly at the sky, each peak a sharp tooth sawing into the gray above it.

I know this place.

That didn't make sense, since he'd never trekked out here, but...

Wait. He turned, doing his best to find the sun, invisible behind a fresh blanket of clouds.

He *had* been here.

"Intense." Angel came up beside him, breathing hard from the climb.

"I've been here."

"In your wildest dreams?"

She'd had him laughing for days, but this was different. There wasn't just humor in her words, but a thread of hope, thin as a spiderweb.

"We didn't come from this direction, though." He spun in a full circle. "From that way. Volkov."

"Wait." She straightened. "Are we closer than we realized?"

"No. No, but we stayed in a place out here. A hut."

He turned to find her watching him closely. Maybe she wasn't quite ready to pull on that fiber-thin thread yet, but he was.

"One of the Russians called this place Baba Yaga's Lock." He leaned back and admired the sharp peaks. What appeared high and aggressive from this direction smoothed out on the other side. "I see it now. See how they look like the edge of a key?"

"Yeah," she breathed. "So, how far is this hut?"

"Just over that rise." It was hard not to let excitement buoy his flagging muscles. "Don't get excited, though. If they've cleaned it out for the winter, we'll..." *Die anyway.* He couldn't finish the sentence. And it apparently didn't matter to Angel, who'd already set off for the summit.

They didn't crest until late in the afternoon. And even then, it took a while to find the hut.

At first, he thought it was a sastrugi or some other impermanent geographical structure.

"I see it! There. I see it!"

Please, God. Let there be food. A fucking cracker could hold them for another day.

The closer they got, the boxier the structure appeared, with a second smaller building close beside it.

Hope pushed his legs a little harder, lightened the load behind him.

This was it—the field research hut, built by Norwegians maybe a couple decades before.

The hope he'd kept tamped down strengthened into a lifeline, pulling him toward the place.

Ice and snow had piled up around the bigger building, so high that only one roof corner remained visible. Was the door accessible? Shit, where was it? Maybe on the other side? He dropped the sled line, kicked off his skis, and sped around the corner, Angel right beside him.

He stopped and stared at the mound of snow, with the barest peek of metal showing. How the hell were they supposed to find the door, much less get in?

Angel grabbed his hand, as naturally as if they did this every day. Which he guessed they did.

"What's it for?"

"Field research camp, originally, but I heard trekking companies sometimes use it as a way station. Russians come out pretty much every year to run some tests."

Silently, they stared.

"There, where it's sticking out," she said.

As good a place to start as any. He squeezed her hand before heading back around for the shovel and ice axe.

For ages, they chipped away at what revealed itself to be the door. Ford hacked and Angel hauled, their rhythm steady but slow. The last thing they needed was to break into a sweat.

He took a swig of water and looked around. Had it gotten darker?

"What's it like in there?"

"Bare bones—just an insulated steel hut and a generator. Which is…" He pointed to the other building. "There."

"You think…"

"I don't know, Angel. I don't know."

There was a chance, after all this, that it would be empty, without a crumb, a lick of fuel, or a spark of hope inside. He remembered with surprising clarity that when he'd been here, someone had left one of those megapacks of cheese puffs. The little balls that melted on your tongue and provided absolutely no nutritional value.

His mouth watered as he let himself go a little, picturing all those foods he'd never gotten to eat as a kid. Dad was strict about junk food. Sugar, as far as he was concerned, was utterly useless. He shook his head and did his best to blink back the memory, which was harder than usual.

It didn't make it any easier, knowing that this was hunger playing tricks on him. As if, while his body metabolized its own musculature, his brain turned to memories for sustenance. Big, fat, unexplored memories, so long-buried they felt new. So new, he could taste them.

Forty-five minutes later, they'd uncovered the door. It was frozen firmly closed. After a good fifteen minutes' struggle, bringing into service their hands, then the axe, and finally the shovel, it still wouldn't budge. Hopelessness had just started to settle over them when Angel disappeared and returned, holding one of her chef's knives like a magic wand.

She chiseled away at the seam, he yanked, and... *halle-freaking-lujah*!

The door flew open to reveal...more snow. A three-foot pile of it right in their path. Angel groaned, but he'd expected this, since he'd seen storms shove ice through cracks in doors and windows. The layer of ice around the door was probably the only reason the inside hadn't packed any fuller than this.

He didn't care, though, because beyond the obstacle, the place was remarkably clear. And there, at the farthest end of the room, was a kitchen corner. On the shelves were boxes and cans and bags of food. He stepped over the mound and stomped across the snow-dusted floor, hoping against hope that the boxes weren't empties left by some lazy asshole. He picked up a can. Full. A package of what looked like cookies or crackers or something—impossible to tell from the Cyrillic writing—also full. Beside it, some kind of dried stew, Indian food, curries in packets... Food for days.

He turned, startled to find Angel right beside him instead of back in the doorway. She'd come in so quietly.

His mouth opened and closed when he met those big warm eyes fixed not on the food, but on him. *Him.*

And her expression—he couldn't explain it exactly, but it did something to him, made him feel…different. Alive and whole and responsible, somehow, for this miracle.

"I didn't put this here," he said, one hand up to keep her from putting too much faith in him. "Didn't even remember this place."

"I know," she said with a funny half smile and a nod. She stepped around him and reached for a can, which she slapped onto the counter with a satisfying thud. "Let's eat."

CHAPTER 34

Day 13—Norwegian Field Research Camp, 142 Miles from Volkov Station

THERE WAS A STRANGE THING HAPPENING IN ANGEL'S body. Or maybe her mind.

The feeling, she thought, might be happiness.

They'd eaten first, scarfing crackers like animals in the frigid hut, then found the generator and fuel. Not a lot, but enough, maybe, to warm the place for a couple days and, probably most important of all, to charge up Ford's sat phone.

He was out there now, hopefully getting the generator up and running.

She emptied the packet of freeze-dried whatever it was into the pot on their camp stove. Now that they'd slaked that first rabid hunger with some dry, bark-like crackers, they'd eat something hot.

A few seconds later, she groaned at the moist warmth wafting up to her. She had no idea what it was she was heating. It could have been dog food for all she knew. Didn't matter.

Just as she spooned the contents into two bowls, an engine started growling, the sound so out of place it took her a dozen beats to realize what it was. Breath held, hope suspended, she waited for a few seconds for it to sputter out. When it didn't, she put down the pan, turned—

And there he was in the doorway, like magic. He slammed the door shut and took a couple steps inside.

Holy crap, the generator worked.

But that wasn't what made her heart clench. It was the smile on Ford's face when he wrenched off his mask—wide and open and honest, an echo of that boy he'd described, fishing on the island with his brother.

That smile split his face and hit her with the blinding force of a gale.

It took every bit of willpower not to run and throw herself into his arms. And then, because willpower was for staying alive, not for fighting the inevitable or denying the truth, she tripped forward and let her body collide with his, wrap around it, sink into him. She wanted to celebrate every vital, warm piece of him, to revel in him as if *he* were the feast.

Speaking of which… "You need hot food." She started to pull back.

"Yeah." He didn't let go.

"Ford."

"Just…"

Just this. Just them. Here, holding each other up, breathing together. Just breathing.

Alive.

One of them pulled away, eventually, probably him since the man was an expert at denial. Or waiting or hiding or whatever he'd been doing all these years.

She led him to the room's single table, where they sat, still suited up, and ate.

The first swallow was too quick, barely making it to her stomach before she went for another. This one laid a warm path, waking up taste buds while it made way for the third—a long, slow slide into bliss. She groaned.

"Jesus." Ford sounded angry.

"What?" She lifted surprised eyes to his. "Don't like it?"

"No. It's good. Perfect."

"Then—"

"That noise. The sound you made."

She watched him. "What?"

He blinked the fierceness away. "Never mind."

"No. What was wrong with—"

"Forget it."

"O-kay." She went back to the stew...and groaned again. "Best thing I've ever eaten."

"Right." Even with his face half-covered in ice, he looked skeptical.

"What?"

"You're a gourmet chef and *this* is the best?"

"It's all relative, isn't it?" She sucked in a deep breath and forced herself to take it easy. "I mean, the best thing I've probably eaten, taste-wise..." Holding the next warm, fragrant bite in her mouth, she put her head back, let it thaw her to life, and remembered. "Tomatoes. Fresh from the garden."

He didn't respond, so she went on. "Big beefsteaks, sliced, with nothing but a drizzle of olive oil. Dash of salt. Or better yet, those tiny sun golds. The orange ones? Right off the vine. One in the basket, one in your mouth. Warm from the sun." She paused, her brain hitching on something. An idea or memory or notion that seemed obvious, though she couldn't quite grasp it.

"When did you know you wanted to become a chef?"

"A chef?" She paused, that elusive thing just out of reach, like a scent she couldn't identify, the way tomato stems smelled like summer, but the fruit itself provided the taste. "I never wanted to be a chef. I wanted to *cook*."

"Not the same thing?"

She shook her head. "No. One's about status and accomplishments. Who people think you are." Hugh. Hugh was a chef. "The other's about…" Understanding shimmered through her, real and pure and brand-new, but old as that first taste of Mama's pupusas. "Cooking's like making music." She threw him a smile. "It's the perfect storm of smell and touch and taste and even sound, you know? That sizzle in the pan, the pop of spices. The moment you turn the heat off and there, *right there*, the ingredients let off a warm, enveloping steam." He watched her with a puzzled look on his face, like she spoke a foreign language that he wanted to understand. "Cooking is knowing to let that tomato speak for itself, to leave it alone instead of piling a bunch of crap on top."

"When'd you start cooking?"

Her eyes shifted to the side. "Everyone else ate junk out of boxes, but Mama and I had a garden. Had to or we'd starve. Late summer, we canned, pickled, preserved. Everything we grew got put up for the winter. Worked till our hands were raw." She squinted at the memory. "Weird." Overwhelmed by something that felt an awful lot like loss, she shoved another bite in her mouth. This one tasted bitter and bland, cloying and salty.

"What?"

"Guess I lost it somewhere." In that kitchen with Hugh, striving for something she'd never really wanted.

"I eat to survive," he said matter-of-factly.

Something inside her clenched, hard. "Oh."

"Why do you look like that?"

"It's…sad."

"Is it?" He truly seemed to be asking.

She opened her mouth, then shut it. Was it sad to eat for survival? That was exactly what they were doing right here and the pleasure of it was almost blinding. In a way, it fed directly into what she'd been saying—that the best parts of food and cooking were the basics—need, ingredients, a little chemistry. "Guess not."

It put a sad spin on her previous life and an even sadder one on Hugh's, with its layers of wants and needs, disappointments and other complications.

She must have sat there for a while, because when Ford finally spoke, she had to shake herself free from the sticky web of memories and regrets.

"You like making people happy."

Her eyes flew to him. "Huh?"

"There's the actual cooking, but there's also the people part. That's why you do it."

Why would he say that?

Her first instinct was to deny it, because wanting to please people wasn't all that flattering a reason to do anything. It made her feel stripped. Naked.

Another moment came back to her. "I grew up in rural Pennsylvania. Green, sweet, innocent."

He nodded at her to go on.

"I remember being nine or ten. Second day of school, there was this new kid. He was different. Harder than most of us. Scruffy and lean. His clothes were worn, like mine, but not as nice. Mama wouldn't let me out of the house with a hole or a ripped seam. He was one of the free lunch kids." She shrugged. "Me too, technically, except Mama would never let me eat that stuff. I had my lunch box every day. Anyway, Travis—that was his name—sat at my table one day with a processed sloppy joe on his plate. I'll never forget the way he stared. At a peach." Just the word felt like biting into one— the hard *p* of teeth through skin, the tart, fresh, sweet blast to the tongue, and there at the end, a soft sink into flesh.

"You're right," she said, weirdly shell-shocked, like Ford had split her open and seen her own soft insides. "It's *not* about the food. I mean, it is, but it's about people. I used to have this fantasy, like, giving someone their first…I don't know, perfectly cooked green bean with butter. You know?"

"Stop it," he groaned. "My mouth's like a fountain."

"Thought you didn't care about food, Ford Cooper."

"Maybe I do now."

She let those words sink in and then hardened her voice with a sly little smile. "Avocados with salt."

"Don't."

"Mango." She gave him an innocent look. "Fresh off the tree, so ripe you bite right in, juice dripping down your—"

"You're evil."

"No. No, you are."

"How so?" he said, looking mock-offended.

"Come on. Last night. All that talk of warm nights and fishing with your brother under the stars when we're in this constant daylight."

"Wanna see stars? Stay here for the winter. Nothing but stars. The aurora australis, man, it's…"

She couldn't tear her eyes from him, but her mouth opened on its own, offering up a word. "Dreamy?"

"Like all your life, the sky's been hiding in plain sight." He put down his food and leaned back, giving her a rare shot of his neck, bisected by angry red scar tissue. "Wearing funeral clothes or something. Dark, thick fabric, with just a glimmer of diamonds. And suddenly, one night, you look up and she's letting you in on her big secret, doing the dance of the seven veils. Wrapping them around you until you're caught in her ephemeral net." He swallowed, lowered his head, and met Angel's eyes with his, and they were rife with the complexity and hidden secrets of this constantly shifting place. "That's the ice, Angel. Infinite, ever-changing, magical." She could get addicted to this man. Maybe she already was. "With depths none of us will ever get to plumb."

A sound escaped her—half gasp, half sob. She covered her mouth, but not quickly enough.

"You okay? Angel?"

"Why'd you have to go and do that?"

"Do what?" he said with a puzzled smile.

"Be so…" Beautiful, solid. *Good.* She could only shake her head, finally tearing her eyes away. "Never mind."

He rose. "Come here."

Like a moth to a flame, mesmerized or hypnotized or something, Angel went to him, giving herself up to Ford Cooper's ephemeral net.

CHAPTER 35

"Come here," Coop said, shocked at his own words and the way he met her halfway.

Honestly, though, this wasn't him. Ford Cooper didn't hug. He shook hands or shared body heat. The one because society dictated it, the other to survive. And sex, of course, was peppered in there because his libido wanted it. But that was just the occasional itch he scratched.

None of it could have prepared him for what he felt now. This hunger was different, as strong as the one gnawing at his belly, but more widespread, impossible to pin down. It filled his head and lungs, only calming when she stepped into his arms.

He didn't just want her body. He wanted *her*.

He'd denied it out there, turned it into something else, about survival and body heat and closeness that saved lives. But here, in the growing warmth from the heaters, with enough space to breathe, he couldn't lie. Couldn't look away.

He bent his head, let his eyes roam her soft features—a novelty after touching only in the dark—and, like a man still starving, kissed her.

For three long seconds, he felt nothing, as if the jolt was too much, the connection too hot, too electric, to register. And Jesus, it was. *She* was. Like defibrillator paddles to his chest. He sucked at her, took a life-giving breath from her lungs, gave his own.

Don't blink. Don't forget a second of this.

Watching her kiss him, watching her watch him, was one of those never-ending mirror portraits, with no beginning and no end. He was lost in it. Like he'd fallen into a maze. Ensnared. No way in, no way out.

No way out.

With a gasp like a drowning man, he stumbled back a step and put his hand to his mouth—not to wipe her away, but to hold her there.

"You okay?" She was upset. He'd upset her.

He nodded. "Let me…" A blind look around supplied an answer. "Get water. For a bath." He almost groaned at that image. Clean, fresh, warm skin. Shit, there was something wrong with him. He'd short-circuited himself with that kiss, blown some neural connections that he'd never get back.

"Be right back," he mumbled, barely remembering to snag his mittens and pull on his hood before heading out.

With relief, he let the cold soak into him. Wake him up. Only it didn't clear his mind the way it always did. It didn't push the feelings back to where he could handle them, in the shadowed confines of a sleeping bag. It froze away the bullshit, let it crackle and fall, leaving nothing but the ice-cold core of reality.

Which was what? That he was an idiot? Scared of a woman because she let her emotions show? Because she lured out his own?

Thwack, thwack. He dug deeper at the ice, pushed his body harder, instinct the only thing stopping him from going over the edge into sweat.

He stood. Looked across the ice—*his* ice—and waited for his usual distance to take hold. The aloofness that let him separate things out enough to handle them one at a time.

Instead, all he could see were those warm dark eyes,

open, defenseless—swirling with a mixed-up mess of emotions, with him at the center.

He wasn't anybody's sun. He didn't want to be. He certainly *shouldn't* be. A sun was warm, giving, constant.

The opposite of him.

Shit, it was dark out here. He reached to yank off his goggles, surprised to find that he wasn't wearing them.

So, what the hell was—

A long, slow scan of the horizon confirmed what his eyes were trying to tell him: the sun was setting, melting into the earth like the world's longest-burning candle.

Night had come to Antarctica.

He threw down the shovel, grabbed the bucket of ice, and stomped back inside to tell her about the sunset.

He shut the door and opened his mouth. "I like you." Not what he'd planned to say.

She stopped what she was doing. "I like you, too." Her words came out slower than his, more careful.

"Okay." Relief spread through him, warm and slow. "Here." He set the ice down, overcome by an absurd flash of himself as a caveman, throwing some freshly killed beast at his woman's feet. An offering. "Make water. For you."

Jesus, how eloquent. He rubbed his hand over his face, surprised to hear the tinkle of frost falling from his beard to the floor. He hadn't been out there long enough to freeze over, had he?

Probably.

Goddamn, he was screwed, in ways he didn't even understand.

"Be right back." He threw open the door and paused at the explosion of color. Wait. He'd meant to show her. "Look, Angel."

With a gasp, she hurried to his side. "It's like a painting."

He nodded. The colors sizzled on the surface, looking hot enough to burn a hole in the earth, but the second they disappeared, the temperature would drop. Thankfully for just a couple hours tonight, then more the next night and the next. Eventually, it would dip below the horizon and wouldn't come back up until spring. Close to four months of darkness.

Did she know how cold it would get now? Did she understand how lucky they were to have found this place today of all days?

A glance at the awe on her expressive face told him that she knew.

Another wave of protectiveness overtook him and he moved to close the door, to keep the heat in, to keep her safe. "I'll get more ice." At her nod, he stepped outside, calmer than before, more accepting of his emotions, though he couldn't begin to control them any more than he could stop the sun from setting.

He didn't believe in fate or a higher power or any of that other crap, but something had brought them together here and now.

Inevitable. That was how it felt. And he was tired of fighting it. He wouldn't win. He couldn't. Not against this unavoidable pull. Even now, with a metal wall between them, he felt her tug, as sure as gravity, as inexorable as the ebb and flow of the tides.

As the last rays of light faded from the sky, he took his bucket and went back inside, floating on a warm wave of surrender.

CHAPTER 36

SHE WAS BEHIND A CURTAIN, TAKING A SPONGE BATH. This would have been fine if she didn't groan. In pleasure, Coop thought, though he stilled, head tilted, and waited for confirmation.

Within seconds, he was pure steel, big and heavy and hungry.

There'd been no room for lust in the enforced closeness of the tent. Here, though, in seconds, it overflowed, overwhelmed, overstimulated.

He collapsed into a chair and put his hands to his ears. He needed earplugs so he could stop hearing those noises. So he could stop picturing her back there, all warm and wet and fresh-smelling. Ready.

What felt like hours later, but was probably about eight minutes, she emerged, looking scrubbed and relaxed, rosy and happy. It was all he could do not to take her into his arms and soak some of that in.

Without a word, he grabbed his only change of clothes, the pan of freshly warmed water, and went behind the curtain to take care of his own business.

Which was even more of a nightmare than he'd imagined, because no matter what he did, he couldn't get his erection to go down. He swiped himself with soap and choked back a noise. Another swipe, another sound barely swallowed.

Had she been doing this back here? Touching her own skin for the first time in days and reveling in it? Were her nerve endings this sensitive to every little thing? He could swear he felt the individual soap bubbles popping against his goose-bumped skin. Heavenly torture.

An uncontrollable sound broke from his mouth—a growl. Dammit. He would come if he kept picturing her lathered in soap, pleasuring herself and—

"You okay in there?" There was humor in her voice. Which was understandable, but it also made him a little bitter. How could she stand out there and listen to him suffer, with absolutely no idea of what he was going through? How could she just sit there and giggle, controlling his feelings, working his insides like a master puppeteer, while he stood here in anguish?

"How…" The sound of her voice made him still, breath solid in his lungs. "How should I set up these beds? Should I…" *Do it. Do what you're thinking. Don't ask, don't make me acknowledge this thing. Any more than I have.* "Put them together?" Another long silence. "For warmth, I mean."

The dam broke and his hand slid tightly down his cock, then back up. Could she hear the slick sound through the generator's hum? "Prob'ly should." The words came out as a grunt, punctuated at the end by a hard-fisted turn at the crown.

"Yeah." Was she as breathless as she sounded or was he imagining that? "Definitely…safer."

The camp bed scraped on the rough metal floor and he gritted his teeth against a wave of pleasure-pain, shooting up from his dick to the rest of him. Christ, this would hurt if he came. He couldn't though. He couldn't come with just a curtain between them. It would be—

"I might as well zip the bags together, too. I mean, I can see my breath in here, so…" A hiccup of sound. "For the best."

His next "yeah" was more of a grunt than a word, and Jesus Christ, she *had* to know what he was doing.

———————————

Angel had dried off from her bath, but she was soaking. Not just wet, but heavy and warm and downright horny. Like back-seat-of-a-car horny. Like do-it-against-a-wall, just-put-it-in-me-before-I-die turned on.

And he'd clearly enjoyed bathing as much as she had.

He was out now, flushed and fresh and young-looking. A glance at her hand showed that she was visibly shaking. Nerves. Excitement. Anticipation.

Shoving it all down, she slid into the bag, turned on her side, and shut her eyes. Sleep would fix this. Or whatever else might happen.

It didn't take long for him to join her, at once familiar and a stranger. The smell of his skin enveloped her, as comforting as fresh bedsheets, hot like sunshine on sand. She'd never forget this smell. Never.

He lay behind her, utterly still. No arm around her. Just breathing, a little lighter than his usual deep, steady rhythm—faster, too, maybe.

Was he nervous? Or was she imagining it? Projecting, probably.

Her neck grew warm from his exhalations. Was he drawing closer? Was that…

Angel shuddered at the feel of his lips on her nape, and though she wanted to press back into him, she forced herself to wait instead. Let him give without pushing too hard in return. He liked giving, her lone wolf, needed to take the first step in his own good time.

He moved in, set his chin on her shoulder, and whispered, "I can't..."

When he didn't go on, she turned slightly to the right, enough to put the tips of their noses together. "Can't what?"

"Can't stop wanting you."

"Why would you want to?" She swallowed, for the first time worried about what kind of terrible answer he might come up with.

Instead of something dire, he puffed out a laugh and rubbed his nose gently against her temple. "You mess with my self-control." A pause and a shift and then his hand was on her hip, just resting there. Slowly, he stroked under her shirt, then up her waist, to where she was braless and more than ready. She gasped, he inhaled, the sounds harsh. "Afraid I'll lose it."

"You won't be alone."

"No?" Lightly, he held her breast, just held it, and it felt like the opposite of losing it. The Ice Man, weighing her, sussing her, assessing her. That sent a tingling rush down her spine, to the hot, heavy place between her legs. "You feel a loss of control?"

"Never..." She lost track of her words when his hand twisted to run the back of his knuckles along her achingly hard nipple. "Never had control to begin with."

He paused, her nipple caught between two fingers, just trapped there, but even that arrested position was torment—no movement, no pull, nothing.

She couldn't help the low sound that escaped her open mouth, which she had no memory of opening.

Painfully slow, he twisted his hand, just enough to tweak her there and everything inside her tightened, already gearing up for orgasm.

More rushed now, he let her go, reached down for the bottom of her shirt and pulled it to just over her breasts, exposing them to the cold air. His face turned, his mouth found the bare, tender skin just under her ear, and he licked her. "Shit happens when I lose control." His busy right hand went from one breast to the other, squeezing, weighing, stroking. Every move still measured—cold, almost—and very, very focused.

What was it about the coolness of him that made her so damned hot? All stern and seductively scientific, as he melted her into a useless puddle of want, right here, in the middle of nowhere.

The center of her universe.

A light pinch to her left breast shoved a gasp from her lungs and pushed her bottom back into his crotch. He was hard behind her. And she was ready.

It was cold here, but they could take off their clothes for a bit without risking frostbite. And she wanted to.

She turned her head. "Ford?" His arm tightened around her chest, making her think of a kid with a toy he wouldn't let go of or a dog with a bone who'd rather die than drop it.

"What?" Oh, he sounded mean. A good mean. Scary in a way that made her grit her teeth and push her breast harder into that proprietary grip.

"I've got an IUD. Not the copper kind. One of those…" *Shut up. He doesn't need the details.* Or maybe he did. A man like him would want to know. "The plastic ones. With hormones."

"Mm-hm." She couldn't see him, but she could picture his serious face, fiercely concentrated.

"So we can…have sex." She paused. Had she gone too far? "If you want."

"If I want." A hard tweak, a press of his hips, and his hand ran over her stomach to the waist of her pants. "Is that what *you* want?"

Slowly, carefully, callused fingers went lower, and though she could have sworn his breath hitched when he didn't encounter underwear, the hand didn't waver. Down, through her curls, to where she awaited him, heavier and wetter than she'd ever been.

Quickly, as if he couldn't wait any longer now that she'd broached the subject, he parted her lips, ran his fingers back and forth through all that moisture, and found her clit.

"Oh God. That's good." It was good. But it was just his hand and she wanted more.

She gasped when he picked up speed. Jesus, right to the point, wasn't he?

"Is it?"

Bleary and confused, she half turned to where he hunched over her, close enough to see his eyes, intense and demanding. "Is what?"

"Is that what you want, Angel? Me inside you?"

CHAPTER 37

THERE WERE RULES TO SEX. RULES THAT COOP HAD PUT into place in order to maintain the order in his brain. In his life.

And Angel was doing her best to bust right through them.

Step one: make sure she's wet. Step two: hit the erogenous zones to get her wetter. Step three: make her come. Step four: slip on condom…and so on. Sex was great that way. Neat, reciprocal, consensual. Free of all that messy emotional shit.

While he wanted to turn this woman over, rip off her pants, and pound into her, he couldn't and still be the man he'd fought to become all these years in Antarctica.

So he pushed her to the edge with his fingers, his only concession to his own pleasure the lazy circles his pelvis rubbed against her ass.

And this ass… He sighed, though the sound came out harsher than that. This ass was the stuff his dreams were made of. The ass of a woman who enjoyed her food. Who cooked it and tasted it and shared it with others. He tightened his hips, pulled his hand from between her legs, and yanked at her pants—two layers of fabric. With her help, he got them down, past the ass in question, and… *Damn.*

He gave it a light squeeze, just to feel the way it moved. "Got to calm down." He was breathing like he'd run a race.

"Why?"

"Don't want to get too worked up."

"What'll happen?"

His only response was a single shake of his head.

"Maybe I want to see you worked up."

He squeezed her again, to still her, maybe. But of course, with her, it had the opposite effect. She undulated against him, half turning onto her back, forcing him back, too. And then, he just had to see her, so he unzipped the bag, letting in air so cold it made them both gasp.

Her breasts were big, their tips dark and tight. "Damn, you're beautiful." Beneath them, her ribs were visible, definitely sharper than they'd been back at the base. Two weeks of hard trekking would do that to a person. But he could picture the way she'd looked with more meat on her bones, and he liked it. He liked everything about her from the warm, bright sparkle in her eyes to the fact that she was kicking her pants the rest of the way off without any prompting. Her eagerness was a mirror of his—a magnifying glass.

And maybe, just maybe he could let loose with Angel. Maybe he could be himself. If he could find that person under the layers and layers of restraint.

"Yours, too."

"Hm?" He blinked blearily.

"Your pants. Get 'em off."

He hurried to do it, the movements awkward and rushed, and reminiscent of his first time. This sort of felt like a first time. Or the last.

They could die here, still miles from safety.

I want you before I die.

Half-naked, he settled in the junction of her legs, his erection between their bellies. Just as he was about to shift down to remedy that, she tugged at his shirt. "This, too. Off. Or up, if you're—"

Cold, she'd been about to say. But he didn't give her time. He was up, shirt shucked, then back over her before she could finish.

Her giggle snapped his eyes to hers.

"What?"

"You're amazing."

He frowned. Was she kidding? "What are you—"

"You were always such a detached jerk. On the outside." When he opened his mouth to interrupt, she put a hand to his lips and stopped him. "But it was an act. I get that now." Straining up, she put her lips to his and kissed him so tenderly he couldn't hold himself up anymore. He sifted his fingers through her thick, soft hair and gave in. Gently at first, then deeper, their tongues playing, exploring, they finally learned each other's faces in the murky light of this place. Their bodies did the same, shifting, sliding, pressing together. Skin to skin. Bliss.

They were in a shitty research hut in Antarctica, but it felt like a five-star hotel. In Paris, he thought. Or someplace like that. Wherever she wanted. Another deep kiss, a shimmy, a wordless promise. He'd take her there.

If they survived this, he'd take her anywhere.

When he opened his eyes, it was like he'd walked through a wall and come out the other side different.

"You're crying." He wiped a tear from her cheek with the back of his finger.

"No I'm not." She smiled and he smiled back, wiping another tear as it leaked straight from her eye. The next one he kissed.

It took a while for him to notice the way her body twisted under his, seeking him out.

He lifted, shifted, then lost his air when her hand reached

into the space between them and grasped his erection. She pressed it down, rubbed herself, covering him in her wetness, and notched him against her. Right where he wanted to be.

He emptied his lungs and pressed in. Slowly, caught in her eyes, in her body's embrace, the slow, tight perfection of it.

One of them moaned.

"Feel so good," he said.

She bit her bottom lip and nodded.

He couldn't get purchase with his foot on the too-short cot, so he bent his knees, lifting her thighs, and pressed in. Oh God, that…that was better than his hand. Better than the first time. Better than any sex he'd ever had.

Another push, this one satisfyingly deep. All the way in, though he craved more—an amorphous, inexplicable something else that floated just beyond his comprehension.

But Jesus, Coop wouldn't trade *this* for the world. Nothing about it. Not the struggle across the ice, not the moment he'd almost lost her. He'd starved for this experience. And he'd suffer again for it. Over and over, if he had to.

On that terrifying thought, he wrapped one hand around the edge of the cot, slid the other under her unbelievably fine ass, and completely lost it.

Angel couldn't stop crying.

It wasn't from hurt, exactly, although her knee would regret this in the morning, but it felt close to it. Like pain, deep and untouched and really, really hard to face. Like pleasure so deep and tender that it came full circle to brush the other side.

Something snapped inside Ford. She watched him go from calculating, to a little lost, then finally a bit…feral.

The thing was, she really liked this animal part. Pounding into her, twisting her body, turning it, bending, pushing, all so he could get closer, deeper. Thrusting into her like he'd die if he didn't.

And she felt it, too. She needed this thing. *Passion*, she'd call it, if it hadn't felt more primal than that.

She was seeing him for the first time. The real Ford. She'd cracked the shell to find the man inside.

Carefully, she swiped a drop of sweat from his forehead and cradled his head for a few seconds, until it became necessary to grasp his shoulder, then his hip, and finally, when he hit that magic spot inside her, his ass.

Each of his hard thrusts scooted the cot toward the metal wall, where it banged like thunder, causing cans and boxes to crash to the floor.

It was hilarious on one level. On another, when she looked him in the eye and he hit that high, bright place just right… No hilarity. Just frightening intensity and a deadly seriousness.

She let out a sound—weak and a little frantic.

He leaned down in response and kissed her again, slowed his movements, twisting his hips, so he got the spot every time and, rather than getting screams now, he forced her into one long, low moan of pleasure. She managed to slip her hand between them, slid along their hot and cold skins to her clit, touched herself once, and…

Fireworks. Blasting, bright, over-the-top. *Everything*.

Every nerve, every pore, every cell focused hard on this connection they shared. Or rather the two connections that mattered right this second—the one between their legs and the one up top—gazes entwined, caught, never letting go.

Oh my God, I do love him.

The thought came and went, a quick, potent electric jolt, the current so fast she almost didn't notice it. After he'd held still, riding out the craziest, most emotional orgasm of her life, she urged him with her hand to keep going. Prodded him to his own pleasure, so she wouldn't feel so alone with all of these feelings.

He pushed faster, harder, the expression on his wide-boned face so close to pain she almost worried for him. But she'd seen him in pain and this was something else. She had to stroke him, from his flank up to his chest, over those big, hard planes—the chest she'd thought about way too often out on the ice. Or maybe just often enough to keep her going.

Saved by his massive pecs.

She smiled at that and he smiled back, slowing, breathing hard. Way too sweaty to be safe in Antarctica. His eyes flicked between hers, a question there.

"Don't have to stop," she said. "IUD, remember?"

They shared another kiss and he picked up the pace again. Determination in his features this time—a race to the finish. And though she hadn't expected to go there with him, it started to feel like maybe she had another orgasm in her.

Her hips lifted to meet his thrust for thrust, each one shoving the cot farther along the floor while it shook her to her foundations. This time she came without her hands, with only the friction of their bodies and the intensity of those eyes pushing her over the edge.

No explosions this time. No way could she crest that high again. But the *feelings* were there…the rush, the tightness, the tingling. He pumped into her a few messy times and then one final, deep press, his head cradled against her shoulder before he collapsed. Not quite a dead weight but almost.

Around them lay the destruction of a room fucked to pieces, their stuff everywhere. Like a storm had come through.

Above her, Ford's body heaved. Exhausted and probably overcome.

She wrapped around him and held on to him—this big, tender loner of a man. The man who'd saved her life more than once. Funny how somehow, suddenly, right this moment, she felt like he'd torn it all apart.

CHAPTER 38

It took Coop forever to fight his way through the fog of emotion, find his muscles and lift his weight off her. But he finally did, figuring they hadn't gotten this far for him to crush her to death.

He leaned back, expecting to have to explain his outburst. The frantic fucking hard enough to move the damn bed across the room. They hadn't discussed any of that ahead of time. Not that he could've warned her anyway, since he hadn't planned it.

It all felt so big, so good, that it hurt.

When he finally let himself focus on Angel, the last thing he expected to see was a smile on her face.

She'd come. He was sure of that. Twice, even.

"What?"

"The…the…" She gasped, caught her breath, and went on. "The Ice Man…cometh." She descended into giggles again and he smiled.

"Hm?"

"It's a play. A movie, too, I think." When he didn't respond, she stopped laughing and cleared her throat. "Guess you haven't heard of it."

He shook his head, surprised to find a happy smile glued to his face now. "Nope," he tried to say, but crap, nothing came out. His voice was gone. Shot to hell from sex. From her.

"Too bad. It was pretty funny. In my head at least." She tightened around his softening cock and he shut his eyes to isolate the sensation.

"It *is* funny," he whispered. His chest was all strange—big and hollow. "You're funny."

"Yeah?" What was it about her expression that made him think she was asking something else? Something more serious.

He lost the grin and nodded. *Yes. Yes, whatever your question is. Though it hurts to feel like this, I'm right here with you.*

Damn, she was beautiful. Tough, strong, and so tender he didn't know what to do with her.

Maybe nothing. Maybe they'd die out here and he wouldn't have to commit to anything beyond this.

That made him feel shitty again. Would he seriously rather die than get emotionally involved with a woman?

Pathetic.

"You're still inside me and already you're gone." She caressed the side of his face, those big wet dark eyes boring into him like one of his drills. "Aren't you?"

"What do you mean?" He hated having to whisper. It made him seem weak, though he was just…

Weak.

"You were Ford and now you're back to being the Ice Man. Removed from it all. Above it, maybe."

That was how she saw him? Removed? It sent a strangely mixed response through him—guilt, because he didn't want to make her feel bad, but a thin strain of pride that the control was still there. He hadn't lost it by giving himself up to her. Good.

Something sad ghosted over her features and she turned away.

"What?" He half smiled, trying to catch her eye.

"I like the *real* Ford."

He started to shake his head and stopped. Opened his mouth and shut it. Twice.

"Okay." He finally gave in because she made him happy in a way he couldn't begin to understand. And who knew how much time they had?

He leaned forward and kissed her, hardening again.

Her brows rose. "You're kidding."

"Not even a little," he told her with a grin.

Day 14—Chronos Corporation Headquarters, Stromville, West Virginia

"My team found something, ma'am."

Irritated at the interruption, Katherine Henley Harper lifted her head from perusing the day's paper, blinking. Another school killing, which only confirmed what she knew to be true—the world needed cleansing. Not a bomb, because Mother Earth didn't deserve that. More like antibodies attacking a disease. A good, clean surgical intervention.

And like any good surgeon, she'd identified the problem. Or problems. A segment of the population needed eradication. It was as simple as that.

Pull the weeds and a garden would flourish. Leave them to grow and the precious plants would be choked out. The plants needed water—which was exactly how she planned to deliver her blow. Over the past few years, Chronos had formed partnerships with water companies throughout the nation, becoming an essential part of the country's very infrastructure. Water treatment and purification.

Population purification.

Exactly like pulling weeds. Those given the vaccine

would flourish, and the others would simply...wilt away to nothing. Good would prevail. The earth would prevail.

Her eyes closed as she pictured her father's garden, where she'd spent her most formative years. Every flower had its place, with—

"Ma'am."

She blinked a few times before narrowing her eyes at the middle-aged woman standing in her door. Bonnie? No. Brenda. Brenda Lassiter. A good find. Not groveling like that Tenny shithead or frightening like the military men the senator sent her way. Women, she found, were generally better employees than men. Smarter, less ego, more willing to work together. Unfortunately, they often had a strong, though skewed, sense of right and wrong. Which was why she was forced to work with people like Tenny. Men whose moral compass had broken somewhere along the way.

She eyed Brenda. Though short and a little fat at the hips, the woman had a steel core. Unflinching.

"Yes?"

"We located them."

Katherine racked her sluggish brain. "Them?" She hated how wobbly her voice had gotten with old age. Weak.

"I had my people do a grid search of the area between Burke-Ruhe and Volkov—and there's someone out there."

The fog she spent most of her time in cleared and everything came back—those fools losing the precious virus samples and heading back to the station, where they'd found nothing. Days—no, weeks—of searching had produced nothing.

She would have to let the entire security team go once this was over. They'd failed on all levels. Spectacularly. And then there was Clive Tenny to contend with—a holdout from her father's era. He'd stuck with the company, but goodness, the man was irritating.

"Could they be ours?"

"I confirmed that ours returned to the Harper Research Facility. I believe the people we have located are on foot."

Her eyes widened in surprise. "On foot!"

She put a hand on the arm of the settee and pushed, keeping her face blank, though the pain was excruciating. Worse every day. Which made this delay even more of an aggravation. She had to be here to see everything come to fruition. She turned to the photo on her desk—her two smiling babies, whose lives had been snuffed out so quickly, so unfairly.

For them. She would see this through for them.

"Show me." Despite the pain, she was proud to note her breathing was even. If it weren't for the cane, there'd be no outward sign of her own physical frailness.

Slowly, with the help of the damned stick, she followed Brenda out the door, down the short, bright hall, past what she thought of as the Widow's Window, overlooking the formal front garden, with its fountains and centuries-old boxwood allée, and through what appeared to be a simple paneled wooden door. Only it wasn't, of course.

Katherine watched Brenda enter her personal code, swipe, and press her hand to the scanner before swinging open the heavy steel panel to reveal the New Wing. A misnomer if ever she'd heard one. There was nothing wing-like about this great glass, metal, and concrete structure, dug deep into the mountain and rising to soar above it. If anything, the original house was the anomaly now. A wart more than a wing, regrettably, but the company's stature had required an update.

And there were certain things Katherine wouldn't—or couldn't—do, since she'd lost her babies. Such as leave her home to go to the office. Therefore, the office had come to her. Naturally.

After her home's warm woods, glowing lamps, and antique florals, the New Wing's bright modern glass and hard stone sheen put a slight hitch in her gait. She pushed through it, of course, lest her employee think she was anything but the strong, steadfast leader she'd always been.

They made their way down the hall, Brenda slowing to match Katherine's pace, which annoyed her to no end. They stopped at the elevator, again delivering handprints, retinal scans, and pass codes—necessary modern annoyances in this line of work—and descended to Floor -4, where this type of operation was handled.

In the bowels of her company's building, they entered to find the logistics team hard at work. Silent, staring, concentrated, most of them with those tiny plastic listening devices stuffed into their ears, there was nothing but the clicking of keys to prove that they were, in fact, in the realm of the living. Modern zombies.

He'd worn one of those ridiculous contraptions, the murderer who'd taken the lives of her grandchildren. His bullets had torn through their perfect little bodies, along with those of other children, their teachers, some parents—including her own daughter—all while piping music directly into his ears.

Something hard and heavy and electronic, no doubt. Although she didn't know. The police had never confirmed what he'd been listening to. And now, suddenly, she wanted to know. Desperately.

She'd turned to go, fueled by a dim idea of calling the

police superintendent, when Brenda's hand on her arm stopped her.

"Todd's the one who found them, ma'am."

Katherine blinked at the zombies, sitting in their expensive ergonomic chairs, bobbing their heads to the kind of music she'd never been able to stand. No artistry at all. Just the loud, constant thump of drumbeats.

At least these zombies worked for her. Though some of them, she knew from detailed reports, had somewhat distasteful pastimes outside these walls, they all excelled at their jobs.

Flustered by the way her mind had drifted, Katherine forced a smile to her stiff lips and focused on Brenda's pleasantly mature countenance.

"Todd, could you bring up the satellite photos you showed me earlier?" Brenda asked, voice as poised and modulated as Katherine's once was.

Without a word, the man did as he was told. There was perhaps a touch of hubris in the tilt of his head, but she laid that at the door of his youth.

Katherine turned and squinted at the screen, seeing nothing at first. What were they looking at? She wouldn't ask. Asking would make her appear weak in the mind. As much as she hated depending on a cane for ambulation, a failing body was nothing compared to a failing brain.

"This location is about halfway between Burke-Ruhe and our facility. This morning. Zoom in, please." Brenda stepped back to let Katherine look. "This"—she indicated with a laser pointer—"is evidently some structure. We have no record of ownership. Probably Russian. And *that*," she said, more excitedly, "is exhaust."

The screen wasn't entirely clear, the image blurry at the

edges, but still a miracle that they'd taken this photo from space. She could hardly fathom it.

"What else?"

"Close in, Todd." Brenda smiled, walked to the big screen, leaned up, and slapped something. "This."

Katherine squinted irritably. Could the woman not just spell it out, for heaven's sake? These images were minuscule and—

She couldn't contain a gasp. There, in the middle of the image, tiny but clear as day alongside an unidentifiable orange square, was a neat pile of metal tubes. "The—" *Virus*, she'd almost said, which wouldn't do, since keeping the various departments in the dark about this project was imperative. *Need to know* was of the essence when one was planning a mass cleansing of the world's population. All for the greater good, of course. She settled for "tubes" instead.

"Yep. We've got the samples. And the location. The clear solution is to prepare a team to go in as soon as the weather warms."

"I don't have *time* for that." She inhaled slowly to steady herself. Appearing erratic in front of the staff was hardly the best way to handle this. But good *God*, the frustration she'd felt when those imbeciles had flown the wrong samples to the Facility.

For the sake of appearances, she forced a smile to her parched lips and turned to Brenda. "Please send Sampson's team."

"No planes will fly in this—"

"They flew last week, didn't they? And again a few days ago? And I understand we've made airdrops in the dead of polar winter. Surely, now that we've located the samples, they can…" She shook her hand vaguely. "Parachute in or something. Take them. And return to the Facility."

Mutiny shone in Brenda's eyes and her dark skin took on a heated cast, her cheeks going pink. When Brenda opened her mouth, Katherine wasn't entirely sure which way she'd go, but the words "yes, ma'am" assuaged her fears.

Greater good. Those words, that idea, mattered to people like Brenda, who'd lost her mother to disease.

"Good." Orders given, she turned to go, then stopped and swiveled painfully. "And you, young man. What's your name again?"

He glanced at Brenda before looking back at her, which was both a good and bad sign—not so big for his britches that he'd overreach, though he clearly needed a lesson on who the boss was around here.

"Todd. Todd Jenkins, ma'am."

"Good work, Todd." She smiled a genuine, heartfelt smile. "You can expect a bonus for your efforts."

And possibly, just possibly, I'll let you keep your life when all of this is over.

CHAPTER 39

Day 14—Norwegian Field Research Camp, 142 Miles from Volkov Station

ANGEL WAS IN TROUBLE. DEEP, DEEP TROUBLE. WITH NO way out. Literally no way out, since she was stuck here with the object of her…affections? Gosh, that didn't really seem to encompass it. Obsession, maybe, although *hunger* felt more like it, given that what she felt for Ford was on a par with the stomach-gnawing pangs of starvation.

She turned from the percolating coffee to look at him now, sleeping, and had to swallow back a hot, mixed-up wave of feelings.

Crap. This wasn't supposed to happen. None of it, obviously, was *supposed* to happen, but *this* least of all.

Because this was going to hurt.

She poured a cup and went to one of the plastic chairs by the metal table, grabbed a blanket, and wrapped herself in it. It was a rough plaid, a little dusty, left by some previous traveler. A researcher like Ford, maybe.

Except not. Because nobody was like him.

Oh geez. Shut up!

For a few self-pitying seconds, she couldn't decide which was worse: the idea of the two of them dying in this place together or the certainty that they'd make it out—somehow—and this thing they had would fizzle to nothing. She'd head back to Pittsburgh to start over. And he'd stay.

"Drama queen," she whispered, sitting up straight.

How crazy was it to realize, in the middle of nowhere, at the ass end of the world, that happiness couldn't be measured in financial success or critics' reviews or stars. It was something else entirely.

It wasn't until Ford had said the words that she'd truly understood: Happiness, for her, was making meals for people. For people who appreciated her food, not just to *ooh* and *ahh* over absurdly hard-to-get ingredients—although, she thought with humor, that was certainly the case here— but for people who needed the sustenance. *Feeding* people. Their souls, their bodies. Their hearts. And helping them to feed their people.

Sounds emerged from the cot, where Ford stirred in the sleeping bag.

She counted silently to three, preparing for the impact before giving in to her urge to look his way.

Didn't work. At all. His sleepy smile hit her like a fist to the belly.

His eyes, a little puffy from a full night's sleep, were adorable. In fact, he'd never looked so soft and sweet. But even as she thought that, her gaze traveled over those thick, hard-looking shoulders, the muscles flexing with a raw-boned, lupine grace as he stretched. Even through the base layer he'd eventually put on, she could make out the deep divots and thick curves of his strong body.

They were so constrained in here, stuck in the cots, since the floor was frigid. She wanted to taste him everywhere, from that big slab of a chest, over each individual stomach muscle, then down that dark trail of hair to his... erection.

Her eyes flew up to meet his. They were focused and

intense now, not exactly his usual remote expression, but neither was he the soft, just-woken-up Ford she'd been lucky enough to catch seconds earlier.

"When you look at me like that…" Only half his words were vocalized, the rest carried out on a dark growl.

"What? What happens?" *What do you feel? Tell me.*

"Come here. I'll show you." Of course she couldn't deny him. Or *this*. The pull between them, so unbelievably shocking after the coolness from before.

She stood and walked the few steps, dropping the plaid and stripping off her pants as she went.

The chill enveloped her like an old friend, delivering shivers of cold mixed with pleasure. Would she feel this need, this ache in her soul, every winter for the rest of her life?

And maybe this pull wasn't shocking, actually. Maybe *he* had known, on some level, that this would happen if they got together. This explosive nuclear attraction that even two weeks on the ice couldn't kill. It was stronger than anything she'd felt—ever. And maybe he'd been afraid of it. Afraid like she was, now that she'd experienced it.

She pulled the sleeping bag from him, straddled his thighs, and tugged at his pants just enough to release his erection, which was—

Uh-oh. She had it bad when she thought a man's penis was beautiful, right? Penises weren't beautiful. They were floppy and ridiculous or weirdly slanted or too thick, too thin, too aggressive. But this one… She sighed and, rather than take him into her body as she'd planned, scooted lower to put her mouth on him.

He was half-hard now, not as big and stiff as he'd been pretty much all night, and she liked that, too. Liked every state of him. Each kiss and lick, each gentle suck sent blood to fill him, turned him to steel against her cheek, her lips. It made her feel softer, more delicate.

He tasted so human here, like sex, like her, the way he'd smelled in the tent—a scent specially blended for her.

She took him deep, enjoying the helpless, low, raspy sounds he let out. With a groan of her own, she took him in down, then back, until she wasn't thinking, just giving and taking pleasure. Though she wasn't sure at any specific moment who took and who received. She reached down and wasn't surprised to find herself soaking wet.

Even sucking him satisfied something inside her. His hand pushed her hair out of her face and held it there, gently. *Tighter*, she begged internally, *harder*.

Maybe she pulled away from him, because he complied by gripping her hair. That forced more sounds from her mouth, made her rub herself faster, and made her twist her head in his grip.

When his other hand urged her up, she let him go with a frown and he laughed. Or at least, he would have if he could make any noise.

"Come here," he mouthed, as he nudged her up and over him, so perfectly aligned that when she dropped her pelvis, she found him ready, right where she wanted.

Her eyes captured by his, she lowered her body as slowly as she could, needing to feel every second, every millimeter of this coming together. To hold on to, to remember, to unpack it later when she was gone and this man was just a memory carved out of the ice.

Sex with Angel was a whole new experience for Coop. Oh, the movements were the same—the in and out, the kissing and licking and rubbing and stroking—but the feelings were different.

She flexed over him, sliding up and down him as if she had all the time in the world.

Clearly, the situation had gotten to him. Fighting for survival, he understood, would do that to a person. It made emotions spring up from out of nowhere. It inspired sensations, even in his body, that he hadn't previously experienced. Thoughts, even.

Thoughts about the future. Like, maybe they had one.

Which was utter crap. He knew this, she no doubt knew it, but the part of him that he preferred to leave buried, the part she'd forced him to acknowledge, couldn't seem to get the picture.

He envisioned sharing a room together back at Burke-Ruhe. Or another station. Hell, he'd settle for the crowds at McMurdo, if she were a part of it. Maybe.

Jesus, he was doing this. He was considering changing his life for a woman. For *this* woman, the one who'd made him feel so threatened he couldn't talk to her.

Suddenly over this slow, sliding thing, he tightened his hands on her waist and pushed down hard, lifting his hips to get as deep as he could.

He needed to cut the hopeful bullshit. She wouldn't move here permanently.

And absolutely no way in hell would he leave this place for more than his yearly vacation to New Zealand and the States. Maybe, for that month or so, they could...what? Hang out?

He pressed harder, that thing inside him growing hopeless and grim. *No. It won't work.*

When she bent forward, probably to kiss him, he took over, turning it into a rough, harsh joining, rather than the sultry one she'd started. Their teeth clashed, their tongues battled, but then she pulled away, looking...hurt, maybe?

No. Angel was tough. She'd be fine.

In fact, she probably hadn't thought once about a future with him. She'd told him often enough that he was cold or whatever. The Ice Man, she called him.

She did a twisty thing with her pelvis, and rather than think about going back to civilization, he lost another little chunk of control, grabbed her body, and pivoted so he was on top.

This was better. He slowed, caught his breath, made his movements measured and deliberate. *Okay. Okay.*

He could do this. A few long, slow strokes to recenter himself. Good.

A hand on her breast. Hot and soft... He dipped, sucked her nipple into his mouth, and gasped at the way she tightened around him. A quick nip, then on to the other breast. He barely noticed his hips picking up speed, hardly felt the way his heartbeat went with it.

When he bent to meet her lush lips with a frantic kiss, it occurred to him that he'd sunk back into her siren's pull. She was so precious beneath him, her eyes full of life and affection and a good dose of challenge.

I can take you on, the look said. *I can turn you inside out and make you like it.*

And it was true. The problem was that he didn't know how he'd find himself again when this was all over.

CHAPTER 40

Day 15—Norwegian Field Research Camp, 142 Miles from Volkov Station

WHAT WAS THAT?

Angel awoke with a gasp, mouth open, heart thudding.

The beep came again, loud as a siren in the absolute quiet of the hut.

When it happened a third time, she shook Ford, who sprang awake immediately.

"Something beeped." The tension in his face made her add, "Like a phone. Maybe a phone."

Without a second's hesitation, he was up and out of their bed, racing to the communication console in the corner, with no care for his feet. She followed him, slower, grabbing shoes, warmer tops, and a blanket to put over his shoulders.

Apparently fully awake, he fiddled with buttons on what she'd have bet might have been the oldest communication system in the world. Was it a shortwave radio or something? No idea. It was hard to look away from his face and the sweet cowlick that had sprung up from the top of his head. She wanted to reach out—not to smooth it into submission, but just to feel the soft slide of it.

He let out an irritated breath and turned. "Where'd it come from?"

"What?" She blinked blearily at him before understanding kicked in. "Oh. Over here, definitely. I'm not sure whe—"

When it came again, he turned and snatched up his sat phone, which, miraculously, lit up when he hit a button. "*Goddammit!* No signal."

"Cloud cover, maybe. Is it even the right time of day?"

"No idea." He squinted at the screen. It was an almost impossible-to-read jumble of letters and numbers. "Got some charge, at least." He shook it and caught her side-eye. "What? Scientific method."

"Right." She stood and headed toward the pantry shelves, favoring her knee. "Coffee?"

He nodded and went back to fiddling with the phone while she heated water, doing her best to ignore the tightness in her abdomen.

Why did she feel like throwing up? It took a few seconds for the realization to happen.

Real life. The outside world.

They were saved!

Too soon. The guilty little thought threaded through her brain like a serpent, making her wish for all the wrong things.

She'd imagined them stuck here for a while, making love, eating crappy food, talking. Getting to know each other, at least until their fuel ran out. Then they could set off to join other people.

A glance showed him pushing buttons and muttering silently to himself. The sweetness of that cowlick twisted her insides in a way that wasn't sweet anymore. It hurt.

Pathetic. Stop it.

Right. So they'd leave here, get to safety—preferably away from this continent, although he might not agree— and then it would all be over. An end in sight. Okay, good. This would make it easier.

"Got it!" He dialed, put the phone to his ear, and waited. "Shit," he muttered, then cleared his throat and spoke, loudly, pushing the sound out through tight-sounding vocal cords. "Eric. Need your help. Burke-Ruhe was attacked. I think they're linked to the Chronos Corporation. The company I told you funded some of my research. We're headed to Volkov Station. You've got to find out what they're doing." He pulled the phone away, glanced at it, and shoved it back to his ear. "Can you hear me? Shit. Volkov. Call Volkov Station. Tell them we're less than one hundred fifty miles out, at the old Norwegian Field Research site. The Russians know it. We could use help. And hey, could you figure out what Chronos Corp wants with my fucking virus?" He yelled for a second but went quiet as he wrapped up the call. "Love you, Bro, whatever happens. Love you."

With a hard expelled breath, he met her eyes, managing to look both hopeless and feverish with energy. "Can't stay here forever."

The words probably weren't meant as an accusation, but they felt like one nonetheless. Like she wanted to stay here—which wasn't a lie—and he was blaming her, somehow, for enjoying it.

It all hit pretty close to home.

"Can you call—"

He lifted the phone, pushed a couple buttons, checked the charger, and dropped it again. "Dead."

"Battery?"

"Probably. Didn't always keep it warm while we were out there."

"You were otherwise occupied."

"Yeah." His smile was tight. "Lucky I could call out at all."

"Definitely."

"Listen, Angel."

Uh-oh. Why did she think she wouldn't like what he was about to say?

"We need to go."

"I know."

"With the sun going down every night, we're gonna lose degrees fast. And—What?"

"The food won't last forever, either." Tears ghosted over her eyes, disappearing just as quickly. "Right?"

At his nod, she turned to look at everything they'd be leaving behind. Rusty metal walls, the mismatched collection of folding chairs around a flimsy, scarred wood table. Fluttering overhead was a multicolored streamer of pennant flags. Along one side, lopsided shelves contained a random assortment of comic books in languages she'd never learn, but she could spend hours looking at the pictures, so bright and interesting after all these days on the ice. The same way she'd enjoyed the novelty of sipping coffee from an enormous mug that said BEER in bold letters.

"I'll miss this place." She went for light, but she couldn't help the hint of sadness in her voice.

In the slow beat of silence that followed, she lifted her eyes and caught her breath at the unguarded hunger on Ford's face. "So will I, Angel," he said before turning away.

Day 15—Harper Research and Testing Facility, East Antarctic Ice Sheet

Someone thumped at the lab door.

"Hm?" Clive pulled off his headphones and turned slowly from his laptop. The connection was too crap to watch porn, so he'd downloaded a Russian language program. Anything to keep busy.

He counted five long seconds as he walked to the door and fiddled at the handle for a few more, just to watch Sampson's face redden. Over the past week, the man's smirk had disappeared, along with his movie-star good looks. He'd grown surlier by the day, while his face got puffy, chapped, and sunburned. His overgrown scruff couldn't hide the herpes sore at the corner of his mouth. His knuckles were swollen, scabbed, and purple, which made sense given the dents Clive had spotted around the facility's walls—a visible trail of rage left in his wake.

Bradley Sampson was falling apart.

Unsurprising, given the week he'd had. Clive wasn't the only one who'd fallen out of the director's favor. After the big storm, frozen fuel had stopped the plane from going back out, then not one, but two of Sampson's men had injured themselves during their daily searches. Sampson himself had suffered a fall, leaving him with a noticeable limp. To top it off, a *mysterious* virus had put three of them out of commission, leaving them vomiting and feverish for a good portion of that time.

That would teach the bastard not to mess with a virologist.

Maybe he wouldn't have to fall back on his bigger contingency plan after all. If he played his cards right, the man would anger himself into cardiac arrest.

But then Clive remembered the bruises on his neck, still visible more than a week after Sampson's barbaric manhandling. No. He wanted the man to suffer.

Pasting an interested smile on his face, Clive asked, "What can I—"

"They've been spotted. Just got the call."

Ah, that would explain the almost feverish light in the man's gaze, the frenetic aura of excitement.

He didn't even glance at his own sat phone to see if he'd somehow missed a call from the director. He hadn't. "I'll be here," he sang. *Not holding my breath.*

"Yeah. You're so useful." The dickwad looked over Clive's shoulder at the living space he'd created right here in the lab, then slowly scanned the crowded holding cells beyond with an oily smile. "What? You just watching 'em now?" He leaned in. "Enjoying their fear? Didn't take you for the type."

"Ha-ha." Clive moved to close the door but was halted by Sampson's booted foot.

For one long, hate-imbued moment, they watched each other.

Oh yes, they'd moved on from wary to outright hostile. While Clive realized that a frustrated, caged Sampson wasn't a beast to be toyed with, the idiot didn't seem to understand that he too had crossed a line.

"You feeling all right?" Clive asked lightly, his eyes skimming over Sampson's pasty features, the pallor behind the sunburn, the bloodshot eyes. Was that a slight tremor in his hands?

"Great," the man lied, narrowing his eyes.

Though he didn't move, something in his stance changed, almost imperceptibly. He was a brute, but he wasn't stupid exactly, which Clive would do well to remember. He tightened his hand on the hypodermic needle he kept hidden in his pocket.

"Are you taking all the men?"

"Yep. Everyone wants a piece of these guys." Still, he didn't move.

Just leave, dammit. "You waiting for me to bid you Godspeed, or something?"

"Godspeed?" Sampson raised his brows and finally pulled his foot from the door. It was all Clive could do not to slam it in his face. Christ, Sampson could barely speak English.

"You know. Like, farewell?" He scarcely kept his eyes from rolling. "For your journey across the ice to do God's work?" All of this was said tongue in cheek, obviously, but Sampson didn't get it. Everything to him was straightforward. First degree.

"That what this is?" Sampson smiled, his teeth big and bright and especially carnivorous in his now-gaunt face. "Seems more like the devil's."

CHAPTER 41

Day 15—137 Miles to Volkov Station—16 Days of Food Remaining

IT WAS SO QUIET ON THE ICE, SO BRIGHT AND STILL, THAT Coop heard it immediately—the far-off drone of engines.

Within seconds, it grew louder, and when he turned to look at Angel, he could tell that she'd heard it, too.

Her stance was straight, tall, excited. Safety. Civilization. He could read her mind. The phone call worked! Eric got through to Volkov. This was over. *Finally.* He could understand that relief, especially given the way she'd limped all morning. Clearly, walking in those snowshoes had been harder on her body than skiing.

Which would make running all the more difficult if these didn't turn out to be allies.

He scanned all three hundred sixty degrees of horizon. Avoiding an enormous crevasse field, along with sastrugi, some as tall and impossible to navigate as ocean waves, had put them slightly off course, which wasn't a bad thing, given how little he trusted whoever approached.

So, was this help on the way?

Or the opposite?

Louder. Chainsaws busting through a quiet forest, bees swarming, coming together to play an off-key chord.

Something sliced through it. Disquiet, fear, an odd, otherworldly awareness. He couldn't say what exactly, but

suddenly, he was sure—more certain than he'd ever been—
that this was not a friendly approach.

Several machines—snowmobiles, he'd guess—coming
from the direction of Volkov. It could mean that Eric had
gotten his message and had somehow made this happen. But
even with his brother's connections, this was awfully quick.

Everything happened fast, after that, as his old instincts
kicked in.

A quick scan of the horizon showed nothing to hide
behind, nothing to put between them and whatever weapons those assholes were packing.

The closer the engines got, the stronger the certainty
that this was very, very bad.

He slowed his breathing and took another look, a full
three sixty, more deliberate this time. Nothing but the Great
Wall of Sastrugi that they'd just avoided. They'd have to
drag the sled over there and hope for a place to hide on the
other side. If they could make it to the forest of frozen wavelike structures, they'd have a chance of going undetected.
Slim, but a chance.

"Run!" he bellowed, making sure Angel was with him
before he took off with the sled behind him, pushing his
body harder than he ever had, stretching his lungs to their
maximum capacity. Even that didn't feel like enough as the
droning grew more strident, angrier.

Definitely more than one engine. Snowmobiles, gun-
ning toward them.

He dared a look back, and Angel was right there with
him, struggling in those snowshoes, limping but pushing
herself as hard as he was. Thank God.

Only a few yards to go. Yoked like a strongman in one of
those truck pulls, he forged his way up, up the steep, short

slope, to the top, then… His breath left him in a whoosh as he took in the sheer drop on the other side. With adrenaline-enhanced muscles, he grabbed the sled and threw it over, then turned just in time to see one of Angel's unwieldy snowshoes catch on the uneven ice, forcing her leg out at an unnatural angle.

I'm fine, Angel chanted in her head. *I'll be fine.*

The first step on her bum knee told her otherwise, sending her halfway to the ground with a lung-purging *oof* before she planted the ski pole and pushed herself to standing.

I'm fine. I'll be fine.

In front of her, the ice formed a wide, shallow hill that she'd have to climb in order to get to the other side. Nothing to it. Just an anthill, really.

Behind her, the engines grew steadily louder. She refused to look, took a step, and—*holy shit*. She leaned over her ski pole and threw up onto the pristine ice, the pain like nothing she'd experienced.

She pushed herself back up, though she had no idea how she'd walk.

And then he was there, arm around her waist.

One hopping step at a time, he helped her perch at the top of the sastrugi, lowered himself, then dropped the few feet to the ground, where he held his arms open. "I'll catch you. Jump!"

She glanced back to see several white-clad figures crouched over their snowmobiles, headed unerringly toward them. The horsemen of the apocalypse. And if she could see their pursuers, they could see her.

If he missed her and she landed on her right leg, the pain would be unbearable.

Eyes fixed on Ford, she scooted to the edge and let go.

Oooomph. Not even a second passed, not even a breath, before he plucked her out of the air and held her tightly in his arms. The contact shoved the breath from her lungs and knocked her leg, turning the edges of her vision black.

"Your knee?" he asked, clearly reading on her face at least a fraction of the pain she was feeling.

It took a great deal of effort to answer. "Yeah."

"How fucked?"

"Capital F."

He gave her a quick nod. "They see you?"

"I could see them. And they're moving fast."

Another nod. Grim, she thought, although possibly just matter-of-fact, coming from Ford.

"What do we do?"

"You see those lines?" He pointed at a textured area maybe twenty yards ahead.

She nodded. "More sastrugi."

"No. It's a crevasse field."

Crevasse. The word dropped from his lips like an omen. "You're kidding."

He grabbed her hand in response and squeezed it, telling her everything she didn't want to know. Showing her exactly how things would pan out. As she scrolled through the possibilities in her mind, there weren't many outcomes that involved them getting through this alive.

They could hide here, like sitting ducks, or…

Staring at the lumps and ridges and patterns in the ice, she squeezed him back. Then, nodding once, she grabbed his arm with one hand and her ski pole with her other before setting off for the crevasse field at his side.

And just like that, their mission changed from survival to something much more chilling.

Day 15—Harper Research and Testing Facility, East Antarctic Ice Sheet

"Who is this?" The voice was deep and authoritative. Decidedly not the director.

"Who is *this*?" Clive used his *world-renowned researcher talking to a minion* voice.

"This is Chief Petty Officer Eric Cooper. I'm wondering what the hell an American's doing answering the phone in an unoccupied Russian research station?"

I could be Canadian was the only thing Clive's brain provided, but he knew not to say that. It took a few frantic seconds for him to fall on an adequate response.

"Unoccupied Russian station? You must…are, uh, mistaken… Ahem. Sir." He cleared his throat and tightened his sweaty hand on the receiver. Why, oh why, did he have to answer the damned thing?

"Bullshit. I called Volkov Station. You answered the Volkov line."

"Well, um, Chief…Officer." He pushed out a tight, too-high laugh. "I'm afraid you've gotten your swords crossed and called Burke-Ruhe." Clive breathed through the long pause at the other end.

"Ah. My mistake then." The man appeared to calm. "Who am I speaking to?"

The question came out so lightly, so innocuously, that Clive didn't think twice before giving his name.

"Dr. Tenny. You're a researcher, aren't you? Who do you work with again? It wouldn't be Chronos Corporation, would it?"

The hairs on Clive's body rose and he immediately regretted giving himself away.

"What the hell does the U.S. Navy want with—"

"Not the navy. *Me. I* want you to listen up, Mr. Tenny." Clive bit back the automatic *Doctor* that came to lips. "Listen closely, because this is the only warning you'll get." The voice was deeper now, all friendliness gone. "I don't know what business you and your people have down there, but I know you're up to something and I know exactly where the phone you're using is located." The voice changed again, grew more gravelly, quieter, as if the man on the other end would come through the phone and tear his throat out if he could. "If anything happens to my brother, *Dr.* Ford Cooper, there's no place in this world where you'll be safe from me. I will hunt you down and tear you apart, limb from limb."

Frantic, Clive ended the call, stood, and backed up to the door, then put his face in his shaking hands, closer to crying than he'd been since losing tenure all those years ago. This was bad. Very, very bad.

The second his hands dropped limply to his sides, his gaze landed on the holding cells, where more than a dozen subjects stood or sat, probably plotting their escape as they angrily awaited their fates. Impossibly, one of them—a hard little gray-haired woman with a square jaw—stared right at him through the two-way mirror, the hatred in her eyes potent enough to make him stumble back.

He had to get out…get away. He needed air.

The damned door wouldn't open. Had Sampson messed with it somehow? No. No, he'd input the code wrong. Slower, he tried again, finally wrenching it open and practically falling into the hall, where he leaned against the wall, working hard to slow his frantic pulse.

It took a while—three minutes, maybe, to come up with the solution. When he did, it seemed obvious.

He went to open the lab door and paused when he caught sight of his shaking hands. A drink would be welcome. Or two.

And it wouldn't hurt to be armed for this. Those idiots had surely left a gun behind.

He set off down the hall, eager now that he'd made his decision to set things in motion.

CHAPTER 42

Shit. Coop stared down into the gaping crevasse. If the entire field was this deep, they were screwed.

The engines grew deafening as he helped Angel limp along the yawning crack, to the end, then to the next crevasse and the next, praying that part of this field would be miraculously shallow.

Finally, he breathed a sigh of relief when the ice opened up to reveal openings that were closer together, narrower. Here, the cracks crisscrossed, the pressure turning the pieces between them into geometrically pleasing chunks, as beautiful as quartz crystals.

And infinitely dangerous.

"Right here." He glanced back at the sastrugi just as one of the men appeared at the top. Shit. That was definitely a gun in his hand.

As fast as he could, he dumped the sled into the first shallow crevasse, waited to make sure it held, and followed it down, then turned back, arms outstretched.

"Great," Angel muttered. "Just freaking great." She dropped, clearly in pain, though the only outward sign was her tight hold on his arm.

He gave her a quick squeeze in return and took stock.

"Are these caves?" She didn't sound happy about it. No surprise there.

"Yeah. This is good." He started to move and then paused. "Just don't lean on the walls."

She peered around the light blue labyrinth and mumbled something that he couldn't hear.

Somewhere up there, the last couple of engines shut off. Impossible to tell how many there were in all. Five? Seven?

"This way." There'd been no time to dump the contents of the sled, so he dragged the whole thing deeper into the crevasse field. Carefully. From the look of them, some of these seracs were a light brush away from becoming an icefall. If one fell, it could turn into an avalanche down here, burying them, along with the virus.

At least they'd take a few of those assholes with them, if they were lucky.

He narrowed his eyes. At the far end of this crevasse was a tunnel. And above them, an ice overhang provided the perfect cover for Angel while he stashed the cores. "Wait under here," he whispered. "Be right back."

He dragged the sled into a long cave, glowing pure fluorescent blue at the entrance, turning shadowy the deeper he went. About eight feet in, another crack bisected that one and Coop wasted no time shoving the cores out of sight.

"Ford!" Angel whisper-called. "They're close!"

After grabbing a couple items from the sled, he ran back, put his arm around her waist, and guided her into one of the side crevasses, then left into another, and down another. Deep into the web of ice. And he and Angel were the spiders.

"Mash-up of my two worst nightmares," Angel hissed, then glanced at him. Was she smiling under there? "Remix version."

He grinned unexpectedly, affection tightening his chest. Shit, he had to save her. If not *them* or the virus, at least her.

"I'm with you this time."

"Great." There was definite humor in her voice. "So now I have *you* to worry about, too."

That surprised a laugh from him. Even now, running for their lives, she made him laugh.

Shit. Please don't let that be my last laugh.

By the time they found a spot they could defend, she was trembling. Fear, he thought, not cold.

Well, maybe cold, too.

"You okay?"

"Dandy."

He huffed out a breath and gathered her close, whispering four words against the side of her face. "*Stop, look, listen. Smell.*" When he didn't feel the tension leave her body, he tightened his hands and rasped, "Learned it in the army. Try it. Stop."

She breathed deeply.

"Look."

Slowly, her head swiveled, taking in the electric-blue walls around them, then tilted back to look up at the sky.

"Listen," he whispered into her ear and waited for her breathing to change, to quiet. "Smell."

It was too cold to smell with sinuses like burnt shells, but he imagined he got a whiff of that soap they'd used back at the hut. He shut his eyes hard as the memory assailed him—her behind the curtain. Warmth and food and the woman of his dreams.

After a few seconds, she nodded, the movement minute against him, then gradually, her shaking eased, while his pulse slowed to an almost normal cadence.

"Okay?" The word wasn't even a whisper against the fleece covering her face, but she felt it and gave him another nod, shifting up enough to put her mouth close to his, their neck gaiters barring a kiss. "I smell *you*."

It was insane how his body reacted to that statement, but he shouldn't have been surprised.

This was more than chemistry.

Jesus, was this what love felt like? This hot, hard, twanging burn in his muscles—deeper—his bones? Death was *here* for them—just meters away while they hid in the center of a virtual minefield—and the only thing holding him together was her. Like if he lost her now, he'd be nothing but a Ford soup, melting into the ice to form his own inexplicable layer.

He gripped her harder, pressed her tighter to his chest. Behind the beating of his heart, he heard them, drawing closer. Their feet crunching over the ice. Impatient, he pulled his mask up and over his ears, the better to hear. He shut his eyes and listened, doing his best to separate out the sounds.

Adrenaline flooded his system along with something he'd managed to restrain for so long. Something hungry and violent. His breathing slowed while the beast inside him grew, taking over his heart and lungs, seeping into his limbs.

One man was close, tromping right toward the crevasse field, though he might not even know it. From up there, without the sun's shadows providing depth, everything was flat and white. They might not realize that they were about to fall into—

Someone screamed, the terrible sound followed by yelling and running. Mayhem. He and Angel startled, but that was it.

One down. If they were lucky, maybe two.

More voices, orders being shouted, footsteps fanning

out. They were harder to distinguish now, coming from all sides. But he thought he heard three? Maybe four?

Another yell led to more movement, and for a few odd moments, Coop could feel the ice on their side, helping them.

Absurd, and yet... He pictured the hidden crevasses that he and Angel had bypassed to get here. At least one man had fallen in.

A shot fired. Then another. Angel's body jumped at every sound, shuddering by the time it stopped.

Shit. They were close. If those assholes found them, they were sitting ducks. He had to think of a way to draw their attention away from Angel.

With a final squeeze of her shoulder, he stepped into what was essentially a corridor, maybe six feet below the surface.

"I'm unarmed." Every nerve ending buzzing with energy, Coop eyed the ground above. Hunkered beneath the overhang, he slowly moved until he saw them: four dark-clad silhouettes standing out like giant crows against the blue sky. Or chess pieces, lining up to take down the king and queen.

"No shit." It was Sampson's voice. The man on the left. And, judging from the side-to-side sweep of his head, he hadn't seen Coop.

They've got no idea where I am.

He could use that. Trick them, get them turned around—lead them away. He just needed time and a lure strong enough to keep them hooked. Coop hurriedly said, "I've got the virus."

Was there an echo in here? Maybe. It made sense that they wouldn't be able to pinpoint a sound. He tensed, ready to start moving away from Angel so he could draw danger from her, when he noticed Sampson focusing down toward where she hid—ignoring the bait.

This wasn't going to work. They would find her.

Angel. Shit. His heart was trying to punch its way out of his chest. He only had one card left to play.

"The virus is safe. Far from here." He stepped out from under the overhang, hands in the air. "You get the coordinates when Angel goes free."

"Yeah right." The sound of Sampson's laugh was worse than nails on a chalkboard. It pricked up every one of Angel's hairs, made her want to burrow into the ground and hide.

But then she looked at Ford—fearless warrior, protector, moving out in the open—and hiding was the last thing she wanted to do. No, she'd remain beside him until her last breath. Whatever happened.

"Got you surrounded, you and the girl." *Girl? Who's he calling a girl?* "Ain't got much of a leg to stand on do you, Cooper?"

Actually, that would be me, she thought hysterically, dangerously close to breaking out into laughter. Or doing something stupid, like calling attention to herself to give Ford a chance to attack.

And that would be pointless against four armed men.

"Maybe not." Ford was cool as a cucumber. Unbreakable. "But I've got five metal tubes hidden. And I'm not giving you the GPS coordinates until she's safe."

"Where you reckon safe is right now, huh?" Sampson sounded off in a way she couldn't quite place. Rough. Desperate. With a forced nonchalance that she'd never heard from him before. "You figure she'd be safer with the mad professor and his test subjects?"

Test subjects? Something queasy turned over in her belly.

"On one of your rides, headed away from here. Alone."

Silence for a few long seconds raised Angel's hackles higher, although she wasn't sure how that was even possible.

"Or we could just shoot—"

"Hurt a hair on her body and you'll get noth—"

The next few seconds contained a flurry of sounds. Footsteps from more than one direction. Something thudded down on their level. A groan, then another. That was Ford.

She was sure of it.

Without waiting to find out, she left her secure cubby—the one that was way too reminiscent of that other icy hiding place she'd rather never think of again—and took off the way Ford had gone.

"I've got him!" someone yelled.

Limping as fast as she could, weight on her ski pole, she hopped ahead. There was Ford, standing maybe four feet from a man with a gun aimed at his head.

"Hey!" she yelled, watching in absolute shock as the man turned and Ford exploded into action. He lowered his body, slid to the side, and somehow, while a shot cracked open the sky, kicked the man's feet out from under him. He went down hard and Ford pounced, graceful and brutal as a northern wolf.

The beautiful warm body she'd spent the last two days wrapped around was more weapon than human now, and the bit of his face she could see was so furious she stumbled back a step.

Quickly, efficiently, and more violently than anything she'd ever witnessed, Ford parried one blow after another, his movements both sharp and fluid, before ending the man with a businesslike snap of the neck. She gasped. Holy shit.

Two down.

A white-clad figure landed behind Ford, arm raised, tensing as if to deliver a shot.

"Behind you!" she screamed.

He snatched the downed man's gun, turned, and fired—Angel's hand flew to her mouth to keep a scream in. Ford's shot split the man's goggles down the middle, and painted the ice crimson before he crumpled to the ground.

Three.

Above them was the sound of someone running, and then, getting closer before they leapt down, somewhere to her left.

She went right, toward where Ford waited on his own little battlefield, surrounded by carnage.

She'd just taken a step out from under the overhang when a loud noise made her jerk back, just in time to get showered in glittering confetti. *Shit!* She'd been shot at.

Instinct made her press into the ice wall, but if the man arrived from the left and this one guarded her right, she'd be trapped here.

She turned to follow Ford, screaming when an arm slid around her neck from behind.

"Got her!" The man—it sounded like Ben Wong—yanked her out from under the ice roof, into the open. "Drop it, Cooper."

Ford hesitated just a second, but it was long enough for Ben to press his weapon to her temple, the metal cold through the layers.

"Don't do it, Ford, it's not—!"

Ben shook her so hard her teeth clattered.

Ignoring her, Ford dropped the gun and took a few steps closer before Ben jostled her again and yelled for him to stop right there.

"Got 'em, Sampson!" he yelled.

"On my way." Just his voice made her insides feel like jelly.

At the crunch of approaching footsteps, Angel lost it. She would not let them end her the way they'd ended her friends in the arch. She tightened her fingers around the ski pole, ready to thrust it back the second she dropped. One... two...

She let go, making her body a dead weight, which shocked Ben into releasing her, and in the seconds before he gathered himself again, she listed to the side and thrust her pole up and toward his crotch, using every bit of anger and fear and protectiveness she could muster.

She didn't wait to see how effective she'd been before taking off, slipping and stumbling. A hand to the ice wall broke her fall, but the knee wouldn't hold up.

There! A side alley. She ducked in just as a shot was fired, spewing ice shards in all directions. Another turn, left this time, through a tiny crevasse. No choice. She had to move. Was it leading higher? Was she getting closer to the surface?

Somewhere, not too far, another shot. Another and another. A volley of them, from two different directions. Someone groaned—Ford?

As she rounded the next corner, she saw him, tight against the ice. *Thank God.* Relief washed over her like a warm sunrise. She smiled, moved toward him. He looked her way. Above, someone appeared on the ledge, throwing a long, cool shadow into the maze.

How many left now? Two? Just Ben and Sampson?

She pictured more, pouring in like the bad guys in a martial arts movie. One after another, a never-ending stream of professional killers.

Her eyes flicked up. No way could she identify whoever it was from here, but the shadow moved, raised an arm.

Memories slammed her in an endless loop—Sampson pointing the gun at Alex's head. Alex falling. Dead. Dead. Dead.

Time stalled, went syrupy slow.

Ford put a finger to his lips, meant for her, but she had to tell him about the man behind him. Ben, limping from where she'd hurt him. In sickening slow-motion, he lifted his handgun.

"Behind you, Ford!"

Ford reached for something at his waist and in a flash, spun away from her, the ice axe appearing in his hands, small but deadly. Before she could blink, he'd sent it flying through the air to catch Ben in the head. Ben fell faster than the bright crimson mist of his own blood. It tinkled onto the ice a millisecond after the thump of his body.

Four down.

More death. She should feel bad. She should feel... *something*?

Someone coughed—the sound strangely vulnerable amidst all this violence. Slow as an oil slick, the shadow spread beside her. The closer it got, the more certain she was that it was *him*. Sampson.

"Go!" Ford yelled, just as a shot thundered from overhead and Ford spun back, hit the wall, and slid slowly down, leaving a Technicolor streak behind him.

"Nooooo!" The scream tore from her insides.

Like an angel from hell, the dark-clad figure leapt to the ice beside Ford, and before he could react, delivered a hard kick to his stomach. Another. Another. Ford curled in on himself, but Sampson didn't stop.

Angel's vision narrowed, muscles tensed. She'd kill him.

"Ang—Angel! Get...out..." Sampson grabbed Ford by the coat, hauled him up, and hit him in the face. Over and over again.

She had to stop him. She had to—

"I've got the virus!" the words were out.

Sampson lifted his head and went very, very still, watching her with predatory interest.

The only movement was the slow rise and fall of Ford's chest. He was limp.

"Come and get it, you prick." She took off.

A look over her shoulder showed him dropping Ford to the ground like a sack of potatoes. With Terminator-like inexorability, Sampson came after her, steps starting slow and measured before picking up speed, until she had no choice but to run like hell.

Or stumble, limp, hop, lean, and slide. It wasn't fast enough. She put her foot down, screamed at the explosion of pain, and pushed through, all so he would follow her, so he'd leave Ford alone.

Into the cave.

"Hear that, Coop—or is it Ford now? Your girl's giving me the virus. Ain't that sweet?" Sampson was so close she could almost taste his sad parody of a sigh. "You're walking funny. You in pain, Angel?" Sampson chuckled low, his slow pace insulting when she was working so hard to move.

He wouldn't win. She wouldn't let him, dammit.

Just before turning into the long, low cave, she eyed the thinnest of the ice columns.

Don't lean on them, Ford had told her. With a rage-fueled burst of strength, she shoved at it. Nothing. But a second push made the thing teeter. She tripped back as it collapsed, like a tree going down.

"I can help with—*Bitch!*"

She didn't wait to hear more before forging into the tunnel, where Ford had jammed the yellow sled in vertically.

Her hand slid over the gleaming silver cores and encountered the shovel. She yanked it out and shoved it through the narrow opening between sled and floor, toward the other end of the ice tunnel.

Panting, she dropped to her butt, avoiding her knee so she wouldn't pass out, crawled on her side, worked her way farther into the narrow space, under the sled, beyond it. She crouched to rummage through the last of their belongings—the food they'd been so happy to have, the tent that felt so much like home. Hurriedly, she threw them down. None of it mattered anymore. Nothing mattered but life and death.

A footstep crunched on the ice. She went still.

"Think that was enough to get me?" Sampson growled out a sound possibly meant to be a laugh. "That's okay. I'm fine." *Crunch. Crunch.* Was he limping? Had she hurt him, at least?

Frantically, her hand sought one last thing from the sled.

"Where you at, darlin'? You in *here*?" Sampson asked, entirely too nonchalant for a man who was about to meet his maker. "Really need to stop meeting like this, don't we?"

He coughed, the sound rough and phlegmy. "Sure am glad you decided to bring me in here. Reminds me of last time. Man, that was..." He stopped to cough again, then snorted and spat a wad of something no doubt repulsive. "*Fuck!*"

A deep, loud inhale. He crunched forward and then stopped.

"Holy shit." His whisper reached her where she still searched frantically from the other side of the sled. "Are they right *here*?" He cleared his throat. "Son of a bitch. They are, aren't they?"

Deep inside the tunnel, with nothing but the sled between her and pure evil, Angel's hand finally closed around a flat cloth packet, as familiar as anything she'd ever owned. She pulled it out, unzipped her coat, and shoved it inside, close to her body.

Now she was ready.

Come here. Come here and get me, you piece of shit.

With one elbow jammed into the wall, she pushed herself until she was up, supported by the shovel, shaking—a wreck—but also weirdly solid inside.

He was close, breathing hard, like maybe his lungs hurt. Good, she hoped he hurt, wanted to hurt him worse. Over and over and over again.

She hesitated for one second and then moved away, into the darkest part of the tunnel, turned the corner, and rather than run toward the light as he'd probably expect her to do, stopped, waiting against the ice, just out of sight.

Come on.

Slow footsteps, the scrape of the sled being yanked out of his way.

"Been looking all over for you little bastards." It took her a second to realize he was talking to the ice cores and not to her. "Angel. So sweet of you to bring them here." A painful clearing of his throat and then more footsteps as he closed in with nightmarish speed.

She lifted her arms up and over her head, gripping the shovel like she was batting in a softball game, only with much, much more adrenaline. She counted out two more of his steps, pushed herself off the wall into his path, and took a swing at Sampson's head.

Up, up, keeping it close in the confined tunnel, shifting her weight to her bad knee, which sent a shockwave of pain through her, so hard she had to fight back the darkness… then *thwack*!

Connection, painful, solid, and satisfying.

He staggered back into the wall opposite, shook his head, and let out a low animal moan as she moved back into position again, ready to swing.

He whipped off his goggles and ski mask to swipe his arm over his bloody face, and she stuttered to a surprised stop.

Wait, that's not Sampson, her brain supplied, dumbfounded, followed by the quick realization that it was. This wasn't the smooth, smiling man she'd met at Burke-Ruhe. In the last couple of weeks, he'd become almost unrecognizable, his face swollen, oozing sores scattered over it, red and rough.

She tightened her hands, recovering from the shock just in time to swing again. But he came at her low and astonishingly quick, shoved her back, so she fell to the ice with a brain-shattering thump.

At least now, she thought a split-second later, as Sampson tried to suffocate her to death, his outside matched his evil innards.

His hand was tight around her neck, squeezing every drop of life from her.

Starved of air, her vision blocked by a constellation of shooting stars, the weirdest feeling came over Angel. An out-of-body dreaminess she'd never experienced before. One at a time, the actions to take lit up before her like a neon-yellow brick road.

One: unzip coat. The thought came as she struggled hard against the monster's hold, dragging the zipper down maybe an inch or two, but it was all she needed to reach inside. She pulled at the cloth roll, reached in, slid her hand around the biggest handle—too bulky—before moving to the next one. Boning knife. She pictured herself quickly and efficiently cutting and pulling the membrane from a rack of pork ribs. Slicing sure and straight between flesh and bone.

Perfect.

Strong arms squeezed her and something popped in her back. She tried ignoring the pain, but that just made her vision swim harder, the shooting stars becoming a river of gold. Blinking, she focused on it, used it, let it drive her, along with the litany pouring from Sampson's lips.

"You just had to make this tough, didn't you?" Gasping with effort, he pushed his body into hers, making it impossible to pull her weapon from its sheath. "Angel, huh? You're no goddamn angel. Fuck. I wanna…*hurt* you so bad. Wanna hear you *scream* for leading us around like this. You…useless little *bitch*."

Not just sounds, not just threats, the *words* were fuel to her fire, much-needed oxygen, lighting up muscles that couldn't function without the extra push.

We'll see, she thought, suddenly as sure of her own wind-honed edges as she was of the knife's. She wasn't the wounded woman who'd come to this place all those months ago. No, this experience—surviving—had turned her into a blade, hard and sleek and cutting.

Grasp, pull, lift, then, with every ounce of strength she could muster, down. The blade slid home, into his back, through fabric and skin, between ribs, right to where his heart should be. If the bastard had one.

"*Fuuuuccccc—*" The word ended on a wet gurgle.

Realization hit his face in microsecond bursts: surprise, anger, the decision to retaliate…the effort…impossible…

He couldn't do it.

With his goggles out of the way, his eyes were unavoidable and Angel watched as understanding dawned. He was finished. Ended.

It was justice. For everything he'd done.

But she couldn't feel pride or relief. She felt nothing but the urgent need to get out from under his weight.

Digging deep for the strength, she shoved him off and lay there, gasping for air. It scraped over her throat, rough as a cheese grater. At least she was breathing.

Was Ford?

Swallowing back a rush of bile when her eyes landed on Sampson's grotesque shape, she took off, hoping to God and the ice and every higher power she could think of that she wasn't too late.

CHAPTER 43

Day 15—Chronos Corporation Headquarters, Stromville, West Virginia

"WHAT DO YOU MEAN HE HAS DISAPPEARED?" KATHERINE Harper stood stiffly, one hand pressed to the Victorian mahogany pedestal desk in her office. "I pay him a hefty monthly retainer. He cannot simply stop working for me."

"None of us have heard from him in at least a week." The young woman on the other end of the phone line was barely competent. When she closed her eyes, Katherine could picture the private investigator's secretary in some hovel of an office. Chewing gum. Likely playing one of those time-waster games on her mobile phone. Popping bubbles in some game, or building virtual farms. *Shooting school children.* "He was following a lead for one of your cases, ma'am. Campbell Turner?"

Campbell Turner. The director felt that name in every nerve of her body, even some that she knew without a doubt were long dead. *Followed a lead... Hasn't come back.*

She inhaled long and slow. Best not to get worked up over nothing. The girl's boss could just be a drunken PI on a bender after all. "What, precisely, was the lead?"

"I'm...not sure."

"You are, I believe, an investigator's secretary. Perhaps you could do a little *investigating* yourself? Have you looked at his email? Checked his telephone messages? Oh, I don't know, read his files?"

The child on the other end of the line swallowed. Hopefully that gum hurt going down. "Uh. No...ma'am."

Good God. Fiona as a five-year-old would have been better at this woman's job. She shut her eyes against the wave of resentment that went through her every time she thought of all of the lost potential.

"Well, then, perhaps you should." It occurred to Katherine that she was close to yelling at someone who was not her own employee. With another of those deep breaths in, she pulled back and did her best to channel her mother. Sweet, syrupy, all smiles. Even as she stabbed you in the back.

"I would be so *grateful*, young lady, if you could establish what it was, precisely, that sent your boss wherever he went. That location—or the person with whom he met, for example—would be helpful hints as to his whereabouts. Or a paper trail? Please provide me with that information at your earliest convenience." She didn't mean that last part. But people apparently appreciated the false impression that their time was their own.

Nothing but nervous breathing on the other end of the phone, then finally, "Of course." A pause. "Ms. Harper."

"Now." She stretched a thin smile across her lips, doing her best to ensure it could be heard in her voice as well. Mama would have been proud, but even after all these decades, being friendly felt like trying to fit into someone else's clothing. "Thank you *so much* for the update. I look forward to hearing from you again." *Night or day*, she almost added, but that would be too eager. It would set off alarm bells, if she hadn't done that already. "*Soon*."

But how, oh how could she hold this inside when it was so very momentous? The man who'd stolen the original virus—Daddy's virus—wasn't far now. They'd find him. She felt it with certainty, in her bones.

Because she just had to tell someone, she broke her own rule of not visiting her daughter during working hours and walked out. Grasping her cane tightly in her hand, she went to the end of the hall, down the stairs to the ground floor, then toward the back of the house—away from the mountain and the company's headquarters.

As she always did before entering, she sucked in a deep, preparatory breath. *Serenity.* Everything else, she left at the door.

Slowly, she opened the door, pleased to see that the curtains were open, the view absolutely spectacular, as always. Well, calmly spectacular—an English garden in the middle of West Virginia, not quite in bloom, though buds had started to spring up everywhere.

The nurse, who'd likely been reading to Fiona, stood up quickly. From her lap, hidden beneath *Anne of Green Gables*, a mobile phone dropped to the floor with a thud. So, *not* reading.

She cleared her throat and stared at the young lady, who couldn't quite meet her eyes.

"May I have a moment with my daughter, please… uh…"

"Catherine."

Ah yes. She and the nurse shared a name—though spelled differently. How could she possibly have forgotten?

"Yes. Catherine. Thank you." She smiled as the woman left the room, then waited until the footsteps faded before letting her eyes take in her sweet, perfect baby, frozen, eyes staring blindly ahead.

Every morning and every night, she came through

this door, and every single time, this sight was like a spear through her chest.

She sank into the armchair she kept close to the bed and grasped Fiona's cold thin white hand.

"There's news, pumpkin." She gulped back an unexpected wave of excitement. "Remember that man I told you about, who stole from us all those years ago?"

Fiona moved slightly, giving Katherine quite a start before she realized she was squeezing her hand too tight. She loosened her hold with an effort and leaned forward to stroke her daughter's cheek. "We're so close, my darling. So close to having a viable virus. And you know what this means, don't you?"

Oh my, Katherine was breathing hard. But this was a lot to happen at once. The virus, first of all, showing up after all this time. Goodness, the excitement of that! And while the team at the South Pole wasn't exactly the most efficient, things were happening now. Change was coming. She could feel it.

"All of our hard work is coming to fruition. Men like the ones who hurt you... *Terrorists,*" she breathed, hating the word, but needing to say it aloud every once in a while. Needing to remember the man attacking the school. Needing the ache of memory—the physical blow to her belly when she'd received the call. The news stories she'd watched for hours...days. Until they'd stopped airing them. And the *anger* even at that. *How* dare *you stop talking about the death of my family? The loss of my grandchildren? One daughter dead, the other forever asleep.* Unresponsive wakefulness syndrome, they called it now, which she much preferred to the phrase *vegetative state.*

A syndrome was something she might wake from someday. A vegetable was grated, cut up, cooked into soup.

"We will *obliterate* them." The words emerged harsh and certain. She softened her voice with another long, slow stroke of Fiona's pasty cheek.

Really, Catherine needed to take her out a bit more often. Even with the chill, she should give Fiona a little sunlight instead of sitting in here watching whatever it was on her telephone. Or texting some boyfriend. This generation…good God.

Odd, because Catherine wasn't that much younger than Fiona. But she'd never let her daughters turn into one of the zombies. Never.

"I know you're kinder than me, my dear, but I can't forgive *that man* for stealing from us all those years ago. He took our virus." The man who'd stolen it had called them evil when he'd done it. Vowing they'd never get their hands on it.

Well, he'd been wrong, hadn't he?

Ford was alive.

Pummeled and shot and bleeding out in an underground forest of ice, yes, but alive.

Angel wrapped her arms tighter around him. She needed to keep him warm, then get him to safety. No. No, first she had to stop the bleeding. She could do that. Stop bleeding.

What she couldn't do was lose it right now.

Okay. Okay. She blinked back the tears that threatened to freeze her eyelids shut and took a look around.

As fast as she could, she dragged herself the few dozen feet, over Sampson's body, back to the sled. She pulled out a pack and rifled through it. Clothing. That would work. And the first aid kit. Sleeping bags and mats, too.

She yanked at the bag, dragged it behind her, and started to crab-crawl back to Ford, then thought better of it. The sled would come in handy and she needed to be efficient with her movements. Quickly, haphazardly, she pushed everything she wouldn't need from the sled, then hesitated, staring at the five metal tubes. She ran her hand over the nearest one, gleaming at her like some cursed relic from the past. In a movie, she'd leave them buried for the next poor person to find.

Yeah, well, this isn't a movie. And I'm not cursed.

She hefted the ice core back onto the sled and zipped the whole thing closed. She'd come back for them.

First, she had to help Ford.

Beside him, she unzipped the first aid kit with difficulty, since her stupid glove kept getting in the way, then dumped the contents. Bandages—good. WoundSeal. Yes. Yes, that would work.

Next, she pulled out clothes until she found a couple pairs of her own clean underwear—the only cotton they had—and a few nylon base-layer items. Then she turned to him.

Oh God. Had his chest stopped moving?

"Live, dammit. *Please.* Live. Live, Ford. Live." She said the words like a mantra, sang them like an anthem, over and over. "You're mine now. You hear? So, live. Freaking live."

Wadded-up clothes pressed to the gunshot wound, high at the cusp of his shoulder and chest, which, when she lifted him, appeared to have gone straight through. Shit. Or, no. Was that good? Two wounds to heal, but out was good, right, instead of having to look for a bullet inside? And it didn't appear to be bleeding much, although who could tell when blood immediately froze solid. "*Live, live, live.*"

Shit, he'd freeze if she opened up his coat. But maybe

not. The air felt hot now. Was it her? Was she immune to the cold? *Ha!* Maybe by destroying the evil killer, she'd unlocked the cold resistance achievement. Sure. And Ford was gonna stand up and walk to Volkov like this.

She unzipped him, quickly threw clothes onto his chest to warm him, then put the sleeping bag over top, fighting to pull his arm from his coat. It weighed a ton.

Every move was an effort: ripping open the WoundSeal powder, sprinkling it on, turning him, doing the same on the other side, wadding up the cotton cloth, pressing hard.

"*Live, live, live, live.*"

She unrolled the bandage, lifted Ford's heavy arm away from his body, grunting, wrapped, pressed.

Finally, she zipped him up, and considered collapsing, but if she did that, she'd die here, with him, surrounded by the scattered bodies of the men who'd done this.

Quickly, she sucked down four ibuprofen, stuck the water bottle into her coat, and looked at the bloody labyrinth around them. Before letting herself acknowledge the real problem: How the hell was she going to get them up?

CHAPTER 44

She bent to zip Ford into the second sleeping bag. "Don't you leave me. Don't die. Don't you dare. Because I love you. I love you, you jerk."

At some point, the mantra had changed and Angel couldn't change it back. Didn't matter if he heard or cared or knew how deeply she felt for him. All she wanted was to keep him alive. She figured tough love was just about Ford's speed.

She couldn't lift him, had no idea how to build a pulley, and couldn't climb out of here anyway.

Which left her with one option—they needed a ramp.

She eyed the massive columns of ice above and around her, some wide and long, others thin and fragile-looking.

She'd done it once. She could do it again.

As far as she could see, the ice chunks rose up, intimidating and regal, smooth in places, bumpy in others, looking like they'd sprouted from the earth. She moved away from Ford to a solid-looking rectangle adjacent to an exterior wall. After a fortifying inhale, she shoved it with all her might.

It didn't budge.

Of course it didn't. The thing was massive, much bigger than the one she'd pushed before.

Come on. Come on. I can't—

Her eye landed on a corpse, flicked immediately away and then, with purpose, looked at it again. Their axe stuck out from the man's head.

"Oh, hell no," she complained, even as she moved toward

it. She wrapped her fingers around the handle, braced herself with the shovel...and yanked it out.

She waited for the dry-heaves to pass, working hard to forget all thoughts of meat and cleavers. After a cleansing breath, she went back to the tall column of ice and, because there wasn't any time to lose, let the axe fly, chopping at the base until, with a suddenness that made her fall back on her ass, it collapsed.

There. She smiled to no one. A ramp.

Triumphant, she rushed back to Ford, every movement an awkward fight against her own body. "Okay. How do I do this?"

She'd emptied the sled of everything, piled their sleeping mats on top, and with great difficulty, worked to shift Ford onto it, one leaden body part at a time.

"God, you're heavy," she huffed. "I can't...get you on the damned sled."

A sound stopped her cold. Did he say something?

"What?" She leaned close, heart trying to punch its way out of her chest. Were his eyes open? Oh God, his mouth moved.

Almost sobbing with relief, she put her ear to his neck gaiter and listened.

"Trying." A rasping breath lifted his chest painfully. "You...too..."

"What?"

"Love...you...too."

No time to cry.

"Yeah?" She grasped his face and held it tightly. "Then climb onto this sled."

He huffed out an agonized sound and grimaced, which hurt her insides, but when she pulled this time, he put his arm on the ground, turned to one side, and with a groan, made it on.

"Gonna get you home," she assured him, although she had no freaking clue where home could be. Or how she'd get there. "Get you home."

With Ford loaded on the sled, she took a second to lean back and consider the situation while she caught her breath. No way could she pull him anywhere, home or otherwise. The impossibility of what she had to do crushed her for a good five seconds before she remembered the snowmobiles. Right.

All she had to do was climb up and out of here, then she'd tie the sled to a snowmobile and pull him out.

After that…could they make it to Volkov in a day? Crap, she had no clue.

CHAPTER 45

THEY WERE OUT.

Angel wanted to crawl into the sleeping bag with Ford and take a rest, but there wasn't time. She pictured him freezing to death. Or bleeding. Or maybe the knocks to his head had caused him to—

Shut up and go.

She'd planned to make him lie on the sled and haul him across the ice, but he insisted on bringing the cores with them, so rather than waste time arguing, she'd piled them on the sled and turned to find him slowly, painfully climbing onto the snowmobile.

He caught her eye. "Want me to drive?" he asked, and she honest-to-God laughed. The man could barely stay upright, much less handle a moving vehicle.

"I've got this."

She tucked her feet into the footwells and stared down at the GPS. With fumbling fingers, she twisted the key and got the engine running, its roar extra loud in all this stillness.

Ford wrapped himself around her, leaned into her body, pressed the side of his head to hers, and sighed.

"Let's go," she said.

He nodded.

"Which way?"

He whispered the coordinates into her ear.

She gave a deep, exhausted sigh and lurched toward Volkov Research Station.

Day 15—4 Miles to Volkov Station—No Food, No Shelter

"No. No, no no. Son of a bitch!" The snowmobile came to a slow, lurching stop in the middle of nowhere. Out of gas.

For several mind-numbing seconds, Angel could only press her hand to her mouth and wait for the wave of hopelessness to pass. No. Not hopelessness. She needed that anger back. Only anger.

There. She held it in so tightly that it shook her body.

It wasn't enough to leave five corpses on the ice. To cross miles and miles of nothing, practically freezing to death every night in a sleeping bag for two. To blow out her knee, with no way in hell to get it fixed down here. And then to watch the man she'd unwisely fallen in love with get shot and beaten.

No. Now, they had to _break down_ within miles of their destination.

Goddammit, she'd had enough.

If Ford hadn't been plastered to her back, she'd have— what? Stomped around swearing? She couldn't even do that with her stupid knee.

And now they had to walk.

"Ford." She turned just her head. "Come on. Got to walk." Or crawl, if that was what it took.

"Mm-hm." And it just might.

"Uh-huh. Yes. Up. Let's go."

Shit. They had nothing. Just the water in her coat and a couple bars in her pocket. She hadn't thought…

Tears pricked at her sinuses.

No. Hell no. _First, buck up, get our asses to safety. Then cry like a damn baby._

With one hand gripping Ford's coat to keep him from slumping, she twisted off their ride and eyed him, hysteria bubbling up inside.

I am totally losing it.

"Okay, mister. We're doing this. But I need your help." A pull on his good arm produced no results. "Come on, Ford. Please."

She yanked with every ounce of strength she had, and he slid too fast, his weight nearly crushing her. She caught the handlebar at the last minute, straightened her left leg, and held steady for a few long, agonized seconds.

"Let's go. We need your two legs." She propped him up on the snowmobile. "I'll use the one that I've got." Her next strangled laugh was high and frenzied. "A tripod."

He muttered something.

"What?"

"Go…" He swallowed. "'thout me."

"No."

"Dammit. *Go.*"

"Fuck off, Ford."

"I'm…slow."

"And I can't even walk on my own." Every drop of humor left Angel's body in a rush. She turned to put her head to his, cheek to cheek, her mouth against the opening to his hood. "We'll go at your pace."

"Sweetheart." His words brushed against her ear. "Go. Get…help."

"Remember when I told you to let me die if I weighed you down?" She shook her head, nuzzling him in the process. "Remember that? I didn't want us both to die. Didn't want to be responsible for killing you."

"I remember," he breathed.

"You wouldn't do it. Wouldn't promise." She'd been so close to falling apart that day.

Months ago, Angel Smith had arrived in Antarctica, alone and directionless.

But, man, did riding the razor edge of death change a girl's priorities.

These last two weeks had boiled her life down to exactly one thing: getting their asses to Volkov Station.

No more aimless soul-searching for Angel. Today, she'd drag this man to safety. Or die in the process.

"I'm not leaving you, ding-dong. So it's your choice. We stay here and hang out around this gorgeous snowmobile until we expire." Shaky breath in. "Together." She forced a smile. "Kinda fun, right?"

His long, low "mmmm" was a definite no.

"Then we finish this. Together."

She started to move when he held her back. "You drive…" He coughed, the sound painful. Christ, had Sampson's beating done something to his insides? "A mean bargain…lady."

With a remarkable show of strength, Ford stood, swayed for a few seconds before putting his good arm around her, and took the first step.

He walked, she hopped, using him and her ski pole for balance, and together, they hobbled slowly across the smooth, creaking ice, hauling the virus behind them.

CHAPTER 46

THE SUN WAS SINKING WHEN SOMETHING APPEARED ON the horizon. An anomaly.

Coop blinked. *Couldn't be.* He didn't let himself hope.

He had at least one broken rib, probably a concussion, something very wrong with his lungs, and a bullet hole in his shoulder.

With every exhale, the air forced from his too-heavy chest had to pass through a tight, dry throat before starting over again. The inhales were the worst, a million sharp claws carving themselves a new path. Over and over again, step by dragging step.

But he could do it. Or Angel could at least. He'd have laughed right now if he could—at himself—for not believing in her. The strongest person he'd met in his life.

As another hour passed, marked by the constant stomp-hop of their progress across the ice, the shape turned into a building. It wasn't until they were close enough to make out details that he finally let himself believe.

Volkov. They'd made it.

Or he was hallucinating. Angel stopped and looked up at him. To anyone else, her expression would be just a blank ski mask, but he knew her like he'd never known another person, could *feel* the triumph running through her.

"See?" she croaked. "Told you we'd make it."

"Yeah you did." He sounded absolutely wasted.

It was nothing like the bustling research station he remembered, but then it was supposedly closed for the winter, right? No, he remembered, they were doing renovations or something, which was confirmed by the exhaust puffing up into the air.

They arrived at the first building—a small, boxy metal structure, rougher-looking than anything at Burke-Ruhe. And much older.

Slowly, painfully, they pulled open the door and peered inside. A hangar, filled with a silent fleet of work vehicles. Right. Right, he remembered this. Jameson would never let his babies rust out like this.

They turned, as awkward and slow as a three-legged beast. Fuck, his head hurt.

"Which—"

"There." Coop couldn't do more than whisper the words and lift his chin. "Big one. Stilts."

At the door to the main building, he started to collapse.

"Come on, Ford. Almost there. Stay with me. Not yet." She sounded like hell, her voice rough as granite. "Come on!" She slid her arm around his waist and moved him to the wall.

The interior heat barely registered against his skin.

"Someone's here," he mumbled, hating that she and the wall were the only things holding him up.

Angel opened her mouth to yell but stopped, turned to him, and asked, "Something seem off to you?"

He tried nodding, but it ramped up the pounding. Eyes closed, he cleared his throat and whispered, "Yeah."

As quietly as they could, they made their stumbling way along the wall through the eerily deserted hall. Farther down, light poured from an open door on the right. Coop's pulse picked up. Jesus, he could use a vacation after this.

Someplace calm, where his pulse would stay slow. Nothing exciting at all.

They exchanged a look before crossing the open doorway and, as one, stepping in.

A man sat at a desk, staring at several large screens.

Coop leaned against the doorframe, trying to make his eyes focus right.

What the actual hell?

They weren't screens but windows into what looked like living quarters. Or prison cells.

He stumbled forward. Was that Jameson laid out on a bed? Marlon? Every winter-over from Burke-Ruhe was in there, three to a room, complete with bunks and a toilet. And absolutely zero privacy.

"What the hell?" Angel croaked, her eyes wide. She stood stock-still, like Coop, dependent on the door for support.

Coop pulled his blurry gaze from the cells and focused on the small balding man, who scrabbled at his desk for something.

Disbelief and anger and a desire to do damage made Coop take three unsteady steps before he had to stop and catch his breath.

"Oh, so *now* you make it." The man's mouth let out a fine spray of spittle when he spoke and his eyes seemed to focus somewhere above Coop's head.

Coop squinted past him to the cells, where almost every occupant lolled around like zoo animals on a hot, sunny afternoon.

"Jameson!" he tried to yell. "Pam! Marlon!"

The little man blinked too rapidly and wiped a thin sheen of sweat from his pale forehead.

"What's wrong with them?" Angel asked.

"They're fine," the man said, obviously lying, and then aimed a weapon at Angel. "Now, where's my *fucking virus*?"

Coop shook his head hard to clear the cobwebs and went down like a ton of bricks.

CHAPTER 47

ANGEL RIPPED HER EYES AWAY FROM THE TWO-WAY mirrors just in time to see Ford slide down the wall, bloody, bruised, beaten to a pulp.

She rushed to his side.

"Where's my virus, Ms. Smith?"

Squinting, she turned, slow as molasses, and rose back up to standing. "What did you say?" Every muscle, tendon, and nerve vibrated with hate.

"The Frond virus." One side of the little a-hole's mouth lifted in a condescending smile. "The one your little cohort have been lugging around this—"

"You want the virus?"

There was movement in one of the cells. Out of the corner of her eye, Angel saw Pam and two other women lifting a metal bed between them.

Beside her, Ford shifted with a groan, pressed back against the wall, and pushed slowly up. She glanced back and caught his eye. Down but not dead, his expression said.

More movement in the cell—the bed rocked back.

Ford grabbed Angel's hand. Squeezed *once…twice…*

The metal bed frame swung forward…

Three times.

Metal smacked into reinforced glass with a dull thud. The man startled and spun, half-rising from his seat.

As one, Angel and Ford went after the man.

Another crash of bed to window. The gun swung toward Angel.

Ford dove in front of her as a shot went off, the blast deafening. He went down.

The gun swung up again. Angel shoved it away and threw her elbow into the man's pinched little face. The resulting crunch would have made her sick in another life, but in this one, it satisfied some bloodthirsty desire for revenge. "*You bastard*," she yelled.

Crack! Spiderwebbed glass tinkled outward, raining onto the floor before the next quick swing, which blew the whole thing out into this room. Angel barely noticed as she used every bit of momentum to bash the man's head on the desk.

She didn't stop to protect her face from the flying glass, just thumped his head over and over again.

"Holy shit. Angel. Hon, stop it."

Angel threw off the hands that got in her way.

"Come on. You'll kill him and—"

"Needs to die." She shoved at him, wishing he'd put up more of a fight.

"*Stop!*" One of the women grabbed ahold of Angel. "Finish this after we get the door codes."

Angel's arms dropped heavily to her sides and she sank to the floor, nodding, though she didn't quite get what was happening.

Someone yelled. Another voice joined in.

"Put pressure on the wound."

Wound? Dazed, Angel searched for Ford.

People were suddenly there: legs, sock-clad feet.

Feet.

"Ford?" She swallowed back the taste of blood. Or the smell. She swiped a battered hand to her face. Stared at the deep red staining her hand. "*Ford?*"

Her eyes scanned the room. Where was he? Slowly, her head dropped. What was Pam doing? Was she kissing someone?

Crimson everywhere. Splashes and smears.

Something thick and sour filled her stomach. Dread.

Ford lay in a pool of blood as Pam worked over him.

Angel threw off a hand that tried to grab her—*no, oh no*—fought to crawl to him, pushed against big, rough arms to get to his side. To hold him tight, keep the blood in his veins, the life in his body.

Finally, she got ahold of one cold hand, which she held in both of hers—and though they tried to pull her away, she wouldn't let go.

She wouldn't let Ford go.

Katherine Harper couldn't raise Sampson or Tenny or anyone else on the phone and was beginning to fret. She turned to her computer and pushed a few buttons, but as usual, the absurd contraption didn't work. Why, oh why couldn't she figure this thing out? She was an intelligent woman after all.

Too old, clearly.

After pounding a few more keys, she shut it, hard.

There was too much invested in this project for those idiots to have gone and ruined it. They couldn't possibly have done that, could they?

She pictured Clive Tenny's obsequious little smile and sat back in her chair with a huff. Yes. Yes, that man could certainly have led this mission straight to ruin.

And if they were compromised, there was no doubt in

her mind as to whether the man could keep his mouth shut. None.

Which meant it was time to put an end to it all.

Temporarily.

But temporary, at this stage, was a difficult pill to swallow, since any day could be her last. The stroke had brought that home like nothing else. Well, the stroke and what had happened to the babies.

My God, that Tenny idiot had better be dead.

She leaned forward with difficulty, picked up the framed photo, and set it on the closed laptop.

One worn, wrinkled finger wiped an invisible layer of dust from their sweet faces, eternally frozen at ages five and seven. Two baby girls. Gone. *Poof.* Just like that.

Even after all these years, the emotion swamped her, turning her hands to shaking leaves. Her breath came in quick, uncontrolled bursts, punctuated with sounds she'd have to call whimpers. Except Katherine Henley Harper didn't whimper.

Swallowing back the last of her humanity, she returned the photo to its place and sat back.

Time to abort this failed mission. Luckily, there were other potential sources. Other ways to complete her life's work. The virus could be found again.

She had to believe that, or she might as well give up right this moment.

As soon as the weather cleared, she'd insert another team. In fact, she'd ensure that every person sent by the NSF next season was one of hers.

Too bad she didn't have someone like Cooper on her team. A glaciologist with an understanding of oil drilling. And she should hire more women, since the men all seemed to be mucking up their jobs.

A female geologist, then, for Colorado, hired through a shell company, with an appropriate cover story.

Of course, there were many other things she should have done. Like not trusting Tenny, that greedy, simpering little imbecile, with such an important mission. Father had been the one to hire him, and though he hadn't liked him much, he'd trusted him. Tenny had been perfect, Daddy had said, because he lacked scruples entirely.

A lot of good that had done them.

She sighed, sinking deep into her chair and staring out at the newly burgeoning spring. It made her feel nothing but old.

Time was passing inexorably, and she still didn't have her damned virus.

The world above her was a kaleidoscope of moving people.

Someone spoke. "You okay, babe?"

No. She blinked up at Jameson and tried to nod, though her muscles weren't working. *Probably.*

"Need help?"

She tried to press her lips into a numb smile and shook her head. "Jus' sit for a sec." The words came out slurred. "Right here." Right here being beside Ford, his hand in hers.

He nodded and tilted his head to look at Ford. "Think we can take over from here?"

She tightened her grip on Ford's limp fingers. Feral, protective.

"Crazy-ass shit happening around here, but we've got you now. We found the med clinic. Pam needs to take him there. Fix him up." He looked her over. "Then it's your turn."

"Okay." She managed to push herself to sitting, not letting go of Ford until Jameson forcibly removed her fingers one at a time. With palpable urgency, a group of her friends carried Ford away and she felt his absence like a missing chunk of her heart.

Once he'd gone, reality came back to her, so fast she had to close her eyes.

When, finally, she could open them again, she stared at her feet. God, were those holes in her boots? Her eyes climbed up her legs. Blood, all over her Carhartts. Ford's blood. She swallowed. Or maybe that man's. The one she'd beaten to a pulp.

She let her head flop back against the wall, put her hands flat on the floor, and breathed through a long, deep heaving wave of nausea.

"Wanna get cleaned up?"

She blinked. *Probably should.*

Someone else approached, the steps slowed. Angel focused on the boots first, then slid her way up to the face, which came into focus slowly. *I know her.* Oh, right. Donna. A scientist, from Burke-Ruhe.

"Hey, Donna." She worked hard to smile and possibly managed it.

"Angel, honey." Donna squatted. "Grab my hand?"

It took a few seconds to focus on the woman's hand. No blood there. It was warm and soft against Angel's chapped skin.

"Let's get you a shower."

They lifted her between them somehow.

"Stink that bad, huh?"

"Nah. But you look like hell."

"Thanks, Don—" She tried a step and stumbled, but

they were there to catch her, arms around her waist, under her armpits.

"Any of this blood yours?" Donna asked.

She shrugged. Crap, that hurt.

"You in pain?"

Frostbite, blisters, chafing, missing skin. None of it was worth mentioning. "Head...shoulders..." A laugh cramped her chest, made her double over. "Knees and toes."

"Right." She caught Donna and another woman exchanging a look. They led her, not straight to a shower, as promised, but to a medical facility, where a group worked around a bed.

"Got another patient, Doc." They helped her onto a bed.

"No," Angel tried to protest, batting at their hands, but nobody seemed to hear. Or care.

"Be right over once I'm done here."

They made her lie back.

"Ford." Her mouth flubbed the name, so she licked her cracked, swollen lips and tried again. "Ford. How's Ford?"

"He'll live." That was Pam talking. Or maybe Donna. Angel couldn't quite open her eyes enough to tell. "You done good, Angel. Really, really good."

Somebody patted her shoulder, someone else unzipped her undercoat. She tried to hold it closed.

Couldn't open it on the ice.

"Ford..." She shut her mouth, swallowed, and tried again. "Tell him he's..." *Everything*, she wanted to say, but no sound came out. *Tell him I love him.*

CHAPTER 48

"Aren't you supposed to wake him up?"

"Let me worry about Coop." Pam eyed her with a squint. "You need to rest."

Angel shook her head, which made the room spin.

"I'm not asking. As your doctor, I'm telli—"

"You weren't there, Pam. You weren't there." She grabbed the woman's hand and leaned forward, intense in that way she'd been since they'd gotten here. Or, if she was being honest, since she'd hidden in that ice tunnel back at Burke-Ruhe however many days ago. Weeks ago. A *lifetime* ago. "Won't leave him."

Pam must have seen something stubborn in Angel's face, or maybe it was the fists she'd made with her bandaged hands, because she backed off. "If you're not going to sleep, at least lie down in this cot. It's for you. Yours. Use it."

"You got the tubes?"

"Yes, Angel." Pam spoke slowly, as if she'd already said this a million times. Which, in fact, she had. "The virus is safe. It's safe."

"'kay." Deaf to whatever Pam said next, Angel turned to look at Ford, so pale and still in the bed beside hers.

Angel knew this was kindness, she understood it, felt it, but she couldn't appreciate it. Couldn't care for a damned thing while a piece of her lay shriveled, half-dead in the bed with Ford. Until he woke up, she couldn't revive it.

"Eat this, or you'll—" Pam stopped, her head at an angle. "What's that?"

It took a few seconds, but eventually Angel heard it, too.

Fear churned through her immediately. *I've been here,* she thought. *Out on the ice, more than once.*

"Sounds an awful lot like a plane."

"Oh God." She sat up too fast. "They've sent reinforcements, they'll—"

"They'll nothing." Pam put a hand on Angel's arm and reached for one of the two guns she'd set on a counter. "You think we're going down without a fight?" She squeezed once and let go, hefted the handgun, and handed it to Angel. "We're ready this time, remember? We've got their weapons, we've got their stupid virus, and we've got each other. They shouldn't have messed with a crew of hardened Poleys like us." Were those tears in Pam's eyes? "You proved that more than anyone, Angel. Got that?"

The panic ebbed and Angel nodded. "Okay."

Yesterday, a few of the Poleys had taken snowmobiles out to the site of her face-off with Sampson. They'd returned with the bodies and weapons, along with a newfound respect for Angel.

She'd gotten along fine with these guys back at Burke-Ruhe, before everything had happened, but the way they looked at her had changed. She wasn't just a colleague anymore, they'd told her, but a South Pole legend, like Shackleton or Scott.

"I'll head out to see what the hell's going on." Pam moved to the door. "You hold down the fort here."

"Got it." Angel nodded, gun gripped in her hands.

Pam left her alone with Ford, whose stillness made her want to shake him. Of course that would be the crazy thing to do. Then again, crazy had pretty much saved her life over the last few days, so...

Awkwardly, she stood and shoved her cot right up against his in a way that so closely resembled their time in the hut that she could almost smell it. Vodka, canned stew, and him. Him, all over her, in her, next to her at night.

She rolled onto the cot and got as close to his heat as she could, her back tight to his side, while her front faced the door, ready to protect him.

With her life, if need be.

Retired Navy SEAL Eric Cooper wasn't the type of man to ask for permission before acting. Nor was he the type to ask for forgiveness. He just did what needed to be done. It had been his job once. Now it was his personal mission.

For the greater good. For his nation. And, above all, for his family.

The second he'd heard his brother's garbled message from the South Pole, he'd set to work putting together a rescue mission, pulling in every favor he'd accrued in his years in the military and since. He'd put to work the vast resources available to a man who'd amassed a fortune through hard work and smart investments.

He'd also called in his friends—by far the most important assets at his disposal. A small specialized team, including Leontyne "Leo" Eddowes, once a combat helicopter pilot who could master anything airworthy. She hadn't batted an eye when he'd told her what he needed.

"Fly to Antarctica to save my brother."

"You got it," she'd said, knowing full well what kind of risk she was taking.

He looked around the cavernous, nearly empty aircraft at the people he was tightest with.

They all knew, to the last, that this mission could end before it even began. Fuel could freeze, the fucking plane could stick to the damn ice, making it impossible to take off again. And still they were willing—no, eager—to step up and do it.

He could almost cry if he weren't so fucking pissed off right now.

"Wish you hadn't come," he said to the woman beside him—Zoe, the love of his life and the only person here without combat experience. Well, with a single experience that he'd prefer never to live through again.

"Wish you'd shut up," she replied, and all he could do was squeeze her hand.

Despite the cold in here, they were sweltering in their massive expedition coats. It had been one hell of a scramble to outfit this group on such short notice, but he'd done it, with Zoe's help.

The Herc they flew in was the biggest miracle—a favor he'd be paying off for the rest of his life. But worth it. Anything would be worth getting his brother back, safe and sound, from whatever hellish clusterfuck he'd managed to get himself into down here.

"I'd say cleared for landing." Leo's voice came through the comm device. "Except there's nobody here to clear us. And we are so under the radar, we'll never see daylight again if they catch us."

Around him, his ex-teammates—although there was no ex- about it—seated themselves, strapping in for what they knew would be one hell of a ride to Volkov Station's blue ice runway.

"Take us there, Leo." He held his rifle tight and reached out again with his left hand, not relaxing until Zoe gripped it. "Let's do this."

———————————

"Get me Senator Mitchum," Katherine Harper said into her phone.

"Yes, ma'am."

She hit End and slumped in her seat for a few seconds. How had this spiraled so far out of control? Goodness, it irked her. She shut her eyes, biting back the disappointment and, with it, thoughts of the worst day of her life. They came more and more often recently, these images, almost too visceral to be considered memories.

A minute later, her phone buzzed. She straightened her spine before lifting the receiver. "Senator. We have a problem."

"What is it?" The man's words were deep and polished—television-worthy, unlike Katherine's own broken voice. This man hadn't suffered as she had. He hadn't known loss, didn't understand how deeply it destroyed a person, body and soul.

"The virus has gotten loose in our Antarctic facility."

"The vaccine didn't—"

"The team does not appear to have used it."

"Well, this is—"

"It is *catastrophic*, Teddy. I know. And now, since your soldiers apparently weren't able to fulfill their duties, the United States government needs to contain it."

The senator's pause spoke volumes, but she knew what

he'd say. They'd prepared for this after all. It was a matter of national security.

"It's the worst-case scenario, I know. And as you are aware, the team signed releases for just such an event. I'm afraid the worst has occurred. I received confirmation from Dr. Tenny himself."

"Well, that's absolutely tragic. He was an important man."

Referring to Tenny in the past already, as if the deed were done. Good. That meant there would be no objections. Not that she'd expected any, of course, since they were in this together. But one never knew how people would respond in high-stress moments.

She knew how *she* responded. Parts of her died—love, kindness, emotion. They all shriveled up, to be sloughed off like so much waste, leaving her a hard, empty shell of a person. A carapace protecting pure drive. A mission. That's all she was.

She straightened up and carried on. She moved mountains—literally digging them up—to ensure that her work would continue. When the world needed changing, she changed it.

"Yes. Yes, he was a very important man *indeed*." She nodded for a few beats. Twenty-five seconds, she found, usually conveyed the appropriate sadness. The senator apparently agreed, since he wrapped it up about then. Professional through and through. "And those soldiers will surely be missed."

"Someone will inform their families." Good Lord, the man was already practicing the lines he'd use on television. "Well, then, I suppose we must engage the necessary action." *Speaking of psychopaths...*

"Yes indeed. And I'm especially sad to say it appears Dr. Tenny performed some...clandestine operations on his own. He has gone rogue with the virus." Another fabrication, obviously. But no one could emerge from this operation alive. Letting the senator know that Tenny had gone rogue would ensure he took this straight to DEFCON, rather than settling on an ill-advised rescue mission. "Sampson was apparently on his side. The project must be shut down."

"Is there no one on the ground who can—"

"I'm afraid *all* of your men have been...terminated," she said, sealing their fates.

The senator's breathing continued, long and slow and smooth. Nothing could shock this man. Obviously not, if he was willing to spearhead top-secret missions like this one. Not for the same reasons as Katherine, nor with the same goal. But the result would be the same. Perhaps a bit more drastic than what the senator expected. But he'd get used to it once it was all over. He would come out on the right side of history. It was the survivors, after all, who wrote the books for future generations.

Either way, she couldn't bring herself to care. She'd likely be gone before the full effects had been felt. By then it would be too late. Her work would be done. And she could let herself rest.

She'd join her beloved husband and the babies and she'd take Fiona with her. At peace, finally.

Senator Mitchum sighed regretfully, bringing her back to the room, to here and now. "I'll engage the destruction protocol."

Katherine lowered her brows, tightened her lips, and nodded once in perfect, unconscious imitation of her father, who'd used this look with heads of state once upon a time. President Kennedy had sat in this very room with Father, strategizing much the way Katherine did today. Reagan, Clinton, both Bushes. Nearly every president since the 1960s. "Time is of the essence, of course, considering how dangerous the virus is. How soon do you think we can...?" she trailed off, knowing how important it was, occasionally, to step back and give men like this one a sense of their own power.

"I'll send the request to our man at Defense. We'll make sure all comms are cut. And he'll get those drones out as soon as is humanly possible."

The director nodded. "Perfect. Thank you, Teddy. *Thank you.*"

"Thank *you*, Katherine. I will ensure that your condolences are passed along to the families." He paused before quietly adding, "It's a good thing what you're doing here. For the good of the planet. For the good of mankind. A very good thing."

CHAPTER 49

A KNOCK AT THE DOOR MADE ANGEL SHAKE LIKE SHE was back on the ice again, alone in her own whiteout. She tightened her bandaged hands on the gun, pressed back into Ford's warm body, and waited.

"Ms. Smith? Ma'am? This is Eric Cooper. I understand my brother's inside with you. Am I free to enter?"

Was it a trick? It had to be a trick.

But wait. Eric Cooper. She knew that name.

Oh my God. It's him. It's Ford's brother.

"I'm pointing a weapon at the door," she croaked out, even though she'd never shot one of these in her life. Then again, she hadn't killed a man before this week, either, so… "How do I know it's you?"

"Ford's my little brother, ma'am. Ask me anything."

She wracked her brain for a few seconds and fell upon something he'd told her in the tent. "There's an island. Off the coast of California, where your dad used to take you fishing when you were kids. What's the name of it?"

"San Elias Island." Her hands loosened of their own volition, and she barely tightened them again before letting the gun fall. "In fact, I spent the night there with Zoe recently."

"It's true!" a woman chimed in. "We didn't exactly choose to stay there the first time. But I guess that's a story for some other day."

"Right. Now, I'm gonna open this door. Okay, Ms. Smith? Angel? Slowly." The door latch opened with a clunk and Angel sucked in a breath. It could still be a trick, right? "Appreciate it if you'd hold your fire."

Angel sat up and, because she couldn't control the way her hand shook, pointed the weapon at the ceiling, watching the door with unblinking hawk eyes.

The man who came in did look like Ford, but longer and leaner. Where Ford had those squared off parts—jaw, chest, shoulders—his brother looked like he'd been stretched up. But the tension in the eyes was the same, what she could see of his coloring, too. When he'd given the room a quick once-over, there was no mistaking his anguish as he went to his brother's side.

"I'm so sorry." The apology rushed out. "He was shot. Twice."

"It's not your fault."

"No. You don't get it. I couldn't stop them from—"

Eric squatted in front of her and put a hand on her arm—just a quick pat—then took it away. "You saved his life. Thank you."

"You know how many times he saved mine?"

"Yeah." He tightened his jaw. "Let's get you guys stateside, okay? You good with that?" At her nod, he asked, "Where's home for you?"

She opened her mouth and closed it.

When she pictured home now, all she could see was an orange cocoon, floating on an endless sea of ice, the heat of two bodies, the secret place between them.

A conversation came back to her, the memory infused with the tent's warm glow: *You like making people happy,* Ford had said about her cooking. *That's why you do it.* She'd wanted to argue, to tell him he was wrong.

And then she'd stopped. Because he'd been right. For her,

cooking wasn't about tastes and smells and textures. It was about feeding people. *Giving* to them. And now just thinking about that made her feel seen. As if Ford had peeled her skin away and peered at her quickly beating heart.

Now that escape was actually possible, she didn't want to sell her soul to the highest bidder anymore. She wanted to spread it around, like butter. Like love. To give it to people who wanted it, who needed it.

But first, Ford. Only Ford.

"We're gonna evacuate the base now. You good with that?" Eric asked.

She shook her head, blinking away the close, heated moment. "How'd you even get here? I thought planes couldn't—"

"Took a necessary risk. But we need to go ASAP. Can you make it to the plane on your own?" She stood, reached for the crutches they'd found for her, and nodded. "We'll get Ford loaded up. Rest of the folks, too."

Minutes later, a bundled-up Angel emerged from the building blinking like a mole just out of hibernation.

She peered at the plane, sitting almost on its belly, with nothing but thick skis between it and the ice. The aircraft was a hive of activity, with red-coated people going in and out. Unlike the ones she'd seen before, this Hercules had nothing printed on the side. A ghost.

Her head tilted back just enough to take in the clear blue sky, the sun slanting down on this place as if bad weather never happened.

Her swinging steps were slow, but nowhere near as sluggish as that final slog across the ice, the two of them propping each other up, when neither could have done it alone.

At the open door to the aircraft, she stopped, moved aside for someone to pass, and turned to look at the station's blocky buildings, dwarfed by this place, as inconsequential as a child's toy. For a few emotionally charged moments, she couldn't move, could only stare and say goodbye.

To an old friend? An archenemy? Like with close family, she'd been forced to endure Antarctica's foibles. Now, in a way she'd never be able to put into words, she was connected to this place.

Suppressing a sob, she stepped into the Herc's shadowy interior, where she joined the rest of the Burke-Ruhe winter-overs, settled into a seat, and waited to fly away from this terrible, wonderful continent.

With the help of his teammates—Von and Ans—Eric loaded Ford into the plane and strapped him in under the care of Burke-Ruhe's physician.

He told the big bearded guy—ex-army, like his brother—to do a final count and ran back outside for the prisoner. Halfway there, Leo's voice cut through on their comm devices. "Picking up something weird, guys."

"What?"

"Something small. More than one. Drones, possibly. Headed this way fast."

Eric and Von exchanged a look and quickened their pace.

"How's the fuel?" Eric asked.

"Well, it's not frozen," replied Leo, clipped and sarcastic. "Yet."

"Roger that." Eric turned to Von. "Help Ans get the ice

cores packed up," he yelled, already running back to the building. "I've got the prisoner."

He sprinted down the hall to where Clive Tenny languished in a cell. The asshole had ignored their order to dress for the cold. Which he'd regret.

Eric threw open the door. "Plane's taking off in one minute, dickwad. With or without you on board."

The man stood and walked toward the door, too damned slowly. Eric grabbed his arm and pulled him out, down the hall.

They were halfway to the plane when Leo's voice crackled to life again. "*Eric!*" she barked. "They're closing in. Need you back here. *Now!*"

Shit.

"Faster." Eric broke into a run, dragging the trembling professor-type across the ice to the plane.

This was the place Ford *chose* to come back to every year? Incomprehensible.

"*Move!*" Von met them twenty yards out and hauled the prisoner on board.

"Need to go wheels up." The urgency in Leo's voice told him they had seconds to spare. If that. "Like, *yesterday.*"

Eric gave the sky a cursory glance as he pulled the door closed behind him. "We're in." Time to get the hell out of this hellhole. "*Go!*" he yelled into his comm device.

They were off, bumping across the ice before they could strap in. The prisoner fell to the floor, rolled. Von got him into a seat, secured his harness, and finally buckled up just as they took to the air. Eric worked his way to the cockpit and settled in beside Leo. He exchanged his earpiece for a headset.

"What the hell?"

"Coming in fast."

"What is it?"

She shook her head. "Not sticking around to find out."

They'd just eased into the air, a good distance from the main building, when the first impact sounded—sharp enough to hear through the big headset Eric had put on.

Though she remained expressionless, he could *see* the tension coming off Leo, could feel the airwaves vibrating. Seconds later, the plane dropped, as if it had hit turbulence.

Craning his neck, he could barely make out a dark puff of smoke from the place they'd just left.

Christ. That was close. His heart was thumping fast with adrenaline and a new thing he'd only recently developed on this type of mission—fear. Not for himself, but for his brother, his woman, his friends, and now this group of people who counted on him.

Leo pushed them higher, slowly gaining altitude and distance.

He exchanged a long look with her as she circled the base, giving them a bird's-eye view of a second impact—a missile hit, shifting the air around them and obliterating the station. When he finally turned back to her, he could see the questions, even through her mirrored sunglasses.

"We safe?"

She swiveled left and right, her movements quick and efficient. "Hell if I know."

There was no sound but the drone of engines as they rose.

"What the fuck is going on here, Eric?" He'd never heard Leo sound quite so shaken.

"No fucking idea." He shook his head. "Who the hell has that kind of firepower?"

Whoever it was had just wiped out an entire research station. If his brother's guess was right and Chronos Corporation—a pharmaceutical company—was behind it, then the face of the world had seriously changed. Or not, depending on what kind of conspiracy theories a person believed.

"Think it was government?"

"Doesn't make sense, but it has to be." He nodded slowly, then faster. "We're dealing with more than just a business decision."

"Whoever it is, they just created one hell of a diplomatic incident."

"Yeah." His jaw tensed up as he realized the importance of what they carried on board. "We've got the tubes, on ice, and possibly the only survivor who knows what the hell they were up to down there."

"Hell of a shit sandwich your brother made here, Cooper." Now that they'd gained altitude, Eric could hear the sparkle in Leo's voice. It might sound like a complaint, but now that the initial shock had passed, she was happy. Because although they'd all left the armed forces for one reason or another, his friends ached for a mission as much as he did. And this adrenaline-filled ride was exactly what they'd been missing.

He grinned back at her. "You're telling me."

It had been one hell of a day. Katherine was enjoying a much-needed scotch in front of the fire when the phone rang, interrupting a long, dreamy thread of memories.

She fumbled with the handset. "Yes?"

"Tenny's alive." It was Senator Mitchum, his voice without its usual rich, self-satisfied timbre.

"Excuse me?"

"He's on a plane, headed to U.S. soil as we speak."

Speechless for a few seconds, Katherine's hand trembled so hard she had to set her glass down. "That is a…surprise." She swallowed. "I was told no aircraft could land in Antarctica in this weather. Much less take off."

"No idea how, but some paramilitary organization took the risk. Went in and evacuated the lot of 'em, apparently, in the nick of time. Including the inhabitants of an entire Antarctic research station." She could hear the wry smile in his voice. "There's already talk of a miracle."

She squinted. "*What* paramilitary organization precisely?" If this was Sampson's work, she'd take him out personally. Right in this room, with poison or her letter opener or her daddy's pistol. The man had gone off the reservation entirely, using resources that weren't his to—

"It's unclear. Appears to involve a team of ex-SEALS and a combat pilot. Possibly linked to one of the Antarctic researchers." All right then. So not Sampson. She had been correct in her assumption that he'd never returned to the facility.

Cooper. She felt it, could almost hear his name with absolute certainty. The one Sampson had left behind, along with the station's cook. He'd wanted to wait for the man, but she'd made the call to leave them to die. *My fault then.* Self-flagellation, rather than punishment.

Not nearly as satisfying.

"What can we do?"

"We'll take care of them."

She nodded, tired. So tired. Her vision blurred as she stared at the dancing flames.

And then something occurred to her.

"What about the virus?" Her breathing picked up speed. "Do they have the virus on board?"

"Is that a possibility?" The senator sounded as worked up as she felt.

"There's only one way to find out." She slugged back her scotch and stood, a little bleary. "We need access to that plane."

CHAPTER 50

AN HOUR INTO THE FLIGHT, ERIC WENT INTO THE BACK, motioned to Ans and Von to grab Tenny, and marched him toward the unoccupied section of the plane behind the cockpit.

"What are you doing? You can't… Hey!" The man's protests were almost impossible to hear through the drone of the big plane. "Where are you taking me? This is highly—"

"Not sure I introduced myself down there. I'm Eric Cooper. We talked on the phone a few days back. Remember me, Dr. Tenny?"

He shut his mouth, wisely, and nodded.

"Right now we're a couple hours out from Punta Arenas, Chile. After that, we plan to head to San Diego. Any idea what'll be waiting for us there?"

Tenny eyed the group of big tough men. He must have come to the correct conclusion that they wouldn't let him leave this aircraft without an explanation.

"Not exactly." He paused. "But I know it won't be good."

"All right. Tell me about the virus my brother found."

Tenny's eyes grew shifty, even as he sniffed and wiped his swollen, bandaged nose for the third time. His face, puffy and bruised, sported two black eyes and more than a dozen stitches, all courtesy of Angel Smith. Eric smiled.

Von and Ans stared silently, emanating violence.

"We were sent to test a vaccine."

Eric exchanged a look with his friends.

"Wait, wait. Ford just found the virus, so how the hell'd you set up that operation so quickly?"

"He extracted it over a month before we arrived. And... this wasn't the first time we've seen the *Fronsviridae*. The Frond virus. We call it that because—"

"Focus," Von spat in his Grim Reaper voice.

"Right. Right." Tenny spoke, eyes darting furtively, as if anyone could overhear them. He cleared his throat. "I understand someone stole the original sample before disappearing. Took it with him. Or destroyed it. Not sure which."

"Who?"

He shrugged. "Someone close to the..."

"To what?"

"A company. I'm not sure..."

"Spit it out."

"Well, my funding's through a small—"

"Don't waste our time. We want the top of the totem pole."

Tenny sat looking at his hands for a few long beats, breathing hard, probably considering who scared him most—the entity whose money and influence had created this hell or the motley group currently staring him down.

"Chronos Corporation." He paused. "But it goes higher. Way higher."

Eric met Von's eyes. Shit. Whatever Chronos was up to, it was bad.

"Okay," Eric said. "So explain those cells where you held the others. And tell me about—"

"I had *nothing* to do with that," Tenny insisted.

"Don't lie to us, you murdering *fuck*." Without seeming to move, Von was in Tenny's face. Everything about Von spoke of violence: his voice, his expression, the way he held himself. Clive Tenny could have no doubt of his own mortality when faced with the wrath of Von "The Reaper" Krainik, and he was scared shitless.

"Who gave you orders? Who, specifically, sent you down there, financed the whole thing? Operation must've cost millions." Eric leaned in. "I want names."

"Uh…" Tenny swallowed and swiped at a bead of sweat trickling down his temple. "I'd…rather not say."

"Really?" Eric had managed to keep his rage at bay up until this moment. But here, right now, this little fucking worm making up excuses was the last straw. He'd hurt him if that was what it took. One hand whipped out and wrapped around the man's neck. Eric didn't tighten it yet, but the threat was there. "Because I can't imagine a single person coming to your rescue if some sort of accident were to occur on this plane, can you?"

Tenny's eyes—already round in his bruised and battered face—had bulged out to become almost inhuman orbs, the whites enormous. He looked at Ans, then at Von, who'd pulled out his knife at some point and started cleaning his fingernails. Finally, Tenny faced Eric, his fear stinking up the air between them.

"Tell me. Now. And you keep your fingers. Your toes, your tongue, your ears." Eric's eyes flicked down, the threat implied. "Talk and we return you to American soil. Don't, and we dump chunks of you into the Pacific."

It took about three seconds for Tenny to start spewing names, places, the testing they'd planned to do on the winter-overs—on his *brother*, goddammit. By the end, Eric had the urge to open the door and throw the monster out anyway, air pressure and promises be damned.

Instead, he handed Tenny over to the other guys and returned to the cockpit to fill Leo in.

"Why?" she asked, as freaked out about the whole thing as he was.

"Money, sounds like."

"Right," she said. "That's why he and those goons did it, but what's the virus for?"

"Bioweapon. His guess. Not mine."

"That's some messed-up shit right there."

"Yeah." Eric shared a long look with Leo. "And I've got a funny feeling it's not over."

"This starting to feel like a conspiracy to you, Eric? A big one?"

"Sure is." He thought for a few seconds. "They *can't* let Tenny live."

"Think they'll take us down? Whole aircraft?"

He shivered, thinking about Zoe and Ford back there. All the others. Good people, who didn't deserve to die.

"Shit." His mind was working fast, going into overdrive. "How soon till we land in Punta Arenas?"

"Hour or so."

"All right." He smiled at her. "I've got an idea."

CHAPTER 51

Entering United States Airspace—18 hours later

"GOT COMPANY," LEO MUTTERED WHEN THEY ENTERED U.S. airspace the next day.

Eric heard it—an F-16 darted under them, swooped up and to the side. Circling them like a goddamned shepherd.

"Escort." He eyed the horizon.

"Yeah." Leo didn't have to look at him.

A voice crackled in their headsets. "This is a United States Air Force armed F-16. You are in violation of restricted airspace."

"Restricted airspace my ass," Leo muttered. "I filed a damn flight plan."

"Yeah, well, we all know they don't give a shit about the flight plan," Eric responded.

"This is a United States Air Force armed F-16. You have been intercepted. Please acknowledge or rock your wings."

Eric lifted his phone. "I'm recording."

"Here we go." With an irritated sigh, Leo acknowledged them, asking, "What is the violation?" When she didn't get an answer, she identified herself and went on. "This aircraft is returning home from the Volkov Antarctic Research Station. We have a prisoner on board. And we've got a journalist from the Los Angeles *Times* on the phone. She is recording and live-broadcasting these communications and knows the identity of every person on this aircraft. Please convey that information to…whoever you are currently reporting to."

After a pause, the F-16 pilot replied, "Roger that."

There was no more communication, so she remained on-course, following the tower's instructions as they approached. When they were cleared to land, she did so impeccably. The woman had nerves of steel. Best pilot he'd ever had the pleasure to fly with.

On the ground, Eric stared out at what looked like millions of flashing lights and let out his pent-up breath before heading to the back. Alone, he opened the airplane door to find quite the welcoming committee, weapons trained on him.

ATF, FBI, police. From the looks of it, they were all here. Media organizations crowded the grass beyond the fence. Above them, more than one news helicopter circled.

"We've got one wounded United States citizen," Eric yelled out the door. "In need of immediate medical care."

"Step outside, sir!"

Even from this distance, he could feel the almost palpable weight of this many weapons trained on him. He put his hands on his head and slowly exited the aircraft, right into the biggest goat rodeo he'd encountered on this side of the Pacific.

Within moments, he, Leo, and Dr. Clive Tenny—the plane's only occupants—were facedown on the tarmac. After a quick search of the aircraft, they were dragged to their feet and taken to three separate locations for questioning.

As Eric watched Dr. Clive Tenny being hauled into an ambulance that quickly sped away, he had the distinct feeling that it was the last he'd ever see of the man.

Clínica Sangre de Cristo, Punta Arenas, Chile—the Next Day

"Knock, knock."

Angel's eyes flew open to see a TV screen floating above her. Not the tent. Not Antarctica.

Her hand scrabbled at her side. No Ford.

Where the hell was she?

A beat later it came back.

A private clinic in Chile. They'd checked her in yesterday under a false name. For her own safety, she'd been told. Same for the armed guard at her door.

She blinked a few times and finally focused on Pam, who stood at the foot of the white metal bed. "Hey, Pam."

"Sorry I woke you."

"No. No, it's fine." She hit the button to sit up, still woozy after her knee surgery. "Everything okay?"

With a nod, Pam picked up Angel's chart. "They taking good care of you?"

"Sure." Angel shrugged as nonchalantly as she could manage.

"At least you speak Spanish." Pam squinted at the page she was reading. "I only get half this stuff and I'm a doctor."

Angel forced a smile to her lips. "Is he still outside my door?" she whispered.

"The guard? Yeah. You and Ford."

"What about everybody else?"

"We're heading home today." Pam threw a narrow-eyed look over her shoulder and leaned closer. "You see the news?"

"No." Angel shook her head. "Don't want to."

"Well, we're the big story. The way they're spinning it, it was all Sampson and Tenny. Two evil genius kidnappers. No higher powers involved."

"What about Chronos and the virus and all that—"

"Shhhh." Pam put a hand on Angel's arm, looking...spooked? "First rule of virus is *there is no virus*." She leaned in and whispered, "It's in a safe place. Eric and his team are already planning next steps."

"Next steps? What does that even mean?"

"They need more information on the damned stuff. Nobody knows what it is, why it's been buried under the ice, or what the hell those people want with it. First, they figure that out." She shrugged. "After that, I'm not sure."

Angel shut her eyes and pressed her fingers to them until she saw spots.

The moment she'd hidden in the supply arch and witnessed Alex Stickley getting shot to death, she'd fallen down a rabbit hole of epic proportions. Crossing the world's coldest continent on foot suddenly seemed absurdly simple, child's play compared to the high-level international espionage cover-up crap going on now. Ford's brother, for example. Who the hell was he? A guy with the resources to do what he'd done, who could plan things like next steps? Next steps...who even talked like that? Thought like that?

"Shit is *crazy* right now, Angel." Pam pointed at the dark screen. "News says the president's been on the phone with Russia, smoothing things out."

"Smoothing what out? The missiles that destroyed the—"

"The *official* story is that the explosions were..." Here she used air quotes. "Charges set by Sampson's team of terrorists. *We* know that this clusterfuck has *government involvement* written all over it, but we've been instructed to play dumb."

"Dumb?"

"As a doornail. Look, the president's suggesting a joint effort at Pole. A U.S. and Russian research station. Suddenly—*surprise!*—Chronos Corp's come out of the woodwork, offering up cash for the rebuild. Bigger, better. You—Hey! Angel? Where are you going? You just had surgery, for Christ's sake."

Ignoring her friend, Angel looked around. "I need clothes. Where are my clothes?"

"Whoa, whoa, I'll get you some when you're ready, but this is—"

"We can't let them get away with it, Pam. If Chronos bankrolls a South Pole rebuild, we might as well hand them those freaking ice cores." Angel turned in a circle and, finding nothing to put on, decided to hell with it. She'd go out there like this.

"Wait. Wait, Angel. *Listen!*" Pam's hand on her arm finally stopped her. "You are not alone anymore." She stared her down. "You're not alone on the ice, honey. *I'm* with you on this. Jameson is. Eric and his guys. We all are. We all want to stop them. But you going off half-cocked is not gonna help anyone."

Angel stopped and sagged back onto the bed, face in her hands.

Pam drew close. "What? You in pain? Want me to call the—"

"It's Ford. Coop, I mean." *Just spit it out already.* "Nobody'll tell me what's happening with him and I'm…" She sucked in air. *Breathe.* "Why won't anyone tell me how the surgery went? Is it that bad? Is he…" She couldn't finish her sentence.

"He's out of surgery. And he's good. Conscious."

Then why can't I see him? Hasn't he asked for me?

"Probably won't be hitting the ice anytime soon." Pam looked at a loss for the first time since she'd arrived. "Goes for all of us, I guess."

"Ford won't like that."

"No. He won't." Pam's eyes were so kind it made her feel itchy. Like maybe she had bad news she didn't want to share. "You okay, Angel?"

Her knee hurt like hell, but she was pretty sure that wasn't what Pam was asking. And this outburst, well, she could put it down to fear and frustration, anger, too, at all the crap that had happened. But when it came down to it, she didn't know. Anything.

She barely recognized herself. Everything felt tight and off, like her insides had been pulled out, mixed up, and put back in wrong.

"I'm fine," she lied. "So. Eric and his band of merry soldiers are taking care of things, but then…what?"

"Well, you get PT for that knee."

"No. I mean. With us? Me? You guys? Ford?" Angel whispered his name. After a long, significant look, Angel opened her mouth and shut it again.

"You want to talk about it?" Pam asked.

"What?" Maybe if she played dumb, Pam would let it go.

"What happened out there?" her friend insisted, because that's what good friends did. They didn't accept your bullshit. "With you and Coop."

"I don't…" Angel blinked past one memory after another—the tent that very first night. His smile, with that almost-dimple that she'd wanted to lick. Had she licked it? She didn't think so. *Why was that so upsetting?* "I don't know." *Because maybe she wouldn't get to lick it now. Ever.*

"You okay, hon?"

Angel could only nod, exhausted. "Yeah." She rubbed a hand over the soft hospital sheet. Well, soft if she compared it to what she'd gotten used to sleeping on. Hard ice, with nothing but a couple layers of padding, slippery sleeping bags. Warm, solid man.

Not just any man.

Ford.

He was *it*, the missing piece she couldn't put her finger on, the reason she couldn't get comfortable in this bed or maybe any bed. Ever again.

Because he wasn't in it. And she wanted him there.

But what did *he* want?

Clínica Sangre de Cristo—2 days later

With Von trailing her like a creepy, ghostly guard dog, Angel finally broke down and went to see Ford.

She made her way on crutches down the long corridor, to where Ans stood at Ford's door. She gave him a weak smile and knocked, waited for Ford's rough voice to invite her in, then entered. It hurt to watch him struggle to sit up, but then again, it would hurt a lot more if he were dead.

She'd get over it.

"Angel."

"Hey."

He looked her up and down, frowning. "Shouldn't you be in…"

She closed the door and leaned against it, then lifted a crutch. "Knee's good enough to walk with these, so I'm headed back to the U.S. today." *Invite me farther in.* "What's your status?" *Ask me to stay. To see where this leads.*

"Stuck here for a while. Then PT. Flying out soon. Guess I'll winter at the university. Then head south next summer."

He meant antarctic summer, clearly. So he'd be going back.

"Wow, that sounds…" Dangerous, stupid, absolutely incomprehensible.

She needed air, but the big shaky breath she sucked in felt more like volcanic ash than oxygen. She held it in, wound up tight, knowing that if she let the tiniest bit of pain seep out, it would turn into an unstoppable deluge. A broken dam. She forced a smile to her wooden lips. "Sounds good."

Ford, of course, didn't bother smiling. "What's your plan?"

"I'll figure it out." She shrugged, going for casual but feeling about as smooth as a broken puppet. "A friend asked me to help her start this little farm-to-table place, not too far from Philly. It's…" *Everything I thought I wanted. But it's not you.*

"Great." Another humorless look.

"Yeah." She couldn't face him for fear she'd break down and beg him to—to what? That was the thing, she didn't even know what she wanted from him. There was no common ground for them. Or rather there was, but they'd left it on the ice. The way they'd been, the way they'd lived, what she'd thought of as a relationship, had been nothing but survival. She gulped and forced another stiff, bright smile. "Anyway. Just thought I'd check in. They're discharging me, so I wanted to say—" *Goodbye. Or hold me. Or I love you.* "Okay." She indicated the crutches with a grimace. "I'd hug you but…" She scrabbled at the door, grasped the knob, twisted, and pushed. "Take care, Ford."

She'd just stepped outside when he said—or rather rasped out—her name. "Angel."

She turned, unable to control the swell of hope that blossomed in her chest. "Yeah?"

"Thank you."

She blinked. "For what?" For the sex part? For saving his life? The door closed again with a snick and, just like that, she was back to the Burke-Ruhe kitchen, honing a steel knife blade while he gave her his awkward thanks.

"Ah. For everything."

Could you specify, please? Or maybe not. Maybe she didn't want him thanking her for sex. Which she couldn't even call sex, since it had been so much more than that— the most intimate, most genuine, moments of her life. But maybe to him it hadn't meant a thing. Just a hot body on cold ice.

"Ah. Okay. Well." She tried another smile, so fake it had to look painted on. "You're welcome."

She'd just reached for the door again when he pierced the little armor she'd managed to wrap around herself.

"We couldn't be any—we can't be anything."

Don't do this to me. Don't break my heart.

She didn't even pretend to misunderstand. "Why not?"

"Got a call from the NSF today. They want me to head up rebuilding and research at the station. I'll have access to— I'm going back." He tightened his lips. Was that supposed to be a happy expression? "And you'll be running the kitchen of your dreams. Which is what you deserve. Entirely."

Was it? Even if it wasn't what she wanted anymore? "What if—"

"The ice is where I belong." He nodded once, his expression stubborn, tight. Who was he working so hard to convince? Her or himself? "Heading back as soon as the weather clears."

"Sure. Clean, simple environment where you're in control, right?" This obsession with control drove her crazy. Especially when she'd seen him the other way—out of control. Wild. Real. The man behind the ice.

Somewhere outside, tires screeched.

"Exactly." The forbidding voice, the austere expression, and even in a damned hospital bed, that rigid spine. The eyes. Those inhumanly cold eyes. The Ice Man was back. She wanted to scream, to rail, to beg him to see her. *Her. Them.*

"I call bullshit." When had the first tear fallen? Her cheeks were soaking now, her mouth full of salt, but there was no relief from breaking the seal and letting them flow. "I call *fear.* You're scared of life, Ford. Of this." She flapped her hand between them.

"Not scared. Just not interested."

A yell sounded from not too far off.

Not interested. Those words hurt as deeply as a slap across the face. Deeper. As if he'd taken one of her blades and slid it straight into her already-bruised heart. But they also served to straighten her back and stop the ridiculous tears. She wouldn't cry over him. Wouldn't mourn the loss of another unfeeling asshole. No way.

"Okay then." One last cleansing breath. "Take care."

She'd just put her hand on the door when the window smashed.

CHAPTER 52

AN EXPLOSION, FOLLOWED BY ABSOLUTE SILENCE.

Coop blinked, the movement slow, pushed himself out of bed, swayed, and dropped to his ass again.

The door swung open.

Von's lips moved as he said something, gesticulating. *Now!* Was that it? *Move now!*

This time, Ford stayed standing, though his skull almost cracked from the pressure.

Ans rushed in, weapon drawn, ran to the window, pulled back the tattered blinds, and dove out into the night.

Where was Angel? Had she been hurt?

Was Von talking to him? Coop couldn't hear a fucking thing.

"Where is she?" he yelled. His voice didn't reach his own ears.

His heart beat loudly, the only sound in this strange, silent world. Rhythmic and muted like the far-off chugging of a train. "Dammit! Angel?"

He spun. Couldn't find her. Spun again, fear climbing from his belly to his chest, where it ballooned before sliding into his throat to choke him.

The building shook, smoke poured in from the hallway. Hands grabbed at Ford. He shoved them off. Oh shit. It was Von.

He turned away. "Angel!" he couldn't hear himself. Took a choked breath. "*Angel!*" This time, his roar burst the bubble, letting in an unbearable cacophony.

Christ, he'd break in half if anything happened to her. Worse than that: he'd tear the world apart. Where was she? Von pulled him, struggling and half-blind, up and out the door.

The noise was deafening. Screaming, gunshots, people dashing around, just vague shapes, flashing red lights. Sprinklers. The deafening shriek of an alarm. Smoke, acrid and thick as fog, made him hack. Absolute mayhem.

"Stairs!" Von led the way through the fiery hellscape, through a door, and down a set of steps. Shit. Coop's chest was tight, his lungs a mess. *Not gonna make it.*

Was that Ans and Angel up ahead?

"Move it!" Von yelled. "Your brother'll kill me if I don't get you out of here."

Ford started to laugh, which made him cough so hard his stitches must've popped. The pain in his shoulder was excruciating, but it pushed him through the pain meds fuzzing up his brain. With a clearer head, he picked up the pace, ignoring his unsteady legs, his lightness of breath, and the fact that the gown left his backside open to the elements.

No fucking way was he coming back from what happened in Antarctica to get his bare ass blown up in some fancy Chilean clinic.

Just behind Von, they burst out a fire door into the cool night, and came to an abrupt stop.

Holy crap. He dropped his hands to his knees and bent, gasping for air.

"Come on." Von lifted his chin to where a car idled at the curb. "You can do that in there."

Blindly, he followed him and dove into the back seat.

Angel was inside.

"What…the hell?" He sounded like crap.

The door slammed shut.

"Good to meet you, Dr. Cooper. Good to see you again, Angel." The driver—a dark-skinned woman with closely shorn hair—flicked a quick salute over her shoulder, her words just audible over the deafening buzzing in his ears. "I'm Leo Eddowes. Buckle up."

She pulled away, tires screeching.

The drive to the private airstrip was absolutely silent. Coop glanced at Angel a few times, only to see her staring out at the dimly lit world. Probably angry. Which was good. It was fine. Better this way.

Then why the hell'd he have the urge to crush something with his bare hands?

At the airstrip, Leo led them to a small jet and got them settled. A short while later, Ans and Von joined them, sat in seats, and they took off.

An hour into the flight, Leo made her way back to Angel and Ford, who'd sat on opposite sides of the same row.

"All right, guys. We've got to talk."

Angel watched Leo, completely avoiding Coop.

"There's a hefty price on your heads. Someone wants the two of you dead. Badly." Leo met his eyes. "And now, as far as they're concerned…you are."

"Dead," he repeated, his brain still ten steps behind.

A glance at Angel showed her sitting stiffly in her seat, staring blankly ahead. He wanted to reach for her, to tell her it would be fine. They'd be fine.

But Jesus, that wasn't true, was it? And he'd never been the type to lie about bullshit like that.

"Where are we headed?"

"States. West Coast. We've got passports for both of you. We'll get you in. Then it depends on you." Leo's eyes flicked from Angel to Ford and back. "Your brother's got something he'd like you to see. After that, we can set you up wherever you want. Together or..." She paused, not quite meeting their eyes this time. "So, you two want to disappear together or are we talking multiple destinations?"

Ford opened his mouth to reply, but Angel beat him to it.

"Separate." She didn't even spare him a glance. "Ford and I are going our separate ways."

With a short nod, Leo made her way back to her seat, and all Ford could think was *What the fuck have I done?*

One Week Later—Polaris Platform, Somewhere off the Coast of San Diego

"This sure is something." Coop stared down at the ocean from the top level of the decommissioned Polaris oil platform. "So when did you become a Bond villain?" he asked his brother.

"That's it?" Eric straightened, looking pissed. Or like he'd taken a hit to the face. "I bring you out to show you this place, the project, our plans. I offer you part of..." He shook his head. "That's all you've got? Your only response is a joke?"

"It's impressive, Bro. It's just a lot."

"Right. Sure." Eric looked away. When he turned back, his expression was worried. "Still in pain?"

"No. I'm good," he said through gritted teeth. "Doing great."

"Jesus, man, you're a shitty liar."

He met his brother's eyes, shocked to see absolutely no humor there.

"Pretty sure I know the answer to this, but...what'll it be, Ford?" Eric looked resigned. "Will you consider my offer? Join Polaris? Or are you seriously committing suicide by going back to the ice?"

Coop couldn't quite meet his eye. "I like it there, Eric. I'm comfortable there."

"Yeah, I know, Ford." Eric leaned forward and smacked Coop's good shoulder. The hit wasn't entirely friendly. "But it's too damned dangerous to be you. If you must, find some isolated glacier where nobody knows you, do your field stuff for a month every year, like a normal person, like every other goddamn researcher. Drill your cores and head home to study 'em."

He couldn't do that. Live his life in labs? Didn't matter how attractive that might sound to someone else—it wasn't for him.

"Take the offer. Change your name and join the team. Come on, man. Don't waste your life hiding from the *good stuff*." The way he said those two words made Coop feel like he'd never understand. *Ever.*

Eric turned away to stare out at the endless blue ocean.

Coop started to say something about how he belonged on the ice and that was where he was needed but stopped. When he looked at Eric again, there was nothing between them but the truth. "I'm lost, Eric." He motioned toward the enormous metal structure, currently under massive renovation. "This is...awesome. I mean, magnificent. And Zoe's...great. She doesn't take your crap and she loves you and..."

He stared out at San Elias Island, rising up from the

water just a few miles closer to shore, sucked in the briny sea air, listened to the gulls and the light slap of water far below.

"Why'd you start coming out here again? I mean, why San Elias instead of a million other places you could've picked to go fishing?"

Eric opened his mouth and shut it, as if he'd reconsidered some wisecrack. "I missed him."

Dad. He didn't have to say it for Coop to know who he meant.

"You ever miss him, Ford?"

Tears hit the back of his throat in a rush, stinging his sinuses, blurring his eyes. Shocked, he could only nod in response.

"He was a shitty dad. But he gave us each other." After a weird, awkward pause, he moved in close to put his arm around Ford's shoulders. Aside from the docs in the clinic, nobody'd touched him like this in forever.

Except for Angel.

They stood quietly for a few minutes—long enough for Eric's arm to go from awkward to comfortable and, finally, comforting. All the while, Coop pictured being back on the ice, the way it was before. He could envision it perfectly: heading out to his drills, going back to the station, taking a load off in the galley. The problem was that he couldn't picture anyone but Angel in the kitchen, couldn't see himself sleeping in that same cold single bed every night of his life.

"I miss Angel and it's only been a week."

Eric dropped his arm without stepping away. Shoulder to shoulder, they faced the island that had brought them together as kids.

"You know, life was different before Mom died," Eric

said lightly. "I was little, but I remember it. Not details, but the feel of it. Of having her. Of Dad loving someone and being loved back." Eric leaned forward and Ford couldn't tell if he felt better or worse with the distance between them. "You never saw them together."

"No. But I saw how bad off Dad was. I never knew him happy." Dad had been a lonely, miserable mess of a human being. He'd had no time for anything, anyone. Not even his sons. He was too busy being…alone.

The realization hit him like a ton of bricks. "She scares the shit out of me, Eric. Not *her*, but…" The salt air tasted like tears.

"I'm there, Ford." His brother nodded slowly. "Right there with you."

"What if…what if something…" He shut his eyes. "She's out there on her own right now."

"We've got an eye on her."

Ford huffed out an annoyed breath. At himself, at his efficient brother and his black ops guys. "Don't even know where she is. What name she's using."

A seagull landed on a metal railing and eyed them before squawking. Another responded.

"I know where she is." Eric smiled.

Hope sprang up inside him, big enough to stretch the patchwork of stitches on his body. Oxygen, after suffocating for so long.

"I know that look. Hold on." Eric used his big brother voice. "You can't go after a woman like that without a plan."

"*You* got a plan?"

"Bro, you're the one with the huge brain. Why don't you use it to…*brainstorm* something." Eric compressed his lips, as if holding in a smile, then sniffed. "So, we on or what?"

Ford blinked. "What?"

Eric rolled his eyes. "This. Polaris. You with us? You part of the team?" He lifted his chin, squinting at Ford, looking...insecure maybe? The expression was so unfamiliar on his brother's face that he turned away to cover his surprise, looked at the rig, the ocean, the island, the big, cloud-dotted sky expanding as far as his eye could see, but nowhere near as big as he was used to.

"Better ask Angel what she wants first."

Eric released a humor-laced sigh. "Good answer."

"Yeah?"

"I believe in you." Eric smirked and thumped him on the arm before leading him to the helicopter pad.

Now if he could just convince Angel to believe in him, too.

CHAPTER 53

"HEY, ABS!" BETTY'S GRAVELLY SMOKER'S VOICE CALLED from the dining room. "Got a visitor."

Angel's hand stilled midscrub. *They've found me* shot through her head and body and soul before she shook it off, realizing how unlikely it was.

No one would look for her here. Some fancy restaurant maybe, or the farm-to-table type of place she'd thought she wanted. Not this rundown soup kitchen catering to the poorest of the poor.

And if they had truly found her, they sure wouldn't announce their presence.

"Coming!" She shut off the water, wiped her hands on her apron, and turned, grabbing her knives out of habit. They were all new. The old ones were still in the rubble of Volkov.

And then, inevitably, she thought of the fate of her favorite boning knife. If only she could rid her body of that *feeling*, the sense memory of steel piercing protective layers of fabric to slide deep into human flesh. She stopped halfway to the kitchen door, swallowed back the familiar rush of bile, closed her eyes, and breathed.

Only rather than running recipes through her mind or picturing a perfectly rising dough, she saw white. Eternal white, marred only by a single red dot, solid and sure and more real than anything she'd ever touched in her life.

How long would it take to stop missing that place?

Right. Like it's the place I miss.

With an internal eye-roll, she strode on, craving cool weather like a thirst she couldn't quench. She pushed open the door, stepped through, and froze, barely missing getting hit as it swung closed.

Ford.

He was bigger in this enclosed place than he'd been in the open. His face was pale, as if he'd spent the past couple weeks indoors. Which was likely, given his injuries. And his eyes—they held her captive: crushed ice, melting, dragging her into their depths.

She didn't move, just watched his face, took in that expression, so different from how he'd looked before. Not the harsh, set lines of the person she'd first met, nor the hungry and slightly shell-shocked look he'd worn in their hut, not even the deep, flattering concentration of a man making love. Right now, he looked...totally unsure of himself.

Which softened her up a little, made her protective.

She pasted on a smile, ignoring the curious looks of the other volunteers, and went forward to greet him.

"Hi," he said, looking uncertain. "Heard you were helping out here." He glanced to the side and smiled at Betty, who turned quickly away, wide-eyed, and started scrubbing down a table.

Angel wanted to answer, but she wasn't sure she could. Not if he was here out of some desire to be friendly or out of obligation or some crap. Not with him watching her like that. Not with her rib cage hanging open, exposing her freshly torn, angrily pumping heart. She'd just decided she could cobble herself back together again, but with him here...

"How are you?" His voice was as raw as ever, the scar on his neck exposed, shiny and new-looking. It suddenly occurred to her that he'd have more scars to show for their journey. It also occurred to her that there might be other old ones she'd never seen. Making love in a hut in the Antarctic hadn't lent itself to slow, meandering explorations of each other's skin.

The tragedy of that struck her hard and the stiff smile morphed into a grimace. She turned away and grabbed a saltshaker from a table. It needed filling. Where'd they keep the salt? Crap. She'd seen it earlier, it just—

"Hey." His hand on her shoulder. "Hey, sweetheart."

Oh no. Don't call me that. Don't do this. Don't rip me open where people can see me. See you.

She shut her eyes, held her breath.

"Ang—Shit." He cleared his throat and glanced around, his face red as an antarctic sunburn. "Abby."

Jesus. Betty and Father Stuart and the three daytime volunteers were right there, listening in on this unfolding minidrama. But not mini for her—major as an earthquake. A freaking tsunami tearing at her innards. She didn't want to lose it in front of these people.

She needed to keep it together. For now. Later, in the privacy of her own place, she could blow apart into a billion jagged little chunks.

"Hey," she said with another forced smile. She didn't actually know what to call him. They'd given him a new name, right? Or had he chosen to keep his identity at the risk of losing his life? "How are *you*?"

"I'm okay." He didn't look okay. He looked weak and exhausted, breathing hard, with one arm in a sling.

"Good. So…great." She looked around for something to do, put the salt down, picked it up again. "Look, what are y—"

"Can I help?"

She blinked. "Huh?"

"Can I pitch in? With whatever you're doing?" He motioned toward the kitchen door. "I can do di—"

"You're in no shape to—"

"Sure!" Betty stepped in, all four foot ten of her, bustling around to a cupboard she pulled an apron from. "You can help Abby back there with dishes." She turned. "I need these guys with me in dry storage. Let's go." She threw the apron at Ford and led the volunteers down the hall.

Father Stuart looked a question at Angel, who nodded. He then shuffled off to his office.

Angel watched Ford struggle for a few seconds before helping him tie the thing around his waist.

Which was a mistake, since it put her close, right against his back, her head halfway up.

He smelled good. Of course he did. Different from out on the ice, a more civilized version of the man she'd been with there, but recognizable nonetheless.

He smelled like... *hers*. And it broke her heart that she couldn't have him.

CHAPTER 54

FORD FORCED HIMSELF BACK SO HE WOULDN'T MAKE AN ass of himself. One step and then a second.

Then again, he'd come here to make a fool of himself, hadn't he? He needed her to understand that this was it for him. *She* was it.

He was willing to put himself through anything for her. He had before and he'd do it again. He just needed to gather up the courage to spit out all the words that had been building inside him.

With an exhale, he unbuttoned his too-tight shirt at the collar. "Lead the way."

She shook her head once, more dazed than in denial, and headed back in the door she'd burst through minutes ago, blowing him wide open all over again.

Damn, she was beautiful. Thinner, but gorgeous. Her cheeks sharper, her dark eyes sunk a little deeper in her skull. Was she sleeping? She looked exhausted. Haunted. It was hard to tell with the apron she wore, but he thought her frame might be slighter. Which he didn't like at all.

He wanted to wrap himself around her, to keep her safe.

"Here." She threw him a towel, which he caught one-handed. "I wash, you dry."

He nodded and rolled up his sleeves. "Let's go."

She was good at her job. He knew that. He'd known it the second she'd shown up in that South Pole kitchen, clearly overqualified. They'd never eaten so well as when she'd been in charge. She'd spoiled them with the tastes and smells and sight of her. How had he thought for a second that he could live without any of it? Like an addiction, he needed her to survive. His oxygen.

But seeing her here, doing grunt work in this most unpretentious of kitchens, was like looking deep into her soul. She didn't mind working hard. But then he knew that already.

For the next hour, he wore himself out, wiping and scrubbing dishes and stoves, fryers and floors, until everything sparkled. Every time he tried to talk to her, she gave him another job to do. And then, when they'd done everything they possibly could and he was beyond ready to tell her how he felt, she took the oven apart and had him scour the inside.

When she finally handed him a glass of water, he was out of breath, exhausted, pouring sweat, while Angel was flushed and alive-looking. Every bit of him ached from the movements. Possibly also from the proximity to her and the too-large space between them. Except that space had shrunk at times when she'd passed behind him, putting a hand to his back to let him know she was there. Or when she'd pointed out a hard-to-get-to spot behind the sink.

Everything about her was so perfectly competent, her body a testament to who she was, covered in years of burn scars, the nails neat and short. For a few lost seconds, he'd pictured those fingers wrapped around him, the hand tight on his hip or scratching furrows down his back.

In the last hour, he'd learned how to clean an industrial kitchen from top to bottom. He'd also learned that working alongside this woman made him feel more alive than anything in the world.

There were so many things he should have been saying to her from the beginning. He'd never been particularly eloquent, but maybe a part of him had been building them up, piece by piece, thought by thought, just for her. And he needed to get the words out—he needed to *tell her*.

"Ange—" He gave an annoyed sigh. "Abby."

She turned the water on full blast.

"Hey." He went over and turned it off. "Will you listen to me? For just a minute?"

She huffed out a breath and met his gaze, hers so full of hurt that it almost felled him.

He inhaled and finally forced the words out. "You're the strongest person I've ever met. In my life. Hands down."

Her eyes grew big and round, and her head was shaking side to side, like she knew what he was about to do and she needed him to stop.

He went on. "As far as I'm concerned, you outshine everyone. Everything. In the kitchen and out." He ignored the tight, flat line of her lips and carried on. "And, you know…you were right."

Her exaggerated eye-roll made him smile. Shit, he'd take that from her any day. She was listening at least. It was a start.

"I was a jerk. I was frozen through. Until I met you." He moved toward her, close enough to touch, but he'd let her take that last step. If she chose to. "And now we're about to start new lives, after everything, and…well, you've ruined me, melted me down and made a new man of me. Except I'm useless without you. Useless." The words were spilling out of him now, faster and faster. "You're magnificent, Angel. You're bigger than Antarctica, stronger than the ice, more magnetic than the poles. I'd do anything to be with you. Be anyone. Go anywhere."

"Ford, you don't have to—"

"I *want* to. I want to show you how much you're worth. *Everything.* Absolutely everything I am, everything I have is for you. Tell me where, tell me when, tell me how, and I'm there."

"No."

No? Christ. He put his hand to his chest.

"I won't take you away from the ice."

"You wouldn't be taking me away." He leaned in and whispered. "I was hiding there. You heal me more than the ice ever did. *You're* my home. And I want to be yours. Will you let me be that? Can I be the place you come home to?"

Her skin burned, her eyes watered, and she couldn't stop shaking.

It wasn't fair of him to catch her off-guard like this, after a long shift volunteering at the soup kitchen.

But he'd done it and she knew this was hard for him.

What had he asked? If he could be her home? Of course he could. He *was*. He had been since their first night in the tent. Since they'd parted ways, she hadn't slept more than an hour or two at a time.

He was her missing half.

Her love.

"Come here," she whispered.

The look on his face when he bent toward her and put his forehead to hers filled something that had been empty for a very long time. The way his fingers caught in her hair, the solid feel of his body against hers.

He was right—this was coming home.

"Love you," he whispered, as if he hadn't already flayed himself alive for her. "More than anything."

She nodded, ate him up with her eyes, and whispered, "Me, too," then lifted her lips for a kiss.

Someone applauded and she almost died. A glance to the side showed Betty and Father James and one of the women who helped out at the shelter. A live audience, for goodness' sake. Ford shocked her by kissing her deeper, holding her tighter, and hamming it up just the slightest bit. *Who was this man?*

Good Lord, he's mine. My man.

"Now what?" she asked when he finally pulled away, leaving her hot and breathless.

"You tell me." He stepped back. Took a look around and threw his arms out, as if to say the world was her oyster. "Or better yet, let's figure it out. Together."

CHAPTER 55

"ALASKA?" KATHERINE HAULED HERSELF UP FROM HER father's armchair. "That's all you know?"

"Yes, ma'am. He booked himself a flight to Anchorage, then headed out into the bush with a local pilot. I talked to someone from the airline and apparently the flight went off the radar. Disappeared. They didn't have an emergency number for him, and without a flight plan or any record of it...well, took us a while to track him down."

"I appreciate the information. Please let me know if anything changes."

"Yes, ma'am."

She ended the call and turned to Brenda. "We need to put together another team."

"A new drilling site?" Brenda's brow lifted, but only slightly.

Katherine appreciated the woman's restraint. It served no purpose to show excessive surprise or emotion. Pointless, when they had so much work to do. "No. No, we'll concentrate on getting the new South Pole station up and running again."

"There's been promising data coming out of Colorado."

Interesting. Her father had always pushed for more drilling in the Rockies. The old mines had shown themselves to be promising. "Don't we have a team in Alaska? Permafrost drilling, right?"

"Yes, Director."

"Well, we need to send more resources to the region."
Alaska! She couldn't wait to tell Fiona the news.

"Yes, Director." Brenda wrote a note on her electronic
doodad. "Is this a small team or—"

Katherine laughed—a grizzly, desiccated sound. "You'll
need an army for this one. A dozen men, at least. And
find me someone more capable than the senator's people.
Sampson was big, but his brain wasn't worth a damn."

"Right. I'll inform HR and security that we'll be hiring."

"Actually, let's go through a subcontractor for this one."

More tapped notes and Katherine could feel the wireless
waves in her brain. If she were in charge, there would be no
more tablets, no more of those absurd smartphones that led,
quite frankly, to the opposite of intelligence. Dumbphones.
They'd be back to basics: women and men living simply in a
clean world. Evil eradicated.

The children would inherit.

It was her mission. No more shootings, no more inno-
cents dying. Only the good would survive her cataclysm.
Only the good.

She sank back into Daddy's chair and stared at the
flames. "And I want to see him."

"I'm sorry?" Brenda, intelligent though she was, didn't
always follow.

"The man. I want to see him once they've found him.
Right here, face-to-face. I want him to know."

"I'll make sure our team is briefed." A pause, during
which Katherine felt Brenda's eyes hard on her. Curious,
perhaps. Worried? Resentful? "Anything else?"

"No. No, I believe that is all. For now." She smiled.
"Thank you, Brenda. You're a godsend."

CHAPTER 56

Two Days Later—Polaris Platform

LEONTYNE EDDOWES MUTTERED SOMETHING INTO HER headset that Angel couldn't understand as they settled onto the helipad in the middle of the ocean. Airplanes, helicopters—apparently the woman flew everything.

Angel glanced at Ford and found him watching her with a half smile.

Would she ever get used to seeing that expression on his face? The softness in his eyes? Hopefully not. Because the jolt of surprise it sent through her every time was pure pleasure.

Man, she loved him. So much it hurt.

He grabbed her hand and squeezed briefly before helping her out of the helicopter. Nobody called them choppers, according to Leo. *This is a helicopter or an aircraft. Helo if you're in a rush*, she'd said. *Only people in the movies use chopper.*

Ducking—though in all honesty, she didn't need to—they ran across the helipad, then down a flight of stairs and inside.

"What do you think?" Side by side, they made their way down a long well-lit hall to a thick metal door.

"Reminds me of Burke-Ruhe."

"Yeah?" His face was so wide-open that she wanted to spread little kisses all over it. In deference to the fact that they were here to join his macho brother's underground paramilitary team of good-guy vigilantes, she refrained. Barely.

"Yes." She squeezed his hand back.

"Sure?"

"Yes. Not trying to become a killing machine or anything, but I don't regret what I did. And I'll never regret what happened."

He smiled. "Good. 'Cause Eric's not kidding about recruiting you to the cause."

"I told you. I'm in." She shook her head. "You should know that by now."

They stepped out of the first passageway and she noted that the door wasn't quite the station's refrigerator-styled ones, but more like a submarine's. Not that she'd visited many of those.

But she would, if Ford took her there.

At the end of another long hall, Eric and his girlfriend, Zoe Garcia, met them. It gave her a weird rush of adrenaline to see them both again, especially in this strange, out-of-the-way setting.

"You made it!" Zoe hugged Ford.

"Course." Ford sounded grumpy, as usual, but she saw through him like cellophane. Gruff meant he had something to hide. In this case, it was happiness and affection at the sight of his brother. It was adorable.

God, she hoped she never got over this first-crush feeling.

"It's so good to see you again!" Zoe rushed forward to hug Angel, then Eric gave her a peck on the cheek. Zoe led the way. "Watch your step down here. The place is a work in progress." She turned one last time. "Welcome to Polaris."

This corridor's lighting was markedly different from the others—warmer, more subtle—with three doors at the end. They walked through the central door into—

"Wow." Angel couldn't shut her mouth at the sight of

the massive high-ceilinged living space, with a circular wall of windows overlooking the ocean at one end. At the other end, doors opened onto what appeared to be a central patio, complete with fire pit and—"Is that a pool?"

"Sure is." Eric laughed his deceptively lazy Paul Newman laugh. "You like?"

"This is amazing. It's like a cruise ship or something." Angel spun just as Leo entered behind them. She was beautiful, but no-frills. Her hair was a very short, dark halo. Simple, no-bullshit hair that went with her no-bullshit personality.

"You see the rooms yet?" Leo asked.

"No."

"Don't even think about stealing mine," she said, looking for all the world like she didn't have an ounce of humor— until she winked. She was followed in by Jameson and Pam, who'd apparently flown in the day before.

"Oh, we all know better than to try to take your room away." Zoe threw an arm around Leo's shoulders, which the pilot appeared to suffer through with an affectionate look. "Besides." Zoe glanced back at Ford. "This guy picked your room ages ago."

"Come on." Eric led the way through a side door into a smaller room, where Ans and Von awaited.

They all stood to kiss Angel on the cheek, then the men bro-hugged Ford—on his good side—before pulling chairs out around a pitted, ancient-looking wooden ship's table.

"Thanks for coming out, everyone. Got some new intel we need to brief everyone on."

Ford seemed to sharpen, and suddenly Angel could see exactly how he'd fit in with this bunch. "New intel?"

"Couple things." Eric looked around. "You've probably all heard that Clive Tenny died in federal custody."

Silence. A couple nods. The man may have been an ass-hole, but nobody was happy about this development.

"As far as you two, we thought you could keep your heads down out here for a while. At least until the nation is finished mourning the deaths of Angel Smith and Ford Cooper." Angel caught Ford's eye. He looked different with his new dark hair and thick-framed glasses. So did she, as a redhead. But they'd adjust.

"Now, we know from what Tenny told us in his debrief that Chronos has teams searching the globe for the virus." Eric was the last to sit. "Ans, tell us what else we've got."

Ans, shorter than the other men at maybe five eleven or six feet, had one of those thick builds that looked packed hard with muscle. He was darkly handsome—and he knew it. His black hair was shorn—about the length of his beard—and gelled up.

"Here's what we've got. We believe that Chronos Corp's CEO and director, Katherine Henley Harper, is head honcho in all this. Tenny named her personally. Said he answered directly to her." He looked around. "But this goes higher than that."

Von broke in. He was scarred and mean-looking, rougher than the other guys, his accent pure Texas. Or Deep South, maybe, Angel couldn't tell the difference. "My contacts at Defense are bein' extremely tight-lipped about everything." He gave Angel and Ford an apologetic look. "They're blamin' the murders of Jamie Cortez and Alex Stickley on Tenny and Sampson. No mention of Chronos involvement." Another look around the room. "Murders, kidnapping, Tenny's so-called suicide in lockup. Cover-ups like this… It's some high-level shit."

For a few seconds, nobody spoke. The four Burke-Ruhe survivors exchanged long looks.

Ans took over. "Good news is there's new intel from a possible inside source."

"To be verified." Eric broke in, before pointing at Ans, letting him know he should carry on.

"They've got digging locations elsewhere." Ans paused. "So far, we know of Colorado. The North Sea, off the coast of Scotland. Siberia. We're trying to get more on those. And now we've got a possibly related incident in Alaska."

"This one's mine." Zoe interjected happily. "When we quietly put out word that we were looking for info on Chronos, we got a few bites. This is from a friend of a friend of a friend, but she works—worked—for a private eye out of LA. Says her boss disappeared a few weeks ago. For over a decade, he's been on retainer. Not for Chronos per se, but for a nameless honcho over there. Apparently, he was pretty excited about finally getting a lead and followed it to some remote place in Alaska."

"Bermuda Triangle," muttered Ans in a ghost story voice.

Leo threw him an affectionately annoyed look. "Well, all she knows is that the guy her boss was after stole something from the Chronos bigwig years ago. Says a few days after she notified the client, the entire office was shut down, taken over by some unnamed government agency. Now she's out a job. And she's scared. Weird shit's been happening."

"We've gotten her to safety," Eric said, chiming in. "In the meantime, word is a security contractor's sending a team for a big operation in Alaska. Major firepower. Could be a coincidence."

Ans snorted.

"Anyway, we'll send someone as soon as we pinpoint where." Eric finished up, then looked at his brother.

"For now, our sole mission is to put a stop to this thing before Burke-Ruhe's up and running again," Von said, his voice almost as gruff as Ford's and totally in keeping with his entire persona—a big, scarred, mean-looking warrior.

Angel's brow lifted in surprise. "That's six or seven months? Not a lot of time."

"Given that they'd planned to test the virus on humans, I'd say we need to clear this up as fast as we can. And with Chronos bankrolling the Burke-Ruhe and Volkov rebuilds, we're on borrowed time." Ford tilted his head at Jameson and Pam, who sat two chairs down. "These two'll be on the first flight down there."

"Yep," Jameson boomed. "Eyes on the ground."

"On the *ice*," Pam said with a giggle. The two exchanged a smoldering look.

Ford smiled. He did that a lot now.

"So." Angel looked at the group, a little nervous now that the big moment had come. "I have a proposal. I know you've probably got a better solution, but I was thinking...when I'm not working on getting my nonprofit together"—she glanced at Ford, who gave her an encouraging nod—"you guys got room for a chef out here?"

"Oh thank God." Leo whooped. "Thought you'd never ask!"

"Hold on. Hold on." Eric put out a hand. "Did we pressure you in any way? I don't want you to feel like it's an obligation. We're perfectly cap—"

"Are you kidding? This is perfect. Like the South Pole without the cold. And I've got my day job." Just thinking about the nonprofit she'd decided to create gave her a warm feeling. As soon as the kitchen was set up, she'd be doing healthy, inexpensive family-cooking sessions with folks from low-income households. Helping people, making them happy, sharing her love of food with them. "Seriously, guys. Working with the families onshore and then cooking out here, being part of this gang—it's a dream."

Everything about her life and this moment—the man beside her, this odd band of people, their crazy HQ in the middle of the Pacific, their mission—made her feel alive and in charge of her destiny. "This is what I want."

"It's settled, then. Executive chef." Eric smiled at her, then looked at his brother. "And chief science officer. Welcome to Polaris Team."

"You don't miss the ice all that much, do you?" Angel flopped down beside Coop on the bed in the ridiculously swank suite they'd been given in the repurposed oil platform. Even unfinished, it was nicer than anyplace he'd stayed in his life.

"What makes you say that?"

"I don't think I've ever seen you look as excited as you were in that meeting today."

Excited. Coop hadn't known the meaning of the word until this woman had come into his life.

He wrapped an arm around her and pulled her to his side, gentle with her and himself. Their bodies were still healing after all.

"This feels right for me."

"Being an underground global superhero living under a false identity? Yeah. The old Ford might have balked, but this guy's into it. With your brilliant mind, you're basically their in-house science geek."

"I'm not a virologist."

"No, but you know where to find one."

"I do." He ran a hand from her strong shoulder, along the gentle curve of her back, to the perfect dip above her ass. "And I—*we*—have the one thing everyone seems to want."

"The virus."

She stretched and rubbed her face on his chest like a cat. "Where's your brother getting the funds for all this?"

He half shrugged with his good shoulder. "Eric's loaded. Apparently a couple of the others are pretty well-off, too."

"*This* loaded? Redo-an-oil-rig-and-finance-a-secret-mercenary-team loaded?"

"They prefer to be called security specialists."

"Whatever. You know what I mean."

"I do." He smoothed a gentle hand down her face and thought *I'm a lucky bastard* for the millionth time. That day. "They've got backers. You heard them—Polaris is more than us. It's a coalition."

"Mm-hm. Just a bunch of masked heroes hanging out, secretly fighting for the common good." She sighed. "Why aren't you kissing me right now?"

"That what I'm supposed to be doing, Angel Smith?" *Angel Cooper* one day, if he had his say.

He broke out into a cold sweat. *He hoped.* Because he couldn't stand to live without her.

Suddenly, he needed to hear her say it. "I love you, sweetheart."

Her smile lit up her face like magic. And to think he hadn't believed in this sort of thing once upon a time. "I love you, too, Ford. And, in case you've forgotten, I told you first."

"Well, obviously. You're smarter than I am."

"It's an EQ thing."

"EQ?"

"Emotional Intelligence." She craned her neck up, reaching for him. "Now kiss me."

He dropped his lips to hers and kissed her the way he did every time—like he meant it. Like he'd cross the world for her, brave anything for her. Like it could be their last kiss, their last breath, and he wanted to spend it with her.

When he pulled away, she followed him partway and then dropped her head back to her pillow, as if it weighed a ton.

"This place..." She rolled her eyes to one side, then the other. "It's like a resort or something. You think it was Zoe's idea?"

"I know for a fact it wasn't."

"Eric's?"

"Yeah. My brother—Navy SEAL, roughneck, billionaire owner of...whatever this is."

"Polaris. The mothership."

He laughed and bent to rub his nose against hers, loving the way she bubbled through him, humor, smiles, warmth, desire. All the things he'd thought he had to give up in order to survive in the world.

"You're *my* mothership."

She turned and gave him a side-eye. "I know that was meant to be romantic, but it came out a little weird."

"I'm a science guy. We're weird by our very nature."

"You can say that again." She sat up. "Hey. Didn't Zoe mention a balcony?"

He grabbed a sweater and followed her outside, where he dropped it on her shoulders. And then, because keeping her warm was a pleasure he'd never get sick of, he wrapped himself around her and looked up at the night sky. "There's only one thing I regret."

"Yeah? What's that?"

"I never got to show you the aurora australis."

With a sigh, she scooted even closer, snuggling into his chest in that way she had that made him feel huge and strong, like a man who could take on the world and survive.

"Right. The southern lights. Oh, I bet we'll make it there one day." She kissed his chest in that spot that felt like *hers* since he'd first held her all those weeks ago in Antarctica. "As far as I'm concerned, Ford Cooper, our adventure is just beginning."

When she put it that way, he knew for a fact that he could—and would—take on anything in the world for her. And he'd do it with a smile on his face.

EPILOGUE

One month later—Familia Kitchen, San Diego, California

ANGEL HUMMED TO HERSELF AS SHE SHOVED THE LEFT-
over cilantro into the fridge, pleased at how it had grown
out in the middle of nowhere, along with the tomatoes and
basil and everything else she'd planted in the Polaris platform's massive interior courtyard. With the chickens she'd
just brought out there and the goats she'd harassed Eric
into considering, Polaris was quickly turning into a farm.

An offshore farm. The world's first, maybe? Now all
they needed was a puppy. The thought of grumpy, stoic
Von holding some cute tiny fuzzball decided her. They were
getting a puppy.

The phone jangled, startling her into dropping a can of
coconut milk, which rolled under a counter. She clapped a
hand to her chest and glanced at the clock. Her last group of
moms and kids had just left Familia. Had someone forgotten something?

The phone rang again, way too loud in this space. She
ran to the office and grabbed it. Too late. Of course.

She checked the number. Who was that? Not an area
code she knew.

It rang again just after she'd set it down. This time, she
snapped it up. "Familia, this is Abby."

"Ang—Sorry. Abby."

"Uh…" Her fingers and toes tingled. No one knew her
real name. "You must have the wrong—"

"It's Leo. Listen, I can't get through to anyone else and they're closing in fast, but it's the virus." Something moved on the other end. A scuffle of some sort and then Leo was back on. "Shit. They're coming. Listen, tell Eric. And Ford. Tell them all. There's something about the virus you need to know."

Something banged—loudly. Then again and again, the pops so familiar that Angel had to fight not to duck for cover.

"I'm listening, Leo." She squeezed the phone in her hand. "I'm here."

"Ford was right about the virus," she whispered. "It's deadly. But it can also..." Another loud pop, this one followed by a crash.

"Leo. Leo!" The line was dead.

Angel hit Redial and raced to the kitchen, where she grabbed her cell phone and tapped out a quick message to Ford.

At her ear, the phone rang once, again, and finally someone picked up.

"Leo, you—"

"'allo." It was a male voice. "With whom do I have the pleasure of speaking?"

"Who are you?" she asked.

"I'm the man who just took down your pilot friend." He huffed out an audible breath. Something beeped in her ear and he spoke again, sounding exceptionally satisfied. "Shame. Had quite a way with an aircraft, she did." Another annoying beep and he sucked in a breath. "Ah! Grand. And now, love, I've got your number, too. All right, then. Afraid I'd better go." His voice lowered, quieted, going from friendly to menacing. "Don't bother looking for her. There won't be anything left for you to find."

Familia's front door opened and Ford stepped in just as the man hung up. He froze as soon as he saw her expression, then rushed to her, instantly concerned. "What's going on?"

"Leo's in trouble." She sank to the floor, numb. It was all starting again: the fear, the violence, the uncertain future. She looked up at Ford. "And I think we're too late to help."

ACKNOWLEDGMENTS

Thank you, above all, to Mary Altman, who has carved, shaped, sculpted, and scoured this book into what it is today. You are amazing.

The wonderful crew at Sourcebooks is, as always, a pleasure to work with. Thank you for all your hard work.

To my lovely beta readers, support network, and author friends Amanda Bouchet, Molly O'Keefe, Alleyne Dickens, Jennifer Sable, Kasey Lane, Jennifer Sable, Madeline Iva, Callie Russell, and Andie J. Christopher. Without you, this book would never have happened.

Merci, Arnaud. Je t'aime.

A million thanks to Jake Cerese and Kate Claeys, owners of the Stargazer Inn and Kerouac's, in the heart of Nevada's Great Basin. Your insight into life as a cook at the South Pole was invaluable. Thank you to Tobi Doyle for your guidance and perspective on viruses, among other things. I have so much more to learn, but you set me on the right path. And finally, my apologies to those Antarctica experts out there. I've moved mountains for this book, dug crevasses, and created icefalls, all for the sake of the story. I hope you don't mind that I messed with the Ice.

To my readers: you are the best. Thank you for coming on this journey.

ABOUT THE AUTHOR

Adriana Anders is the award-winning author of the Love at Last series and Blank Canvas series. *Under Her Skin*, a *Publishers Weekly* Best Book of 2017 and double recipient of the HOLT Medallion award, was featured in *Bustle*, *USA Today* Happy Ever After, and *Book Riot*. And *Loving the Secret Billionaire* was a Romance Writers of America 2019 Rita® Award Finalist. Today, she resides with her husband and two small children on the coast of France, where she writes the gritty, emotional love stories of her heart.

ON HIS WATCH

KATIE RUGGLE

"DON'T YOU THINK THIS PUNISHMENT IS A LITTLE harsh?" Derek asked under his breath, eyeing the yellow school bus pulling into the gravel parking lot.

His dive-team leader, Callum, didn't hesitate. "No."

"I think you're blowing this way out of proportion." The kids started flowing off the bus, and Derek had to resist the impulse to take a step back. Any show of fear would be like blood in the water. They'd devour him alive. "It was funny. You need to work on your sense of humor. Laughter makes you live longer. They've done scientific studies."

"It wasn't funny."

"C'mon." Since the chaperones had the kids contained to the parking lot, Derek risked taking his eyes off the horde to shoot a smirk in Callum's direction. "It was a *little* funny. Admit it. Your face…man. When you opened your truck door and saw that goat, I nearly pissed myself laughing."

"It ate the seats." Derek wasn't sure how Callum managed to speak while clamping his jaw muscles so tightly. The man had a gift. "I can't take my truck to Denver to be reupholstered until next week." Now a forehead vein was throbbing in time with the clenching of his jaw. "Nine days. Until then, my seats are being held together with duct tape." Callum slowly turned his head to focus his chilly blue gaze on Derek. "Duct. Tape."

Forcing his face into serious lines with some difficulty, Derek donned his most contrite expression. "Hey, I'm paying for that new upholstery. Isn't that punishment enough?" Cal just narrowed his eyes a little more. "I was trying to do a good thing. Maybelle needed a home, and I thought the dive team could use a mascot."

"Why would the dive team need a mascot?"

"To improve morale? I mean, laughter is good for morale, right? And since Steve ended up taking Maybelle, now the Fire guys are going to be the ones with awesome morale. We lost out."

"How would a goat…never mind." Callum gave his head a single shake. "You put the thing in my truck. How could you *ever* think that was a good idea?"

Since he was losing the battle to control his grin, Derek rubbed his hand over his mouth to hide it. "Uh…didn't really think about it, boss. I mean, I'd just picked up the goat, and we got a call—I had to put her somewhere."

"Why not leave it in *your* truck?"

"Are you kidding?" Derek snorted. "Maybelle would've wrecked it."

Callum's expression cooled until it was positively glacial. "I've changed my mind."

"Really?" Hope replaced the amusement in Derek's voice. In his peripheral vision, he could see that the kids, now organized in semi-straight lines, had started their advance. Time was running out. He needed to escape— quickly. "I don't have to do this?"

"Oh, no," Callum said silkily, "you *do* have to do this. But I've decided that this punishment isn't sufficient. It ate. My. Truck."

"But—"

A blond woman appeared at Callum's side before Derek could say more. "Hi! Are you Callum Cook?"

Turning his head, Callum focused the full power of his arctic glare on the woman. If he hadn't been so relieved not to be the target of that stare, Derek would've felt bad for her. Several uncomfortable seconds ticked past before Callum dipped his head, finally answering her question.

"Great! Fire Chief Early said I'd find you here." Her grin was still as wide as ever, and Derek couldn't help but be impressed. It had taken Derek years to build up the nerve to go toe-to-toe with Callum. "I'm Lou Sparks. I'd like to join the dive team, and the fire chief told me you're the one I need to hook up with." Her brown eyes widened as her smile finally began to falter. "Uh, not hook up with as in a *dirty* way or anything. I meant talk. Chief Early said I should *talk* to you."

Derek tilted his head, forcing his expression into severe lines as he clucked his tongue. "Don't think you're getting on this team that easy. Every one of us divers had to make it through the casting couch interview. There's no shortcut to wearing the neoprene uniform."

He'd been concentrating so hard on the woman that

Derek didn't see the hand swinging toward the back of his head until it was too late to duck.

"Ignore him," Callum said, dropping his arm. "Do you have any dive experience?"

"Sure." Although her smile started to return, Lou's cheeks remained pink. "In tropical places, that is—I've never done any cold-water diving. Mainly because of the… um, coldness." She gestured toward the icy reservoir behind them. "I'm guessing that's different than diving in just scuba gear and a bikini." She squeezed her eyes closed. "Frick. What is wrong with my mouth right now? I promise I'm not an oversexed bimbo. And now I just said 'sex' and 'bimbo.' Wow, what a great first impression I'm making. Please make me shut up immediately."

As Callum blinked at her, looking bemused, Derek couldn't hold back his laughter any longer.

"Lou," he said, holding out a hand. "Welcome to the dive team. I'm Derek, and I can already tell that I'm going to like you."

She grinned with obvious relief as she shook his hand.

"Meet me at Fire Station One at six thirty tomorrow evening for your official"—Callum shot Derek a scowl—"*interview*. Team training begins at seven."

She nodded, looking nervous again.

Derek stage-whispered, "Interview-shminterview. You're in. He's just trying to play the hard-ass." He glanced up and barely restrained a flinch. The kids had formed a half circle around them, eliminating any chance of escape.

Lou laughed. "I imagine it's a role he's comfortable playing."

Callum narrowed his eyes. "Since the two of you have apparently bonded, your first task can be to help Derek with this presentation."

Her mouth dropped open as she gave the encircling crowd a hunted glance. "Uh...presentation? To kids? I'm not...well, very good with kids. In fact, they tend to hate me." The terror in her voice matched what Derek felt, and he gave her a commiserating smile.

"They're waiting for you to begin." Jerking his chin toward the group, Callum turned and began walking away.

"Wait!" Despite his best effort at not showing fear, Derek knew his panic was obvious. "You're leaving me here? Alone?"

"You're not alone," Callum said, tipping his head toward Lou. "And I'll be right over there. Observing. Weren't you just saying that I should laugh more? I'm thinking this might be an excellent opportunity."

Well, shit. He couldn't argue with that.

Reluctantly turning back, Derek faced his audience. A funny-looking kid in the front licked at snot running from his nose to his upper lip. Holding back a wince, Derek forced a smile.

"Hey, kids. How's it going?"

All thirty-eight of the Simpson Elementary School third- and fourth-graders stared at him, unsmiling. Despite the December chill, Derek felt sweat prickle his forehead. When he shot Lou a desperate glance, she returned an equally fraught one and shifted behind him, putting his body between her and the kids.

Derek cleared his throat, making a mental note never to seriously piss off Callum again. The man was positively diabolical when it came to punishments. "I'm Derek Warner, and I'm going to tell you about the Field County Rescue Dive Team."

"Where are the firemen?" demanded a girl with dark

curls poking out from under her stocking hat. "Ms. Belcher said we were going to see firemen."

"No firemen." Derek frowned. Apparently, even girls under ten had a thing for firefighters. "Divers are way better."

"Nuh-uh." The girl scowled at him.

"Uh-huh."

"Nuh-uh."

"Totally better."

"Are not."

Lou's amused snort interrupted the argument, and Derek took a deep breath. "When people fall into the water, the dive team rescues them. We also…" His words trailed off as he turned his head toward Lou. Out of the corner of his mouth, he muttered, "How do I explain body recovery to kids without traumatizing them?"

"Um…I don't think it's possible," Lou whispered. "Maybe you could use Barbie and Ken dolls to demonstrate?"

"What?" Realizing that his voice had risen, he lowered it to a hiss. "That's a stupid idea. Besides, I don't carry dolls around with me."

"Just don't mention dead people then!" she whispered back.

"Where are your fire trucks?" asked the snot-licker.

"We don't have fire trucks. We have a dive van." He waved toward the converted ambulance parked ten feet away.

The kids looked unimpressed. One mini-Neanderthal toward the back wasn't paying attention at all, too busy stuffing a fistful of snow down the neck of the girl in front of him. The girl yelped when it touched her skin.

"Hey!" Derek snapped. "Knock it off."

"Chase DuBois!" The all-too-familiar voice made Derek stiffen. How had he missed that *she* was here? Usually he had a divining rod crossed with a cattle prod inside him, giving him electric shocks whenever Artemis Rey was near. "If you can't behave, you'll be sitting in the bus with me for the remainder of the presentation."

Derek allowed himself a quick look. She was at the back of the group, standing next to the fourth-grade teacher, Marnie Belcher. Artie towered over the kids, and he wondered once again how he'd missed seeing her. After all, she was *Artie*, and he'd been panting after her since he'd been old enough to know that "hot" meant more than just a temperature. He gave her a nod of appreciation, and she smiled back at him, her delicate features somehow looking even more striking in contrast to her lumpy, hot-pink stocking hat. It appeared that she was attacking a new knitting hobby with more determination than skill.

A jab to his back brought him out of his Artie-inspired daze. "You have to do something, or there's going to be a mutiny," Lou whispered. "And that wouldn't go well, since there are more little people than big people. They'd have a chance at winning this thing."

He glanced around the crowd; the natives were indeed getting restless. The only other adults besides him, Lou, Artie, and Marnie were the two chaperones standing off to the side, too busy with their whispered conversation to pay much attention to the kids. Lou was right—the grown-ups were completely outnumbered. "What exactly do you think I should do? Dance? Sing? Magic tricks?"

"I don't know." She sounded irritated. "Does that poor excuse for an emergency vehicle have a siren? Maybe we can startle them into submission."

Derek sent a frantic glance over the crowd and noticed that Callum was leaning against the school bus, arms crossed over his chest and a tiny smile curling the corners of his mouth. For Callum, that small grin was the equivalent of belly laughter.

Scowling, Derek gave a short nod. "Code Three it is."

Using the flashing lights as a distraction, Zoe reached over and grabbed Maya's arm, towing her little sister several feet away from stupid Chase.

"I hate him," Maya said matter-of-factly, her voice just loud enough for Zoe to hear. She pulled at the back of her coat in an attempt to dislodge the last of the melting snow.

"Me too." Zoe wiped the moisture off the back of her sister's neck with her glove. "If Micah were here, Chase would've been too chicken to do anything to you."

"That's because Micah would've punched him in the face and made Chase cry in front of everyone." Releasing the hem in defeat, Maya gave a full-body shiver. "I wish the fifth-graders got to come today, too."

"It'll be okay. We'll watch him. If he gets too close, we'll go stand by Ms. Rey."

"Fine." Despite her reluctant agreement, Maya's face screwed up in a scowl. "I wish that dork-brain would fall in the water, though."

With a grin, Zoe eyed the reservoir with its thin coat of ice. "Yeah. It looks really cold."

Their gazes met, and the two girls started to giggle.

"Zoe and Maya Springfield!" Ms. Rey's crisp voice stopped their laughter. "Listening ears."

With slightly guilty nods, they turned back to the pair of presenters.

"Derek is really bad at this," Zoe whispered as the man struggled to talk while donning a goofy-looking suit.

"Yeah. Remember when he babysat us that one time?"

Clapping a hand over her mouth to hold back renewed giggles, Zoe nodded. "The spaghetti," she managed to say between her fingers, and it was Maya's turn to try to muffle her laughter.

A sharp poke at her side turned Zoe's repressed giggles into a grunt of pain. Chase was standing right next to her, holding a slimy-looking stick. She took a quick step away from the smirking boy, pulling Maya along with her.

"Leave us alone," Zoe whispered, but Chase just reached out with the stick again. She barely jumped back in time to dodge getting a slime trail across the leg of her jeans. When Zoe craned her neck to check for Ms. Rey, hoping the teacher would notice and put a stop to Chase's latest stupid behavior, she noticed Ms. Rey was staring at Derek.

Zoe looked back and forth between Ms. Rey and Derek, trying to figure out why the teacher was watching him so closely. It wasn't like Derek was doing anything *interesting*. He'd managed to get the funny-looking suit on all the way, and he'd taken a few steps out on the ice.

Ms. Belcher was trying to make Julius—who was always too hot—put his coat back on, and the two parent chaperones were all the way on the other side of the group, talking to each other. There wasn't any help coming from the grownups, so Zoe was going to have to take care of this herself.

The stick whacked the side of her boot, and Zoe refocused on Chase.

"I'm going to tell," she lied. Her brothers had taught her never to rat out anyone. "Then you'll have to sit on the bus. Ms. Rey said so."

With a shrug, Chase dragged the tip of the stick through a puddle of partially frozen mud. "Don't care. This is dumb, anyway."

That time, when he swung, he aimed at Maya. Pulling her sister behind her, Zoe kicked at the stick, trying to knock it out of Chase's hand, but she missed. Instead, mud spattered across her jeans. Rage-inspired heat prickled along the back of her neck and across her cheeks.

"You're such a *bully*, Chase DuBois!" Even in her flush of anger, Zoe remembered to keep her voice low so as not to incur the wrath of Ms. Rey. "Why don't you just go jump in the reservoir?"

"Like that guy?" Chase scoffed, pointing his muddy stick at Derek, who was back on shore, explaining different pieces of equipment. It actually looked kind of interesting, and Zoe wished that Chase would leave them alone so she could move closer to the presenters for a better view. "He's a tool. His stupid suit looks like something a baby would wear."

Zoe rolled her eyes. "Like you could do what he does."

His smirk fading, Chase swung the stick through the air next to his leg, the accelerating *swish-swish* revealing his growing temper. "I bet I could."

She made a contemptuous sound. "Ha. You'd be too scared even to walk out on the ice."

"Am not." Despite the denial, his expression was dubious as he eyed the reservoir.

"Then *do it*." Even as she spoke, Zoe's stomach started to feel like she'd eaten something rotten. "Not just on the edge, though. If you're really not scared, you have to walk…thirty steps across the ice."

When Maya sucked in a breath behind her, Zoe almost

lost her nerve and told Chase to forget about it. Before she could, he tossed down his stick.

"Fine. But I'm only going to do ten steps."

"Bock, bock!" she mocked.

"I'm not a chicken!" he almost yelled. They both paused and looked around to see if they'd attracted any attention, but the main group had pulled in more closely around the dive van. Zoe, Maya, and Chase were a good distance from anyone else.

"Twenty-five steps." As Zoe waited for his response, she made quiet clucking sounds under her breath.

"Okay. Twenty-five." Flushing darkly, Chase checked the teachers again, but all the others were focused on Derek and the woman presenter. Chase made a wide circle around the crowd, heading toward the edge of the ice.

"You shouldn't have dared him," Maya whispered, grabbing Zoe's gloved hand with both of hers.

"I know." She thought she'd enjoy watching Chase fall into the water, but now she just felt sick. Swallowing the sour remains of her lunch, she kept her gaze locked on the boy moving closer and closer to the ice.

Chase turned and glanced at them, and Zoe's nerve broke. She waved toward Chase, gesturing for him to return to safety. As if that had made up his mind, he shook his head and took a step onto the ice.

"One," Zoe counted under her breath. His other foot left the rocky security of the beach and he took another step. "Two."

Maya joined her in counting under their breath, each step feeling like it took an eternity. When they reached twenty-two, the band of fear around Zoe's chest loosened slightly.

"Almost there," she said quietly. "Twenty-three. Oh!" Her breath sucked harshly into her throat as she saw Chase drop to his knees. He turned his head to look at them, eyes huge in his pale face. For once, his constant smirk was gone.

"What happened?" Maya demanded. "Why'd he fall down like that?"

"I don't know." Her voice sounded strange—not like hers at all. She had to do something, had to help him. All at once he looked so pale and scared—not at all like the boy who constantly teased her.

But as she took a step closer to the reservoir, Chase dropped through the ice and disappeared.

It was completely unfair. Even in a ridiculous-looking neoprene onesie, Derek still managed to look hot. With the hood covering his short brown hair, only his face showed, but that was enough. His wicked smile and those eyes that couldn't decide if they were blue or green still had the ability to reduce her to a pile of mush. The universe obviously enjoyed rubbing Artie's long ago mistakes in her face.

When she'd noticed Derek standing by the reservoir with Callum Cook and a blond woman she didn't know, Artie couldn't react as she usually did to a Derek spotting—forget how to breathe and then run in the opposite direction. As badly as she'd wanted to scurry back to the bus and hide, she had to act like an adult. Derek didn't make it easy, though, as he started the presentation, so tall and beautiful and adorably flustered. She'd forgotten how hopeless he was at public speaking.

After that rough start, Derek appeared to have found a

rhythm and was actually out of the running for worst presenter of the year. He explained the steps of an ice rescue as he hooked a rope harness around his body.

"Once I'm in the water, I get behind the victim"—he stepped behind the blond woman who'd shakily introduced herself to the kids as Lou at the beginning of the presentation—"and loop this around her like so."

Lou glanced at the half circle of students, looking nervous—and gorgeous. Artie wondered if she and Derek were dating and then immediately clamped down on that line of thought. Things had ended between them four years ago. As much as she wished it had been otherwise, Artie had no right to be jealous. None.

A child screamed.

In her job, she heard kids yelling a lot—while they were playing or arguing or pretending to be scared. This, though, *this* scream was so truly terrified, life-in-danger, rip-her-heart-out scream that it made all the hair rise on Artie's arms as her stomach contracted into a hard ball. Artie started running toward Zoe Springfield almost before she realized who had made that horrified—and horrifying—sound.

"Zoe!" She dropped to her knees in front of the girl, gaze darting over her, scanning for any visible injuries. "What's wrong, sweetie? Are you hurt?"

"Not me!" Her skin was so pale it almost had a blue tint as she pointed over Artie's shoulder. "Chase!"

Twisting around, Artie stared at the reservoir and a dark jagged hole about forty feet from shore. It took her a second to understand what that opening in the ice meant. When realization struck, her breathing stuttered, ragged and painful. Marnie ran toward them, her face white with fright. Artie's gaze darted toward the panting teacher, breaking her stare that had been locked on that horrible, yawning hole in the reservoir.

"Zoe!" Artie whipped back to the girl again. "Did Chase fall through the ice?"

Zoe's eyes were huge as she nodded. As soon as she had confirmation, Artie was stumbling to her feet and running again, this time toward the shore. Before she reached the ice, something hit her from the right with the force of a freight train. She staggered sideways and would've fallen if two arms hadn't wrapped around her. Her eyes fixed on that dark hole, she struggled against the iron hold.

"Artie, stop!" Derek's voice brought her out of her panic, and she turned her head to look at him. His normally cheerful face was stern, almost fierce. "If you go out there, it won't help. You'll go through the ice, and then we'll have a second victim."

She stared at him, breathing hard. Although she understood his words, it seemed wrong not to run across the ice, to pull Chase out of that freezing water. He was one of her students, one of *her* kids, and she was supposed to keep him safe. She couldn't just stand there and watch as he drowned.

"Do you want to help him? Do you?" Derek demanded, giving her a little shake. She nodded, her chin trembling. "Then promise you'll stay on shore and let me get him. Don't distract me by putting yourself in danger."

"Okay." Her voice was harsh and raspy. "I get it. I'll stay here. Just go save Chase."

"Promise?"

"I promise."

After a final hard look, he nodded, releasing her, and ran toward the dive van. Lou was already helping Callum Cook don a dry suit similar to the one Derek was wearing. Their efforts were hampered by Callum barking orders into a portable radio. The men exchanged a quick word, and then Derek moved back toward the ice with Callum and Lou holding the end of the rope.

"Stay back, kids!" Callum warned, and his crisp order snapped Artie out of her useless daze. A glance showed that Marnie had returned to the group and was lining up the children. Betsy and Lorna, the two parent chaperones, were just gaping at the rescue preparations. The small corner of Artie's brain that wasn't completely overwhelmed with panic made a mental note never to ask those women to chaperone again.

"Students," Artie barked, clapping her hands. "Everyone back to the bus. Let's go!"

With Marnie herding them, the kids moved reluctantly away from the shore, watching over their shoulders as Derek carefully made his way closer to the broken ice. The two other chaperones finally tore their own horrified gazes from what was happening on the reservoir and began helping Marnie usher the children toward the parking lot.

As Artie nudged the stragglers farther away from shore, she couldn't help but turn to check on Derek's progress. When he was ten feet from the spot where Chase had disappeared, he lowered himself to his hands and knees and started to crawl. The ice cracked beneath his knee, the far side of a slab rising out of the water under his weight, and his lower body slid into the water.

Artie sucked in a breath, her feet freezing to the ground. Even though she knew he was in a dry suit that would keep him warm, the sight of him dropping into the frigid depths made her heart thunder in her ears.

Bracing his gloved hands on the edge of the hole he'd

just created, Derek boosted himself out of the water. For a moment, Artie thought that he was in the clear, but then the ice folded, dropping him back into the reservoir. Air hissed between her teeth as he was submerged up to his neck.

"Adults!" Callum's bark was loud and commanding, dragging her attention away from Derek's struggle to reach Chase. "I need you on the line."

"Betsy, stay with the kids!" Artie ordered as she hurried over to join Callum and Lou. "Marnie and Lorna, you're with me." She was relieved that she would be able to do *something* to help. Her gaze kept moving to Derek. On his next attempt, he managed to slide across the ice on his belly for several feet before it broke apart beneath him. As she watched him drop into the water, Artie's own insides froze with cold, as if she were being dunked along with Derek.

"Kids!" Callum snapped. Every student clustered next to the bus stared at him with wide eyes. "If any of you takes even a single step closer to the water, I promise that you will regret it." He sounded like he meant it. The children froze in place.

Derek broke through the last section of ice separating him from the spot where Chase had fallen through. His head disappeared, and a small sound escaped Artie.

"He'll be fine," Callum said. "Derek knows what he's doing."

His confidence eased the churning acid in her stomach slightly, and she gave him a pathetic attempt at a smile.

"Everyone take a place on the rope," he ordered. "Help's on the way, but we'll most likely get everybody out of the water before the rest of the team arrives."

Artie found herself in front of Lou.

"This is my first day," Lou muttered. "I haven't even passed the freaking dive-team interview yet. I don't know what I'm doing!"

The scary thing was that none of them—except for Callum and Derek—knew what they were doing. A little boy's life depended on them, and Artie could do nothing to help. She hadn't even been able to keep him from going into the water. What kind of horrible, irresponsible teacher was she? How could something so awful have happened on her watch?

Artie's gaze was drawn inexorably back to the reservoir, and she stared at the dark water, the broken ice floating in miniature icebergs above where Derek had gone under. It seemed like forever since he'd disappeared. How long could he hold his breath? What if he got disoriented and couldn't find his way back to the opening in the ice? The horrific image of him trying to surface but being blocked by a ceiling of solid ice filled her mind, and she bit the inside of her cheek hard enough to draw blood.

"Artemis." Even Callum's commanding tone couldn't mute the nightmarish scene playing in her brain. "Artie!" His hand closed around her forearm, and he gave her a shake, jerking her out of her thoughts.

"Sorry." Squeezing her eyes closed for a moment, she dragged in a deep breath. When she met Callum's gaze, he looked at her closely and then released her arm.

"I'll need you to pull soon. You with me?"

Derek suddenly popped out of the water. As he took a breath, he tapped his fist against the top of his head in some sort of signal and then dove under again. The sight of him, alive and not trapped under an impenetrable sheet of ice, made her next breath easier.

"Yes." She grimaced. "Sorry. I'm usually calmer in emergency situations."

"You're doing fine." Callum's attention turned to the radio chattering on the ground by his feet. "Fire and Med will be here in less than five minutes."

Five minutes suddenly felt endless.

The sound of quiet sobs made her look behind her. Marnie released the rope with one hand so she could wipe the tears from her face. Artie reached back and squeezed the other teacher's arm before turning around so she could watch for Derek to reemerge. She couldn't escape the crazy feeling that he *needed* her to keep watch, as if her hope and fear was all that was drawing him back. *Please oh please oh please. Derek, please.*

The seconds ticked by, the silence broken only by the incomprehensible voices on the radio and Marnie's sniffles. Then Derek's head broke the surface, followed by his shoulders. Tucked against his chest was a limp Chase.

"Got him." Callum's voice was thick with satisfaction. "Get ready to pull. I'll tell you when."

Everyone on the line cheered. Artie's vision blurred, but she blinked away the wetness, determined not to dissolve into a weepy, relieved heap until everyone was safe and dry and home.

Pushing at the chunks of ice blocking his path with one hand as he kept the other wrapped around the boy, Derek made his way to the edge of the hole and signaled.

"Pull!"

They hauled on the rope as Derek boosted himself and the boy onto the ice. It immediately collapsed beneath their weight, dropping them back into the water. Shoving the newly broken pieces aside, Derek reached the edge and tried again.

"Pull!"

The ice started folding under Derek and Chase. Artie bit the inside of her cheek to stifle the panicked sound that wanted to escape.

"Pull!"

Artie threw her weight back as she yanked the rope as hard as she could, putting all her strength into it. The pair slid out of the chasm forming in the ice, with only Derek's feet dropping back into the water.

"Pull!"

Her arms shook with adrenaline and fatigue, but she ignored the quaking of her muscles. Each yank on the rope drew the man and boy closer. The ice held beneath them, and they slid across the solid ice toward safety. Once they were just a few feet from the shore, Callum unhooked the foam strap looped around the boy and lifted him in his arms.

"Sparks! Get blankets from the warmer and the med kit," Callum ordered, and Lou scrambled toward the dive van. Artie tore her eyes from Chase's blue-tinted face to check on Derek. He'd gotten to his feet and was following Callum to a level area next to the van. Lou emerged from the back, blankets in one arm and a white case in the other. Derek grabbed a blanket from her, spreading it on the ground, and then took the kit from her.

"Artie, grab the radio." Callum laid Chase on his back on top of the blanket. She scrambled to find the radio sitting on the ground where Callum had left it.

"Got it!"

"Press the big button on the side and tell dispatch that the victim is out of the water. He's unresponsive and not breathing. Say that 1210 and 1228 are starting CPR."

Not breathing. Her fingers went numb as she fumbled with the radio. Frustrated, she ripped off her glove and finally managed to press the button. Her lungs didn't want to work, but she opened her mouth and forced out the words. Derek and Callum were doing freaking CPR. The least she could do was talk.

"Copy," a calm female voice responded when Artie finished relaying the information. "Ambulance Two, did you copy?"

"Ambulance Two, we copied. ETA one minute."

Radio still clutched in her fingers, Artie stared as Callum did chest compressions, counting out loud as he did so. When he reached thirty, Derek placed the bag valve mask over the boy's face and squeezed twice. She watched Chase's tiny chest rise and fall with each ventilation, which made it seem only that much more still afterward.

"C'mon, Chase," she muttered. "Breathe. You can do it, sweetie. Just take a breath."

Callum started compressions again, but he'd only reached nine when he pulled his hands away. The small body convulsed as Chase choked, and Derek pulled the mask off his face while Callum turned him onto his side.

As the boy coughed and vomited, Derek grabbed another blanket and wrapped it around Chase's heaving form. Artie pressed her hand to her mouth, not sure if she was holding back relieved laughter or sobs.

"Artie." Callum rubbed the boy's back over the blanket as he turned toward her. "Let them know he's breathing independently."

Lifting the radio, she took a quavering breath and pushed the button.

"He's breathing," she said, her voice hoarse. Artie met Derek's eyes and returned his relieved grin. "He's *breathing*."

The ambulance arrived just seconds later, quickly followed by two fire rescue trucks and a sheriff's department squad car. Derek stepped back to allow the EMTs access to the shivering, crying boy.

A gust of wind reminded Derek that he was wet and getting colder by the second, so he headed for the dive van. The earlier winter sunshine was now blocked by a bank of dark clouds that cast a shadow over the distant peaks. After shutting himself in the back of the vehicle, he stripped off the dry suit and the damp layers beneath. Shivering, he hurried to dress in his street clothes.

By the time he reemerged, the EMTs had Chase bundled into the ambulance. As the emergency vehicle left the reservoir, lights and sirens flashing, Derek found himself moving toward a shell-shocked-looking Artie. He couldn't help it. When she was close, she drew him toward her. It had been that way since kindergarten.

"Guess that little girl gets her wish about seeing some firemen," he said.

Artie blinked and then turned her head toward him. She was so beautiful. Each time he looked at her, it was like getting punched in the stomach. "What?"

In answer, he just gestured at the crowd of students still clustered next to the bus. Their eyes were all fixed on the big red trucks, although their feet hadn't moved an inch since Callum had ordered them to stay still.

Her laugh was more of a gasp. "Right. At least Amber's day is made."

"Amber? Is that the fireman fan?"

She nodded, but Callum stepped in front of her before she could say more.

"I'll take this. Thanks for your help, Artie," he said,

gently pulling the portable radio from her grip. She looked down at her now-empty hand, as if she'd forgotten that she'd been holding it.

"If I'd been doing my job," she said, her eyes still fixed on her fingers as they tightened into a fist, "then he wouldn't have gotten onto the ice in the first place."

"No use in killing yourself over 'ifs.'" Derek resisted the urge to wrap his arm around her shoulders. She wouldn't welcome the touch—they'd barely spoken in years. "Besides, I count three other chaperones and three dive-team members who're just as responsible. Put your glove on."

Although she did as he asked without any argument, her expression showed she still blamed herself. "I should get back to the others."

Feeling like a needy idiot, Derek followed when she walked away, taking a couple of quick strides so he caught up to her. "How've you been?"

"Okay."

It was such an obvious lie that he snorted. "Let's try this again. How've you been, Artie? The truth, this time."

Her exasperated huff made him smile. He didn't like seeing her looking so...defeated. "Honestly? There are good days and bad days. Overall, though, it's an uphill progression, so I'm sticking with my original answer. What's wrong?"

Derek blinked at the question before realizing that it was directed at Marnie Belcher, who'd hurried to catch them a few feet away from the group of students. Although her tears from earlier were gone, she looked unsettled.

"I've counted over and over, and there are only thirty-five kids," Marnie said in a low voice.

"There should be thirty-seven." Squeezing her eyes shut for a second, Artie took an audible breath. "Okay. Who's missing?"

Marnie grimaced. "I'm trying to figure that out, but, after what happened with Chase, my brain is fried. Maybe I'm just skipping over a couple of the short ones. Could you do a count?"

"Sure." Artie raised her voice to address the group. "Students! Line up in two rows. Ms. Belcher's class, line up here next to her." She nudged Marnie a few feet to the side. "My class, line up in front of me."

The kids hesitated, sending fearful looks toward the dive van. "That man said we shouldn't move," one of the girls said, pointing at Callum. "He's scary."

Derek had to turn his head to hide his grin.

"That was just for when we were getting Chase out of the reservoir," Artie explained. "It's okay to move now."

None of the students took even a single step.

Coughing to mask a laugh, Derek turned and bellowed, "Yo! Cal! Tell the kids the game of freeze tag is over."

Turning away from his discussion with Lou, Callum eyed the group of petrified students. "As long as you stay off the ice"—his crisp voice carried easily—"you may move."

The kids hurried to get into their appropriate lines. Artie leaned closer to Derek and murmured, "Callum needs to visit my classroom on a regular basis. That was amazing."

The admiration in her voice caused a pang in his chest, but Derek shook it off. He should be used to jealousy when it came to Artemis. To cover, he forced a laugh. "His magic works on adults, too."

She smiled as she began counting, walking along each line and touching each child on the shoulder. As she started on Ms. Belcher's class, her eyebrows drew together. Uh-oh. That didn't look good. Derek swallowed

the swearword—multiple swearwords, actually—trying
to bubble up in his throat. This day was going from bad to
worse.

At the end of Ms. Belcher's line, she turned and caught
his eyes. He saw a flash of worry before she smoothed her
expression and moved in front of the group.

"Students," she said calmly, although Derek could sense
the tension vibrating through her. "Does anyone know
where Zoe and Maya Springfield are?"

The response was a mixture of shaking heads and blank
looks.

"Are you sure? This is very important. I promise that
neither you nor the Springfield girls will get into trouble."

When none of the kids said anything, Derek saw Artie's
shoulders fall with a silent sigh. "Okay. Everyone on the bus,
please."

He took a step toward Artie as she supervised the board-
ing. Leaning close to her ear, he said quietly, "Steve's girls
are missing?"

"They're probably close by," she said in an equally
hushed—but tense—tone. "We'll look around, but I want to
get the rest of the kids on the bus before any more disappear."

"Good idea."

When the last child climbed onto the bus, Artie waved
over Marnie and the two other women, who were looking
a little worse for wear. Derek figured they probably hadn't
been prepared for the field trip from hell when they'd vol-
unteered to chaperone.

"Lorna, could you stay here with the driver and watch
the students?" At Lorna's nod, Artie turned to the other
two. "Betsy, would you mind checking over there? It's closest to where I last saw the girls, right after Chase fell in."

"Sure." As Betsy hurried in the direction indicated, Artie looked at Derek.

"Since you're the diving expert, could you look for the girls closer to the shore?"

"What about me?" Marnie asked.

Holding out her fist, Artie sighed. "One of us has to call Chase's parents. The other one will search opposite from where Betsy's looking."

With a groan, Marnie put her fist next to Artie's.

"Rock, paper, scissors, go!"

Artie picked paper and gave a tiny, pleased yelp when she saw Marnie's rock.

"Wish me luck," Marnie muttered, retreating to the bus.

"Good luck!" Artie called after her before lowering her voice so only Derek could hear. "Although it doesn't seem to be in plentiful supply today."

"I don't know about that," Derek said as he started walking back toward the reservoir. "Chase is alive, isn't he?"

"True." She gave him a smile that was only slightly pained. "And we're going to find the girls in no time and get their wandering little butts on the bus."

As they split, heading to their designated areas, Derek couldn't stop himself from turning his head so his gaze could follow her. Despite the knowledge that he wouldn't ever have her, he couldn't seem *not* to watch Artie whenever she was within view. Maybe it was his punishment for almost wrecking her life four years ago.

He shook off his thoughts. There were kids to find; it was not the time for him to dwell on his biggest regret.

Shaking off his distraction, he noticed Sheriff Rob Coughlin heading to intercept her. Derek immediately reversed direction so he could join the pair. A part of him felt a twinge of guilt. It wasn't Rob's fault that most of the female—and a few of the male—Simpson residents were tempted to commit crimes just so they could be arrested by the rugged, good-looking sheriff. Rob was a decent cop, too, and Derek normally would rather deal with him than anyone else in the sheriff's department. It was just that Artie's smile was awfully big. And was it really necessary that they stand so close together?

As he stopped behind Artie, Derek caught the tail end of Rob's sentence—something about a report.

"I promise I'll give you my statement in just a few minutes," Artie said. "Right now, I have to track down Zoe and Maya Springfield."

Wrinkles appeared between the sheriff's eyebrows. "Steve's girls are missing? Hey, Derek."

Although all of Rob's attention was focused on Artie, Derek returned the greeting with a lift of his chin.

"Yes." Artie scanned the area as she spoke. "Zoe was the first to notice Chase had fallen through the ice. I don't know if they're scared and hiding somewhere or what."

"I'll help you look. Where do you need me?"

"You can help me…" Her voice trailed away as Derek caught her hand. When she looked up at him questioningly, he shifted his gaze to Rob. He knew that there was no excuse for his possessive behavior, especially when he should be focused on tracking down the missing kids, but Derek couldn't seem to stop himself from tugging her a step farther away from the sheriff.

"We'll check the shore if you could look over there?" Derek gestured toward the area where Artie had originally planned to search.

"Sure," Rob said with a faint smile before striding

away. Still holding Artie's hand, Derek turned toward the reservoir.

As they walked, Derek kept his gaze forward, even though Artie's scrutiny was making his skin prickle.

"Why don't you look in the dive van?" she suggested. "There aren't many places to hide around here. Maybe they crawled into the back?"

Relieved that she wasn't going to bring up his strangely territorial behavior, he grunted an agreement and reluctantly released her hand. As he strode toward the dive van, he blew out an exasperated breath. Following her around, yanking her away from Rob, grunting—since when had he gone full-on Cro-Magnon man?

He'd ended things years ago because she'd deserved better. Afterward, Derek had punched a hole in the wall and stayed drunk for a solid month before he'd started pulling himself out of that pit of self-pitying despair. He'd thought he'd finally gotten over her, but an hour in her company had proven how wrong he was.

Forcing himself to concentrate on finding the girls, he checked the back of the dive van, looking in all the places big enough to hide a little kid or two. When he was satisfied that the van was child free, he hopped out of the back and looked underneath. He circled the van to check the front, and almost ran into Callum and Lou. The dive-team leader broke off in the middle of a sentence.

Derek stopped abruptly and eyed the two, who were standing a little too close together. *That* was interesting.

"What is it?" Callum asked sharply. Since that was his usual tone, Derek wasn't offended, although Lou looked slightly alarmed.

Grimacing, Derek explained, "Steve's girls decided to go

on a walkabout. Artie managed to get the rest of the monkeys on the bus, but they're still two short."

Callum's only outward reaction was a twitching muscle in his cheek. "No more dive-team presentations. Fire can talk to the kids from now on."

"I'm not going to argue with that." Derek pulled open the driver's door and peered into the cab. It was empty.

Lou sucked in a breath. "What if they fell in, too?"

"Zoe, the older girl, sounded the alarm when Chase went under." Slamming the van door, Derek headed toward the shore. He saw that Artie had gone east, so he headed in the opposite direction. Callum and Lou followed. "After that, there were a lot of eyes focused on the reservoir. Someone would've spotted them if they'd gone onto the ice. Besides, it'd take a pretty dumb kid to step onto the reservoir after watching someone else fall through, and the Springfield girls aren't stupid."

Callum nodded, although his gaze still raked the frozen surface of the reservoir. "Why do you think they wandered off, then?"

"My guess? They're the ones who talked Chase into going out on the ice. Now they think they're in trouble, so they're hiding."

Frowning, Lou asked, "You think they convinced him to walk on the ice? That seems a little budding-psycho-like. Why would they do that?"

"Maya was the one who got a load of snow down her back earlier, thanks to Chase. I've babysat the Springfield kids. They're…uh, feisty."

Derek stopped and looked around. There really wasn't anywhere for the girls to hide nearby. The rocky shore changed to scrub, which winter had stripped to skeletons.

The closest concealment was the evergreens almost a quarter mile away. Wind sent powdery snow swirling across the ground as Derek eyed the dark gray clouds hanging over the forest. The cold, empty landscape sent a trickle of unease down his spine.

"Zoe!" he bellowed. "Maya!" Their names echoed over the reservoir, but there was no response. Turning, he could see Artie and Betsy still searching, and Derek's stomach twisted. For the first time since Artie had discovered that the girls weren't at the bus, it occurred to him that they might *not* be hiding close by. The heavy snow clouds and whipping wind could quickly turn this situation from an annoyance into a tragedy.

He met Callum's gaze. By the other man's grim expression, Derek could tell he was having similar thoughts.

"Should we ask the firemen to help look?" Lou asked.

With a nod, Derek turned toward the red truck. It appeared that the firefighters were packing up to leave, so he quickened his steps. "I didn't see Steve with them. Is he here, do you know?"

"Springfield's on nights," Callum said, pulling out his cell. "I'll call him."

Derek tapped the screen on his own phone. "I'll call Rob."

"Who's Rob?" Lou's face was tight with worry.

"He's an obnoxiously handsome man whose tortured soul and tragic past make all women want to fix him." When she stared at him, confused, Derek added, "And he's the sheriff. He's already here, but he'll mobilize Search and Rescue."

Her eyes widened. "Search and Rescue? Do you think the girls are really missing, then?"

"I'm thinking," Derek answered as the phone rang, "that the sooner we find those kids, the better."

As she walked, calling their names every so often, Artie felt her impatience slowly morph into true fear. She knew both girls well. Zoe had been in her class a year earlier, and Maya was currently one of her students. Although Artie could understand their initial impulse to panic and hide, she honestly didn't think either of the girls would stay hidden if they could hear so many frantic voices calling their names.

"Zoe!" she called, trying to mask the shrill note of worry. It was getting harder and harder to do as the minutes ticked past. "Maya! You're not in trouble! Please come back to the bus so we can go!"

"Artie." Derek's voice behind her made her turn. His normally teasing expression held nothing but concern. "Steve's on his way. Rob's calling in Search and Rescue, too."

His gentle tone made tears burn her eyes, but she fought them back. There were two students to find before she could finally have the nervous breakdown that had been building all afternoon.

"That's probably best." Starting to walk back toward the parking lot, she ignored the betraying thickness in her throat. "I'm going to send Marnie and the two chaperones back to school with the kids. If they leave now, they'll get there in time to catch their buses."

"Good idea." Although he still used that meltingly kind voice, a reassuringly Derek-like smirk curled the corners of his mouth. It made her realize how terribly she'd missed that grin. "Let someone else keep track of them for a while."

Her laugh had a hiccup in the middle, and Derek threw an arm around her shoulders. "We'll find them."

The urge to melt into his side was incredibly strong, but

she stiffened her spine instead. "I know. And after we do, I'm never taking the students on another field trip again."

It was his turn to chuckle, although his sounded less watery than hers. "Callum said pretty much the exact same thing. Fire is getting all the school visits from now on."

"The firefighters can come to the school, then. Once the kids are inside, I'm not letting them go anywhere."

"What about recess?"

"Canceled."

Giving her shoulders a squeeze, he laughed again and then dropped his arm. Artie instantly missed it. "Did you call Randy?"

Her forehead wrinkled with confusion. "Why would I do that?"

He kept his eyes directed forward. "I just thought you might need some support during all of this. He'd probably want to help search, too."

Artie opened her mouth and then closed it again. How was she supposed to condense years' worth of heartache and rage into a couple of sentences? "You must be out of the Simpson gossip loop."

"What?" That made him look at her, although she couldn't read his expression.

"Randy's been living in California for over six months. The divorce was finalized more than a year ago."

"He left?"

He sounded so stunned that she shot him an incredulous look. "How did you not hear about it? I couldn't even go to the grocery store without someone trapping me in the condiment aisle, trying to worm the gory details out of me."

"Whenever someone mentioned you, I'd...well"—he rubbed the back of his neck, not meeting her gaze—"I'd walk away. Or say something rude. Hearing details about you and Randy—" He focused on something over her shoulder, his relief obvious. "Hey, Rob."

The sheriff gave a short nod as he moved to join them. "The team's on their way. Janelle is bringing her younger dog." From his frown, this wasn't good news.

"Why not Tank?" Derek asked.

"He had surgery yesterday to remove a bowel obstruction."

Derek groaned. "What'd that dumb dog eat this time?"

"Janelle said it was her kid's bike tire."

With a shake of his head, Derek asked, "How many of these surgeries has Tank had? Six? Seven?"

"Something like that," Rob said. "The vet should install a zipper in Tank's belly to save some time."

"How's the new dog coming along?"

Artie followed the two men's gazes to a woman with graying brown hair who was standing next to a deputy. She held the lead of a medium-size, black-and-white dog that Artie guessed was a border collie mix. As Janelle talked with the deputy, the dog spun in excited circles, occasionally catching his tail in his mouth.

"Puck is...improving?" the sheriff said doubtfully. "He's still a little, well, unfocused."

The three watched as the dog pulled hard enough on his tail that he lost his balance and tumbled over sideways.

"Better than not having a tracking dog at all, I guess." Derek sighed before turning back to Rob. "Are you taking incident command?"

"Already called it in." Striding away, Rob lifted his hand to his mouth and gave a two-fingered whistle, the kind Derek and Randy had tried to teach Artie when they were kids. She'd never been able to master the skill.

The group that gathered around Rob was already large, and more vehicles were pulling into the parking lot. The sight of the school bus reminded Artie of her plan to send the rest of the kids and chaperones back to Simpson Elementary. She jogged over to the bus. The driver must have seen her coming, since the door was open when Artie reached it.

Marnie and the two other chaperones met her next to the driver, all four looking worried.

"You didn't find them?" Betsy asked. "There was no sign of them in my area, and I went almost all the way to the woods."

"Not yet." Artie kept her voice low so as not to freak out the students. "We're going to keep looking. Can you take everyone else back so they'll be on time to catch their buses home? There's a storm coming, too. If the bus doesn't leave soon, they'll all be stuck here for who knows how long." Unlike Maya and Zoe, the kids on the bus would at least be warm and safe. Artie squeezed her eyes shut for a second, banishing the image of the girls huddled in the midst of a blizzard. Panic was too close, and she couldn't let it consume her.

"I can stay and help search," Marnie offered, glancing through the back window that framed an approaching bank of black clouds, but Artie shook her head.

"Someone needs to go back, and I have on warmer clothes." When Marnie opened her mouth as if to argue, Artie said even more quietly, "If they haven't been found by then, you can come back to help after all the kids get home."

After a moment, Marnie gave a reluctant nod. "Go find those little girls then."

"Thanks, Marn." Artie moved down the steps as she

spoke, pushed by the urgent need to find Maya and Zoe before they were lost in the oncoming storm. "And we will."

The confidence in her voice surprised her. If only her heart was as sure.

The sheriff had barely managed to get two words out before a battered pickup came flying into the parking lot, almost side-swiping a fire truck as it fishtailed to a crooked halt. Before the pickup had completely stopped, the driver had the door open and was charging toward the group of rescue workers.

"Frantic father incoming," Derek warned, and everyone turned toward Steve Springfield.

"Where are my girls?" Steve was demanding when he reached them. "How long have they been missing? Where've you looked so far? Did you check the ice? Could they have gone under? How could they have wandered off? Why wasn't someone watching?"

Derek blinked at the torrent of words coming from the mouth of a normally quiet Steve. Ian Walsh, another fire-man, put a hand on Springfield's back.

"We'll find them," Ian soothed, but Steve stepped out of the other man's reach.

"Why's everyone standing around? Why isn't anyone looking for my baby girls?" He threw an arm toward the western sky, where the clouds looked even darker and more ominous than just a few minutes earlier. "It's about to snow, and they'll be out there, alone and cold and scared—" The final word ended abruptly, as if it had choked him.

"Steve." Rob's clipped voice swung the agitated firefight-er's attention around to him. "We were waiting for you to start the search. Did you bring something that smells like the girls?"

Either the commanding tone or the question seemed to settle Steve a little. "Yes. I...yes." He dug in his coat pocket and pulled out two freezer bags, each with what looked like a shirt inside. The smallness of the items made Derek's chest hurt, and he couldn't help a glance at the western sky. If those tiny girls were caught in a blizzard... He gritted his teeth, forcing back the mental image. Panic would just make him useless.

Janelle took the bags from Steve with a gentle smile. "Where were the girls last seen?"

"I'll show you," Artie said, hurrying the last few strides to join their group. The school bus rumbled to life behind her. Artie, Janelle, and the dog headed for the area where the girls had been standing when Chase had fallen into the reservoir. Steve started to follow, but Rob grabbed his arm.

"Stay here," he ordered. When Steve turned furiously toward him, Rob let go and raised his hands to chest level, palms out. "We're working on our plan of action. I figured you'd want to be part of the search."

With a final glance at the women and dog, Steve gave a grudging nod.

"Okay," Rob said. "We have about two and a half hours of daylight left, but that storm's coming in faster than expected. Let's see how far the dog gets. Best case, he'll lead us right to them. Worst case, well, George here is almost as good at picking up a trail." He gave the huge bearded man to his right a slap on the shoulder. If George hadn't been George, Derek would've thought he rolled his eyes. Derek couldn't blame him. After all, Rob had just compared him—unfavorably—to a dog.

A shout from Janelle caught their attention, and Derek

looked over to see Puck plunging toward the east, the twenty-foot lead fully extended between the dog's harness and Janelle, who was working to keep up. Artie was a few feet behind the handler. Derek knew Artie, with her long legs and love of running, could easily outpace Janelle, so he assumed she was staying back to keep out of the way.

The whole group rushed after them, their excitement almost a physical presence. Ian kept Steve from passing Janelle and distracting the dog. It only took a couple of body checks before Steve fell in behind Janelle, still simmering but resigned to the controlled pace.

Derek caught up to Artie, running just behind her and to her right. She threw him a grin that glowed with anticipation and relief. It was impossible not to smile back, although he wasn't counting his missing chicks until they were back in their dad's arms.

Sure enough, Puck lost the trail at the first line of trees. After a few aborted attempts at picking it up again, he started spinning in circles.

"Sorry, guys," Janelle said with an apologetic grimace as she reeled in the extra line until he was next to her. "He's done."

"He gave us a direction," Rob told her. "That reduces our search area by about seventy-five percent. Not bad for a puppy in training. George? Any sign?"

While Puck had been trying to find the lost trail, George had been hunting for footprints or broken twigs—any indication of which way the girls had gone. Without pausing in his search, the big man shook his head.

"Shoot," Artie muttered. "I'd already been picturing the magical reunion scene with the girls, Steve, and the dog."

Derek squeezed her shoulder and then reluctantly let

his hand drop. He couldn't help touching her whenever an opportunity presented itself. "Nothing's ever easy, is it?"

"Since we don't have a trail, let's start a grid search." As the sheriff unfolded a map, the wind snapped at it, almost ripping it from his fingers. He looked up, taking in the descending clouds that were swallowing the tops of the evergreens. "Pair up. With this weather coming, I don't want anyone out there alone."

Taking a half step closer to Artie, Derek bumped her with his shoulder. "Partners?" he mouthed, feeling like a junior high kid teaming up in gym class. He felt a surge of pleasure when Artie nodded.

Rob divided the search area on the map into four squares.

"How does he know how big to make it?" Artie whispered.

"He estimated how fast the girls could travel and multiplied that by how long they've been missing."

She made a face. "Oh. Sorry for the stupid question."

Although Derek had a joke about being used to her stupid questions hovering at the tip of his tongue, he swallowed it back and just smiled at her. It felt too soon to start teasing her like that again, especially in the current situation.

When Janelle returned after putting Puck in her SUV, she had four more people with her.

"Chief and the rest of the guys'll be here as soon as they can," one of them said, giving Steve a sympathetic clap on the upper arm. "Another arson."

The rest of the firefighters groaned.

"That little shit, whoever he is, picked a hell of a day to play with matches again," Ian grumbled.

"The chief's wife went to your house," the first firefighter told Steve. "She'll watch the boys and be there in case the girls circled around and managed to get home."

"Good." Steve's voice was rusty, and he couldn't quite manage a smile of thanks.

The sheriff cleared his throat, drawing everyone's attention back to him. "Let's get started. We'll divide into four groups, each one led by a Search and Rescue member. I'll be staying at base camp, heading up command."

Derek and Artie ended up in group three, along with Callum and Lou—an odd couple pairing that Derek made a mental note to mock as soon as the crisis was over. Judging by the frequent bewildered glances Cal was shooting the newest dive-team member, he was well on his way to being smitten. Steve and Ian rounded out their group, with George in the lead.

"Shouldn't you have a partner?" Artie asked George as the seven of them headed to the start point of their quadrant. The burly man just gave her a look and walked between two trees, forcing her to drop behind him or run face-first into a trunk. Derek held back a laugh at her expression.

"I don't think George Holloway does the whole partner thing," he whispered once he caught up with her.

"Or the whole talking thing," she muttered back, making it even harder not to snicker.

"Zoe!" Steve called. "Maya!" The crack in his voice erased any desire to laugh. Derek focused on looking around him as he walked, trying to pick up any movement or color that was out of place, which might possibly belong to one of the missing girls. There was a dusting of snow, although not enough to hold a boot print, and the ground was more rocks than dirt. It felt as if they were on a slight upward incline as they made their way between the thickening trees.

At George's grunt, they stopped. Derek assumed that they were at the eastern border of their quadrant. Between billows of wind, he could hear the other groups calling the girls' names.

George lined them up by pointing at each pair and then at the spot where he wanted them. The big guy acted like every word cost him a million bucks. The three couples were spread far enough apart that Derek could see only an occasional flash of purple from Lou's coat, and he couldn't make out Steve and Ian at all. The clouds had fully descended, draping them in a gray fog, and Derek suddenly felt isolated. He took a step closer to Artie.

"You okay?" she asked without looking at him. She was concentrating on the compass in her hand.

"Fine." His voice sounded tense even to his own ears as he looked around at their rapidly decreasing circle of visibility. "Just don't like this weather."

A high-pitched, crooning howl pierced the fog, joined by several other animal voices and ending with a series of yips.

"The coyotes aren't helping either," Artie grumbled. "We're supposed to walk directly west, right?"

"Right." Derek released the breath he'd been holding. It was nice to have Artie there, breaking the uneasy eeriness with her practical questions. "George will use the radio to give us a shout when we reach the western border of our quadrant. Then we'll head south fifty feet before going east, searching the next strip of our section."

"Got it." She started walking, and Derek followed. Although he tried to keep his attention focused, calling out the girls' names every so often, he couldn't help but notice that Artie's pants cupped her ass in a very distracting way.

It didn't help that her down jacket was not long enough to fall much past her waist. Shit. Now was not the time. He jerked his gaze off her posterior for the hundredth time and scoured the area for any hints of the kids.

It had been easier to look for Maya and Zoe by the shore, where the scrub and small rocks didn't provide any kind of concealment. Now, it seemed like every tree could hide a small body, and the wind competed with him in volume each time he tried to yell for the girls.

He and Artie scrambled over a couple of good-size boulders before stopping abruptly. A rocky crevice divided the path like a wedge.

"Which way?" Artie shouted over the growing wind, tipping her face to protect it from the ice and dirt particles carried in the gusts.

Turning so his back was to the wind, Derek pulled his radio off his belt and held it close to his face. When they'd divided into groups, everyone had turned their portables to the channel dedicated to the search.

"Warner to Holloway."

Instead of George, the dispatcher answered. "Unit calling, you're unreadable."

Mentally swearing at the wind, Derek hunched his shoulders, trying to shelter the radio as much as possible. Artie shuffled to stand in front of him, so close that Derek had to clear his throat before he could try talking on the radio again.

"Warner to Holloway!"

"Holloway," George's raspy bass responded, making Derek's shoulders dip in relief.

"There's a ravine in our path. Do you want us to go around it to the north or south?" Without climbing equipment, there was no way they could go directly through. They'd need to shift fifty feet either north or south before they could head west again.

The radio was silent for a moment, and Derek prayed that George had been able to understand the question. To his relief, the radio crackled before George's clipped, "South."

"Copy."

As they moved left to skirt the yawning hole, Derek saw Artie shoot an anxious glance toward the direction of the rest of their group. He couldn't blame her. It felt wrong to be moving away from their team, but they weren't really *that* far apart. It was just the low-lying clouds and the wind and those damn coyotes that were making it seem as if he and Artie were the only two people left alive.

The snow started, icy flakes peppering Derek's face. Twisting away from the blasting wind, he turned to check on Artie. She was obviously fighting to keep her head up so she could look for the girls, despite the pummeling ice crystals. He'd never seen her look so miserable.

Impulsively wrapping an arm around her shoulders, Derek curled her in so she faced his chest with only a bare inch separating them. It was unnervingly too close and too far at the same time. She tilted her face to give him a questioning look.

"Let's give it a minute. Maybe the wind will settle down." He took a couple of steps back until they were semi-sheltered by the broad, twisted trunk of a bristlecone pine.

"But we need to keep looking," she protested, trying to crane her neck to see over her shoulder. An especially fierce gust shot tiny pellets of snow at them, and she quickly turned back to bury her face in Derek's neck.

He sighed. It was nice having her pressed against him... really nice. Her tall body was a perfect fit to his, with the top of her head not quite reaching his chin. "We can't find the girls if we're getting smacked in the eyeballs with snowflakes."

Her small laugh puffed against his throat, sending a rush of pleasure across his skin. Flushing with heat, he fought the urge to fidget.

"Fine. But just for a few minutes."

"Just until this wind goes from sixty miles an hour to something more reasonable. Like fifty-five." Artie rewarded his lame joke with another shiver-inducing laugh. Since she seemed okay with using him for a wind block, he inched a little closer and wrapped his other arm around her back. Although he'd braced for her reaction, half-expecting her to shove him away, she didn't seem to mind. Instead, she settled more securely against him.

It was like the past four years hadn't happened. The press of Artie's body against his, even with the multiple layers of clothes separating them, brought back all the times he'd held her. His world had revolved around Artie—when he wasn't with her, he was thinking of her or dreaming of her. Until the day he'd sent her away.

"What happened between you and Randy?"

She stiffened and pulled away. "We should look for the girls."

He forced himself to let her go. Each time, it got harder.

"Maya! Zoe!" Her voice was growing hoarse, the air rubbing painfully against her throat each time she shouted. Artie accepted it as part of her punishment for being an inattentive chaperone. No, she hadn't been inattentive—she'd just been attending to the wrong things, like how broad Derek's shoulders were and how great his legs looked in neoprene.

She wasn't sure how much use her calls were, anyway, since the wind had increased in volume to a wailing roar. Her boot slid on a loose rock, and she stumbled. Derek caught her upper arm before she could fall. Grimacing at her clumsiness, Artie gave him a tight smile of thanks. All they needed was for her to sprain her ankle and have to be carried out of there.

After dropping south, they'd turned west again and followed the edge of the crevice for a while. Now their course was taking them through a thickly wooded area. The trees swayed and thrashed in the wind, turning the usual tranquil scenery into something nightmarish. The clouds and fog had darkened the afternoon to dusk, and Artie couldn't stop herself from thinking of how scared the lost girls must be.

Although the radio had chirped a few times, no one had announced that they'd found the missing kids yet. Despite the sandblasting effect of the wind, Artie forced herself to keep her head lifted so she could look for any glimpse of the girls. It got harder when they moved into an area that had been ravaged by the previous summer's fire, the black skeletons of the pines stripped bare of any green needles that might've helped block some of the wind.

"Zoe! Maya!" Cupping her hands around her mouth, she screamed the names, trying to make them heard above the howling gusts. It was pointless. Her throat ached from yelling and the wind snatched away her voice. It was as if nature itself was against her. Now that the forest had the girls, it wasn't about to give them back without a fight.

A flash of movement in her peripheral vision caught her attention. Her heart pounding, she grabbed Derek's arm.

"What?" he shouted.

"There!" Artie pointed in the direction where she'd seen something move, already jogging toward it. "Zoe! Is that you? Come on out! You're not in trouble, I promise!"

Derek wrapped his arm around her waist, pulling her to a stop.

"Derek, let go!" Artie strained against his hold. "I saw something moving over there!"

"Wait," he ordered, his mouth so close to her ear that his hot breath warmed her skin, even through the knit of her hat. "Go slowly. The girls aren't the only living things in these mountains."

The sense of his words penetrated, and she stopped fighting his hold. As soon as her struggling ceased, he released her. Continuing more cautiously toward the spot where she'd seen the motion, Artie scanned the trees and brush, desperately hoping to get a glimpse of one of the girls. There was nothing there, though, and her shoulders slumped.

"Sorry." She turned toward Derek. There was a lull in the wind, so she didn't have to scream to be heard. "I must have imagined it."

Each disappointment—not finding the girls hiding by the reservoir, the dog losing their trail, this latest false alarm—was harder to take, especially as the snow began to swirl again as the wind resumed its howling. Her feet stopped moving as frustration and worry settled heavily on her shoulders.

Derek brushed past her, his eyes on the ground. He moved through the trees, apparently searching for something.

"What?" She was back to yelling. Her abused throat complained, making her wince.

Instead of answering out loud, Derek pointed at the ground. Moving toward him, Artie saw an impression in the sheltered area between two protruding tree roots. She crouched for a better look, and Derek followed suit.

"Shoe print?" The snow was dry and shallow, but there was a definite top and bottom curve to the impression. The problem was that it wasn't a child-size print. The snow was new, so the shoe print was, too. Artie couldn't stop herself from looking around the gathering gloom. Her neck prickled with the feeling of being watched.

"Yes." Derek looked grim as he scanned the area. "And not from a little girl's boot."

"Could it be from one of the other searchers?"

"Not unless someone got lost." His gaze raked the trees surrounding them again. "Really lost." Taking his cell phone from his pocket, he crouched and took a picture. As he started to rise, Artie put a hand on his knee, stopping him.

"Wait." She dug in her own coat pocket and pulled out a pack of gum that she placed by the print, careful not to smudge the edges. "Take another picture. The gum package will help scale it."

"You've been watching those cop shows again?" he teased, but he took a couple more photos before putting away his phone.

She returned the gum to her pocket, giving the boot print a final worried look. "We did a unit on forensics last month."

"You taught third-graders about blood spatter and

gunshot residue?" Derek stared at her, although the corner of his mouth was twitching.

With a shrug, she said, "It was more fingerprints and photographs, but sure. They loved it."

He grinned, tapping the screen on his phone. "I'm sure they did."

When his brief smile disappeared, Artie asked, "What's wrong?"

"No cell reception," he explained, returning his phone to his pocket. "I was trying to text one of those pictures to the sheriff."

Artie shivered, and bile burned the base of her throat. "Do you think someone...took them?" Just the act of saying the words out loud made awful images play in her mind.

After glancing at her face, which she was sure was a nasty shade of green, Derek slid an arm around her shoulders. "Doubtful. Can you imagine someone trying to snatch those girls against their will? They'd scream their heads off at the very least, if not take the guy down. C'mon, let's go find them."

"Sure." Forcing a smile, Artie began walking again. As she called for the girls, blinking small, biting snowflakes from her eyes, she turned her head back and forth, searching for any movement. When she glanced back at Derek, she saw he'd regained his grim expression, and his gaze was cautious, watchful. Swallowing hard, she went back to scanning for the children...and whoever else was out there in the storm.

A burst of sound from the radio made Artie jump.

"Unit calling, you're unreadable," Derek shouted into the mic as he tried to shield the portable from the wind.

"Warne...ay." The scratchy sound of George's voice

broke through the static, but just bits and pieces of the words were understandable. Artie met Derek's gaze and saw her own frustration mirrored in his eyes.

"Re...base...ound..."

"Wait." Leaning closer to the radio, Artie strained her ears, mentally cursing the wind. "Did he say 'found,' as in the girls are found?"

"Not sure." Despite his doubtful words, his face lit with hope. "Holloway, please repeat."

The connection was even worse that time. At the end, though, three words were as clear as could be.

"Return to base."

"They must be found," Artie said, starting to smile. "If they're pulling us in, they must have the girls."

"Copy, return to base," Derek said loudly into the radio before grinning at her as he hooked the portable onto his belt. "They could just be pulling us in because of this storm, but—"

"But I heard 'found.' I definitely heard 'found'!" With a squeal that would've embarrassed Artie at any other moment, she grabbed him in a hug. He didn't hesitate to pull her tight to his chest. Pressing her forehead against his breastbone, she relaxed for the first time in what felt like days. She'd missed Derek's hugs. They'd always made her feel so cherished and safe. Even during that long, awful night in jail, she'd felt like everything would be okay because Derek was with her. Nothing had been okay after that, though, since he'd broken up with her the very next day.

Reality returned, and Artie, feeling awkward, extricated herself from the embrace. Turning to face the way they'd come, she started walking.

"Artemis."

Derek's shout made her stop and turn.

"This way." He continued in the direction they'd been going.

Confused, Artie hurried to catch up with him. "Aren't we returning to base?"

"Not until the storm settles," he told her.

That didn't lessen her confusion, and her brows drew together. "So we're going to walk the wrong way until then?"

He laughed. "The remains of an old cabin are a quarter mile from here. There won't be any heat—or much of a roof—but it'll provide a little shelter until the wind lets up."

Shelter of any kind sounded wonderful, so Artie fell in behind him. The wind ripped through the trees, peppering any exposed skin with snow. The stinging cold took away her breath, and she tilted her head down and to the side to avoid the worst of the impact.

Snowflakes clumped on her lashes, making it even harder to see through the snow-laden gusts. Even though Derek was only a few feet in front of her, she had a panicked image of him disappearing into the storm, leaving her alone. She ran a couple of steps until she was right behind him and grabbed the back of his jacket.

"What's wrong?" he asked, looking over his shoulder at her.

Great. Now I'll have to tell him I'm a big chicken. "Nothing."

His mouth quirked, and she braced herself for his teasing, but he just faced forward. Despite the embarrassing moment of getting caught clinging to his back like a baby opossum, she didn't let go. Instead, she walked as close behind him as she could, appreciating the way his broad back cut the wind.

When he stopped, she bumped into him. Derek reached a hand back to steady her and didn't remove it from her hip even after she'd regained her bearings. She wasn't about to complain.

"This is it," he said, and she peered around his arm to see the crumbling shack in front of them.

Artie blinked. "Wow." The tiny cabin looked as if the next strong gust would knock it down. The roof sagged, and there were sections missing. The structure had shifted, and the tattered, cockeyed door was propped open. Artie doubted that it would even close anymore, judging by the lopsided shape of the frame.

"Told you it was pretty far gone." He ducked through the low entrance into the darkness. After a second of hesitation, she followed, stopping just inside to allow her eyes to adjust to the dim light. The relief from the battering wind was immediate.

"As long as we're not sharing it with a bear, I'll take it." She looked around the tiny space. To her relief, no bears or any other woodland creatures were present.

Derek gave a distracted smile as he crouched on the other side of the cabin, examining something on the floor.

"What'd you find?" she asked, squatting next to him.

"Lighter." He held it up so she could see. "And cigarette butts. Someone else was in here not too long ago."

The shiver making its way down her spine had nothing to do with the cold. "Define 'not too long ago.'"

He moved one of the butts with his gloved finger. "Sometime over the last few months, I'm guessing." His expression was teasing when he glanced at her. "Although I could be wrong, since I didn't get to take your forensics class."

Standing, she bumped his boot lightly with one of hers. "Funny."

His hand curled around her calf as he grinned up at her, and both her heart and her stomach did a roller-coaster swoop. As he released her and straightened to his full height, Artie remembered how it felt to have him next to her, so strong and protective.

Trying to shake off the longing he inspired so easily, she asked, "No picture for the sheriff this time?"

"Nope. I'll let him know about it, though. It's probably kids, but we can't have them burning down the forest. Enough damage was done by the wildland fire this past summer." He roamed to the other side of the cabin, examining old bits and pieces of furniture that remained from the long-ago homeowners. "Hang on."

"What is it?" Joining him next to an old wooden crate, she crouched beside him again. "Wow. This is ancient."

"Yeah, but this isn't." He carefully opened a plastic grocery bag inside the antique box. "Neither are these."

As she leaned forward to peer at the contents of the bag, she teetered and put her hand out to catch her balance. His thigh muscle tightened under her palm, and she flushed red as she removed her fingers from his leg as casually as possible. Risking a glance at his face, she saw that he was staring at her, not the plastic bag. Their gazes caught for a few seconds before she managed to tear hers away and focus blindly on the crate. When she realized what the plastic bag contained, she blinked.

"That's strange." She pushed the plastic out of the way more so she could see all of the items. "And random. Nail polish remover, hair spray, rubbing alcohol, paint thinner, linseed oil…it's like a medicine cabinet and a wood shop got together."

Pulling a box of matches from between two of the

containers, Derek held it so she could see. "Not that random. These are all very flammable."

Her breath caught in her chest as she realized the ramifications of what they'd found. "The wildland fire." When she met his unusually grim gaze, she almost didn't want to ask. "Do you think it was set by the person who left this stuff here?"

"The fire chief's official word was that the cause was inconclusive, but I'm pretty sure he had a feeling in his gut that screamed 'arson.' We've been having a string of those, actually." Derek pulled out his radio and attempted to reach Rob, but only silence followed his transmissions. Swearing under his breath, he pulled out his phone and took some pictures before straightening. When he offered his hand to her, she gripped it and let him pull her to her feet. Once she was standing, neither one of them let go.

"So we might be in an arsonist's lair." Her words had a tremor, thanks to her chattering teeth. Now that she knew the girls were safe and she wasn't walking, the cold had crept under her clothes. She told herself that her shakiness had nothing to do with worry that a criminal might return at any moment.

Derek looked at her sharply. "Come here." He reached out and caught her hands, pulling her toward him.

"I'm fine," she protested, although her words were contradicted by a hard shudder that rocked through her.

"Quit being stubborn." His tone was affectionate as he caught her against his chest, backing them into the corner with the fewest holes in the walls. Although she frowned at his bossiness, she couldn't resist tucking her face against his neck and warming her cold nose.

When he reached between them and unzipped his coat, she pulled back, startled. "What are you doing?"

He switched to unzipping her jacket, and she flinched as the cold air instantly chilled her middle. "I'm sharing my body heat. And I was hoping to steal a little of yours."

Derek pulled her close again as she opened her mouth to respond. The hard warmth that pressed against her belly and breasts made her close her mouth before she did something embarrassing, like moan with pleasure. As he wrapped the edges of his coat around her back, she returned her face to the spot under his chin. The heat made her realize how very cold she'd been.

"Tuck in a little closer," he said, his voice low. He and his fabulous warmth were too tempting to refuse. Sliding her arms around him under his coat, she squeezed, flattening her front to his. "Perfect." His voice sounded rough.

Artie heard the slide of the zipper behind her. It was a tight fit in his zipped coat, but she basked in his heat and comfort.

"We could've just used the emergency blanket from the backpack," she said without moving.

"Sure, but this way's more fun."

Wrapped up in his heat, Artie had to agree. As she grew warmer, she realized how tired she was.

"Can we sit?" she asked, her words muffled against his throat.

"We can try." Amusement touched his voice as he shifted to lean against the rough wall and started to lower his body. She came along with him, since they were bound together by his coat.

Tipping her head back a little so she could see his face, she couldn't help but laugh. "Suddenly, I have empathy for conjoined twins."

"I know. Here." His hands caught the backs of her thighs,

lifting her feet off the floor before she even processed what he was doing. "Put your legs around me."

As she followed his direction, she flashed back to other times with Derek where her legs had been wrapped around him. Flushing, she pressed her face against his shoulder to hide her expression. With surprising ease, he lowered himself to a sitting position with Artie on his lap, her legs still tangled around his waist.

For a long minute, they sat quietly as the wind howled outside their dilapidated shelter.

"Shit, Artie," Derek finally sighed. "I've missed this."

So had she...so much that it was scary to admit out loud. She tried to force a chuckle. "What? Sitting in frozen squirrel poop in the middle of a blizzard?"

"No." For once, he sounded completely serious. "I've missed holding you. I've missed *you*."

His words stripped her bare. She leaned back as far as his zipped coat would allow so she could meet his gaze. "Derek..."

Tucking a strand of her hair back under her cap, he gave her a crooked smile. "You're so beautiful, Artemis Rey."

Whatever she'd been about to say was forgotten, wiped away by his expression. It was hunger and wistfulness and longing, all directed at her. How had she managed to let him go four years ago? After just a few minutes in his arms, she didn't ever want to leave him again. All she wanted was to stay wrapped in his coat and his arms forever.

Her face must've revealed her thoughts, because his breath caught. He leaned closer, and Artie fought to keep her eyes from closing, not wanting to look away from him. It'd been so long. She didn't want to miss a second of his kiss.

Their lips met lightly, and she sighed, contentment

underlying the excitement and need churning inside her. He pulled back, and Artie's stomach clenched, worried that it was over already, but he just checked her expression before leaning in for a second kiss, as sweet and delicate as the one before.

The featherlight contact lasted only two seconds before Artie was pressing closer, her arms and legs tightening around him, trying to increase the contact. His lips turned up in a smile under hers, and he palmed the back of her head. He felt so familiar and, at the same time, so thrilling. After nipping at her lower lip, Derek soothed it with his tongue. She groaned into his mouth, loving that he remembered what she liked.

As he deepened the kiss, he dropped his other hand to the small of her back, and then lower to cup her ass. He tucked her closer, digging his fingers into her flesh. Even through all of their layers, he felt amazing, comfortable yet new. Artie rocked her hips into his, wanting more, needing him, not caring about the freezing temperature and screaming wind.

His hands and mouth were urgent, as if desperate to make up for the years of separation in just one kiss. Artie didn't mind, since she was just as eager and needy. When he touched his lips beneath her jaw, she tilted her head back with a low groan. He kissed the hollow of her throat and then worked his way back toward her mouth.

"God, Artie," he muttered barely an inch from her skin, his breath so hot it burned. "I'm still crazy about you. Even when I knew I was dragging you down, the hardest thing I'd ever done was to break things off with you."

Inhaling sharply, she parted her lips, meaning to tell him how she'd fallen apart when he'd left, how she hadn't been able to stop mentally comparing Randy to Derek, and how every time she had done so, her husband—her *husband*—had come up short. When she'd signed the divorce papers, her first thought, quickly quashed, had been of Derek, and how maybe they could get a second chance.

All she managed to get out, though, was a choked, "I—" before his mouth crashed down on hers. The kiss was even more frantic this time, consuming her with its urgency. Feelings that had stayed dormant, hiding deep inside of her, woke in a fury, roaring to the surface and making her dig her nails into his shirt as a moan escaped her throat.

At the sound, he answered her with a hungry groan and pulled her even more tightly against him. From the time they were kids, Derek had always seemed so easygoing and carefree, but the man kissing her was neither of those things. He was desperate and intense and possessive, instead. In fact, he was acting like a man in love.

At that thought, she startled, yanking her head back and breaking the kiss.

"What?" His voice was rough and husky, his gaze locked on her mouth.

"Uh…" How could she explain her thoughts without dying of embarrassment? The decreased noise from outside registered as her head cleared slightly, and she seized on the distraction. "The wind's quieter. If we don't get back to base sometime soon, they're going to send people out after us." All the events of the day rushed back to her, and she marveled at how simply kissing Derek could erase all her thoughts and worries so easily.

"Right." He blew out a short breath, as if preparing to return to reality, but his grip didn't ease. "You're right. But I don't want to move."

Tipping forward so her forehead could rest on his shoulder, she found it was easier to be brutally honest with him when she wasn't meeting his gaze. "I don't want to move, either."

He chuckled, although there was still a gritty sound to it. "So it's settled. We're staying here for infinity. It *would* be nice to be somewhere with heat, though." Glancing around the cabin, he grimaced. "And walls."

"And fewer rodents."

"A hole-free roof."

"Maybe a bed?"

Laughing, he hugged her close. "God, I've missed you, Artie."

"I've missed you, too. So much." Still hiding her face against his shoulder, she admitted, "If I'd refused to let you go, I would've saved myself so much heartache and misery."

"What happened? Between you and Randy, I mean?"

Artie groaned. Everything had been perfect—Derek, the kisses, the bear-free semi shelter—until the mention of Randy made her stomach knot. "It really is getting late. We should be heading back to base camp."

"Nice try." Ignoring her attempt at redirecting the conversation, he didn't make any move to rise. "Tell me."

She sighed, knowing he was stubborn enough to keep them there until they froze into ice statues or she spilled her guts. "You're not going to drop this, are you?"

"Nope." His arms tightened around her. "Dog with a bone here."

Although she hated talking about the mess her former marriage had become, Artie realized that she wanted Derek to know. Except for the past four years, he'd been her best friend. She missed that, missed telling him everything and knowing he wouldn't judge her. After a few seconds of struggling to figure out where to begin, she just blurted, "Remember how Randy was always so…intense?"

He snorted. "Yeah. He was a competitive bastard, too. Everything had to be a bet, and then he always had to win. Who could spit the farthest or yell the loudest or run the fastest…" Even as he shook his head, a nostalgic smile curled his lips. Artie understood. He, Randy, and Artie'd had a lot of fun growing up—at least until he'd dumped her, leaving Artie heartbroken.

"Or whose ant could cross the line in the dirt first."

"And then he stomped on yours just before you won."

"Yeah." Her body sagged a little, and Derek held her tighter. Despite the terror and stress of the day, with Chase falling in the water and the girls going missing, being able to press against him like that was a single bright spark in a dismal day.

"So…?"

"So, he kind of swept me up in that intensity. He loved me so much, and wanted me so much, I kind of figured, who was I to turn him down?"

Derek choked. "What?"

"I know." She shifted so she could press her temple to his shoulder while keeping her face hidden in his neck. That was really nice, too. "I was young and dumb and, I don't know, malleable, I guess. You'd just dumped me—"

"Not because I didn't want you!" he protested. "I'd gotten you arrested. *Arrested*, Artie. If you'd been convicted, no school would've hired you. Teaching has been your dream since I've known you, and I almost wrecked your life."

That brought her head up so she could meet his gaze. "Is *that* why you broke up with me? Because you thought you were bad for me? And I just let you, too young and stupid and scared to fight back." She closed her eyes for a second, angry with the both of them for letting youth and inexperience ruin what they could have had these last four years. "It wasn't your fault, Derek. How could you have known that the motorcycle your dad gave you for your birthday was stolen?"

"Because I know my dad." His face tightened into furious lines. "He's never paid for anything. Ever. I should've known that bike was hot, and I definitely never should've let you ride on it."

She scowled at him. "You weren't the only one with an operable brain back then, you know. I knew all about your dad's business, about the hidden compartments in his semi-trailer. Everyone in Field County knows that your dad's long-haul trucking business is just a front for moving whatever illegal goods need to be transported across the country."

His expression didn't lighten. "My dad wasn't the one who picked you up that day on a stolen bike. He wasn't the one you trusted to keep you safe."

She wanted to smack him, but her hands were trapped under his coat, so she had to settle for pinching his side... hard.

"Ow!" His body jolted beneath her. "What's with the violence?"

"Quit trying to make me the victim. You'd told me about your dad's sticky fingers and then showed up on a motorcycle he'd given to you. I knew what I was getting into when I got on that bike, but I did it anyway because it was exciting and exhilarating and I wanted to be with you." Familiar regret overtook her, and she dropped her eyes to his throat. "I'm sorry I didn't fight for you when you ended things the next day. I, well, I guess I was still pretty freaked out about getting arrested. I'd never even gotten *detention* in high school, so that night in jail was kind of overwhelming."

"I'm sorry." The same regret she felt was echoed in his words.

She pinched him again. "Stop it, stupid. It wasn't your fault. I'm sorry I didn't stick with you. I'm sorry I didn't fight to know why you were leaving and just assumed the worst. Instead, I took your words at face value and figured I had to find a way to get over you, so I kind of latched onto Randy."

"Right." He cleared his throat, but his voice still sounded tight. "How did that happen?"

"Now that I look back on it, I was such an idiot. Randy was there and interested and seemed like the safer choice, despite all his drama and jealousy."

"Safer?"

Her cheeks flushed as she admitted, "I knew I'd never love Randy enough for him to hurt me like you had."

He groaned. "Artie…"

"Quit with the self-flagellation, or I'm not going to tell you what happened."

"Self-flagellation?" Although he wasn't smiling, his frown lightened a little. "I'd forgotten how much I loved it when you used your vocabulary on me."

"Stop." Her face felt like it was on fire. "I have to get through this. As much as I hate talking about it, I want you to know everything. I think Randy always knew he was my second choice, and it kind of drove him crazy. He always had to know where I was and who I was with. I almost broke up with him a bunch of times, but it scared me."

His muscles tightened. "He scared you?"

Instead of answering, she hunched her shoulders in a tiny shrug. "Mostly, I was scared of being alone. It's tough for me to make new friends, for some reason. Maybe because I never had to as a kid. I had you and Randy, and I didn't need anyone else. After you ended things, you just disappeared. That was"—her inhale shook—"hard. I missed you so much, and I didn't know if I could handle losing Randy, too."

He opened his mouth, but she hurried to speak before he could say anything. It was hard to talk about the last four years, and she needed just to get it out before she lost her nerve. "Once I got my teaching job, things went from tense to, well, really tense. I love my job, love the kids, but it's hard to turn off bossy-teacher mode."

"Why would you want to?" he asked, sounding honestly stumped. "I love it when you're in bossy-teacher mode. It's almost as sexy as when you use your big words."

"Thanks, Derek." She relaxed a little, sinking against him as he rubbed her back. "Randy felt like he was losing control, so he tried to regain it. I'm different than I was when we got together, though, and I didn't—don't—want to be controlled. He started really pushing me about having a baby. I'd love to have kids, but the thought of Randy as a father... No. So we split."

She heard Derek's molars grind together. "How exactly"—each word came out clearly and precisely—"did he try to 'regain control'?"

"It doesn't matter." Her forehead rubbed his coat as she shook her head against his shoulder. "It's done."

"Did he hit you?"

The silence went on long enough to be an answer in itself. His muscles tensed against her, turning his body to rock. Artie wasn't scared of him, though. She could never fear him—he was her Derek, and he'd protect her with his life.

"Once," she confirmed. "First and last time. I left him

and stayed with my parents for a couple of months while I got my life together."

"He just let you go?" Derek's voice didn't sound like his.

Her laugh, quick and silent, seemed to relax him a little. "Not exactly. It took a restraining order and a few chats with Sheriff Rob, but he finally moved to California. He said it was too hard to see me all the time when we weren't together. I told him that he wouldn't see me all the time if he weren't stalking me."

Derek's sharp bark of laughter surprised her. "Good point. Has he left you alone since he moved?"

"Pretty much." She shrugged. "There were a couple of texts and calls and emails, all of which I ignored. Everything's been quiet the last few months. I have a feeling he has a new girlfriend."

"You okay with that?"

"Definitely," she said honestly. "Any remaining love for him faded before the divorce was final—probably even before his fist hit my face."

Just like that, all his furious tension returned. "Where in California is he?"

She snorted. "Don't try that oh-so-casual tone with me. I'm not telling you."

Pulling back just far enough to meet her eyes, he put on his most innocent expression. "Why not? Figured I'd just go catch up with my good friend Randy."

"Hah." Smirking, she gave him another light pinch in the side. "'Catch up' as in kill him?"

"Of course not. Hurt him, sure, but I'd leave him alive. Maybe."

"Thanks for the offer, but I've already gotten revenge for that punch." Her lips curled in a smug smile.

"Yeah?" His eyes strayed to her mouth.

"Yeah. I had an awesome divorce lawyer. I'm now the proud owner of a Ducati Scrambler."

After a stunned second, a laugh burst from him. "But you don't even know how to ride one. You said you *never* wanted to learn."

"I don't *ride* it." She shrugged, unable to stop her grin from lingering. It might've been petty and small-minded of her, but owning that motorcycle still warmed her insides. "I just go into the garage and look at it. It makes me happy that I have it and he doesn't. He really loved that bike."

Laughing again, he hugged her hard. "I'm glad it makes you happy. That doesn't make me want to kill him any less, though. How about you text me his address once we're out of the forest-of-no-cell-reception?"

"Nope. It's a good life lesson to know that you can't always get what you want."

His laugh faded. "All I ever wanted was you."

Her heart was tripping so fast that her heartbeats merged into a single sound. "You've always had me."

She felt his chest expand with his rapid inhale. "Do you mean it? Because if I get another chance with you, Artie, I'm never letting you go."

Her laugh was thick with the threat of happy tears. "I've been warned, and I accept your terms."

Despite the cold, all of Artie felt warm when his lips touched hers. This was it. She never thought she'd get another chance with him, not after Derek had dumped her and she'd screwed up her life with a series of Randy-based bad decisions. But here they were, older and wiser—or at least willing to try.

"Is this real?" she asked, her words muffled by his mouth.

He pulled back slightly, just enough for her to see his

smile. "Doesn't it feel real? Let me try again." Dipping his head, he kissed her harder and thoroughly enough to leave her gasping by the time he raised his head. "Better?"

It took her a moment to pick up the thread of their conversation. "I'm not sure. It could be that I'm freezing to death and having a cold-induced hallucination. You'd better try again."

She could feel the curve of his mouth as he pressed it to hers, and she marveled at how wonderful it was to kiss happy Derek, although she wouldn't turn down mopey Derek or angsty Derek or teasing Derek or serious Derek or... The kiss intensified, and her thoughts were lost in a swirl of love and need and sheer joy.

A crackle of static from the radio brought them out of their blissful world and back to the cold, dilapidated cabin. They both gave a sigh and then laughed at their mutual obvious disappointment.

"The wind's died down a little," Derek said, his mouth still temptingly close to hers.

"We need to let the others know we're safe," she sighed, wishing for a slightly less developed sense of responsibility. She would've been happy staying all night with Derek in the cabin.

Although he groaned, he unzipped his coat. Before she could stand, though, he pulled her back for a final peck and a hard hug. Artie got to her feet quickly, knowing each second she stayed in his embrace would make it that much harder to leave it.

As she zipped her coat, she couldn't stop shooting quick glances at him, feeling weirdly shy and not quite believing that they'd just made out like a couple of teenagers. After four years, they were actually back together! The thought sent a surge of happiness and anticipation through her, making her bounce lightly on her numb toes. During the past four years, she'd had a hollow, Derek-shaped place in her heart, and it was finally filled again.

They ducked through the low, lopsided doorway, and Artie shot a final look at the sad remains of the cabin. It had given them a windbreak and a chance to reconnect, and she felt almost fond of the slowly collapsing structure.

She felt Derek's gloved fingers wrap around her own. Turning toward him, she smiled, using her free hand to push stray strands of hair out of her face. Although the wind wasn't as ferocious as it had been earlier, it still snapped around them, making the tree branches sway and moan.

The afternoon had slipped away while they'd been happily occupied in the cabin, and dusk was fast approaching, lending an eerie cast to the forest. The pines were black against a dark gray sky. Normally, Artie enjoyed hiking, but she'd never tried walking in the forest this close to nighttime, especially in a snowstorm.

The previous summer's forest fire had decimated the area, and the dead trees still stood in blackened groups, needleless and foreboding. They wove their way between the lifeless trunks, the wind loud enough to erase any other sound.

Uneasy, Artie tightened her fingers around Derek's hand, wishing they were already home. Her mind returned to the fresh footprint from earlier and the flammable materials in the cabin. With the frantic urgency to find Zoe and Maya eased, Artie's mind moved to the possible dangers in the forest—dangers to her and Derek.

Every shadow between the trees became a bear to her unsettled imagination, and every squeak and tap of branches turned into footsteps.

"You okay?" Derek asked when she jumped for the umpteenth time, squeezing the life out of his hand as she did so.

"Sure."

"Artie."

"I'm fine. Just a little spooked."

"Don't blame you." His gaze swept back and forth with a watchfulness that didn't help settle Artie's nerves. "I'll be happy to get back to base."

"Me too." Something smacked against her leg, and she flinched before she realized it was just a cluster of dead leaves tossed by the wind. When she glanced at Derek to see if he noticed her scare, his smirk was obvious, even in the increasing gloom.

"Shut it."

"I didn't say a word." The humor left his face quickly as he drew to a halt. "I'm going to see if we get radio reception here so we can let the sheriff know where we are."

Derek checked their GPS coordinates and lifted his radio, moving to face the blackened trunk of a dead tree to block the wind. Artie tipped her head back, watching the trees bend under a strong gust.

A sharp crack rang out, and Artie spun around, startled. It had sounded almost like a gunshot. Another loud crash above them made her look up and suck in a hard breath.

An enormous branch had been torn from the tree by the wind. It smashed through lower branches, the weight of it snapping the smaller limbs without slowing its fall.

Grabbing the back of Derek's coat, she ran, dragging him with her. After a few stumbling, backward steps, Derek twisted out of her grip and latched onto Artie's arm, propelling her forward even faster—but not fast enough. The huge branch plunged to the ground, knocking both of them down with it.

Artie landed facedown, hitting hard enough to knock the air and the sense out of her for a minute. She was vaguely aware of Derek's pained grunt as he fell next to her, but she was concentrating too hard on trying to breathe for the sound to really register. The best she could do was suck in small gulps of air. It felt as if her lungs had shrunk to kidney-bean-size, refusing to take in enough oxygen.

She finally managed a deeper inhale, and then two. When she was breathing seminormally again, she struggled to take stock. Her face throbbed, there was a metallic taste at the back of her throat, and her stomach hurt where she'd landed on a protruding rock. Everything else just ached dully and could be ignored.

"Artemis." Derek's anxious voice made her turn her head toward him. "You okay?"

"Just had…the breath…knocked…out of me." Talking made her realize that her lungs weren't quite functioning normally. "You?"

"Nothing serious."

She tried to push up to her knees, but something was across her back, flattening her against the ground.

"We didn't run fast enough," Derek said. "You're bleeding."

"I'm fine." Once he said it, she realized that her face was wet. There were other, more urgent things to worry about, though, like getting free of the enormous branch that pinned them down. Even as she thought it, she saw Derek work his arms higher so he could belly crawl. She tried to copy him, but her left arm didn't want to move. Pressing her right elbow against the ground, she pushed her body upward against the restraining bark.

It lifted very slightly, but that was enough for her to drag her left arm free. The rough wood tore the fabric of her coat sleeve, and Artie had to bite back a sound of annoyance. On the scale of things-to-worry-about-now, a ripped jacket did not even rate, even if it was her favorite coat…and the temperature was dropping rapidly.

With both arms mobile, she managed to drag her body forward. Her right knee throbbed when she bent it, so she used her forearms and her left knee to wiggle out from under the branch. She was almost free when the weight on her legs disappeared. Turning her head, she saw Derek holding up the branch. From her position, he looked obnoxiously superhero-like, and she scrunched her nose.

"What was that face?" he complained. "I rescue you and that's my reward?"

Artie scooted the rest of the way clear, and he let it drop. "You know I hate to be rescued."

He laughed, offering a hand to help her stand. "I remember. You always refused to be the damsel in distress when we played together as kids."

"So did you." Her knee protested when she climbed to her feet, and she clung to his hand a second too long. Derek lost his smile, eyeing her intently, and she started talking to distract him from her wobble. "It's no fun to wait for the hero to swoop in and save me. I wanted to be part of the action."

"What's wrong? Is it your bad knee?" Obviously, her efforts at diverting his attention from her injury hadn't worked.

"I'm fine. I just need to walk it off." She looked past him to where the branch was lying on the ground. "Whoa. It's good that thing just nicked us. That's as big as a good-size tree."

Derek was digging in his pack. Before they'd started searching, Rob had handed out backpacks with basic survival gear—a first-aid kit, matches, an emergency blanket, flares, water, energy bars, and flashlights. After a brief tug-of-war, Artie had given in and let Derek carry the pack. It hadn't been worth spending time arguing about it, not with the girls missing.

Pulling out the first-aid kit, Derek opened it and extracted some gauze squares. As she accepted them, she gave him a confused look.

"Your nose is bleeding," he said, and she remembered the wetness on her face earlier, and the metallic taste.

Artie dabbed under her nose. The flow seemed to have stopped, so she wiped up the remaining blood and tucked the soiled gauze into her pocket.

"Ready?" she asked.

"Sure you're okay to walk back?" he asked.

The thought of hiking to base made her want to bawl like a baby, but she straightened her aching shoulders instead. "Of course. Let's go."

"Hang on a second. Let me tell Rob we'll take a little longer to get back than expected." After shouldering the pack, Derek reached for something at his side...then frowned. "Shit. The radio must've been knocked off my belt. Do you see it?"

They both started searching the area around where they'd been laid flat, and Artie made a conscious effort not to limp. By the way her knee was refusing to bend, it was already starting to swell. If she'd been at home, she could've elevated it and iced it, but now she just had to deal with it. The wind was cold enough to act as an ice pack, at least, although Artie was pretty sure that wouldn't be helpful.

"This is one time when more snow would've been useful," Artie said, her eyes sweeping the ground. The earlier icy snowfall had stopped before much had accumulated. Before Derek could reply, she finally spotted the black rectangle. "Found it!"

Derek swept it up and then swore a few seconds later.

"Broken?" she guessed, watching as he turned it off and on a few times.

"Broken." After messing with it for a couple of minutes, he tucked the still-nonfunctional radio into his pack and turned to Artie. "Are you going to be able to make it to base camp?"

"Didn't we already cover this?" she snapped, trying to disguise her own doubts. There was no way she was going to make Derek carry her back to safety like some pampered princess. She was going to get there on her own steam, even if her leg fell *off*.

Instead of taking offense, Derek grinned at her. "Okay, my feisty goddess. Lead the way, then." He gestured toward what used to be the trail.

"Uh…this way isn't going to work." A cliff on one side, heavy brush on the other, and the huge fallen limb in front of them blocked the way as cleanly as a barred door. "We're going to need to drop south to go around this."

After eyeing the downed, tree-size branch, he nodded. "You're right. It'll definitely be easier going around than through. I knew there was a reason I picked you as my partner."

Her snort was covered by another blast of wind.

Even as it grew closer to full dark, Derek still couldn't stop looking at her. After being reminded what her lips felt like against his, all those feelings he'd shoved into a mental drawer four years earlier came rushing back. His love for her filled his chest, blocking out the cold and making it impossible to keep the grin off his face.

It was worse now that she was pretending not to limp, reminding him of the stubborn, competitive girl with whom he'd shared the majority of his childhood and college years. Apparently, she hadn't changed much. After hearing how possessive and controlling that asshole Randy had turned out to be, it shocked him that she'd put up with him for so long.

"Let me carry you."

Artie didn't even turn around when she answered. "No."

"Stubborn," he muttered, although the corners of his lips curled, once again, into a smile. As much as he wished she'd accept his help, he loved her mule-headedness. Pulling his gaze from her profile, Derek reminded himself that they still needed to get back to base. There'd be plenty of time to admire Artie later, especially since they were back together. The thought boggled his mind. After all those years of frustrated longing, he finally, *finally*, got to keep her. His jaw firmed. This time she'd be safe with him. He'd make sure of that.

As he strode through the gathering darkness, passing the remains of their temporary shelter again, he stayed alert. The newly formed boot print, and the cigarette butts and incendiary supplies in the cabin made him uneasy. He scanned the trees for movement, but the shadowed near-darkness could hide anything—or anyone—that didn't want to be seen. His ears strained to pick up the snap of a twig or the scrape of pine needles against a moving body, but the wind covered any other sound.

Snow began to fall again, but it wasn't the fluffy, soft flakes shown at the end of Christmas movies. Instead, icy pellets stung his exposed skin, and he tugged his hat lower to protect the back of his neck.

Their shift to the south had been an uphill slog, and now they were following the side of a ridge. Their vantage point allowed them to see farther than they could on the way out, and Derek took advantage of the openness, scanning the area for any flash of color or movement. He realized that he wasn't just squinting to keep the stinging snowflakes out of his eyes. The storm had hurried the day along, and it was almost dark.

"Hold up!" he called to Artie, and she turned around, looking relieved to be able to put her back to the brutal wind for a minute. He pulled two flashlights out of his pack and handed her one.

"Thanks." Flicking on the light, she aimed the beam at the ground. "I didn't realize how dark it'd gotten."

He turned on his own light, following Artie as she started walking east along the ridge again, swinging her bad leg ever so slightly to the side with each stride. If he hadn't been watching for it, he would've missed her tiny limp. He was tempted to sling her over his shoulder, despite her protests, but he knew she'd much rather take care of herself. Clenching his free hand into a fist to keep from picking her up, he concentrated on the dark path ahead.

With a yelp, she started to fall, and Derek leaped forward, catching the back of her coat just before her body hit the ground. He hauled her to her feet, turned her around, and lifted her in a fireman's carry. Except for a grunt, she didn't protest, which meant her knee was *really* hurting.

Pivoting, he turned back the way they'd just come.

"Where are you going?" Artie asked.

"Back to the cabin. Once the storm dies down again and you rest your knee for a while, we'll try again."

In the few seconds of silence that followed, Derek wasn't sure if she was planning to protest or agree with the plan. His arm tightened around the backs of her thighs. It didn't matter what she said. There was no way she could hike all the way back to base on a slippery, narrow ledge in a snowstorm while injured.

"Okay."

He blinked. He'd been braced for a fight, but Artie had managed to surprise him yet again. Grinning, he gave her legs another squeeze, this one affectionate. Life with Artemis Rey would never be boring.

Even with his slow pace from carrying Artie, the cabin came back into view quickly. It was a little disheartening to know just how short of a distance they'd covered, but Derek didn't say anything out loud. From Artie's uncharacteristic silence, he knew she was in a lot of pain, and she didn't need his Gloomy Gus comments bringing her down.

"Home, sweet home," he said grimly, carefully maneuvering through the doorway so none of Artie's parts bumped the wood.

Although she laughed, it sounded like she was gritting her teeth. "I was thinking fond thoughts about this place when we left it, but I have to admit I'm not too excited to be back."

"Yeah, me either." Carefully easing her off his shoulder, he helped her sit on the floor and then grabbed an old piece of four-by-four wood that he propped under her outstretched leg to elevate it.

"Thanks." Her expression was flat, and he recognized the look from when she'd been eight and had fallen while trying to climb a six-foot fence. It was Artie's attempting-not-to-cry face, and it made him frantic. Ripping off his gloves, he dug through the pack and pulled out the first-aid kit. Frowning at the frozen water bottles, he returned them to the pack.

"Here. Take these." He held out a couple of over-the-counter painkillers. After removing her own gloves, she held out a shaking hand for the pills. As she dry-swallowed the tablets, he eyed her face, not liking the pale undertone of her naturally tan complexion. Derek wondered if she was going into shock or was just cold and tired. Either way, he need to warm her.

Yanking out the emergency blanket, he eased behind her, lifting Artie on his lap without dislodging her leg from the supporting piece of wood. As he opened the blanket and wrapped it around both of them, she settled against his chest with a silent sigh. Alarmed at her atypical docility, he wrapped his arms around her under the blanket, pulling her as close as possible.

He felt her shivering and released her to unzip his jacket and then hers. Artie grabbed his hands, stopping them.

"Hey! I need that," she protested through chattering teeth. "Unless we could build a fire?"

"I'm just rearranging things," he said, "so you can take advantage of my incredible hotness. And no fire. Not with all this dry wood and the firebug's box of accelerants."

As she made a disappointed sound, he slid her coat off her arms and quickly moved it around to her front, wrapping it around her like a reversed cape. When she leaned her back against his chest, their bodies now separated only by a few thin layers, she gave a purr of contentment. The sound was so unintentionally sexy that he had to close his eyes and take a couple of deep breaths to get his body under control.

"Not to feed your ego," she said, apparently unaware of what she was doing to him, "but you really are incredibly hot."

His laugh was rough around the edges as he rearranged the emergency blanket to cover them. "Told you."

By the time he snaked his arms around her waist under her draped coat, Artie had stopped shivering. They both fell silent as she rested against him, finally getting warm again in their nest of coats and blanket and body heat. Derek realized his palms had flattened against her belly and one of his fingers just brushed her bare skin where the hem of her shirt had bunched. As if his hands had a life of their own, they slid a little lower, until that fingertip had slipped under the waistband of her jeans.

"Derek," she breathed, and it clearly wasn't a protest.

As his hands rubbed up and down her stomach, slipping farther in each direction with every pass, she tilted her face toward him. In the indirect light from the flashlight lying next to them, he could see the kaleidoscope of emotions playing across her face. There was so much love and longing in her expression that he couldn't breathe for a long second. Moving one hand from her stomach so he could cup her cheek, he lowered his mouth to hers.

As soon as they touched, it was as if a match had been tossed in the bag of flammables sharing the cabin with them. He couldn't kiss her deeply enough, couldn't touch her enough. The truth finally sank in, striking him hard—she was actually his again. Artie—gorgeous, smart, funny, sexy-as-hell Artemis Rey—was in his arms and, from the way she squirmed and moaned under his touch, she wanted him.

The knowledge triggered an inferno that blazed through his body. His mouth met hers with bruising force, and she kissed him back just as hard. Their tongues battled for dominance, and their teeth nipped and pulled. Derek loved it. It was her bossy side coming out to play, and nothing turned him on more than when she showed just how strong and fierce she truly was.

Needing to touch her, he slid one hand under her shirt, brushing her soft, soft skin until he cupped her breast through her bra. The sound she made against his lips vibrated through him, making his hips lift and press against her. His fingers tugged the fabric down, desperately wanting to really feel her, skin to skin.

Her teeth sank almost painfully into his bottom lip as his thumb strummed her rigid nipple, and she moaned her approval into his mouth. He repeated the move, loving how sensitive she was, how quickly his touch excited her. Freeing her other breast, he divided his attention between her perfect chest and her just-as-perfect mouth.

Touching her, kissing her, feeling her respond—it was all driving him crazy. He'd never been so hard and, at the same time, so focused on someone else. It didn't matter if he got off or not—this was all about Artie. He'd waited too long to have her in his arms again, and he was determined to make her so happy that she never wanted to leave.

This is Artie, he thought, amazed and exhilarated. All his memories and dreams of her were nothing compared to the reality of actually holding her, both of them shaking from arousal instead of the cold. His other hand unbuttoned her pants and worked beneath the layers of fabric, until his fingers found her wet and so, so warm.

Tearing his mouth from hers, he buried his face in

the side of her neck, breathing hard. The feel of her was destroying his control, and he fought to get it back, even as his fingers slid into her. Her body tightened around him, and he groaned, closing his teeth gently on her shoulder. Giving her pleasure was more arousing to him than actual sex with anyone else.

He tried to ignore the desperate need coursing through his body as he lightly circled and stroked, his fingers effortlessly remembering what she liked best. Clenching his teeth as he tried to cling to his control, he lifted his head so he could watch her face. He was rock hard and hurting, but it didn't change his focus. Her hips lifted toward his hand, and she made those soft sounds that drove him wild. He moved his hand faster, drove his fingers deeper, until her gasps and cries filled his ears. Her body arched and shuddered as she came, so beautiful in the dim light that he couldn't look away.

His fingers slowed as her body softened and her breathing grew more even. Reluctantly, he withdrew his hands, although he kept his arms wrapped around her. Letting her go was not an option. Never again.

"Your name fits you," he said quietly when she finally slumped, boneless, against his chest. "You really are a goddess."

Her reply was a sleepy chuckle. "It doesn't really fit anymore."

"Why not?" He straightened her clothes and rearranged the coats and blankets to cover them.

"Artemis was the *virgin* goddess," she explained in a yawn, making him laugh. Her eyelids started to droop, but then she straightened. "Wait. What about you?"

"What about me? I'm no virgin goddess either."

She snorted, blushing at the same time. "That's for sure.

I meant that you didn't..." She gestured in the general vicinity of his aching lap.

"What?" he teased. "Don't tell me your extensive vocabulary is failing you?"

"Stop it." She tried to swat at him, but the muffling layers of coats and the blanket thwarted her efforts. "You know what I mean. You didn't get to come."

"I'm fine."

"Liar."

Shifting uncomfortably, he amended, "I'll *be* fine. I wanted this to be about you. Quit worrying and take a nap. I'll wake you once the storm lightens up."

"Okay," she grumbled, settling back against his chest. "But I'm keeping track. There's a sticky note in my brain that says, 'I owe Derek one happy ending.'"

He laughed. "I'm definitely collecting on that. Now sleep."

Without any further argument, she closed her eyes and almost instantly went limp. Then, he just held her, loving that he could.

All of this—Chase falling through the ice, running off, getting lost—was her fault. Zoe tightened her arms around Maya, knowing that it wouldn't help, that it wouldn't make them be warm or safe at home. She was a bad sister. Now it was getting dark. Although she hated to admit it, Zoe was terrified of the dark.

Her seat was numb under her jeans, thanks to the cold rock under her. Even though she'd always been told to stay in one spot if she got lost, she knew there was no way they could be seen where they were. When the wind had really started raging, Maya had almost been blown off the edge of a ledge. Zoe knew they couldn't keep walking, so they'd wedged themselves into a hidden spot between two large boulders. Now, though, it sounded as if the wind had died down a little.

"Maya." When her little sister didn't respond, Zoe jostled her lightly. "C'mon. We have to move."

"C-can't w-w-we stay h-here?" Maya was shaking so hard that the words were interrupted by her teeth clicking together.

"No one'll find us in here." As she stood, Zoe unsuccessfully tried to pull Maya to her feet. It was amazing how much her tiny sister weighed when she went limp. Tears threatened, but Zoe forced them back. "Maya. We need to walk. You'll stay warmer that way, too."

"I th-thought we didn't w-want anyone to f-f-find us," Maya whined through chattering teeth, but she allowed Zoe to pull her to standing.

A jolt of fear shot through Zoe at the thought of what would happen when they were found. Looking at her shivering sister made her more scared of what would happen if they *weren't* found, though, so she took Maya's hand and led her back to the path.

Between the low light and the snow, it was hard to see things on the trail, and Zoe kept tripping. As she walked, her toes went from numb to painful pins and needles. She wished they'd stayed numb. She wished she had a flashlight. She wished her dad was there. She wished she'd never had the stupid, stupid idea to egg Chase into walking out onto the ice. She wished she'd just stayed and taken her punishment, so that Maya wouldn't be here, cold and hungry and scared, just like Zoe.

Something moved in front of them.

"What w-was that?" Maya whispered.

Squinting through the dusk, Zoe opened her mouth, ready to tell her sister that she didn't know, that it was nothing, just a shadow or a trick of the dark. Then it shifted closer, morphing into the terrifying shape of a mountain lion, and the reassuring words she was about to utter turned into a scream.

Every step hurt. She knew that Derek was watching her carefully. He'd wanted to stay at the cabin longer, but she couldn't stay cuddled with Derek while their friends were slogging through the snow, searching for them. It had been almost impossible, though, to force herself to leave his arms and the tiny, ramshackle cabin.

Trying to mask her limp was making it worse, but Artie was worried what would happen if she stopped trying to hide it. He'd either insist on carrying her or make her stop so he could light a flare, and then all the searchers would converge on them, endangering everyone for the second time that day for an injured would-be rescuer who'd gotten all of them into this mess in the first place by being such a crappy chaperone.

Gritting her teeth against the pain and the guilt, she swept her flashlight in a steady rhythm, watching for obstacles on the trail and boogeymen in the bushes. Instead, the light reflected against the swirling snow. The toe of her boot caught on the edge of a rock, making her stumble and sending a shock of agony through her right knee.

"Artemis…"

"I'm fine," she barked, focusing the beam of her flashlight on the area ahead of her. The wind had eased slightly, to her relief, allowing a half inch of snow to settle on the ground. Then an odd depression in the white blanket caught the light, and Artie stopped abruptly, her bad knee forgotten.

"What is it?" Derek asked from right behind her.

"Prints." Keeping the light focused on it, she forced herself to step closer. Crouching, she extended her right leg to the side so she wouldn't have to bend her bad knee. It was a total giveaway that she was hurting, but the new discovery trumped hiding her injury from Derek. "What does that look like to you?"

Even with her attention focused on the impression in the snow, she could tell he stiffened. He leaned closer to look over her shoulder at the print, his chest lightly brushing her back. "That"—his voice was quiet and eerily calm— "looks like the paw print of a really big cat."

Not wanting to be crouching and vulnerable any longer, Artie stood so quickly that she clipped Derek's chin with her shoulder.

"Ow."

"Sorry." She moved her flashlight, searching farther along the trail. Her stomach dipped when she found them—neat, even rows of overlapping paw prints. "Mountain lion?"

"Yep."

"Really fresh prints."

"Uh-huh."

"Shit."

"Exactly."

Artie realized that she was breathing much too fast. "Okay. Since there's a mountain lion a scarily short distance in front of us, we should go in a different direction, right?"

"That's a good idea." He let out a grumbly sigh. "We're going to have to backtrack."

"Why?" she asked before turning her flashlight toward the left and the right. "Oh." The ridge had narrowed, and the rock to the right rose in a vertical wall, while the left side dropped straight down into blackness. Without climbing equipment, there was no way to go either up or down. The only choice was retracing their steps. Again.

With a resigned groan, she turned around, prepared to follow Derek back the way they'd come. Her knee started throbbing again. It felt like it hurt worse when they walked over ground they'd already traveled. Suddenly, the idea of being rescued and carried out of there didn't seem so bad.

A cry ripped through the snowstorm, jerking both of them to an instant halt. The sound was horribly familiar. For the second time that day, Artie heard Zoe's terrified scream.

Pivoting around, Artie took off toward the sound. She didn't even pause to wonder why Zoe was still out there, screaming, rather than tucked up in bed like the earlier static-filled radio transmission had led them to believe. The light from her flashlight bobbed with her sprinting strides, reflecting off Derek's back as he ran in front of her. Everything disappeared—the pain in her knee, the cougar tracks they were following, the slickness of the snowy path. All that mattered was getting to the girls and saving them from whatever had made Zoe scream like that.

Her foot slid to the left, and she scrambled to keep her balance. The bobble allowed Derek to pull farther ahead. Artie pushed for more speed, digging for that last final burst of power like she had during high school track meets, and closed the gap between them.

When Derek slid to a halt, she almost crashed into him, barely managing to stop in time. His broad shoulders blocked her view, so she shifted to the side and then sucked in a breath.

Their flashlights turned the tawny coat of the mountain lion almost white. It turned its head to look at them, eyes reflecting eerie brightness. Artie bit the inside of her cheek hard. The sharp pinch cut off the scream that was building in her chest.

The cougar was slightly crouched, its long tail twitching like an annoyed house cat's. A high-pitched whimper from twenty feet in front of the lion caught its attention, making its rounded ears swivel toward the sound. Artie raised her flashlight slightly to find the source of the noise.

When she saw Zoe and Maya's tiny, huddled forms, tucked against the flat face of a boulder, she had to swallow her own frightened cry.

"Zoe." Derek's voice was loud enough to make everyone, including the big cat, startle. "Stand up slowly. You too, Maya."

The girls didn't move, but Artie understood what he was doing and stepped to his side. "Girls." She used her stern-teacher voice. "Get up. I know you're scared, but you need to be brave." Zoe was the first to respond, wobbling to her feet and tugging a reluctant Maya with her.

"Good job." Derek's tone was more soothing, and Artie had to hold back a semi-hysterical laugh. Apparently, she was the bad cop in this situation. "Now, unzip your coats. Move slowly, though."

As Derek gave instructions, Artie started inching to the left. Her fingers clutched Derek's arm, both to tug him over with her and because she needed to cling to him. Her heart was beating so loudly in her ears that it was hard to hear anything else. Both girls had managed to unzip their coats, but Maya started crying, making squeaky, high-pitched sounds. When Artie looked at the cougar, she noticed the animal's attention was fixed on the children again. She wasn't sure if it was her imagination, but Artie was pretty sure the lion crouched lower.

"Maya. Stop," Artie snapped, startling the little girl into silence. "You need to act like a lion, not a little mouse. Be big. Spread your jackets open. Arms over your heads. Pretend you're ten feet tall and have teeth like a shark, got it?"

Neither girl said anything, but the tears had stopped completely. Their shaking hands extended over their heads. Artie sucked a relieved breath through her teeth as she and Derek made painfully slow progress circling around the cougar.

"That's perfect," Derek crooned in his good-cop voice. "You two are so brave. We're coming to get you now."

He and Artie had shuffled as far as they could to the side. It wasn't nearly far enough away from the animal—barely fifteen feet—but a wall of stone blocked their retreat.

With their backs facing a steep rock slope, they inched toward the girls. Artie's heart was beating fast—much too fast—and she could barely hold in the terrified noises that wanted to escape her lungs. *Be a lion,* she mentally repeated her own advice. *The girls need you. Be a lion.*

She and Derek drew parallel to the mountain lion's side, and it turned to stare at them with eyes that reflected the light. Artie could barely breathe as they made their impossibly slow progress toward the girls while the cat watched. It was almost impossible not to sprint to the girls, snatch them up, and run. Panicked instinct fought reason in her head as her vision narrowed until all she could see was the cougar, crouched to attack her kids.

Artie's eyes and flashlight flicked back and forth between the predator and the children. They looked so small, even with their jackets opened and their hands stretched bravely toward the sky.

She and Derek passed the cougar's midsection and then its shoulder. Each careful sideways step moved them closer to the children but also put them more directly in front of a mountain lion that looked ready to pounce. If the animal had to attack, though, Artie would rather be the victim than Maya, Zoe, or Derek. Her fear for her own safety was overwhelmed by the lung-squeezing terror at the thought of the others being mauled.

They were twenty feet from the girls and then fifteen. *Oh, please God, please let them stay safe!* After one agonizingly slow shift to the side and then another, they were in front of the lion. Finally, *finally*, they were close enough that Artie raised her arms above her head. When they'd been behind it, she'd been afraid of driving the animal toward the girls. Now that they were on the same end, she was hoping the cougar would take advantage of the opening behind it and leave.

Instead, it lifted one enormous paw and shifted forward a half step. Artie's heart started beating in triple time. Terror sped through her body until it was hard to think. She stomped down her fear and shifted the flashlight so it skipped over the area around the two girls.

"Zoe." She was shocked at how calm and even her voice sounded when her brain was in hysterics. "Use your left hand to reach for that rock on the ledge behind you. Go slow. Do you see it?" Artie kept the light aimed at the notch in the boulder where a few small rocks were piled.

Keeping her wide eyes locked on the cougar, Zoe lowered her trembling hand to grope along the surface of the boulder. It took everything inside of Artie to keep from screaming at the little girl to hurry. She clenched her jaw and swallowed.

"A little higher and to the left," Derek guided, although he kept his light aimed at the mountain lion. "There. You've got it."

"It's too heavy," she whimpered, and the cat shifted another oversize paw.

"No squeaking, Zoe." Artie put a snap in her voice. It had worked to yank Maya out of her tears, so hopefully it would keep Zoe from falling apart, too. "Use both hands. Got it?"

Zoe lifted the rock just over her head in silent response.

"That's awesome, Zoe. You have a weapon now. That's like Thor's hammer. This is the time when you get to act like a superhero." Derek edged closer, moving a little faster now that they were so close to the girls. It was impossibly hard for Artie not to break and dash for the children.

No running, she told herself, taking a sideways baby step. *No running. It's like you told the girls. Don't be a mouse. Predators don't run away. Don't run.*

Despite her mental lecture, keeping her pace to a creeping shuffle was painfully difficult. They were five feet away, then three, then Derek was picking up Zoe, and Artie finally could reach for Maya, lifting the girl into her arms without bending down. Derek stretched his free arm behind Artie and pulled them close.

"Now we'll be really tall," Artie told the trembling child, trying to keep her own voice from shaking. "Arms up. We'll look like a giant. A four-headed giant."

"You too, Zoe," Derek said. "Hold that magic hammer as high as you can."

Artie met the mountain lion's eyes, her fingers tightening around the flashlight. Like Zoe's rock, it could be used as a weapon, if necessary. "We are not mice."

"We're superheroes," Zoe piped up, her voice quavering just a little.

Although the prey-like high pitch of the girl's voice made Artie wince internally, she couldn't hold back a puff of startled laughter. "Exactly."

The big cat stared at them as Artie held her breath and tried not to shake. Each second felt like an eternity as the mountain lion studied them, unmoving except for the twitch of its tail. *Please let the kids be safe. Please let Derek survive this. If we all get out of this okay, I'll never take my eyes off any of my kids ever again.*

Her breath caught. Had the lion just crouched? Was it preparing to lunge? Clutching Maya tighter, she raised the flashlight, trying to shove the panic down so she could strategize in her mind. If the cougar pounced, she'd turn her body so Maya would be away from the animal, then she'd swing the flashlight at its head. Realizing that her shoulders were rounding, Artie shoved them back, standing tall.

"Go!" Maya's usually piping voice had lowered to her best attempt at a growly roar. "Shoo! Bad kitty! Go!"

The mountain lion's tail twitched, its haunches lowering even farther. Resisting the urge to squeeze her eyes closed, Artie stared at the enormous cat, watching for movement, anything to give her some warning before it attacked.

Its hindquarter's bunched, and Artie flinched slightly, ready for the charge. With a flick of its tail, the cougar turned and bounded away, quickly leaving the range of their lights until it was swallowed by the darkness.

Artie stared after it in disbelief. *Did it really just…leave?*

They all stood in silence for a solid minute after the lion had disappeared. Derek was the first to move, twisting until he could wrap his other arm around Artie and Maya, sandwiching the two girls between them in a four-person hug.

Maya burst into tears. "Sorry," she wailed between sobs. "I'm…being a…mouse!"

Squeezing the girl tighter, Artie gasped out a laugh. "It's okay to be a mouse now, sweetie. The cat is gone."

"Can I drop my hammer?" Zoe asked.

"Just don't drop it on anyone's foot." Taking the rock from her two-handed grip, Derek tossed it away from their huddle, and it landed on the snowy ground with a dull thud. A clump of snow jostled free and fell to cover it in a muffled *fwump fwump fwump*, like an echo.

Artie wasn't sure who started it, but they all began laughing, which led to the girls crying. Although Artie was close to tears too, she held them back. Tonight, when everyone was safe in bed, she could break down. For now, she still needed to be the invincible teacher, Ms. Rey.

When Derek withdrew his embracing arm, cupping her shoulder for a moment on the way, she turned her head to smile at him. At least the invincible Ms. Rey had a pretty awesome sidekick.

Derek placed Zoe on her feet. "You okay to walk? It'll keep you warmer." He didn't tell her that the main reason he put her down was because he'd started shaking as the adrenaline rush faded, and he didn't want her to know.

"Yes." She wiped her face with the back of her glove. Her stoic expression wavered a little as she asked, "Is it far?"

"No. We're just going to find a sheltered spot where we can light some flares and then wait for your dad to find us."

"Can we go *that* way?" Maya asked through chattering teeth, pointing in the opposite direction from the cougar's deep tracks.

"Definitely." Artie gave a choked laugh, and he eyed her carefully. There was an edge to her voice that made him worry she was about to lose it. After the day from hell, she fully deserved to have a complete breakdown, but it would help if she could hold it together for another couple of hours.

"You good?" Although he kept the words light, so as not to scare the girls, Artie must have caught the serious undertone, because she took a deep breath and met his gaze squarely.

"Yes," was all she said, but it was steady and resolute enough to send a burst of warm pride through Derek. He wanted to hug her, to tell her how amazing he thought she was, how brave and smart and simply *awesome*, but he had to be satisfied with holding his fist out to her.

As she bumped it, her lips tugged up into a shaky smile.

"How about you, Maya? Can you walk a little longer?" Derek asked, careful not to shine the flashlight in her eyes as he looked her over carefully. Both children had been dressed for the cold, and he was pretty sure that Maya's trembling was from the encounter with the mountain lion rather than the beginning of hypothermia.

"Okay. My hands are cold, though."

Derek glanced at Artie over the kids' heads, and they shared a concerned look. Crouching down by the smaller girl, Artie tugged off her own gloves and then Maya's mittens, while Derek directed his flashlight beam at their bare hands.

Maya hissed between her teeth as her tiny fingers were sandwiched between Artie's palms. "Your hands are really hot, Ms. Rey."

"I know it hurts," she said with brisk sympathy, "but we need to warm yours up fast. There's no sign of frostbite, so that's good. They'll sting a little, but you'll be okay."

Derek loved how she was with her students, like a kindly drill sergeant. After warming Maya's hands and replacing her mittens, Artie stood and pulled on her gloves.

"Any cold parts on you, Zoe?" she asked. Although the girl shook her head, Derek frowned. It might have been the blanching effect of the flashlight, but Zoe's face looked pale and pinched.

"Let's move, then. The quicker we light those flares, the sooner we'll get you home to your warm beds."

"And hot chocolate?" Maya asked.

"And soup," Zoe added.

"And pizza."

"And macaroni and cheese."

Apparently, the kids were hungry. As they started walking, with Derek leading the way, the two girls in the middle and Artie taking up the rear, he made a mental note to give them a protein bar when they found a good place to wait for rescue.

"What happened?" Artie asked when the girls stopped naming foods. "Why'd you run off like that?"

Silence greeted her question, but Artie didn't push.

Instead, she waited them out, and Derek grinned. He wasn't surprised that she was skilled at interrogation.

"Is Chase dead?" Zoe finally asked in a small voice.

"No," Derek assured her, a little startled by the question. "He'll be fine. The doctors will have him stay at the hospital overnight just to make sure, but he should be back at school and harassing you again really soon."

Zoe started sniffling, and Maya's sobs soon joined her. Unnerved by the tear fest behind him, Derek kept his gaze on the trail ahead of him.

"Enough," Artie said firmly. "You can cry later. Right now, it'll just make your faces cold. How about we sing a song? That way, our voices will warn any wildlife to stay away."

With a snort, Derek said, "Especially yours, Ms. Rey. I've heard you sing. The animals will run like they're fleeing from a forest fire when they hear you."

Although they were watery, there were two distinct giggles behind him.

"You shouldn't be throwing stones in that glass house of yours, Mr. Warner." Her voice had a frosty edge, but he heard the laughter she was hiding underneath. "You forget that I've heard *you* as well. You sounded like a sick walrus."

Now the girls were definitely laughing.

Racking his brain for a kid-appropriate song, Derek said, "How about 'The Itsy-Bitsy Spider'?" His suggestion was greeted by three groans.

"That's a *baby* song." Maya's voice was full of condescension. "Can we sing something by Taylor Swift?"

"No Taylor Swift," Artie and Derek said in unison, making him grin again.

The beam of his flashlight illuminated a protected area,

and he headed toward the spot. After scrambling over some loose rocks, he turned and helped the kids negotiate the tricky footing. When he reached a hand toward Artie, however, she gave him a look and climbed over the rocks without assistance. Biting back a smile, Derek returned to the front of their little group.

"Look, girls," Artie said. "Derek's found us the perfect spot to hang out and wait for your dad."

He grinned. "It is perfect, isn't it?" A rock overhang and a nearby tree created a natural shelter, blocking most of the wind and intermittent snow. Shucking the backpack, he reached inside and handed Artie some protein bars and the emergency blanket. When he pulled out one of the water bottles, he frowned.

"I forgot. The water's frozen." He started to return it to the pack, but Artie grabbed it before he could.

"I'll put it under my clothes, against my skin," she said, ushering the girls into the protected nook. "It'll melt."

The mental image made Derek's brain take an inappropriate leap. "Lucky water bottle," he muttered.

"What was that?"

"Nothing." He hurried to grab the aerial flare, as well as a couple of spiked ones. "I'll announce our presence."

Holding back a smile, Artie put her arms around both of the girls. "Watch. It's kind of like fireworks. Well, boring fireworks."

Derek launched the aerial flare into the dark sky, where it glowed red as it rose and fell.

"Your dad and the other searchers will see that," Artie

said, hugging the kids against her sides. "It'll tell them where we are and that we've found you."

It took a couple of tries before Derek found a spot soft enough to drive the first spike connected to the bottom of a flare into the ground. He climbed above their improvised shelter to place the second flare. Once both were lit, he returned to their spot under the overhang.

They arranged themselves under the emergency blanket with Derek and Artie sitting with the girls on their laps. Artie winced at the hard and lumpy rock under her, made worse by Maya's weight on her legs, and the icy bottle tucked under her clothes that was numbing her side. To add to her misery, she had to take off her gloves in order to unwrap the protein bars. Despite all the discomforts, though, her relief that the girls were found and safe outweighed everything.

"Eat this," she said, passing out the protein bars and donning her gloves, "and tell me what happened."

Zoe and Maya chewed mulishly for a while, but Artie waited patiently, eating her own bar in three eager bites. She hadn't realized how hungry she was until the food touched her lips.

Surprisingly, Maya was the one to break the silence. "Zoe told him to do it."

"Maya!"

"What? You did!"

"I didn't *mean* it!" Zoe sounded like she was about to cry again. "I waved at him to come back."

"You told Chase to go out on the ice?" Artie wasn't surprised. She'd figured it was something along those lines.

"I dared him," Zoe admitted, the words rushing out as if a dam had broken. "And then he fell in, and Derek pulled him out, but he wasn't moving. They took him away in an ambulance, and we thought he was dead." She finished on a wail.

Her sister's tears set off Maya, as well.

"It's not crying time yet." Artie tried to keep her voice stern, even when all she wanted to do was hug them close and join them in shedding buckets of tears. "You need to be brave for a little longer."

"Suh-superheroes." Maya hiccuped, wiping her nose on her cuff.

"Exactly," Artie said, hugging the girl tightly.

"Is that why you ran?" Derek asked Zoe, who was making a valiant effort to stop her sobs. "Because you thought it was your fault?"

She nodded, her breath shuddering with leftover tears. "I thought the sheriff would arrest me for m-murder."

Biting her cheek to hold back a completely inappropriate laugh, Artie said, "Zoe Springfield. Who is responsible for our actions?"

"We are," the girls chorused, and their rote response made Artie swallow another grin. It was obvious that both sisters had been in her class. Personal accountability was one of her preaching points.

"So who was responsible for Chase walking out onto the ice?"

That didn't received the instant response that the first question did. "But I dared him," Zoe finally protested.

"Which you shouldn't have done. Chase can be obnoxious, but that doesn't make it okay for you to be a bully."

"I know." Her voice was small.

"But no matter what you said, Chase was the one who made the decision to walk out on the ice. You are not responsible for his actions."

The girls were quiet for a long minute. "Okay," Zoe finally said, the one word weighed down with relief and exhaustion.

"So Zoe's not going to jail?" Maya shoved the last bit of her protein bar into her mouth.

"Neither of you are going to jail," Artie confirmed, pulling the water bottle away from her numb side, "but I have a feeling that you're going to be grounded for *years* after your dad hugs the stuffing out of you. You really scared him by running off like that."

Both girls ducked their heads.

"I think this has melted a little. Anyone thirsty?"

After everyone had an inadequate sip of the water, the kids dozed off. Artie snuggled Maya a little closer. She had to keep all the day's emotions, even the good ones, tucked away for a little longer. As she'd told the girls, it wasn't crying time yet. And it wasn't the time or place to let her heart run away with her, no matter how aware she was of Derek's proximity.

"Is there anything more uncomfortable than sitting on rock with a kid on top of you?" she asked Derek quietly.

His low laugh made her skin feel warm. "Sitting on hot coals, maybe? Or sharpened stakes?"

Their arms were pressed together as they shared body heat and blanket space, and Derek's shoulder was too tempting. Artie's head tipped to the side until it rested on him.

"Maybe, but I doubt it," she grumbled, making him laugh again. "Do you think you should send up another flare?"

"I will in ten minutes or so. By then, everyone should be close." He rested his cheek against the crown of her head. "Today turned out pretty well, don't you think?"

She snorted. "At times, it felt like we'd entered a hell

dimension, but the kids are all safe, so we can call this a definite win."

"I wouldn't mind visiting hell dimensions as long as you're with me."

Her skin prickled with goose bumps at the admission. "Aw...thanks. I have to admit that you made a dilapidated shack seem like a palace. A *pleasure* palace." His soft laugh warmed her insides.

"I can't believe you're back with me."

"Why is that so hard to believe?" she asked. "After all, *you* broke up with *me*."

"Only because I convinced myself you were better off without me and my criminal relations." His voice held a note of bitterness. "Life without you, though...I didn't think I'd survive it. After being drunk for a month, I sobered up and told my dad I wouldn't be part of his business any longer. I was done."

"What'd he say?"

"He laughed."

She winced. "Sorry."

Her head lifted, following his shoulder as he shrugged. "He stopped laughing when I quit taking jobs. I worked for Donnie at his auto shop for a while, and then Malcolm— you remember Mal?"

With a huff of a laugh, she asked, "How could I forget your darling brother, Mal? He used to call me Fartie."

"I'd forgotten about that." She could tell he was restraining a laugh. "Anyway, Mal was fed up with Dad's shit, too, so we started our small-engine repair shop. It's not the kind of money I could have made if I'd stayed with Dad, but I like the work, and there's no threat of prison. Plus, since I'm the boss, I can drop everything to go on dive-team calls."

"Sounds like you got your life together." She tried to keep her voice casual, but her heart actually ached with pride.

"Too late. By the time I got my shit sorted, you and Randy were engaged. I figured you deserved better than me, anyway."

Trying not to jostle Maya, she pulled far enough away to punch Derek in the arm. "Dumb ass. Why would you think that?"

"C'mon, look at you. You're perfect. You're smart and funny and driven. Ever since we were kids, you always knew you wanted to be a teacher. You know what you want, and you go get it."

Artie opened her mouth to respond, but shock kept her silent.

"Me, on the other hand," he continued, "everyone knows I'm the screwup."

"You've never been a screwup," she protested, her voice a little higher pitched than usual. She'd never imagined that Derek saw either of them that way. "You're just as smart as I am, Derek. Probably smarter. And you're clever and self-less and brave and you risk your life every day to save other people. You turned your entire life around when it would've been easier just to join your dad in his business. How could you think you're a screwup?"

"Right. So I didn't get you into all that trouble when we were kids."

She laughed. "That's true. You did get me in trouble all the time."

"See? Screwup. If we hadn't been friends, you probably would've started the Simpson Junior Social Services Club and eliminated poverty in Field County or some shit before you were out of junior high. Instead, I dragged you down into delinquency with me."

His melodramatic tone made her laugh again. "Derek. Stop. Sure, we got in trouble a lot, and the stuff we did was usually your idea, but I don't regret it at all. You were the reason I had any fun growing up."

He studied her for a minute before one corner of his mouth lifted, just a shadow of his usual smirk. "Yeah?"

"Yeah." Grinning at him, she added, "Besides, your version of my ideal childhood sounds hella boring."

Finally, he laughed, leaning closer so he could kiss her. "You're amazing, Artemis Rey."

"I know."

With his lips still close to hers, he chuckled again. Warm air brushed her skin, and she closed her eyes, clinging to the moment.

"You're pretty incredible yourself, Derek Warner," she said, her voice husky. "I'm sorry I let you break up with me."

"I'm sorry I didn't get my shit together sooner." With a final kiss, he raised his head. "And I'm sorry I didn't steal you away from Randy and tell you that I've loved you since we were thirteen."

Her eyes went wide. "Nuh-uh."

"Yeah-huh."

"You have not."

"Have too."

Why does Derek always reduce me to an eight-year-old when we argue? she wondered, trying to frown. Her lips kept insisting on curling upward, however. "Well, I've loved you since we were *twelve*."

Shifting a sleeping Zoe, he freed the arm closer to Artie

and curled it around her shoulders. "So you're really okay with being stuck with me for good?"

"Just try to get rid of me." Knowing that Derek was hers again was making her giddy. "I'm a barnacle. A leech. A wood tick. A—"

"Okay, okay." He laughed, kissing her temple. "I get the picture. You're stuck with me, and I'm stuck with you. Forever."

"Forever." As she cuddled closer to Derek, tightening her arms around the sleeping child in her lap, she smiled so hard her cheeks hurt. Forever with Derek. It sounded wonderful.

Steve's was the first voice they heard. "Zoe! Maya!"

"Here!" Derek bellowed, making both girls startle awake. "We're here!"

After gently moving a dazed Maya off her lap, Artie scrambled to her feet and grabbed both flashlights, waving them above her head. Distant shouts indicated that they'd spotted the beams of light.

"Dad!" Zoe yelled, jumping to her feet.

"Zoe? You okay?"

"Yes!" Her voice broke mid-word.

"Maya, too?"

"Yes, Daddy!" Maya shouted, standing up and grabbing her sister's hand.

"Hang on!" Steve sounded jubilant. "I'm coming, babies!"

The voices quickly grew louder and more distinct as the searchers drew nearer. Artie and Derek had to hold the girls back when they tried to dash into the darkness toward their father's voice.

"Whoa!" That sounded like Ian Walsh. "Springfield, you can't go that way unless you've turned into Spider-Man."

Either Steve discovered he had some latent superhero skills, or the searchers found another, more mortal-friendly trail, but Steve barreled toward them just minutes later. Falling to his knees, he scooped both girls into his arms and hugged them against him. Maya and Zoe wrapped their arms around his neck as all three of them cried.

"My babies," Steve rasped, kissing first one head and then the other. "My sweet girls. Are you okay?" He pulled back to check them for injuries. Zoe nodded, tears tracking down her cheeks, but Maya just sobbed. Wrapping them into another hug, Steve squeezed them tight to his chest. "Ian!"

"Right here, Steve." The firefighter standing behind them pulled a medical kit out of his pack. "Hey, princesses. I'm glad a bear didn't eat your faces."

"Watch your mouth," Steve growled. If his arms hadn't been full of little girls, Artie was pretty sure Ian would've gotten smacked upside the head.

"We didn't see any bears," Zoe said. "Just a mountain lion."

"A mountain lion, huh?" Ian's voice was amused, his disbelief obvious. "That must've been scary."

"It was." Maya turned her head so she could talk, although she kept a tight grip on her father. "But we turned into a four-headed giant, so it ran away."

Zoe made an impatient noise. "We weren't a giant; we were superheroes."

"A *giant* superhero."

Exchanging a "kids have the best imaginations" look

with Steve, Ian chuckled. "Well, giant superheroes, mind if I make sure you're healthy after your big adventure?"

Shifting closer to Derek, Artie whispered, "Should we tell them there really *was* a mountain lion?"

"Later," he said out of the side of his mouth. "Steve's heart probably can't take one more shock right now."

"Good idea."

Despite her exhausted, sore, and cold body, Artie couldn't stop grinning. The searchers, buoyed by relief and residual adrenaline, joked and laughed as Ian gave the girls a quick check over. Derek slung his arm around her shoulders, and she leaned against him, taking her weight off her sore knee.

"Hey, Rob." Derek waved at the sheriff. "Come here a second."

Rob carefully picked his way over the snowy trail until he was in front of them. "Glad you're okay." His gaze flicked over to Maya and Zoe. "All of you."

"Me too." Lowering his voice, Derek said, "You might want to check out who's been stashing fire accelerants in the remains of that old Forest Service cabin."

The sheriff's eyebrows rose. "Accelerants?"

Derek nodded. "Rubbing alcohol, nail polish remover, linseed oil, and some other things right next to a big box of matches and across the cabin from recently smoked cigarette butts. Maybe it has nothing to do with the wildland fire this past summer, but it seems awfully suspicious."

Rob's expression darkened. "Agreed. Thank you for telling me."

Clearing her throat, Artie added, "Someone else was out there while we were searching, too. We saw a fresh footprint."

"Another searcher?" Rob shifted a half step closer, his voice quiet.

"Nope," Derek answered. "We got some pictures of it for you, though."

"Good. Email them to me, and I'll check them out." Rob started heading toward one of the firefighters who was waving him over. "Thanks."

They were quiet as they watched the sheriff walk toward the beckoning man. After a few minutes, Derek shifted back a few steps, tugging her with him. Although she gave him a curious glance, she followed willingly enough as he maneuvered them into the shadow of a lodgepole pine.

"What are you doing?" she finally asked.

Turning, he backed her against the tree trunk. Even in the dimness, she saw the flash of his wicked grin. "Something I've wanted to do since we left the cabin."

"Wh—" His mouth landed on hers, cutting off her words. It took only a few seconds before she completely forgot what she'd been about to say. In the years before and after Derek, she'd never experienced anything like his kisses. They'd always brought to mind every romantic cliché she'd ever heard.

Her arms rose of their own accord to circle his neck. When her tongue met his, he made a low sound and pressed her harder against the tree. He kneaded her hips as he leaned against her, trapping her in the very best way.

Their earlier conversation ran through her mind, and the knowledge that he still loved her made the kiss even more intense. She squeezed him, hard, never wanting to lose him again.

"Ahem."

Her fingers worked their way under his hat into his hair,

pressing against his scalp to keep his mouth on hers, where it should be.

"*Ahem!*"

He nipped at her lower lip, making her moan. His kisses made the entire world disappear, until they were the only two people in it. Heat rose quickly, burning through her as she pulled him even closer, never wanting the embrace to end.

A female voice intruded on Artie's bliss. "Too bad the fire trucks are at base camp. We might have to hose these two down to separate them."

Artie knew she was still floating in some other world, because she thought she heard Callum laugh. Callum Cook *never* laughed. The odd sound was enough to jar her out of her Derek-induced daze, and she turned her head toward the interrupting voices.

"Come back," Derek grumbled, kissing the line of her jaw.

It was tempting to melt back into Derek's embrace, but the sight of Callum and a grinning Lou was as effective as a shot from the aforementioned firehose in returning her to reality.

"Derek." She moved her hands from his head to his shoulders so she could push against him. It was like shoving a boulder—a boulder that was kissing a sensitive spot just under her ear that brought a whole host of pleasurable goose bumps. "Derek!"

Grumbling, he shifted away a fraction of an inch and glared at the intruders. If Artie was to take a deep breath, their chests would touch. "What?"

"We're in the middle of a search and rescue mission." Any hint of laughter was totally missing from Callum's tone. Artie decided that she'd just imagined his chuckle earlier.

Huh. Instead of *bells ringing* when Derek had kissed her—like in all the stories—she'd heard *Callum laughing*. That was a disturbing thought.

"Fine." Derek stepped back, sliding his hand down her arm to interlace their fingers. "This isn't really fair, though, Cal. I tried to get you set up with online dating last week, and you kiss-block me. I feel like I'm doing all the giving, and you're doing all the taking in this relationship."

Biting her lip so she didn't laugh, Artie looked anywhere except at Derek. After giving Derek an arctic glower, Callum stalked away, his shoulders rigid.

"Let's go!" he barked.

Artie made the mistake of meeting Lou's gaze, and they started snickering. Tossing an arm over both women's shoulders, Derek steered them toward the rest of the group.

"Time to go home," he said, pressing a kiss to the side of Artie's hat. "We'll eat, sleep, and"—he cleared his throat—"do…other things before someone else needs rescuing."

Trying to ignore the way her heart thumped faster at his mention of "other things," Artie directed her flashlight at the ground, carefully placing each step. It would only take one loose rock to completely destroy her knee. Artie still had a good chance of getting to base camp without being carried, and she wanted to keep it that way.

As they fell into a single-file line to descend the narrow path, a distant chorus of coyotes echoed in the darkness. Artie glanced up at the towering cliffs, wondering if the mountain lion was perched somewhere high above them. Or maybe the person who'd left the boot print in the snow was still close by, watching.

With a shiver, she refocused on where she was putting her feet. The downward slope made it tricky to keep her balance, and she winced as a tiny slide jarred her knee. Derek put a steadying hand on her back, reminding her that he was with her—for good, this time.

Smiling, she took another step toward home.

ABOUT THE AUTHOR

A fan of the old adage "write what you know," Katie Ruggle lived in an off-grid, solar- and wind-powered house in the Rocky Mountains until her family lured her back to Minnesota. When she's not writing, Katie rides horses, shoots guns, cross-country skis (badly), and travels to warm places where she can scuba dive. A graduate of the Police Academy, Katie received her ice-rescue certification and can attest that the reservoirs in the Colorado mountains really are that cold. A fan of anything that makes her feel like a badass, she has trained in Krav Maga, boxing, and gymnastics. You can connect with Katie at katieruggle.com, facebook.com/katierugglebooks, or on Twitter @KatieRuggle.

Also by Adriana Anders

Blank Canvas
Under Her Skin
By Her Touch
In His Hands

Survival Instincts
"Deep Blue" in the *Turn the Tide* anthology